COAL BLACK SOUL

M.P. WRIGHT

To Steven
Thanks for all the kind
Support
Best Wishes
M.P. Wright

SPELLBOUND
BOOKS

First Published by in 2024 by SpellBound Books

First Published by SpellBound Books 2024

PRINT ISBN:
978-1-0686655-8-5

For my lovely, devoted wife,
Jen
And
To my literary agent,
Phil Patterson.
Still both believers

CHAPTER ONE

Salonica. 1976

IT WAS THE KIND OF MORNING THAT HAD ME WISHING I WERE someplace else, doing a different kind of job and getting a lot better paid for it. It was the first Monday in September, still officially summer, but it felt like the dead of winter. Outside it was lashing it down with rain and cold enough for a thick overcoat and woollen scarf.

I had neither.

This latest storm had crept in like a whisper before dawn. Earlier in the day I'd watched it slowly grow on the horizon as I was sat looking out of my third-floor office window in the police headquarters building on the *Via Egnatia*. Dirty, sullen clouds lay over the mountain villages that bordered the city. By midday the deluge had blown south, rolling across the valley of the Vardar River, and within less than half an hour the downpour had reached my stomping ground, Thessaloniki.

To the world at large I'm known as a senior police official. A fancy name for a very grubby job. I'm beholden to a reclusive master but not the boundaries of the law. There's no uniform, gold braid or brass plate outside my door to announce who I am, or for that matter, what I do. I'm not kosher and nor is the particular section I operate for. I dwell in the grisly realm of the *'Matatzides'* or the MAT division, part of the feral *Unit for the Reinstatement of Order*. The department's existence was only ever spoken of in hushed tones and governed by one man. Its role was simple. Bribery, coercion, extortion, fit-ups and death. Worse still, if it was called for. And it often was.

In a city with an old quarter known as the *Bara,* the largest red-light district in Eastern Europe, there was always plenty of work for an honest policeman. Especially a tolerant sort of officer who settled matters before they got out of hand, believed in due process and never took a kickback.

I'm not that kind of law enforcer.

If truth be told, I'd never intended to become policeman.

And, once I'd fallen into becoming a cop, never a detective.

And after promotion to that position ... never what I was now.

I'm given a wide berth by both crook and copper alike. Neither would piss on me if I was on fire. What I do for a living could never be called decent... and most of the time, neither am I. In a town filled with so many delinquent lepers, I'm the errant pariah with the most fingers, and I like to keep it that way.

To the rank and file on the force, the great and the good at city hall and in the mayor's office, to those on the streets, the huge criminal underbelly of Salonika, I am simply referred to as '*that bastard Remis.*'

• • •

I'd clocked on just after nine-thirty, before the heavens opened, feeling like dog shit. My head drumming away. An irritating droning sound fizzing in my ears, the dull humming working in unison with the pulsating throb of my newly forming hangover. I took my time on the stairs that led up to the squad room, dreading each step, my chest tight, sweating and breathing fast, a cigarette burning down to the skin just below my nail. I'd have happily turned around, walked over to the bar across the road and got comfy with a bottle of Metaxa until it was punching out time, but instead I stubbed out the butt of my Santé on the top step and headed on into purgatory.

Police headquarters are the same the world over: impersonal, worn, malodorous, busy; and Salonica Central was no different. Away from my office, the squad room was full of smoke. It hung straight up in the air in thin lines, like a curtain of small clear beads. It didn't dissolve; didn't float off; didn't move. I stared out across rows of desks, toward a dozen or so men, each with sweat-stained shirt-backs and armpits, who were busying themselves with so-called police work. There were pats on the back, handshakes here, winks there, like some fucking reunion. No nods or smiles for me, and that's just the way I liked it.

There wasn't a decent detective amongst them. Plenty of brawn, very little brains. Most on the take, and every one of them cheap. Everyone in Greece likes money. It was the Greeks who invented the damn stuff, but corrupt Greek coppers like the feel of cash in their hip pocket more than the average schmuck. Especially when it's money that they haven't had to sweat for.

I riffled through my desk draw, pulled out a small brown medicine bottle, flicked open the lid and tipped a couple of aspirin into the palm of my hand. I chucked them into my mouth and swallowed. Whilst the tablets struggled to make their way down my gullet, I stared at the faces of the wanted and the dead on the cork board that was screwed to the back wall, then spent the better part of an hour leaning against a battered steel filing cabinet, smoking, drinking coffee, ignoring the two big manila files on the table and the pile of paperwork in my 'in tray'. I listened to chairs scrape, papers rustle, typewriters clatter. The telephone on my desk had the air of something that knew it was being watched and I had the kind of nasty sinking feeling in my gut telling me that my day was just about to hit the skids.

The Black Raven: that's what I called it. A hunch inside of me that more often than not brought on an unpleasant prickling sensation that would run down the back of my neck, along my arms and tingle through to the tips of my fingers. A sixth sense. Portent. Omen. Call it what you will, it all boiled down to the fact that somewhere down the line, either bad news or bad luck was heading my way.

I closed my eyes against the harsh bright office lights and the white noise that filled my thoughts. It took me a moment to pick out the sound of the phone ringing. I sat down, leant forward in my chair, my elbows on the desk, I reached for the telephone, lifting the handset to my ear.

"Major Remis speaking,"

There was a long pause. I felt my scalp recede against my skull when the female switchboard operator finally spoke.

"The provost wants to see you, immediately."

I sat upright in my chair, wiping the sweat off my palm on my trouser leg. My first thought was that I was in some kind of trouble. It's a notion that comes naturally to anyone who has as much to hide as I do. I cradled the phone between my ear and my chin before replying.

"I'm on my way." I ground my back teeth down tight together.

The line went dead.

I replaced the receiver, glanced down at my wristwatch; ten past eleven. I mouthed a curse and got to my feet, patted my hand against the left side of my jacket, feeling for the Walther cradled in its shoulder holster. I snatched my cigarettes and Ronson lighter off the desk, lit another smoke and walked out of my office, heading back down the stairs, out into the street, thinking to myself ... *fuck the provost and this cloak and dagger horseshit.*

CHAPTER TWO

There was a time when the living covered the mouths of their dead with a single coin before their final goodbye. The image of metal glinting over lifeless lips still makes the living shiver. It has become a part of our collective subconscious, possibly because the ritual appeared in different traditions, and continues to survive here in Greece. The coins had a purpose: to allow the dead to pay for their passage to the Otherworld. This was the realm of Hades, separated from the land of the living by five rivers. It was a perilous journey, and there was only one guide to take the recently departed to their final destination. He was known as the *Ferryman*, his name, Charon: he of the keen gaze.

The man who had just requested my presence had been keeping a hungry eye on me for a long time. I was about to enter a familiar domain to hold court with him, a retreat that was both welcome and repellent. A dusky and sombre Elysium fit for the most malevolent of Gods.

I'd been with the Hellenic Gendarmerie since leaving the regular army in the spring of 1963. The gendarmerie has strong historical connections to the army. The rest of the country has the *'City Police'*, which were something very different to the mob I'd joined. Both organisations cooperated as separate forces, of course. At least that was the rumour. After wearing out my shoe leather on the city's streets for what seemed like the better part of an eternity I was finally promoted to sergeant, and after showing the powers that be an aptitude for investigative work, three years later, to detective. Back then, even with a couple of pips on each shoulder and a reputation for being hard-nosed with crooks and subordinates alike, I was, in the eyes of my superiors, still little more than a suit instead of a uniform. That said, with my feet under the table with the C.I.D., I began to hit lucky, broke a few decent cases. A minor reputation slowly began to build as did my status within the ranks.

My rising star came to an abrupt halt in the spring of 1967, all thanks to an unexpected coup d'état courtesy of a group of right-wing army officers led by General Stylianos Pattakos. *The Regime of the Colonels,* as the brutal junta became known, moved swiftly to seize control of the nation.

By the early morning hours of April 21st, the whole of Greece was in the hands of five senior military leaders; the army gaining control of all communication centres, the parliament, the royal palace, and within days arresting over 10,000 people. All leading politicians, including the acting Prime Minister, were taken into custody and held incommunicado by the conspirators. At six the next day the Greek constitution was suspended.

The consequences of such a drastic abeyance of the state laws meant that anyone could be arrested without warrant at any time and brought before a military court to be tried. Every politician, every man, every anarchist or communist considered a threat to the new cabal could be rounded up and dealt with accordingly. It was a simple, diabolical, callous, plan. With tanks and paratroopers on the streets, curfews imposed, a black-out of information to the rest of the world, Greece had quickly become a police state, and I was now being ordered to run with a very savage pack in order to do my job.

With the shit still hitting the fan, and only weeks into the new confederacy being set up, I decided to throw in the towel. Get out of policing forever whilst my conscience was clean, and my hands were still relatively free from the blood of others. My decision to quit was greeted with both disdain and suspicion by my division commander, and for a brief time I thought I might end up either banged up in a cell or worst still, face down in a ditch some place.

Although unaware at the time, I had a secret benefactor. Someone watching over me; an overseer with a vested interest in my career. This surreptitious figure no-doubt kept me out of the *Heptapyrgion*, the infamous *Fortress of the Seven Towers* prison overlooking the city or being carried off out into the sticks to be shot.

There was an expression from the time of the Turkish occupation, that it was most fortunate to have a *Bara Sto Palatti*, an 'uncle in the palace', and it turned out to my surprise that my unknown family mentor was none other than the head of the gendarmerie, Manolis Callas, a near mystic presence in the city. At that time Provost Callas was at least sixty-five, some said older, with a fearsome reputation. For almost twenty years nothing had gone down in Thessaloniki that the old man didn't know about and that included my ascending career on the force. Instead of being placed under lock and key or executed, Callas bid me into his lair and to my great surprise offered me a promotion. One that got me my own office and a much-improved salary.

Now with the rank of major, my advancement and elevation into the league of the *'Matatzides'* would come at a very heavy personal cost. A heady mix of hubris and stupidity at the time prevented me from seeing how much of a heavy toll both personal duty to the state and my unstinting obligation to the provost would exact upon me in the years to come.

Like the Ferryman of old, Callas expected to be rewarded for his guidance, counsel and protection.

And I have paid dearly in receipt of such rare gifts.

Only the wealthy could afford to live in the north-eastern district of Polichni, a select neighbourhood of private homes with showy gardens. Only one venerable creature resided at the *Salem Mansion* on Vasilissis Street. The houses around it were powerfully built, of sober imported stone or red brick, often three storeys high, sometimes with elegant verandas and high corner towers, while the lawns and plantings were kept with the sort of precision achieved only by the employment of forelock-tugging gardeners. I pulled my battered Lancia up at a pair of huge wrought-iron gates which hung between massive walls.

A uniformed officer with an M3 sub-machine gun slung over his shoulder marched out of the tiny gatehouse and eyeballed me. I flashed my warrant card and waited whilst the guard gave it the once over. I drove along a short avenue of cherry trees before arriving at a wide, gravel courtyard. The *Salem Mansion* was white with pebbledash walls and a flat roof. It was the size of a beach-front hotel; five star and not the kind of pile I could have afforded to bed down in. Somewhere in the trees behind the house a peacock screeched out a warning to the good souls inside that one of the unwashed had managed to set foot inside its hallowed ground.

I drew up next to a pair of date palms, which stood like unkempt custodians on either side of the mansion's entrance. I grabbed my fedora off the passenger seat next to me and stepped out on to the washed gravel. Another deadpan guard approached and asked me for identification. I went through the motions of establishing my credentials again. Both the goon on the gate and this latest sour-faced minion already knew who I was, they were no doubt even probably expecting me. Nevertheless, both officers were expected to run everything by the book. Meticulous, observant, bureaucratic. A real pain in the butt.

My papers now bona fide by the sentry, I was ushered up to the house and parked outside a big oak door. I didn't have to wait long to gain entry. It swung open to reveal a faint-looking police adjutant. Medium height, dark-haired and shadowy downcast eyes. I didn't speak to him nor him to me. He stood aside as I crossed the threshold and stepped inside the wide entrance hall. It was the kind of lobby that made you feel lucky just to have got through the door. A single, wide-flight staircase with gleaming pearl-white banisters led up to where Callas held court. On the ceiling above my head hung a huge chandelier that the palace of Versailles would have envied, and which looked more lurid than a trollop's earrings.

The adjutant saluted me and asked for my hat.

"I'll hang on to it if you don't mind," I said, feeding its brim through my fingers. I gestured my head upwards towards the ornate light fitting. “It’ll help me keep my hands off all the crystal.”

The pasty-faced lackey ignored the patter. He held out an effete hand before escorting me across the polished agate tile-work and upstairs. The second floor felt overbearing, grandiose with a bucolic air which belied its up-market location. I didn’t get chance to eye-up the two new pieces of art that had been put up on display since I’d last paid a visit; the flunky escorting me was all too eager to sling my carcass into the lion’s den. I watched the attendant give a single, short cuff on the wood-panelled, formal double-door that led into the inner sanctum.

Beyond the door I knew there was a sofa made by Sheraton, an Aubusson carpet, and a little Renoir oil of a ballet-girl tying her slipper. They were possessions that had once been in Callas’ home, and in a sense they still were. The mansion house was his home. I waited until a calm voice said, “Come in.” The voice was always calm, just as the man was always scarily serene, no matter what instructions he gave you, no matter who ran the risk of death.

Manolis Callas’ office wasn’t big by the standards of say Aristotle Onassis, you certainly couldn’t have parked more than four cars between his antique mahogany Partners desk and the door. It was decorated in the neo-classical style, with great white beams at each corner of the room, a grand marble chimneypiece and wall-mounted weaponry. There were plenty of books, of the sort you buy by the metre: plenty of Greek poets and philosophers and tomes written by historians with whom I could claim a degree of familiarity, but only as the names of back alleys and hanging over the ingresses of dilapidated public buildings. I took a hike around the room before heading towards the chief.

"Sit down, Major."

I did as I was ordered. No salute required, just blind obedience. I peeked over the green-leather surface of the desk as I sat. There was a copy of the *Makedonia* newspaper, well read, a pair of half-moon spectacles; a fountain pen alongside a pile of correspondence, a heavy bronze ashtray containing the butts of half a dozen *Aupa* menthol cigarettes and several silver-framed photographs featuring Callas with various dignitaries and heads of state standing at his side.

My arse had barely had chance to settle into the cushion of the expensive leather upholstery before my boss was up on his feet and moving around the furniture. Callas was the kind of man who took great pleasure in looking down on his subordinates. He was tall and heavy, balding and sombre, with a thick grey moustache. Aristocratic and intelligent. He was given to well-cut, dark-blue suits, formal language, and, if the mood took him, cold-eyed stares.

He looked what he was, a senior civil servant with a good family background. A planner and decision-maker. Only his planning was the arrangement of the downfall of others. Callas never responded immediately to anything you said, a dead moment always hanging in the air before he offered a reply or comment.

"Smoke?" The expensive inlay cigarette box with the kingfishers of wood grain was wafted across my face. I lifted one out, an expensive *Georgopulo & Co* American brand coffin nail, stuck it in my mouth and fished my Ronson out of my jacket pocket. Callas waited until I'd lit it and taken a heavy draw, speaking to me as I blew some smoke at the high ceiling.

"We'd like you to handle a rather delicate assignment."

I nodded my head. "As long as it doesn't demand a classical education, I might be able to stumble my way round it."

I watched the old man scowl. "And perhaps you could undertake it without your usual sarcasm or complaint?"

I cocked a smile. "It wouldn't be the same if I didn't grumble just a little,"

Callas gave me a calculated look before continuing. "You're going to have to navigate through some rather unpleasant waters, I'm afraid."

"Unpleasant?" There was a moment or so of silence before Callas answered my query. He spoke slowly, carefully articulating each syllable.

"We have a body that needs to be ousted off Greek soil," he said, bitterly.

I inhaled and snorted smoke down my nostrils. "That'll be fun."

Callas tugged at one of his loose, elephantine ears, before thrusting his gnarled hands into the pockets of his jacket. "When I say disappear, I don't want this carcass finding its way into some deep pit or at the bottom of the Thermaic Gulf. This particular body needs to be handled in the appropriate manner, but with as few questions asked about the cause of death as possible."

"Okay. May I ask who the stiff is?"

I got a cold stare. Callas' tone became a low growl. "A man of no importance. An American. Cause of death yet to be ascertained. The body was found early this morning in an empty storage silo by workers out at Ptolemaida-Florina coal mine."

"Did this dead fellow work for the mining company?"

Callas shrugged. "To my knowledge, no."

"So, we're talking about a heap of cold meat that's been dumped up there. That doesn't bode well."

"That maybe so. Nevertheless, we'd like a swift repatriation of the deceased without any protracted agitation."

I shifted awkwardly in my seat. "That may not be easy to achieve."

Callas was silent for a moment. "How so?"

"In my experience, the Yanks like to dot the 'I's and cross the 'T's. Americans tend to pay a great deal of attention to the little things. You know, the specific details and points of fact and description ..." I watched my boss sniff the air indignantly before continuing. "Especially when it comes to the death of one of their own. There's nothing quite like the homicide of a fellow native on foreign soil to set the cat among the pigeons. Brings out the worst in people.

"I always think that skilful pilots win their reputation from storms and tempest, major. You've gained your considerable élan weathering greater squalls in the past. Try not to put anyone's back up. We have every faith in your abilities to placate our American friends."

"You keep saying we. Am I missing something here?"

Callas drew his hands together, the cuffs of his shirt gleaming like icing. "Cautious as ever, Remis. Due to the rather unusual nature of this investigation, and the fact that the mining authorities have in their infinite wisdom seen fit to contact the National Intelligence Service, it's unfortunate that the spooks have been drawn into what is a police matter."

"That is, unfortunate."

"Brigadier Kyril Grivas of the Salonica *N.I.S* will be accompanying you up to Florina."

"Will he now."

Callas looked quizzically at me. "In a purely advisory role, of course."

"Of course."

"Consider Grivas tagging along as two heads being better than one, especially a head as grey as yours."

I took the advice proffered with a hefty pinch of salt. "Don't think my grey hairs make this head of mine wise, sir. They just make me old. And tired. That's why I'm still sat here bootlicking and you're there giving the orders."

"If you say so. Remember major, Greece has never been a country for young men. It's old heads that have always mattered here."

I nodded in obeyance; went to rise out of my seat.

"Oh, there's one more thing," Callas said, turning around and making his way around the desk to stand behind his chair. I dropped my arse down, looked back up towards the impassive features staring at me. "Grivas has kindly offered to escort you up to Florina. He and his driver will collect you from outside police headquarters at four pm." The old man peered down at his wristwatch. "You'll need to get a move on. Grivas likes to be prompt. Slave to the clock. Not one for insolence, either. And he doesn't have my sense of humour."

I made a mental note to crack a joke as soon as I came to face with the Brigadier. "Yes, sir. I'll bear that in mind, sir."

Callas, straightening his back, ushered me to rise with a flap of his hand. I got to my feet, took a few paces across the antique floor-covering then stopped to stare out of the window. I turned and looked back at Callas who was now sat on his throne. "You know ... you ought to get out more." I watched Callas raise an eyebrow. I began to make my escape, backing away toward the door. "All this talk of corpses can't be good for you." I pointed toward the shuttered window. "In case you hadn't notice, it's still summertime outside."

Callas feigned the briefest of smiles. "Yes, I'd observed earlier that the rain was a little warmer than usual. At least a filthy summer is one thing the Americans won't be blaming on us."

I turned on my heels in retreat. *"Oh, don't you fucking believe it,"* I muttered under my breath.

CHAPTER
THREE

DETECTIVE WORK IS A LITTLE LIKE WALKING INTO A CINEMA WHEN THE film's already started. You don't know what's happened already and, as you try to find your way in the dark, it's inevitable that you're going to stand on someone's toes or get in the way. I was sure that I was about to put someone's back up. No doubt the esteemed government inquisitor. Brigadier Grivas would, I was sure, be the first to take offence at my presence, let alone any snooping around I may or may not be doing. The way I saw it, if I was going to hack anyone off, it may as well be some officious prick from the National Intelligence Service.

I stood on the corner of the Via Egnatia, outside police headquarters, my booze-induced headache still nagging at my temples, being the dutiful public employee waiting on my lift to Florina. It was a little before four and still raining; no downpour now, but enough to make the road surface shine and the gutters roll with excess water. The Vardari, the wind that blew down from the valley, rattled around me. It was one of those cold, biting winds with an edge like a new razor blade. I turned away from it, faced the port and watched the lightning as it lit the clouds above the sea. Moments later thunder followed, distant rumblings, far to the south.

I stubbed out my cigarette with the toe of my shoe, looked at my watch. Out of the corner of my eye I saw a staff car heading down the street toward me. A Russian-built Chaika limousine, old and boxy, a relic with a blue and white Greek pennant flown from a whippy radio aerial. My ride drew up in front of me, the engine still running. A gaunt-looking man in the passenger seat opened the rear door from inside. "Major Remis," he said. I saluted, ducked my head and climbed in. Inside the air was thick with stale cigarette smoke and cheap cologne. Brigadier Grivas moved over to make room for me and held out his hand.

"Well, this is a pleasant surprise." Grivas gave me a nasty, curt smile which revealed a row of badly decaying front teeth and a single gold-plated incisor. The emissary was probably in his late-sixties, skinny with high cheek bones, a thin, short snout, old-fashioned side-whiskers and an angry expression. He was wearing a tight-fitting grey-flannel suit. A military-style black greatcoat rested across his lap; the embroidered insignia of the Greek Military Phoenix adorned his breast pocket. Ignoring the pleasantries, I shook the brigadier's mitt and found it being held for an uncomfortably long time as the Brigadier's eyes investigated my face. I find I get a lot of officials who do that: they reckon themselves as judges of a man's character if they gawk at you long enough. As the car pulled away Grivas finally released my palm. "Help yourself to a drink or a cigarette." He flipped open a cocktail cabinet and produced a silver cigarette carrier. "The unfiltered Turkish are sadly rather poor quality; I'd stick to the American brand at the back of the box if I were you."

I said yes to the smoke and no to any of the booze. I understood it paid to keep your wits about you when in the presence of a shifty piece of work like Grivas. "Would you be so kind as to light me, please Major?" The Brigadier held out his hand, the tobacco-filled paper tube clenched between two gloved fingers. The man's voice was fastidious, suave even: soft and slow, with just a hint of cruelty. The sort of voice, I thought, that could lead you into incriminating yourself quite nicely, thank you. The sort of voice that belonged to an interrogator. I lit our cigarettes and settled back into the Chaika's big seat.

"You are from Salonika, Major?"

I shook my head. "No, not originally."

"Then where, originally?"

"Sparti."

"Ah, a Laconian. That perhaps explains your reputation for verbal austerity."

"I have a habit of being a little blunt at times."

"Yes, so I've heard."

Grivas pulled a heavy hit of nicotine inside him, holding onto the smoke in his mouth for a dog's age. When he finally exhaled, the vapour that drifted out had a dull, flat hue, as if the spymaster had sucked every cruel toxin from the dried leaf. I listened to him clear mucus from his throat before addressing me again. "The N. I. S is very grateful to have your investigative prowess to rely upon."

"Oh, I'm not paid to investigate, Brigadier. Just to clear up the messes other people leave behind."

Grivas tried to look thoughtful but only succeeded in

looking bad-tempered. "Then, I trust this particular muck can be easily mopped up?"

I shrugged. "No-one's ever complained about my housekeeping skills in the past."

Grivas' smile widened before turning to stare out of the window. "That's comforting to hear, Major."

We drove northwest. The driver working hard, his foot to the floor, eager to get us to our destination. The Chaika quickly headed out of the city sprawl, up into the mountains on darkening, rain-soaked roads, the wiper brushing slowly across the windscreen. The rural highway was deserted until we came up behind a plodding army truck. Soldiers, with rifles between their knees, sat on two benches that ran the length of the truck bed. Their ceremonial uniforms, white kilts and hats with tassels gave away their regimental standing, *Evzones*. Sharpshooters, an elite breed. Killers to a man and feared on the streets during the junta. One of them waved at our driver. Grivas was clearly enjoying his brief bout of self-imposed silence, hoping, I guessed, to elicit a sense of unease. I thought now was as good a time as any to quiz my taciturn travelling companion, see if I could rattle his gruff exterior a little.

"Perhaps you could throw a little more light on the deceased?"

The Brigadier's cheeks went a mottled red. He turned to face me, gesturing expansively, turning his palms upwards, like a man showing he has nothing to hide.

"A little."

I waited for the professional Judas to start spilling the beans.

"The deceased is an American citizen. Name of Tafel ... Konrad Tafel. He's been successfully identified from the passport found on his body. At the moment the man's death is being treated as suicide. That really is about the sum of it."

"Suicide, really? Topping yourself down a coal mine. That seems a little curious, don't you think?"

A terse sniff dismissed my questioning, any hint of the previous smile long gone. "Why should you care about where some stranger choses to snuff out their life?"

I paused briefly, looked out of the rear window. Jagged walls of stone rose above us. I turned and watched the driver swing over into the left lane and pass the crawling military vehicle, then focussed my attention back on the Brigadier.

"In my experience, here in Greece, this kind of unusual tragedy usually involves someone being murdered. We practically invented the idea of the noble hero brought low by some flaw of character."

"Well Konrad Tafel wasn't murdered. He certainly isn't Greek and there appears to be nothing heroic about his rather miserable demise."

"Not a very Yankee sounding name, Tafel?"

"Is that a fact?" Grivas smirked, inhaled noisily, like he was sucking a spoonful of soup then blew a smoke ring at my face. If I could have caught it, I would have liked to have wrapped it round his scraggy, little neck.

"It's just an observation, that's all."

"I, nor the Provost, need your observations, Major. You do as you have been ordered. Worry about making sure the stars and stripes are draped over the damn casket when the body's shipped out."

. . .

I took a last puff of my cigarette before extinguishing it in a silver ashtray in the door panel. “So, no digging the dirt then?”

Grivas shook his head. “That’s always the problem with digging about in other people’s business, Major. Once you start, it’s knowing when to stop.” The Brigadier smiled a decayed smile, which served to remind me of just how rotten his soul probably was. Among all Grivas’ perished teeth, a single, gleaming flash of gold resembled a tiny nugget found in the dirt in some grizzled Klondike prospector’s pan, and in his brutally cynical mouth, gold could not have seemed less precious.

CHAPTER FOUR

IT WAS WELL-KNOWN THAT THE SUN COULD BARELY EVER BE SEEN IN the sky over the Ptolemaida mine. The heavy industrial haze that was always suspended in the air didn't allow you to see far, even on a good day. But on a day like today, with thick black clouds, a biting mountain air current and the rain pissing down, we may as well have been driving through the Siberian wilderness.

Ptolemaida was owned by the Public Power Corporation and was the biggest mine in the Balkans, responsible for thirty percent of the country's electricity production. The grim landscape around the sprawling black colliery spanned over six-hundred-and-twenty-five square miles and included, at its heart, more than a dozen deserted villages. One of the last towns still standing amidst the thick carbon ash and cinder was Florina, a small, beaten-up municipality on the outskirts of the mine and one of the few inhabited settlements in the region. Florina was also one of the coldest towns in Greece, because of its elevation and geographic position. Heavy snowfalls, thick fog and below-freezing temperatures were common during the winter months, while the summers were smog-filled and stifling hot.

I am only aware of these facts because Gravis had been rattling on about the damn place for the better part of half an hour.

What the Brigadier had failed to impress upon me was how Florina had fallen into rack and ruin. It was now a ghostly, godforsaken slum; deserted, all but forgotten except for the miners who had been forced to remain.

From what I could gather, the rest of the town's inhabitants were made up of various off-the-books militia, a few reckless scientists, shady scavengers and a handful of elderly Greeks who would rather ignore the toxic fumes than be forced to relocate. It was a hardscrabble enclave, one that was now lost in an unwelcoming black terrain, gutted by the mining of lignite, the nation's brown coal.

The roads, mainly unlit, were an obstacle course of potholes. As we drove through, I could see for myself that most of the town was made up of half-demolished houses, a few hungry stray dogs, dilapidated churches. The cemetery lay deep in an embrace of brambles and weeds. Many of the buildings we'd past on the outskirts had either been vacated years ago or looked fit to crumble: door frames shifted, exterior walls and foundations cracked beyond repair. Ruin and decay were everywhere.

A real shithole.

The mine itself hadn't fared any better aesthetically or, from the look of it, in its upkeep either. To call the surroundings and site construction depressed-looking was an understatement. After introducing ourselves to a disinterested sentry at the main gate we headed into the workings along a bleak stretch of black road and parked outside a grubby two-storey concrete building with a sign directing you to the manager's office that was so discreet it might have been signalling the way to a public toilet. As we climbed out of the car a barrel-chested little man who looked like he'd been ironed into his ill-fitting, brown-serge suit, shambled down some steps from the office quarters and slowly headed across the lot towards us. Clearly sunburned, his balding head slathered with cream, every step taken towards us looked painful. As he drew closer the man held out his hand in greeting, the scorching on his scalp clearly raw and inflamed. He gestured with his head toward the sky.

"Enough of fucking Crete and its fucking sun!"

I smiled and pointed at the man's vicious-looking suntan. "Not a good trip then?"

"Fucking awful holiday. And it was full of Germans too!

Grivas, his expression as grave as a hangman, swiftly interrupted. "You are?"

The man stuttered a wary response. "I'm Pattakos ... Leon Pattakos, the site manager."

Grivas held his warrant card up in front of the site manager's blistered face for all of a gnat's breath before wading into him. "We've not travelled up from Salonica to this miserable damn hole to hear you complain about your holiday." The Brigadier shifted a thumb in my direction. "This is Major Remis of the Hellenic Gendarmerie."

The overseer nodded apologetically. "I'm sorry, gentlemen. We've been expecting you." He shuffled on his feet nervously before turning and pointing back to where he had limped from. "Please, if you'd like to follow me."

We left Grivas' men to guard the motor and headed

across the car park, climbing the cement-flagged steps to enter a dingy corner office that was filled with the fetid odour of stale food and perspiration. The inside of the cramped room was decorated with greasy notice boards, dusty photographs of forgotten comrades, old bulletins curled into yellow scrolls, new bulletins slung into the wastebasket and a tired-looking metal desk marked with coffee stains. A small window sat in the centre of the wall, which was papered with peeling, damp anaglypta. Filthy net curtains and torn, green and purple drapes had been drawn back against one wall. The glass in the window looked like it hadn't seen a wet rag in years but, surprisingly, was still fighting off the grime to offer up an impressive view of the coke heap at the back of the building.

Leon Pattakos made a beeline for his wretched bureau and snatched up the tail end of a thick Cuban corona that was burning in a glass ashtray. He nervously stuck the stogie between his lips and took a hefty pull on it before pulling open a drawer underneath the desk. He lifted out a blue passport, walked back around his desk to Grivas and handed over the travel document to the Brigadier.

"This was found next to the body." Pattakos waved away a wreath of cigar smoke, flashing a ruby that Pope Paul would have got down on his knees to kiss. The tubby executive looked at me nervously. "Please, take a seat." He raised an arm and pointed to one of two dreary-looking orange easy chairs. I refused the offer. Both recliners resembled a dyer's experiment gone wrong. The rest of the office was a celebration of bad taste and filth, and it had the urine-coloured Persian rug to prove it. My feet searched for landing space amongst the spread of clutter that was pitched across the floor.

I watched Grivas scrutinise the contents of the passport before handing it over to me.

"Where is the body?" the Brigadier barked.

"We have a small infirmary and mortuary." Pattakos took a moment to consider his next words. "Sadly, accidents at the mine are common and sometimes fatal."

I waved the passport out in front of me. "And you think this man's death was an accident, do you?"

I saw the Brigadier give Pattakos the evil eye. "I don't think our friend here should be expected to answer to such a complex question, do you Major?" The site manager cleared his throat nervously, flashing a twitchy smile at me. I kept schtum and simply nodded my head in agreement. The Brigadier stiffened his back and gestured an open palm toward the door. "Now, if you would kindly take us to the deceased." Grivas snatched back the passport and gave me a withering glare before stepping away. He took my silence as an indicator of my subordination then continued with his own inquisitorial enquiry as he ushered Pattakos out of the office. I shadowed after them. Mute for now.

Who was I to disagree or interrupt a man who liked the sound of his own voice so much?

It is difficult to form any clear impression of a man who has been hanged that is not grotesque. The tongue is normally always turgid and protruding like a third lip, the eyes as prominent as a Doberman's balls – these things tend to colour your thoughts a little. So, on first impressions standing in the mortuary doorway looking at the corpse stretch out on the metal table, there wasn't much to say about Konrad Tafel except what his passport already told me.

He was thirty-eight years old, white, a citizen of the United

States of America and possibly, if it was true that he'd hung himself, thanks in part to his necktie, getting on for tall.

Clear cut enough you'd think. In my experience hanging is almost always suicide: there are far easier ways to kill a man than choking him to death. I have seen few exceptions, those that had been accidental cases, where the victim had encountered the mishap of vagal inhibition while going about some sado-masochistic perversion. These sexual non-conformists were usually found naked or clothed in female underwear with a spread of pornographic literature to sticky hand.

I lit a Santé and walked on inside; the reek of death was overwhelming. The site manager stood close to the door; his eyes fixed on the ground. Cigarette butts littered the red concrete floor under a sign that said ***No Smoking***. The walls were white tiled and in desperate need of hot soapy water and a scrub. I watched Grivas sniff the air then cover his mouth with the back of his hand. "My God, it stinks in here."

I lifted my hand. "It's this cheap Greek tobacco." I filled my lungs with smoke and offered the packet to Grivas. "You want one?"

The Brigadier waved a gloved hand in my face. I stood over the body and shook my head slowly at Grivas. "It makes you think doesn't it."

"About mortality?"

"No. About how I should open up a flower shop, the number of corpses I see in a month." I walked slowly around the gurney, taking in horrific injuries that had been inflicted on the dead man's body. "In my game people are either dead or dying. They always need flowers. I could make more money a month as a florist."

Grivas didn't care for my glib remarks. He briskly turned his attention back to Leon Pattakos.

"Who found the body?"

The site manager looked up uneasily to address the Brigadier. "Two of my overmen coming on to the early shift." He took a step forward, glanced across at the body then decided against it. He wiped the back of his hand across his mouth and took a deep breath before continuing to answer. "They said the poor bastard was stretched out on the ground out by number two silo, right next to the pit brow."

"At what time was this, approximately?" Grivas barked.

"Around 6am this morning."

I took out my fountain pen from my inside jacket pocket. "6am, you say?" Pattakos stayed put, nodding his head in agreement at my question. I continued my stroll around the table, making a mental note of the injuries on the body, aware that Grivas was scrutinizing every move I made, waiting to block any awkward or probing query I may have for the mining official. I pointed at the corpse as I addressed Grivas. "From the stink coming off his hide, I'd say that this fella's been dead for more than a couple of days."

"In your opinion, how long?"

"I'm not a medical examiner. I'd just be hazarding a guess based on the stiffs I've seen in the same kind of state previously."

Grivas' steely countenance didn't care for my irreverent description. "So, damn it, how long?"

I shrugged. "Maybe, three, four days, judging by the post-mortem decay."

I stood at the top of the table and viewed the length of corpse from head to toe. The body was still fully clothed. A once white shirt, now smeared in coal dirt, dried saliva and blood, ripped open to the waist, most of the buttons gone, the cuffs un-done and sleeves rolled up to the elbows. A necktie that had originally been Windsor knotted was dragged away from the collar and likewise drenched in the man's blood and desiccated snot. Torn, black, linen trousers, the hem of each leg rolled above the ankles revealing socks that had been shoved down toward the feet. The man's flies were unzipped and the fabric around the groin still clearly sodden wet. The left shoe was missing, the right heavily scuffed and caked-in mud at the heel. Severe facial abrasions covered one side of the man's face, as well as on the chin and the front and lefthand side of the neck. There were ligature marks and burns on the neck indicating strangulation as the possible cause of death. I leaned across the man's face and carefully pushed the tip of my pen inside the mouth pressing down to see inside.

The tongue had been gouged by the man's teeth as he'd died strangling. From the state he was in, he'd probably been unconscious by the time the final force was applied. There were further cord marks on both the ankles and wrists. Both sets of imprints had drawn blood from deep cuts, suggesting that the victim had fought his attacker for a length of time. The palm of each hand had also been pierced through, possibly by a large nail or similar metal instrument and it appeared that unsuccessful attempts had been made to inflict the same injury to the left foot, resulting in only a partial piercing.

Unsuccessful or perhaps Konrad Tafel had just given up the information he'd been tortured for and there was no need for the interrogator to continue.

I wiped the top of my pen on some paper towel that had been scrunched up and discarded on a metal bench next to the gurney and slid it back into my jacket pocket. I lit another cigarette from the dying embers of the old butt I still had clenched between my fingers and drew the smoke in sharply making my eyes tear. I glanced over my shoulder at the site manager. “Would you mind leaving us for a moment, Mister Pattakos?” The peaky-looking foreman didn’t need asking twice and backed out into the corridor and was out of sight before I had chance to thank him. I turned to Grivas, pointing down at the butchered corpse.

“I’m going to have a real fucking problem convincing anyone that this was suicide.”

Grivas looked at me narrowly and smiled before marching away toward the exit. He called after me as he turned into the hallway.

“Well, as you rightly say, Major. It’s your problem now.”

CHAPTER
FIVE

An old soldier once told me, *"Hungry dogs will always bolt down a dirty pudding".* It was sage like advice, the aged trooper extolling the virtue that we should always look at ourselves first before criticising others. After spending time with Grivas it was difficult to tell who was the unfed dog or who was the grimy pudding.

The only thing I was certain of was that I didn't trust the Brigadier as far as I could have thrown him.

I had no appetite for the fishy assignment I'd been given, but Grivas' craving for me to execute the Provost's orders in double-quick time left me with little choice but to carry out my directives without scrutiny or complaint. The hacked-up cadaver laying on the gurney back at the infirmary had been anything other than suicide. Something stank to high-heaven, I just didn't know what, and I was in no position to begin investigating a crime or start questioning my betters. The drive back to Salonica had been one of awkward silences and painful, half-hearted small talk. Before departing the mine, Grivas had snatched back the dead man's passport from me and decamped to the site manager's office, swiftly arranging for Konrad Tafel's body to be collected that evening without further delay. The corpse to be taken under police escort in an unmarked N.I.S vehicle and deposited at the city morgue. After that, as Grivas had briskly stressed to me; the dead American was my problem.

It was a little after nine when Grivas' wordless driver and his accompanying and equally tight-lipped aide dropped me off outside police headquarters on Republic Square. The Brigadier and I shared no fond farewells. No salutes. The stuffy spy chief didn't need to utter another word. He knew what was expected of me, and the sooner I got on with the state's grunt work, the better. There was no way in hell that I was going back to my desk to bust my gut into the small hours or worse still, return to my fleapit apartment to mull over the shitty day I'd just had. Instead, I got in my car and headed out to an old haunt in search of something cool to pour inside me.

Salonika's different at night: the air smells better, it's harder to see that the building sites and cranes now outnumber the harbour-front palm trees; it's almost like the good old days, at least the way I'd like to remember them. Stay in my business long enough and every street leads to a place you'd like to forget, every new case brings back memories of what you should have done and what might have been, and every skirt reminds you of another woman... or, if you've got it bad enough, the same woman.

The Tsinari bar on Alexandras Place in the Ano Poli district of the city was one of the few places I felt happy drinking in, and where I could forget about work. The bar owner, Billy

Krifakis was a born-again ex-con who'd acquired the deed and keys to the Tsinari from a debt-ridden cell mate whom he'd been holed up with for a five-year stretch in Athens' notorious Korydallos prison. Billy, not being an over familiar fella, had given me the barest nod when I came in. I doubted if he knew my first name, but I was sure he knew what I did for a living.

It was a slow night and there were few customers in the place, which suited me perfectly. When the bar was busy, Billy had a way of standing with his hands spread on the bar top, his big square head lowered, gazing out through the open doorway into the street with a far-away look in his eyes, as if he was remembering a long-lost love or a guardhouse fight, he'd won one time. He didn't say much. He was neither dumb nor very wise. I could never decide which. Either way, I liked him.

I sidled onto a stool and ordered a Mythos beer. There was a bowl of pitted black olives on the bar. I took a handful and chomped on them. The saltiness left my tongue feeling like a piece of chalk. Billy returned with my drink and slid the glass toward me on a white paper serviette. I thanked him, knocked the heavy pitcher of lager straight back and ordered a refill.

"Gonna be one of those nights, is it?"

"Been one of those fucking days."

The barman shook his head, picked up a white cloth and began polishing a glass. "You ain't gonna get canned and start abusing my customers like last time."

I turned and stared around the almost empty Taverna. "What customers?"

Billy flexed his muscleman's shoulders in a shrug. "Just don't start any of your shit tonight. I don't wanna have to sling your arse out into the street again. Got it?"

I studied my beer glass, rotating it on its base. Nodded my head. "Got it."

A man walked in, signalled from the far end of the bar and Billy went off to serve him. I heard the fella begin speaking in pigeon Greek, with a heavy German accent thrown in for good measure but quickly blocked out the chit-chat, becoming lost in my own thoughts, mulling over my latest assignment and considering the bigger questions in life; like why the first sip of beer always tasted so much better than the second. This was the kind of philosophical speculation I was prone to, hence my reputation as the thinking man's detective, abuser of fellow drinkers and bar room brawler. Hearing the Provost mention Gravis' name earlier and how he'd be tagging along with me to the mine had quickly set me on edge, starting me thinking about my past, about all those old secrets kept, the veiled cases worked, cruel deeds undertaken, the beatings and torture witnessed and the fact that being at the behest of powerful and unscrupulous men, like Provost Callas and the Brigadier meant that you quickly learn never to trust a living soul. Storing up so many bad memories was as unpredictable as nitro-glycerine; you never know what was going to set one off. Being around Grivas had stirred up black thoughts, got me thinking about my former sinful conduct in the line of duty; the shitty stuff that I'd rather have kept under lock and key. I'd hoped a few more beers would dull such unwelcome reveries, and if the Mythos lager didn't staunch such miserable thinking there was a bottle of seventy per cent proof Metaxa brandy back at my place that would more than take the edge off.

I lit a cigarette, took in a chest-full of the cheap nicotine and slowly released the dull vapour out of my nostrils.

"How'd you like those smokes?" said the voice with the German accent.

I stared at the Santé in between my fingers. "They're alright. I've been smoking 'em for so long I hardly notice how bad they are anymore."

The kraut at the opposite end of the bar picked up his glass of red wine and headed toward me. He was slim and balding, in his mid-to-late forties, with a hooked nose, short moustache and chin beard. He was wearing a well-cut navy sports jacket, dark polo-necked sweater and formal cavalry twill trousers. His black brogues looked as if they had been polished to a glass shine by hired help. He pushed a packet of cigarettes along the marble-topped bar, nodding his shaven head in greeting. "Eric Hodt. I'm in the tobacco business. At the risk of sounding like a commercial, try one of these. They're new to the Greek market, they'll be sat on every news stand in the country soon."

I turned the pack, reading the brand name out loud. "Juno. Sounds like they should come from the Baltic rather than the Rhineland."

"They're German, but the tobacco's Greek or Turkish, depending on how you look at these things. The man's voice was a nasal baritone with a lot of patience on the edge. The tone sounded like the low growl of a house-trained panther. "Fortunately, they don't smoke like Russian tobacco, thank Christ. These are sweet on the tongue and cool on the throat. One thing I hate is Russian smokes."

My new German friend blinked his lashless eyes slowly: they looked like smaller versions of his almost hairless skull. I watched him take a couple of cigarettes out of the box; he handed one to me. I stubbed out my Santé in the glass ashtray on the bar. Lit up the Juno, liked it, and nodded my genuine appreciation.

"Well, life's full of surprises. The names Michail Remis. And thanks." I pushed the pack back along the bar.

"Keep them," he said. "I've a suitcase full of samples back at my hotel room."

"Whereabouts in Germany are you from Herr Hodt?"

"Köpenick. It's a small-town south-east of Berlin." Hodt took a sip of wine and rested his elbow against the limestone slab. "What line of work are you in, Mister Remis?"

"Civil servant. Public highways maintenance," I lied.

"Important work, no doubt. And is this your regular watering hole?"

"Friend, I've been drinking in this dive for so long I've started to smash the crockery for the tourists when I'm in a good mood."

"And when you are in a bad mood?"

I gestured my head toward the gorilla-sized barman. "Then Billy over there chucks my drunken backside out onto the pavement." I threw the last of my beer back and winked at Billy. I pointed at Hodt's still half-filled wine glass. "Buy you another?"

The German swigged the rest of his drink, pushed the stemmed goblet back across the bar, nodding at Billy. "Same again please."

I took another drag on my hand-out smoke. "How long are you in Salonika, Herr Hodt?"

"Not long, just until the end of the week. I'm here for several meetings with the Karelia Tobacco Corporation. All very formal, and I'm afraid, quite boring." Hodt toasted me with the wine he'd just ordered. "Any tips for a traveller new to the city?"

"Just one. Keep away from the tap water. The hotel staff will tell you it's safe to drink, but it ain't. I'd stick to bottled if I were you. That's unless you want to lose weight fast." I toasted him back. Hodt grinned, stuck his hand inside his jacket pocket, withdrew a business card and handed it to me.

"Sounds like good advice." Hodt looked at his wristwatch then emptied his glass in two swift drafts. "I must be on my way. An early start in the morning." The German backed up a step, pointed at the card in my hand. "If you want any more Junos before they hit the newsstands, give that number a call. I have a guy over here that can do you a good deal on a few cases if you feel like stocking up. Now, I must bid you a very good-night." I nodded my farewell. Hodt stuck out his hand. I took his palm in mine, noted the clammy skin and manicured fingernails. We shook. He clicked his heels together. I cringed and hoped the kraut hadn't see me flinch.

Hodt pointed at the Junos on the bar top. "We smokers have to stick together, right Mister Remis? What does that Greek proverb say? Caught together, hanged together, yes?"

I watched Herr Hodt march across the bar and out into the street. I quickly got to my feet, went over to the window and watched the stranger idle back down the road until he'd disappeared out of sight. I looked at the business card I'd just be given, then glanced over the bar back at Billy Krifakis.

Although neither of us uttered a word, I knew what we both were thinking.

Eric Hodt was about as much of a tobacco salesman, as I was a civil servant.

CHAPTER SIX

THERE'S ONE THING I LEARNED ABOUT THE TRUTH ... A LITTLE BIT GOES a long way.

When I was a young cop, a couple of millennia ago, I used to think I knew what I was doing out on the street. I was aware of the world's caprices, how the good and bad in human nature had to co-exist on a day-to-day basis. Where small-time crime was concerned, I was happy to sometimes allow myself to get thrown off the scent, occasionally turning a blind eye rather than make my own life or some other joker's harder than it needed to be. Back then, where my own actions were concerned, I was confident that I was a good man, doing an honest job. I was sitting square in the driver's seat, with the wheel held firmly in my own two hands.

These days I know different. Things aren't so black and white. Now I know that decisions I think I make are in fact made only in hindsight, and that at the time things are actually happening all I do is either drift or obey orders. It doesn't trouble me much, this awareness of how little control I have over my work and policing affairs. Most of the time I've been content to slide along with the current, do as I'm told, never rock the boat. There are occasions, though, when I wish I'd made at least some kind of effort to be more of a proper copper, to dig deeper and not always turn so many blind eyes.

My chance meeting earlier this evening with the shifty German, the day's curious events, the mutilated corpse, had stirred up the real detective in me and not the fella willing to look the other way or doctor an arrest or charge sheet.

I knew that my new friend Herr Hodt wasn't on the level in the same way that both Brigadier Grivas and the Provost weren't being straight with me. Honesty was not something either my boss or the spy master ever gave much serious thought about; especially when hoodwinking a flunkey like me. Hodt had put on a good show back at the bar, but I can smell a liar a mile off. His impromptu introduction immediately felt feigned, worse still, the German's over-confident manner smacked of old school, inside-man guile.

I knew that both Callas and Grivas had their own reasons for wanting Konrad Tafel's body shipped out of the country quicker than a buttered bullet. I was now left wondering where the shifty kraut fitted into the picture.

I drove back to my rented apartment, which was in spitting distance of the Tsinari bar. I lived in the heart of the *Ano Poli*, the old town of Thessaloniki. The upper town is the most traditional part of the city, preserving much of the Byzantine and Ottoman era homes. The roach trap I dossed down in had been around almost as long as some of those ancient joints, but those relics were in a helluva lot better condition. It was the last tenement on Pileos Avenue. The area was upmarket, but you wouldn't have known it from inside my place. The outside was shielded by a carapace of olive trees and so well-disguised by overgrown weeds and shrubbery that it was hard to believe the building was there at all unless you looked really closely. Inside, you knew it was there but wished it wasn't.

Eric Hodt's slippery handshake had stayed with me all the way to my front door, which is where I was determined to leave it. I turned the key in the lock, let myself in, flicked down the light switch in the hall so that I could treat myself to a look at all the luxury I'd afforded myself over the years. The living room and kitchen were rustic, the ceiling fans just rusty. The wallpaper in all the rooms was yellow, although not by design and the furniture looked as if it was trying to return to nature and join the invading plant-life outside. Poisonous, half-decayed, vaguely fungal, it was the kind of place that belonged in a bottle of formaldehyde. In the bedroom, broken shutters hid a dirty, cobwebbed pane of single glass, a threadbare rug and a decrepit brass bed with a mattress as thin as a pauper's pitta. To call it monastic would have been an understatement.

The inside of my head still felt like it was being sand-blasted. My stomach was in no mood to entertain the thought of food. Nicotine and booze were the only two things to have passed my lips in the past twenty-four hours and all I was longing for before I hit the sack was another hit of liquor and a smoke. I threw my coat and hat on the kitchen counter, kicked off my shoes, grabbed a glass tumbler and headed over to the fake teak sideboard in search of the brandy bottle. I kept pouring the Metaxa until the booze was deep enough in the glass to drown puppies in.

I fell into an armchair and knocked back the fiery spirit in a couple of swift gulps. I gave myself a generous top-up and stayed sat in that old recliner for the better part of an hour mulling over the strange particulars of the day, my thoughts like spiders crawling inside my skull, my mind trying desperately to make sense of all that I'd seen and heard. I sank another three glasses of hooch before my brain finally gave up the ghost and let me relax. I shifted in my seat, felt the damp sensation of cold perspiration sticking to the shirt on my back. The cruel stink rising from underneath my arms and making me gag as good a reason as any to muster up the will and strength to finally shift me up out of my chair.

I staggered into the bathroom, turned on the tap and took off my clothes then stood underneath the head of the shower for ten minutes. I let the hot water run down onto my body until my skin stung and prickled, finally getting out when fatigue got the better of me and I felt my legs could no longer hold me up. I dried off and wiped the palm of my hand across the condensation on the glass and stared at myself. I'd turned forty-five that summer, not a welcome event. My body was still trim with only an inch of belly above my belt. I told myself that I wasn't bad looking if you were after more boxer than movie star. I continued to examine my face without much enthusiasm. What I had against my mug was its air of disappointment, its lived-in look, the bloodshot-eyes and mean expression, as if I was always expecting the tap on the shoulder that might again usher its reluctant owner to undertake yet another unsavoury endeavour.

I went into the bedroom pulled on a loose-fitting, grey T-shirt and a pair of gym shorts then headed for my bed. As I slung back the sheet, I could feel myself slipping toward a darkness that both my body and mind seemed reluctant to enter. I climbed into bed, my head throbbing, my stomach knotted tight. I swallowed hard, then let both arms fall loosely at my side. I looked up toward the ceiling and closed my eyes. My heart beat quickly inside my chest, its dull throbbing like an old clock that was about to bust a vital spring.

I told myself that sleep was the most natural and inevitable condition in the human metabolism. We can abstain from sex and thrive on the thorns of desire, deny ourselves water in the desert, keep silent on the torturer's rack, and fast unto death; but eventually sleep has its way with us.

An army psychiatrist I knew once told me that everyone has a dream store cupboard in their head. He said that sometimes a recent disturbing event provides us with a rusty key to it that we can well do without. I was about to discover that the dead American, Konrad Tafel, would be waiting for me whilst I slept and that he was about to turn all the tumblers in the lock like a perverse nocturnal demiurge.

I am walking in the rain, down a narrow, unlit, brick passageway close to my home. I can smell the damp stone, the mint and oregano growing in the courtyards, see the shadows of the olive trees waving on the cobble-stone path beyond the piked gate that hung open at the end of the alleyway. I can hear the slow-moving low waters flowing along the gutters in the distance, the mortar between the bricks in the wall feel like claws in my back. I work my way up toward my apartment, my Walther service pistol held out in front of me. My hand tightening on the grips, my breath ballooning in my chest. As I step toward the scrolled iron gate it swings into my face, rakes my gun out of my hand and knocks me back into a pool of rainwater.

As I scramble around on the wet path Konrad Tafel walks out of the darkness, his face blackened with coal dust, his hair so thick with blood that his scalp glows in the moonlight. His matted clothes are glued against his body with sweat and bodily fluids. In his hands he holds an antique Marlin 12-gauge shotgun, which is raised out in front of him. He moves slowly as I start to kick out with my legs and try to clamber back away from him. I feel my back suddenly slam against the brick wall. Tafel squats down in front of me, the shotgun resting on his thigh. He looks at me, his eyes red-rimmed, his breath rank with decay.

"Look what your people did to me," he says.

I feel my fingertips bite into the hard ground as he pokes the shotgun towards my face. "Come and beg, beg for your worthless fucking life, as I did." Then he smiles, lifts the point of my chin with the barrel and cocks the hammer.

I wake from my nightmare bolt upright. My T-shirt and shorts damp with perspiration. I sit on the edge of the bed, my head bent down, palms clammy on the tops of my legs, my jaws clenched tight to keep them from shaking. Outside, I could hear late-night revellers in the street, glass breaking, a beer can rolling across the tarmac.

I did not close my eyes again until the birds began to sing and the cedar trees outside were black and stiff with the coming of the grey dawn.

CHAPTER SEVEN

My heart was still thrumming from the nightmare as I pulled up outside the Salonica coroner's office. The city morgue was a rusticated white building on Kordelio Street which came complete with blue door, shutters and a tatty Greek flag out front just in case the colour scheme left room for doubt regarding anyone's sense of patriotism. The front door was nearly always guarded by a pair of enormous, fierce-looking seagulls neither of which ever showed any fear of the scrawny black mutt that permanently lay asleep, or possibly dead, on the step.

The chief coroner, Lakis Vokos, belonged to a species of human that should have died out a century ago. An infamous character, well-known to police officer and surgeon alike, both for his brusque manner, his massive girth and for wearing a black wool cap with a peak in all weathers that was only a little less long and hairy than his nose. Vokos was no respecter of men. To him, heroes, tyrants, holy men were all decaying meat on a stone slab. Alive, they may have been draped in cassocks, military decorations or professor's robes. Dead, their secrets poured out in cheesy rolls of fat, blackened livers and tender brains exposed in a steel bowl; nothing more. The fact that chief medical examiner Vokos was still alive was a relief to other pathologists because nobody ever wanted to carve up a colleague, especially one as fat as Vokos. He had done his part over the past year to keep his arse out of a shallow grave, lost fifty pounds, huffed and puffed around the murky corridors of the soulscot for exercise looking like a half-deflated balloon in slow motion.

I met the pathologist in the morgue's outer office, a cigarette hanging from his lips, a glass of milky-white ouzo in his hand. The sour smell that hung in the air was reminiscent of warm, wet poultry flesh mixed with surgical spirits. It was a sickly cocktail that I felt in my stomach at the same time as I drew it into my nostrils. The office, barely furnished with a couple of chairs and a table, contained nothing to warn the unwary of what lay beyond the two glass doors, except the stench and a sign that simply read **'Morgue: Entrance Forbidden'**.

The hair of the dog cure I imbibed before leaving my apartment had done little to improve my hangover. My skull felt like it had an axe planted in it. Before heading on inside I lit up one of Hodt's fancy German cigarettes in the hope that a quick hit of nicotine would see off the heavy bell sound booming in my head, and the brown spots that were floating in front of my eyes.

Vokos looked up when he heard my Ronson spark. "You going to puke before we go see your Yankee friend?"

"Not if it's going to ruin your day. You need to remember that I'm not getting the kind of drachmas in my pocket like some of us are." I couldn't help reminding Vokos that pathologists were paid thirty percent more than ordinary doctors who worked for a living. It was considered as 'hazard pay' because nothing was so dangerously alive with toxic flora as a rotting corpse. I inhaled deeply on the Juno until my nose and lungs were thoroughly corrupted with smoke.

Ready, I followed Vokos into a heady atmosphere of methanal and surgical spirits. The inside of the mortuary never changed. At its centre was an operating table that was also part trough. It was hard to forget the grubby cement walls, brown stains around the floor, bleached drains and glaring florescent lights that more often than not induced a headache. There was a queue of sorts. Other tables held a young female so drained of claret she was as white as an alabaster sculpture, the blackened remains of a torso, and the ballooned-up carcass of an elderly man topped off a general atmosphere of spoiled meat, vinegar and saltpetre. I sucked on the Juno so hard it sparked the tobacco and still I could taste bile in my throat.

"Quite a collection, isn't it?" Vokos offered an indigent flap of his hand at the row of cadavers. "See anything you like?"

"I'd like to see the exit as soon as possible. Can we make this snappy?"

Vokos grinned and waved his glass in front of me. "Come on, indulge me, Remis. I'm stuck in this hellhole with these dead bastards day and night. A man needs to make light, just to stay sane. The living inside here are worse still. Some of the work that comes out of this place you wouldn't believe.

A meat slaughter's work at a meat traders pace. This place is nothing more than a glorified knacker's yard. I tell you, Remis; these young so-called coroners have no panache. No skill in their surgical technique. No talent for anatomy scrutiny. They excavate the guts and entrails, slit the throat and pull out the craw then drop it in a bucket. I watch these dolts try and run a saw around a skull. It's like watching a drunken carpenter chop off a rotten chair leg. Fucking amateurs the lot of them!" The coroner pulled a face, emptied the last of the ouzo down his throat and ditched the glass in a hand basin. "I've survived two huge coronaries in the last six years. I have acute myocardial infarction. Hypertension that could kill an elephant. I could keel over and die just breaking wind. So these days I do not rush. The cut-up jobs I do for you are the best. Completed by a master."

"What does your doctor say about your health?"

"Same shit the idiot always tells me. Shift my weight. Cut out the raki and tobacco. And, get this, avoid passionate exhilaration. No fucking, the man says. Christ, I haven't had a decent jump in years. Most days I struggle to find my own pecker, just so I can take a leak." Vokos shuffled around the morgue like a woolly mammoth in an operating gown and pointed at the all too familiar corpse. "This the fella you came to visit?"

Konrad Tafel was stretched out on a marble slab that was set slightly at an angle so that fluids from the corpse could drain into the centre and be washed down the drain by water from two tall, murmuring taps. Vokos handed me a wooden clipboard with a half-dozen pieces of paper attached to it. "Here, I can't be bothered to read it."

I gave the papers the once over.

Male. Caucasian. Age 38. Time of death, approximately four days. Cause of death, strangulation. Heavy bone structure with well-developed musculature. Soft facial tissue mutilations to the right-hand side of face and lower neck. Blunt force trauma to the lower left jaw resulting in posterior dislocation with massive extra-

neous bruising. Median Salcus region of the lower tongue lacerated and penetrated. Non-fatal wounds to both hands; each palm punctured, directed via the back of the hands rupturing the hamate and capitate carpal bones. Partial piercing of the left foot. Navicular bone breached and fragmentary rupture. Torso, front and rear, severely contused as result of sustained trauma. Thoracic cavity: ribs, four, five and six broken as a result of repeated direct blows.

I handed the clipboard back to Vokos. "Makes great reading, Lakis. Is there anything not on those papers that I need to know?"

The tubby pathologist winked at me. "There was also a lack of wear on the teeth."

"You've done a dental chart already?"

Vokos handed over the odontology papers. "Done, but they won't help much. This on the other hand might." He flicked the butt of his cigarette across the floor and picked up a stainless-steel kidney bowl from the bench behind him. "Most interesting, this." Vokos hand me the metal dish. Inside was a tooth which had been cracked from crown to root. "From the mandibular dental arcade."

I looked at the pathologist, shrugged my ignorance. Vokos gave a heavy sigh before continuing.

"First molar. Lower jaw. Found upon inspection inside the deceased's mouth. The tooth had practically been dislodged from the gum. No doubt as a result of the heavy pounding the fella's jaw got."

"Are you telling me this guy he was hit hard enough to practically knock out a big tooth like this?"

Vokos nodded. "It's not the first time I've seen it happen, probably won't be the last either. I took a look at it under the microscope. The tooth has been recently worked on and filled with a thin layer of amalgam, which I thought was rather strange."

"Why strange?"

"Because a molar filling would normally require the tooth to be drilled a great deal deeper into the cavity, any decay removed and then filled with a metal alloy mixture. Normally mercury."

"And this tooth wasn't worked on in that way?"

Vokos gave a chuckle. "Hardly. That filling is only surface depth. A slim covering at best. The tooth you have there was healthy. It was drilled and filled for cosmetic purposes."

I felt myself frown. "Cosmetic?"

"Yes." Vokos took the kidney bowl out of my hand, returned it back to the work bench, then picked up a glass petri dish and handed it to me. Inside it were two glass lab slides."

"What the hell?"

"I found that between two tiny sheets of very thin, pliable plastic. Picked it up by chance after a little fine adjustment of the microscope."

"Found what? There's nothing in there but these slides."

"To the naked eye maybe ... It's what's in-between those two plates that really got my attention."

I lifted the dish closer to my face, peered inside. "I can't see a damn thing."

"Vokos laughed and shook his head. He took a thin metal probe out of the top pocket of his overall and tapped it against the side of the glass agar dish.

"That's the point. A micro-dot, Major, isn't meant to be seen."

CHAPTER EIGHT

I SHOULD HAVE LEFT IT THERE; SHOULD HAVE DONE EXACTLY AS THE Provost had ordered me to do and put the body of Konrad Tafel in a casket, cover it in a flag and had it shipped back to the States on the first available flight out of Mikra airport. Instead, I had Vokos stash the Yank's corpse in a refrigerator in one of the remoter parts of the mortuary and told him to inform anyone that came asking, that Tafel's remains had already been shipped out to the aerodrome ready to be repatriated back to the U.S.

Being suspicious becomes a habit; it's also what makes you a good investigator. Lies and deceit come easy to people like me and to my friend, the coroner. Vokos was tighter with words than a Paris waiter with change, more devious than a bucketful of monkeys. The sworn promise of a case of one hundred per cent proof Raki had in no way swayed him to go along with my furtive request.

Rather than go back to the station, I decided to take myself someplace where my phone wasn't ringing off the hook or I could hear cell doors slamming. I needed to think through my next move; consider more carefully the implications of my escalating defiance and duplicity. I couldn't remember the last time I'd sat down to a decent meal. The only things I'd imbibed in recent memory had been poured out of a bottle or shook from a packet. There was a kafeneion, a coffee house, just a short drive across town where I could think things through, grab a bite to eat and knock back a couple of cups of ellinikós kafés, which I hoped would help shift the morning-after feeling that was still plaguing me.

I dodged potholes in the road as I drove along Vasileos Irakliou Street. It was a little after one-thirty, a nice afternoon, too nice to spoil with the car radio but not warm enough to have the window wound down to take in all the car fumes. Yesterday's rain had washed down the pavements of the dust and fly-away trash that was normally caked to them. I headed into the old city, parked the Lancia under a canopy of spruce trees and walked the hundred yards or so into the former Jewish neighbourhood known as the Kadi.

The footprints and signs of the past were everywhere in the old quarter. The unscrupulous, the corrupt and opportunistic, had all been plying their illicit trades inside the Salonica Kadi since the Romans first showed the Greeks the benefits of crazed religion, cheap wine, and a few hundred years of forced labour. Nowadays, the enclosed bazaar was a living piece of history and home to a slightly less unsavoury crowd. Locals shopped alongside tourists, merchants, artists and criminals alike. The archaic slave trade and attic butchery may have long gone, but strangely the Kadi still manages to lure the more unscrupulous members of Thessalonian society. Maybe that's why I always felt so at home wandering through its poorly lit, colonnaded alleyways.

Ouzeri Aristotelous next to the Modiano market was a non-descript little coffee house. Hidden away in a side street, away from the chaos and commotion and the loud haggling voices of hawkers, barrow-boys and peddlers in the agora. The tables outside of the café were in high demand, but I knew that at this time of the day the cosy, antique-filled interior would be quiet and there'd be a seat. I bought a copy of the early edition of the Makedonia from a newsstand opposite the café then headed on inside.

The green-painted interior had been unchanged for decades. A few regulars were sat chatting at rough plank tables, the air dense with cigarette smoke and spilled retsina, a fire of damp coke and grapevine prunings crackled and spluttered in the clay hearth. The flames weren't providing much heat, but it was loud and comforting in its own way. I took off my jacket and sat in the stone inglenook next to the spitting coals and called my order to the taverna's owner, Aris Vezenes, a tall and shambling myopic man, who always viewed the world and his customers through thick-lensed, steel-framed glasses.

I wasn't kept waiting for long before a waiter brought over my coffee in a tiny copper Briki pot along with a plate of mixed mezedes and a glass of chilled water. I knocked back the first cup of strong black coffee in a couple of gulps to get the much-needed caffeine hit inside of me, then went about reading my paper whilst eating.

There was a killing in Chortiatis, a jewellery store robbery in the city's diamond district that resulted in the shop owner taking a beating and three major arrests, but thankfully no mention of a dead foreigner turning up in one of our coal mines.

If I'd learned anything at all from my years as a police officer, it was the simple lesson that most human beings are always more complicated, cruel and devious than we can ever guess, and that none of us completely understands another, no matter how intimate we think we are with them. I thought I knew the Provost well, and what he was capable of. I was also more than aware of the Brigadier's brutal reputation. Yesterday I'd once again found myself waist-high in other people's shit, and as usual was being expected to clean it up. Over the years I'd bent the rules, turned a deaf ear, covered-up and whitewashed just about every kind of crime and immoral transgression you could imagine, and all for the good of Greece, and at my superior's clandestine behest. Konrad Tafel's murder had once again served to drag me into my boss's cruel and debased realm but this time something about the American's death was niggling at my normally hermit-like conscience. Call it a sense of long-lost professional integrity, or just good old plain stupidity.

Although I should have known better, the idea of drawing a veil over this latest can of worms just didn't sit right with me. The petri dish sat in the inside pocket of my jacket, the spur to my current reckless thinking.

I needed to know what was contained on that micro-dot sitting in-between those two glass slides.

I looked across at the wall phone on the other side of the room, knew who I needed to call to get that kind of specialist information. I figured the only way I was ever going find out what had really happened to Konrad Tafel was to look to my past. Search out an old face with a big mouth. Begin asking questions in the gutter.

In my experience, that's where the truth hides.

CHAPTER NINE

I'M NO KNIGHT IN SHINING ARMOUR. JUST A WEATHER-BEATEN MAN IN a crumpled jacket on a street corner with only a grey idea of something you might as well call morality. Sure, I'm none too scrupulous about things that might benefit my pocket, and I could no more inspire a bunch of young thugs to do good works of charity than I could stand up and sing a solo in a church choir. But of one thing, I was sure; I was through being told to look at my fingernails whilst there were thieves in the store.

With that harsh reality in mind, I'd decided to stay clear of police headquarters and my office for the rest of the afternoon. I wasn't known for keeping regular hours and doubted that I would be missed either by my colleagues or the desk sergeant. I'd driven back to my apartment, made a couple of telephone calls and continued to brood over why there was a dead American cooling his dick back at the morgue.

My gut instinct told me that the provost's, *'man of no importance'*, as he'd coolly implied, clearly wasn't the small fry he was making him out to be. Konrad Tafel's murder had been a brutal and sustained assault. The injuries inflicted had been meted out with both sadistic precision and deviant abandon. My boss and Brigadier Grivas clearly had their own reasons for wanting the dead man's demise knocked up to a simple suicide, but Tafel's carving up and clear signs of torture had been anything but self-immolation.

The coroner, Vokos, had offered up a teasing revelation, unearthing the kind of dirt that I knew deep down I'd have been wise to stay well clear of. It was a valuable lead, and one that I simply couldn't dismiss. Over the years, I've learnt that the signs that keep you on the right track are never where you look for them. These kinds of clues generally fall out of the pocket of somebody else's suit that you pick up at the cleaners. They're in the tune you can't stop humming; that you've never heard before. They're at the other end of the wrong number you dial in the middle of the night. The tell-tale signs that something is not as it should be are in those old familiar places you think you've never been before.

But you get used to seeing them out of the corner of your eye, and you end up tripping over the ones that are right in front of you. I knew that once I started sniffing about, following up whatever was photographed on the micro-dot stowed inside the dead yank's tooth, that trouble wouldn't be very far behind.

I was used to wading through deep water.

Getting in over my head.

Shit. Trouble's what I do.

. . .

I didn't remember falling asleep, only waking and still being plagued by a damned headache. My thoughts slowly remerged with the increasing pain behind my eye. I pressed a thumb against my temple and the ache lessened maybe three decibels. I had a time-worn remedy for kicking this kind of pole-axed feeling, and reluctantly slouched down the hall into the crapper.

An ice-cold shower numbers among the one of the most painful experiences I've ever willingly endured, but it does wonders for hangovers and an over-thinking mind. Ten minutes with my head bowed under a hail of bone-chilling water and I came out of the stall shivering like a wet dog and almost ready to hunt.

I went into the bedroom and dressed; a lightweight, navy blue, single-breasted suit, white dress shirt, crisp from the laundry, and an unstained burgundy necktie. I splashed on a little aftershave, ran my fingertips through the front of my hair, straightened my tie. I snatched up the leather shoulder holster that cradled my service-issue Walther from the bed. I slipped on the harness, put on my jacket, and placed a bill fold into my inside breast pocket. I looked at myself in the mirror, smoothing down the material underneath my left arm where the automatic was hidden with the palm of my hand.

Satisfied with my appearance, I reached across to the bedside table, opened it up, grabbed a stiletto switchblade and concealed it out of sight. I looked at my watch. The blue iridescent hands told me that it was seven-ten. I collected my warrant card and keys off the kitchen counter before heading downstairs. On the stone step outside my apartment, I stood for a moment and listened to the evening song of a chorus of crickets chirping in the oregano shrubs at the rear of the tenement.

The sun had already started to slowly drop behind the rooftops, the air warm and heavy. There was no traffic or sound in the streets, only dust and scraps of newspaper whirling in the wind through the tunnel of olive trees at the end of the road. I closed the front door and felt a sudden shiver run through me as I walked across to the car. I got inside, turned the key in the ignition and listened to the engine rumble into life.

My destination was just a short drive away. I was en-route to a location that few people in the city knew existed and fewer still were ever invited or admitted in to. I required no street guide or map to find this elusive domain. I'd trodden over its cloaked threshold many times before. Encased inside these shrouded chambers was an old acquaintance; a disagreeable little man who dealt in very dark arts.

And this evening whilst in his furtive company, I'd be giving him every opportunity to ply his Delphic talents on my behalf.

CHAPTER TEN

IT ONLY TOOK A MINUTE FOR EZRA LIEBERMAN TO DISENGAGE THE lock on the battleship grey, reinforced metal door to his underground apartment/workshop. This door was eight feet below street level on Olgas Boulevard close to the seafront promenade. The electronic lab that had once been a living space was now a series of rooms lined with worktables containing every sort of gadget you could imagine; listening devices, hidden lenses, specialised walkie talkie telephones, infrared sensors and a pile of other gear I couldn't even begin to explain. I walked down the hall, past the one-time master bedroom that now doubled as a dark room and found my normally elusive quarry waiting for me in his junk-filled studio.

I didn't often get the chance to see Lieberman on his feet and away from the massive table that dominated his work-room. He rarely stood up in my presence and was usually happy sat in a high-backed leather chair, surrounded by the tools of his trade; needle-nose pliers, wire cutters, tweezers, oscilloscopes, precision screwdrivers and smoking soldering irons. He was at least two-feet smaller than me, his curly hair longish and unruly.

"Christ, look who it is. The Golem of Salonika." Lieberman was wearing his usual grubby attire; threadbare denim overalls with no shirt, a string vest and a pair of square-framed, grey-tinted glasses that he used to track the goings on in the street above and directly outside his front door via an array of black and white television screen monitors. I guessed he was about sixty-five. His speaking voice, which sounded like dark honey, relied a great deal on his hairy hands, which he tossed around as he chattered.

"Good evening my friend. And how are you?"

"Fuck how I am. Why is it that every time you come knocking at my door, I always feel the urgent need to emigrate?"

"Where the hell would a little shit like you run off to?"

"Why should I care. A Black Sea sanitorium, a winter retreat in Lübeck. Any place where I'd be free of you and your misery."

"I was expecting a warmer welcome."

"Yeah? Well hard luck. You want open arms and a warm embrace; go find one of those scabby whores you knock around with to hug you."

"And here's me thinking we were friends."

"Friends, he says. You're a fucking jinx, you know that? You turn up here whenever you feel like it. You drop a heap of steaming mule shit in my lap and then, when you've got what you want out of me, you creep back to whatever stone you've crawled from under. Afterwards, I'm plagued with misfortune. I curse you!"

We both remained silent for a moment, studying each

other's eyes until Lieberman accepted the fact that he was in over his depth. I watched the little man's shoulders sag as he held up his arms, his palms outstretched in submission.

"Whadda you want, Remis?"

I took the petri dish that Vokos had given me earlier out of my jacket pocket and handed it to Lieberman. He held the circular glass plate up to the naked bulb hanging from the rose above his head.

"What's this shit?"

"That's what I'm darkening your door to find out. A man I trust tells me that there is a microdot sitting between those two slides. I want to know what's on it?"

"Oh, I bet you do." Lieberman turned and headed back into his workroom. I didn't wait to be asked to join him.

They say that a man's bookcase will tell you everything you need to know about him. A businessman has business books, a dreamer has novels and poetry. A revolutionary will have tomes about the minutiae of overthrowing the oppressor. A war monger, the works of Napoleon and Caesar. A person with no books is perhaps inconsequential to his fellow man, but a peasant that reads, now, he is a prince in waiting. Ezra Lieberman was considered royalty in his unusual line of work. A king, rather than a mere prince. He was a master in his field, a specialist in surveillance with a nice little side-line in forgery of all kinds. The diminutive counterfeiter was both reclusive and brilliant. His many bookcases were filled from floor to ceiling with a vast array of scientific texts, electronic and mechanics manuals, as well as volumes of hardbound classics, theological manuscripts and historical publications.

"And where did you encounter such a find?"

"In the cracked molar of a dead man."

"Really." I watched as Lieberman took the thin slides out of the petri dish. He placed them carefully on to the stage of a large electronic microscope, hunched himself over the double eyepiece ports and flicked on a powerful light underneath.

"Wonderful thing the microdot. Not used so often these days. A shame. Did you know that the reduction of image size is such that a page of text can be legibly reproduced on a surface no smaller than a pin head" Lieberman peered up at me over the thin, still frames of his spectacles. "To put that into stupid policeman terms. I could use one of these little bastards to put the entire text of the Bible on and you'd still have room for the Encyclopaedia Britannica. Brilliant, don't you think?"

"I think you should tell me what's on the damn thing."

Lieberman returned his eye to the twin oculars and began to fiddle with the fine lens adjuster. "You have a partial document with a Union Bank of Switzerland letter heading; that's what you have."

"And?"

I saw the old man slowly shake his head before concentrating his sight down the two eyepieces again. "And, you have quite a list of names on here."

"Like who?"

"Like men that a major in the Salonica Gendarme should take no further interest in."

"The names please, Ezra?"

Lieberman remained staring into the microscope's viewfinder as he spoke. "Well for starters, you have that murdering shithouse, Max Merten at the top of the page, then there's a host of other fucking krauts. All of them Nazis. All of them involved in the expropriation of Jewish valuables and property. None of them I want to sully my lips with by speaking their names. I can tell you that the list was at one time more extensive than what has been photographed here. You can see where the document has been torn. Whatever was written underneath was clearly most sensitive, considering the undesirables catalogued above it."

"Write the names down for me."

"If you insist."

"I do."

The forger pulled open a drawer from underneath his workstation, took out a notebook and pencil, and leafed open the cover. I watched as he scribbled down more than half a dozen names. Lieberman lifted his head and pointed to the slide. "Whoever has misplaced such a thing will want it back for sure. And they'll most likely be prepared to do anything to get it, if you catch my drift. I'm surprised that the deceased was able to conceal something so valuable from individuals who would have been quite desperate for its retrieval and safe return."

"How so?"

Ezra Lieberman chuckled to himself. "Come now. A man of your experience must surely realise that it's rare to be able to hide anything with absolute certainty. Given enough time, enough men, anything can be found if it's been hidden in or on the human body, and I mean anywhere. Swallow a metal capsule? Stick a microfilm up your ass, tattoo your skull and let your hair grow over it. Forget it. It can all be found. Why a ground-out tooth that had been capped over wasn't checked, is a schoolboy error in my opinion. A raw deal for whoever was looking for this microdot, and a stroke of bad luck for you. I for one no longer want any part of this." Lieberman tore out the page with the names he'd written down then gestured his head at the paper and petri dish as he handed them back to me. "Be careful with this. Men die for a great deal less."

"I'll bear that in mind."

Lieberman took off his glasses and raised a finger. "I am a Jew, Remis, and I was born in Athens but have lived here in this city for almost twenty years." He looked distant for a moment, as if his mind had transported itself back to the capital. Lieberman rubbed his jaw thoughtfully. He pushed back his wool cap, the hair on his head dark and shiny, with just a hint of silver, and in the light of the workroom it resembled the skin of a mackerel. "You know, it's not an exaggeration to say that this city was once the Jerusalem of the Balkans, perhaps even the mother of Israel. The Nazis ended our lengthy tenure in this place over thirty-five years ago. They called our enforced migration, *Befriedung*, pacification. Germans have a peculiar talent for euphemism, Major. Words like 'resettlement' quickly take on a different meaning spoken in a foreign tongue. The Jews here in Salonica soon found out that those kinds of words meant something very different in the mouths of a German. The names on that microdot were responsible for unmentionable horrors in our past. Obscenities that still haunt this town, and which can never be forgiven. The presence of such savageries still persists in our country, even if such evil is no longer in plain sight. Remember that. I suggest you throw that filthy microdot along with its glass petri dish into the Mediterranean and forget you ever saw it."

I nodded silently, took out my bill fold and unclipped three one-hundred Drachma notes and dropped them on to the workbench.

Ezra Lieberman hawked up a wad of phlegm and spat at my feet. "I don't want your ill fortune pay-off. Keep it."

I shrugged my shoulders. Wiped up the cash from off the table and stuffed it back in my pocket.

"One other thing, Remis."

"Yeah?"

"You can bet every penny you own that the first name written below that tear mark will have been a Greek's." Lieberman bid me good riddance with a flick of his hand.

"Thanks. I owe you one." I turned and headed back down the hall. The old Jew called after me.

"You owe me more than one, you fucking benzona!" He was laughing and coughing at the same time as I walked away.

It had been a while since I'd last been called a son of a bitch.

It hadn't sounded any less of an insult in Hebrew.

CHAPTER ELEVEN

I'D LIKED WALKING THE NIGHT-TIME STREETS OF A CITY EVER SINCE I was a child on the run from the juvenile and foster care bureaucracies. I found the darkness and electric lights soothing. I feel in control when I see bright neon in the shadows. This relaxation allows me to think more deeply about the twisted nature of men and myself.

My father killed my mother in a fit of booze-filled rage in the winter of 1948. I was twelve years old. Haimon Remis went to a wall and met a firing squad in the grounds of Korydallos Prison. My mother, Rhea, to an unmarked grave at the Elos cemetery in the village where we'd lived. During all that madness I was transferred to a 'special institution' for children at the Zanneion Orphanage in Piraeus. There was nothing special about Zanneion. Orphans endured the '*Kipo*' as it was known, more prison than sanctuary. The orphanage was not a place of tenderness and love. Most of us living within its walls were thrashed on a daily basis or tied to our beds so we wouldn't cause any trouble. Any child crying ended up being sedated. Many just rocked back and forth and we rarely spoke to one another. Sometimes kids were thrashed so ferociously that they would end up dead. The caretakers would simply wrap the body in a sheet and remove it like nothing had happened.

Tired of beatings and the stench of piss-soaked mattresses, I chose to take to my heels and get the hell out. The first time I absconded I made it to an olive grove less than a mile down the road. The farmer was quick to take me in, feed me a cold plate of lentils and listen to my pleading for safety before bundling me into the back of his truck and driving me the short distance back to the orphanage to collect the five Drachma reward money for returning a *'lost child'*.

Once back inside, I was given a kicking by one of the wardens, then locked in a dark cellar room for five days. My only companions during my enforced isolation were the cockroaches that scuttered across the ground and over my body. A bucket of stagnant water was left by the door, the occasional crust of stale bread, thrown in to keep me just on the right side of life.

The prospect of another hammering, being tied up, slung back in a holding cell or drinking ditch water never deterred me from making a break for it again. I kept breaking out, running, and in turn, I'd be caught and returned to Zanneion for another pummelling. By the time I was fourteen I'd managed to make a bolt for freedom more than a dozen times, every attempt to flee put paid to by greedy locals eager to pick up a bounty, or juvenile justice workers and beat coppers who'd pick me up on the streets. In the winter of '51 I made a last-ditch attempt to flee. After being picked up so many times in the past, I'd slowly learnt to stay away from public areas or bedding down for the night on Votsalakia beach. I never walked out in sunlight, and only ever crept about in the shade. After weeks of hiding in and around the port area of the city, dossing down overnight in warehouse attics or taverna outhouses I found myself in Trouba, the infamous red-light district of old in Piraeus. One night, starving hungry and not giving a damn if I'd be caught by either the law or low-life reward chaser, I sneaked down a back alley and broke into the rear of what I thought was a taverna and began to rifle through the garbage bins in search of something to fill my aching gut. My frantic search for food was interrupted by Maria Lioudaki, the elderly owner of the trash cans I'd been thieving out of. Weak and emaciated, tired of running, I backed myself into a corner of the tiny courtyard, my hands clinging on to whatever filthy scraps I'd managed to salvage from the old woman's bin and resigned myself to a journey back to the hellhole that was Zanneion and a fresh beating.

That feared journey thankfully never came about. Instead, for whatever reasons, that night I was met with open arms and encouraged to venture into the nebulous world of Maria Lioudaki, or *Ya-Ya*, as she was known to everyone.

I soon found out, was the public face of the *Black Cat*, a bordello creep joint and bar that the city's great and not so good all frequented once the sun had set and the churches and confessionals had closed for the night. The Trouba district had begun life shortly after the German occupation with the appearance of its first brothels. The port of Piraeus and the ever-changing rabble of seafarers was conducive to creating a raft of whorehouses, cabarets and seedy bars.

Ya-Ya took me in, treated me as if I was her own blood. Fed, clothed and educated me and kept me out of the hands of the police or public officials and away from the brutal confines of the Zanneion orphanage. It didn't take long before I felt at home in the infamous neighbourhood, happily living amongst the hordes of wayward servicemen, pickpockets, pimps and shysters. In time I worked the bar at the Black Cat and at the same time, a bookie's runner for Kostas Perrikos, a local moneylender and flesh-peddler. For most of the time I kept my nose clean and when I found myself sailing too close to the wind, made sure never to get caught. At nineteen, despite Ya-Ya's best attempts to prevent it, I was conscripted into the Greek army. I spent the better years of my service with the 1st Raider, parachute brigade. Growing up an orphan had taught me that if I wanted anything, I'd have to fight for it: now I was simply fighting for my country. I served in Cyprus and on the streets of Athens and across the nation's cities and towns, mostly always against poorly armed communist insurgents. And I killed. Mostly right up close so that I could see and smell their fear. When the killing was over, I returned to barracks, kept myself to myself. I drank alone, rarely ever ventured out from my quarters or the confines of the garrison when it was allowed. I never went looking for promotion nor was it offered. Decorations were non-existent. I kept my head down, did as I was ordered and stayed on as a regular soldier until I was demobbed nine years later.

On civvy street, before joining the gendarmerie, I'd silently made a vow never to take another human's life ever again. It was a sincere pledge, one that I swore I would take to my grave, if not beyond.

I'm ashamed to admit that I broke that earnest promise long ago.

. . .

It was a little after nine-thirty. Still early for Salonican nightlife to kick in, before the diehards would begin prowling, the last dancers seeking a smooch, the last toast revellers, the last laugh of the night. I'd emerged from Ezra Lieberman's underground apartment without a smile on my face to find the city in the path of another thunderstorm. Gusts of wind stirred litter in the street and fat drops of rain pinged off car roofs and windshields. A man and woman hustling to beat the storm brushed by me. Another couple ran past, the woman in bare feet to spare the high-heeled shoes she held in her hand. Lieberman's uncovering of the microdot, his warning about walking away had posed a question in my head, one which I desperately needed answering. A nagging query that I was unhappy to leave until morning and which could only be answered by one man. I put my head down, the squall beating at my head and shoulders. I kept on walking until I found a payphone. I hunched underneath the plastic overhead canopy, dropped a coin into the slot and dialled the number for the coroner's office. The phone at the other end rang and rang until finally, Lakis Vokos answered.

"Yeah, spit it out!"

"And a very good evening to you, too."

"Remis. What the fuck do you want, now?"

"Our man in the freezer,"

"Yeah, what about him?"

"Is he snipped?"

"What?"

"Is he snipped ...you know, is his dick circumcised?"

"You're calling me at this time of night to find out whether a corpse has a purple sombrero or not?"

"So, I'm bored. Just indulge me will you." I heard Vokos

curse under his breath then came the sound of him shifting papers on his desk.

"Yeah, for what it's worth, your dead American doesn't have a lid over his cock. You happy now?"

"Ecstatic."

"Then you'll be delirious when you hear about the tattoo, I found on him."

"What tattoo?"

"The one under his left armpit. No printed word. Just a plain, black symbol half a centimetre in length. Small enough, that I had to take a magnifying glass to his skin to read it."

"What kind of symbol?"

"It's what's known as a Shekhinah sigil."

"And what the hell's that?"

Vokos sighed heavily. "A six-pointed Star of David. It's a Kabbalistic protection symbol. Keeps the wearer safe from the evils of man. It clearly didn't work for that poor bastard though."

"Can you photograph it for me?"

"What the dick or the tattoo?"

"You know that I'm not gonna dignify that stupid fucking question with an answer, don't you?"

Vokos was laughing louder than the rain pelting against the plastic shield above my head. He continued talking to me whilst trying to muffle his obvious amusement. "I've already done it, you sour-faced bastard. The roll of film is in my internal mailbox. It'll be developed by one of my lackeys at some point tomorrow."

"Thanks."

"Don't you mention it. I was put on this earth to wait hand and foot on you, Remis. You know how here in the pathology department we consider it an honour to assist the great Salonican gendarmerie."

I ignored Vokos' caustic remarks. "So, I've got a dead Jew with a tattoo, that's hardly a first."

"This one might be."

"What are you talking about?"

I heard the tubby coroner blow out his breath. "Jews have a longstanding aversion to tattoos, Major. No doubt attributed to the tattooing of concentration camp inmates during the Holocaust and the calling that tattooed Jews can't be buried in sacred ground."

"What's that gotta do with our man?"

"I have it on very good authority that the kind of tattoo that's been engraved so stealthily on the deceased is the kind of artwork that is only found etched on the skins of a very select group of men and women."

"Cut with the fucking riddles, Vokos."

"By way of deception thou shalt make war, Major."

"Say what?"

"It's the motto of the Israeli intelligence agency, Mossad, Remis." Vokos fell silent for a moment, the rain hitting hard against my back, the downpour almost deafening me. When the coroner began to speak again, I quickly stuck a finger into one ear so I could catch his words. "If your dead fella is a member of that particularly nasty bunch of individuals, you really are in the shit."

Before I could reply, Vokos had already eased his phone's receiver back into its cradle.

CHAPTER
TWELVE

It was said that the Greek god Zeus rarely heeded warnings from fellow gods because he considered their counsel to be irrelevant to his mighty stature. Greeks these days believe that fools don't heed warnings because they feel such cautions are only there to enhance their imprudent lives in some mysterious way. This evening, in less than two hours, I had been warned by both Ezra Lieberman and Lakis Vokos that I was meddling in matters that I should be leaving well alone.

Snooping around in the affairs of others is an inevitability in my line of work. I've always believed that a good detective is a nosey detective. In the past few years, I'd undertaken very little in the way of investigative policing. Strong-arm tactics were generally the name of the game for me, tipping the odds in favour of the brass, the ultimate goal. I was paid to cover up, rather than rubberneck but something about Konrad Tafel's death had sparked my latent sense of curiosity. Made me feel like a policeman again rather than hired muscle with a badge. Maybe I was poking my nose where it wasn't wanted. Maybe I had suddenly found a long-lost conscience? Maybe I just didn't care anymore.

God.

Fool.

Muckraker.

The way I saw it, two outta three can't be bad.

The Deuce strip club was on the corner of Nikis Avenue and Kastron Street. The shake joint had been plying its seedy trade for over a decade and was a popular late-night haven for the city's criminal demimonde. Pugilist and ponce, felon or fuzz, they all liked The Deuce to view a little skin action. If my old friend Antonia Garbi was getting naked in there and still feeding all the dragons that had lived inside her since she was a little girl, she'd have most probably hit the bar before eight for her first martini. In the years I had known Antonia she'd been one of my very best snitches. Nia, as she liked to be called, had been arrested dozens of times by vice, stabbed through the shoulder by a pimp, and had her jaw broken with a wood mallet by one of her husbands. Like me, she was an orphan. Brought up in the labyrinthine slums around Aghias Sofias Street, the daughter of a half-wit mother and a mentally ill father who used to wrap the piss-soaked sheets around her head when she wet the bed. Now, in her adulthood, she'd managed to move a half mile from the place of her birth and made a living undressing for the city's slime.

But Nia wasn't at the club. In fact, The Deuce was almost empty when I walked out of the rain and through its doors. The mirrored runway behind the bar was darkened; the music instruments of the three-piece band sat unattended in the small pit at the end of the runway; in the empty gloom a strobe light made a revolving shotgun pattern of darkness and light that could be equalled only by seasickness. I asked the barman if she was in. He was in his early thirties, and wore thick side-burns, a grey fisherman's cap and a white T-shirt with an orange *Levi's* logo printed on the front.

"You bet," he said and laughed. Her first show is at ten-thirty. She'll be in soon for her happy hour. You a friend of hers?

"Yes."

"What you drinking?"

"I'll have a bottle of Fix."

"It's eight Drachma. You sure you wanna drink piss-weak lager at that price?"

I put a ten Drachma note on the bar.

"Suit yourself, mister."

The barman took the bottle of beer out of a fridge behind him, uncapped it, poured it into a fluted glass and slid it across the wood panelled surface toward me.

"I know you, right?" He grinned at me.

"Maybe."

"You're a cop, right?"

I shrugged. "Maybe."

"Hey, come on man. I got two big talents; one is a bartender and the other's for faces. But you're not vice, right?"

I took a sip of my beer. "You're getting warmer."

"You remember me, yeah?"

I clicked my fingers a couple of times. "Uh-huh, it's Sakis something or other. Yep, I remember, now. It's gotta be six years ago, you did a three-year stretch for beating an old man with a lead pipe. How'd you like it up there at the Heptapyrgion?"

His brown eyes widened a moment, looked boldly at me from under the brim of his cap, then narrowed and crinkled again. He began drying glasses with a towel, his face turned at a sloping angle.

"It wasn't bad. I was outdoors a lot on the prison farm, lots of fresh air, gave me a chance to get in shape. I like farm work. I grew up on one," he said. "Hey, have another beer on me. You got an impressive memory. A sharp guy like you should have a drink on the house."

"You drink it for me." I picked up my glass and walked to the back of the bar. I watched him light a cigarette, smoke only a few nervous puffs of it, then flip it angrily through the front door onto the street.

Nia came in a half hour later, dressed in high-heeled sandals, blue jeans low on her hips and a white cotton top that exposed her flat, tanned stomach. Unlike most of the strippers, she wore her black hair cut short, like the 1920's silent film star, Louise Brooks. And, in spite of all the booze, coke and speed, she was still good to look at.

"Well, look who it is, my favourite relation." She sat down in the seat opposite me and winked. "How are you Uncle Michail?"

"I'm good. You?"

"Can't complain. I'll be a lot better when I've gotta drink in my hand. Hey, Sakis, does it look like I got the clap down here. It's Nia's glug-glug time."

I hitched forward in my seat. "I'm trying to find out something about a guy."

"Shit, this ain't an information centre, you know."

"Well, when I have questions, you're pretty hot at throwing up the answers for me."

"Not this time, uncle. You really want to do this here?" She lit a cigarette and turned to watch the martini that Sakis was mixing for her down the bar.

"This man I'm talking about, he was an American. Found dead yesterday, up-country in Florina. Someone cut him up pretty badly, left him for the stray dogs to tear to pieces."

Nia shrugged. "What's a stiff found up in the mountains gotta do with a high-rolling city copper like you?"

"This guy had a tiny tattoo branded under one armpit. A six-pointed Star of David. Now, it's a real long-shot, I know. Perhaps this guy may have been hanging around the bars and clubs here in Salonica for a while or if he maybe could have visited a place like this."

"Men pay to see me take my clothes off, Michail. It's not the other way around. Why would I get to see something like that?"

"You know what I'm talking about."

"Oh, that's what it is, huh?" Nia took the glass out of Sakis' hand and drank from it. Her mouth looked wet and cold when she set the crystal tumbler down. "Look, I don't do the other stuff anymore, you know that. I don't have to do that shit. I work this place six months, then I've my job tending bar at the Capsis. Ask your friends in vice."

"They're not my friends." Nia flicked her cigarette ash into the ashtray and didn't answer. "Look, I just need you to do a little snooping around. Speak to a few of the girls you know on the street. See if you can turn anything up.

"There can't be that many yanks in town at this time of year. Perhaps one of the hustlers noticed the tattoo. I'm just trying to get a better fix on the fella if I can. I'm not expecting miracles."

Nia gestured with her head toward the street. "What's stopping you from getting out there and bracing a few hookers?" She exhaled smoke into the spinning circles of light and brushed a strand of hair out of her eye, waiting for me to reply.

"My boss has me on a short leash on this one. That's why I've come to you." I took out my billfold, unfurled a handful of notes out of sight of the barman and passed the cash under the table. "You need to be discreet. You find anything out, bring what you've got to my apartment. Not to police headquarters. Understand?"

Nia grinned, snatched the fifty drachmas from my fingers and swigged back the last of her martini. "Hey Sakis. Can you take it out of slow motion back there? This lady needs herself another gin."

I got to my feet, walked back along the bar, ignoring Sakis and went out into the wet, neon-lit street. The rain had all but stopped, the water now sluicing off the roofs and balconies overhead. The music and chatter of customers from the other bars and clubs around me starting to kick in for the night. In the distance I could just hear a ship's horn blowing across the water.

I looked back at Nia, but her chair was empty.

CHAPTER THIRTEEN

I CAME-TO HALF AWAKE, CONFUSED AND INERT, THE TELEPHONE ringing itself stupid on the other side of the room. My whirling head was still hundreds of fathoms down in the deepest, darkest blackness, somewhere where no absurd sexual fantasy, tormented episode from my childhood or the horrors of police work could have interrupted my once beautiful never-ending, velvet-lined consciousness. I was sprawled, flat out on my living room sofa, still fully dressed, an empty glass tumbler nestling precariously between my legs. The half-bottle of Metaxa I'd knocked back after getting in from The Deuce had done its job, floored me and left my tongue feeling as rough as a bearskin rug. I lifted my arm and squinted down at my wristwatch. Eight twenty a.m. Almost a lie in, but not quite. I slowly raised my head an inch or two off the cushion and watched the room begin to swirl around me. I sat up, swung my feet on to the floor and waited for the groggy feeling to subside a little then got around to wondering why someone was that desperate to speak to me at home. I got to my feet, staggered across the room like a sleep-walker, picked up the receiver and placed it idly against my ear.

"Remis."

"Finally." The tone of Provost Callas' voice on the other end of the line sounded like polished metal, smooth and clean and without a hint of aggression. I pinched at my eyes with my thumb and forefinger, my bewildered retort swiftly interrupted by the old man. "Lakis Vokos has been found dead at his place of work."

"He's what?"

Callas ignored my perplexed enquiry. "Tell me that you weren't stupid enough to entrust our American package to Vokos yesterday?"

I began to breathe deeply, the wires trembling in my chest. I swallowed and kept my voice flat. "Yeah, I did. For safe keeping overnight."

"Did I not make it abundantly clear to you that the package was to be expedited out of the country expeditiously?"

"Yes ... yes you did. Grivas had already given the order to have the package transported over to Vokos' department. I was going to take it from there and undertake your orders."

"I don't really care how it got to where it is. It's what happened to the damn thing after its arrival that's concerning me. I expected the package to be heading back over the Atlantic by now."

I felt my hand slide up and down my flexed thigh. I had to wet my lips before I could speak again. I should have remained silent, said nothing, but the control was gone. "I have everything in hand, sir."

“In hand, do you? Callas was quiet a moment, then spoke again. “My people have informed me that Captain Kampouris from the crime and homicide division has been assigned to the case.”

“Oh, crap.”

“My sentiments exactly. We both know that Kampouris’ loyalties are somewhat, divided. If he’s prowling around in that nasty, little mortuary you can assume anything you left in Vokos’ protection is now no longer as safe as it was. Get over there now and secure the package. Understand?”

“Yes, sir. I understand, sir.”

“A swift repatriation is what I asked for, Major. Just see that it’s done.”

I arrived at the city coroner’s office a little before nine, just as the police photographer was finishing and the ambulance attendants were about to lift Vokos body out of a wide pool of blood and zipper it inside a black bag.

Nick Kampouris was that rare beast, a bent cop who took little or no pleasure in the telling of his untruths or the illicit deeds I knew he undertook for two masters. I’d always got the gut feeling that he was man who’d once prided himself in the integrity of his profession and the even-handed application of judicial ethics.

But that was a long time ago. Now the corrupt detective was little more than a bag man for the Balkan crime syndicate and its boss, Ljuba Zemunac. Kampouris had been coerced into doing the bidding of pitiless men whose only concerns were to stay rich and keep one step ahead of the law. It would have been well-paid but risky work; the kind of employment where mistakes were rarely tolerated and the punishment for making them, brutally meted out. The fact that Kampouris was also an inside man for the gendarmerie made his precarious work all the more high risk. He wore a cheap, grey flannel suit over a candy-striped shirt, his tie pulled loose at the throat. "There's a half bottle of ouzo on his desk and a spilled tub of Valium next to it."

A Beretta 70 semi-automatic pistol lay at the foot of a cream, stuffed chair. The headrest, the wall behind it and the ceiling were streaked with blood. One side of Vokos' face looked perfectly normal, the eye staring straight ahead like a blue marble pressed into dough. The opposite side of his face, where the jawbone should have been, had sunk into the rug like a broken melon. Vokos' right arm was pointed straight out onto the wood floor. At the end of his fingers, painted in red, were the letters, *P H.*

"You're writing this off as suicide, are you?"

"That's the way it looks to me."

"Why would a suicide try to write something in his own blood?"

"Who the hell knows. Maybe the old fucker changed his mind when he knew it was too late. Maybe he was trying to hold on any way he could after he'd pulled the trigger. He was probably trying to message his ex-wife. I'm pretty sure her name was Phaedra."

The ambulance attendants lifted Vokos' body off the rug, then lowered it inside the plastic bag, straightened his arms by his sides, and zippered the bag over his face. Kampouris' eyes fixed on mine. "Look Major, from what I can make out, this fat bastard's career was in the shitter." The detective took a couple of steps backwards as the attendants worked the gurney past him. “His wife left him years ago for a magistrate from Patras. Word has it he was getting freebies from the toms down at the port.

“There are plenty of blabbermouths in this place that say most mornings he was a trembling mess, eating pills and knocking booze back in front of his whole team. You might believe otherwise, but there’s no big mystery to what happened here overnight.”

I felt the heat rise across my face. “Vokos maybe had trouble with the bottle, but I don’t buy it about him using hookers.”

“No? Well, you can think what you want, Major. He was a fucking drunk as far as I’m concerned. That fact’s not going to go away. At least the prick hasn’t got far to go in this place. He can join the rest of the stiffs in his freezers. He’ll be right at home.”

Kampouris took a couple of steps towards me, wiping his nose with the back of his hand then gesturing at the blood on the floor with his finger. “I’m about to seal this place up. Are you done here?”

I could feel my heart beating, felt the blood in the back of my neck and in my temples. I shook my head as I looked around the office. “No, I’m not done. In fact, I’m going to look around a little longer, and in the meantime, I’d like you to do me a favour?”

“Yeah, what’s that?”

“You can get the fuck out of my face and go speak ill of the dead someplace else. Either that or I kick your arse out into the street.”

Kampouris made a grumbling noise at the back of his throat. His breath was stale, his eyes liquid and resentful. Then the interest went out of them and he glanced outside toward the corridor. He reached into his jacket pocket, took out a packet, stuck a cigarette in his mouth, went into the hallway and watched the ambulance crew wheel Vokos' body toward the morgue, not out of fear of me or even personal humiliation; but because he was simply one of those officers for whom insensitivity, cynicism, cruelty and indifference was now firmly ingrained. A dead colleague had no more value or significance than that of a stranger's killing. Such calculated coldness reminded me of myself.

Vokos' office was a mess. A pile of garbage in the wastepaper basket, coffee grounds, spat out olive stones, cigarette butts, crushed beer cans. The top of the coroner's desk was strewn in paperwork and reports. A small notebook with a pencil attachment that he always carried in his shirt pocket sat on top of a pile of manila folders. The first eight pages were filled with notes about a drowning and a dockside stabbing fatality. The next few pages had been torn out. Tiny bits of paper clung to the wire spirals, and the first blank page had no impressions on it from the previous one. Perched on the edge of the desk was a framed photograph of Vokos and his ex-wife taken at a wedding. I rifled through the top drawer and found nothing of interest. There was certainly no sign of Tafel's passport which I'd assumed Grivas would have sent on with the body. In the one below it, a half empty bottle of Plomari ouzo and an unopened carton of *Metro* cigarettes. I stared down again at Vokos' blood on the floor. Someone had tracked through the edge of it and printed their heel a couple of times brightly on the wood. What a way to exit forty years of service to the state, I thought. Dying in a room that was barely fit for human habitation where your colleagues write you off as a womanising drunk and step in your blood.

I looked at the smudged letters *P H* again. What were you trying to tell us, Lakis?"

I mouthed the two letters under my breath, trying to work out in my head what my old friend was attempting to convey to the world as his life ebbed away. My eyes quickly scanned around the room, taking in the grey filing cabinets, cork pinboards and the typewriter sat on the smaller desk to my left. My attention suddenly homed in on the industrial pigeon-hole unit on the back wall. *"The roll of film's in my internal mail-box. It'll be developed by one of my skivvies at some point tomorrow."*

P H... Photograph. The sound of Vokos' voice was still in my head as I headed over to the shelving and began rifling through the various compartments that were crammed with letters and official documentation. In a middle cubicle, tucked behind a blue duplicate docket, was a small, clear plastic bag, inside it, a roll of *Kodak* Tri X black and white film.

I took a quick glance behind me before quickly tearing open the bag and pocketing the cannister then headed out of the office and made my way along the corridor, past the post-mortem rooms and viewing suite. I followed my nose; the rank atmosphere in the hallway that of putrefaction and formalde-hyde. I made my way through a series of double-doors, past the body-room and into the refrigeration area, then eventually along a thinner passageway towards the farthest recesses of the building until I reached what Vokos preferred to call his private study. I entered the small annexe room. At its centre was a stainless-steel autopsy table. Polished surgical instru-ments were lined on a metal bench like shiny, parading soldiers. Galvanised buckets and large bowls stood on the floor. Glass jars filled with alcohol, body parts and organs lined a series of shelves.

The place stank of death. I'd seen plenty of dead bodies in my time, but I could never get used to being inside a mortuary. Some men saunter into a morgue and browse the unliving like viewing rare plants at a flower show. I could never attain such composure. Eager to get out of the place and soaked with perspiration, I made my way over to the two refrigerator cabinets and opened the first drawer. Stretched out, rigid and grey like a piece of decomposing meat, was the body of an elderly woman. Her skin peeled ear to ear across her scalp and dragged back over her forehead. I slammed the cooler hatch shut and immediately grabbed the handle to the second freezer cabinet and snatched open the door. Inside, the cold chamber was empty.

The body of Konrad Tafel had taken a walk.

I was screwed. I knew that Callas would put my head on a spike for fucking this up. Anger and frustration took over. In blind temper I reeled backwards, my right ankle accidently clipping against the wheel of a mobile, two-tier supply cart. I cursed loudly then felt my guts tighten. The bile rose inside my throat, my head suddenly punch-drunk and giddy. For the briefest of moments, I could see my own black-and-blue body on the metal tray staring back at me, even heard the dry, detached tone of the new medical examiner stating how I'd met my untimely demise.

I don't know how long I lingered looking into the vacant compartment before I finally swung the door shut, turned on my heels and left. The one thing that kept me focussed as I made my way out of the building and back toward my car was the sharp pain in my ankle. Every time my foot hit the floor; a shooting sensation would travel almost to the knee. Rather than resent the spasm, I welcomed it, because with each step I was shocked back to clarity. The survivor came out in me. The return of the runaway orphan that never quit. The pain was like a bright red spot on a fading grey plain, a distant sun, a jabbing reminder that my blood was still pumping, that my life, if not a certainty, was at least a possibility.

CHAPTER FOURTEEN

I WAS WEIGHING UP MY NEXT MOVE BEFORE I'D GOT BACK TO MY CAR. I'm not fond of humble pie. It gives me indigestion. So does eating my own words but I knew I'd have to chew on a couple of chalk tablets and head off into the eye of the storm if I was going to save my neck. I don't normally pay a visit to the Provost unless I've been invited. I knew I wasn't going to be able to keep a lid on Konrad Tafel's body vanishing off the face of the earth for long. I decided it was better that I broke the bad news before one of his many grasses got to him first and let the cat out of the bag. I was up to my neck in shit. The way I saw it, better to face the old devil head-on now than wait to be summoned to his hideaway and have to come clean further down the line. I climbed into the Lancia, fired it up with a roar, then hit the gas and felt the car thrust forward as she pulled toward the corner. I turned the steering wheel, sensing the swing of the back end as I straightened out for the main road.

That's when I saw the woman in front of me pushing a baby's pram.

I hit the brakes and felt the backend fishtail. I got a

panorama of the buildings and shops on the east side of the street. The car swung violently before shuddering to a halt. The young mother was yelling at me. "You fucking bastard! You bastard! "

Another car behind me hit his brakes. The squeal seemed to go on forever, but it didn't collide into anything. The woman stopped screaming and gathered up her baby in her arms. She ran for the pavement, leaving the carriage in the middle of the road. My heart was beating fast, the inside of my mouth as dry as lint. The woman was sobbing, trying to calm her hollering baby.

I looked straight ahead of me, started the engine back up and drove off thinking how my life had suddenly slipped out of control.

I was just driving up from the front gates of the mansion house when I spotted Callas walking a big chestnut stallion down the drive. I drew the car to a stop and rolled down the window. He didn't look like a man who had been riding hard for any great length of time. His hair was untousled and his jodhpurs still as pristine as when he'd first walked out of his private quarters. He wasn't even sweating, not so you'd notice. The horse was the one that looked frazzled. It kept rolling its eyes, tossing its huge head and tugging at the reins, which rested in its master's hands as lightly as a child's skipping rope. Callas approached my car, leaned down toward the window and rested a forearm on the doorframe. He curled a top lip at me, briefly showing two small white teeth. It was one of the emptiest smiles I'd had flashed at me in a long time. "I clearly need to have words with the sentry if he's opening up my home to every man coming in off the streets."

"My apologies for the unannounced intrusion, sir. But I wanted to appraise you of the current situation promptly."

There was a dead silence, Callas viewed me suspiciously, as if he already knew what I was thinking. "A situation. That doesn't sound very palatable, Major."

"It isn't. The American's body has been taken."

"Taken. By whom?"

"I have no idea."

"That, you stupid bastard, is not the answer I want to hear." The horse was nuzzling at the Provost's shoulder, but he took no notice.

"I know it isn't. I'm just informing you of the facts."

"Facts you say." Callas glanced at his wristwatch before refocussing his attention on me. "If we're to concentrate on the specifics of this total bloody mess, perhaps you could enlighten me on how the body managed to end up at the city morgue?"

"The Brigadier pulled rank. He clearly wanted to do things his way."

"Did he now?" The Provost stared back at me coldly for a moment. "Go on."

"There's not a lot to say. By the time we got up to Florina, Tafel's body had already been transported to the mine's infirmary. There was no local law around, no scene of crime containment, and apart from the man's passport, to the best of my knowledge, no other evidence had been secured. After I'd briefly examined the corpse and we'd questioned the site manager, Grivas pocketed the passport and had his men collect the body and transport it back to the local morgue. The

N.I.S turned up after we'd left. I assumed I'd be notified by Vokos the next day that the yank was crated up and ready to be shipped home."

Callas raised an eyebrow. "That, on reflection, was a very foolish assumption, Major."

"I realise that now."

"And you're certain that Grivas took charge of the man's passport?"

"Yes, absolutely. I thought the travel document and any other paperwork would end up at the coroner's office to go out with the casket."

"Well, you thought wrong didn't you, you idiot!"

I watched Callas' face twist to one side with malice, like a feeding shark. I was all too aware that whatever I uttered next could easily make my situation dicier. "Before heading over to you, I took the opportunity to root around in the coroner's office, see if I could come up with Tafel's travel papers but there was no sign of them anywhere."

Callas nodded to himself. "Disappointing." The Provost pressed a finger to his lips meditatively. "What about Vokos?"

I shrugged. "Kampouris is certain he's looking at a suicide. I don't buy it."

"No?"

I shook my head. "No. Lakis Vokos would have happily smoked and drank himself to death, but he'd never have put a gun to his head to end his days. Before leaving the mortuary, I learnt that the coroner's body had been discovered by a colleague coming on to the early shift a little before 7am. No other staff were around during the evening. No nightshift workers either. There were no witnesses, no gunshot heard, and it looks like nobody saw Tafel's carcass being snatched off the premises."

"How unfortunate."

A gut feeling told me I'd be better off keeping my mouth shut about my earlier meeting with the pathologist, his uncovering of the microdot in Tafel's tooth, and the roll of film sat in my jacket pocket. There was one other morsel of information about Vokos' death that I knew I had to spill. I swallowed hard with every muscle in my neck and throat before opening my mouth. "There's one other thing. Before Vokos died, he'd daubed the letters P H onto the wall in his own blood."

"P H ... and why would he do that?"

"Again, I'm not sure. Vokos' ex-wife's name was Phaedra. Captain Kampouris thinks it might have been some kind of final, crude suicide note."

The Provost's nose wrinkled in disgust. "Charming." Callas' horse made a loud blowing sound through its nostrils and dragged its front hoof nervously through the gravel.

"Nice beast." The animal rolled an eye my way.

Callas nodded. "Santanas. Eighteen hands, and as strong as the devil himself."

I made a funnel with my lips as if to whistle but didn't. "Impressive. You play polo on him?"

Callas gave a gruff snort. "Polo is played on ponies. Can you imagine trying to get at a ball on the ground from this big bastard's back?" The Provost rubbed his chin with a forefinger. "You've never ridden I take it?"

"Where I come from, a riding crop was never out of our hands."

Callas looked pained. "You know, after a disaster like this, I'd hate to have to lose you, Major. After all, there isn't much demand for men like you once you leave me. I mean, what can you do after all? Use a gun, use your fists. Legally, you're unskilled, Remis."

"You're right. I'd have been better off throwing in my badge and running guns for the Turks."

The old man's look of pain vanished. "Always the joker, Remis."

"You wouldn't expect any less of me, sir."

"I expect you to find that fucking dead American's corpse and end this madness before I end you."

Callas went on looking at me for a while longer. When he narrowed his eyes, a fan of fine wrinkles opened at the outer corner of each side. The he straightened his back, smacked a palm on the door frame.

"Remind me, what's my section for, Major?"

"Getting rid of people."

"Exactly. Getting rid of people. Bribery, blackmail, deportation, frame-ups ..."

"And death," I interrupted.

Callas' eyes narrowed again. "Occasionally. When there's been no other way. I needn't remind you how many of those sanctions you undertook or how easy it would be for you to join the likes of your friend Vokos, need I?"

I shook my head, my eyes avoiding my boss's. "Good. I entrusted you with a simple clean-up job. Do what you're good at, Major. Start mopping this fiasco up."

The nag tossed its head, flapping its big lips as if to tell me to clear off. I put the car in gear and let out the clutch.

"Understood," I said and drove off.

CHAPTER FIFTEEN

I KNOW HOW TO BE PATIENT. KNOW HOW TO WAIT, GIVEN THE WAY I choose to make my living. If I have to, I can waste time, no problem. I can sit in my office for hours, in my swivel chair, gazing out of the window or at one of the secretaries across the way bent over a dictation machine, not even seeing her, half the time. I can dawdle over a game of backgammon until the pieces go blurry and the narrow-pointed patterning on the board sends my brain into a slow spin. I can sit nursing a beer in some musty taverna whilst the bartender tells me how awful his wife is and how his damn kids have no respect for him, and I'll not even break into a yawn. A natural timewaster me, given half the chance. But give me a specific thing that I either have no choice but to wait for, or which is causing me grief, and within five minutes I'm starting to twitch.

I had that tremoring feeling pulsing through me as I drove back from the Provost's mansion house into Salonika. I pulled over at a phone booth on Egnatia Street and made a call to Ezra Lieberman.

"I need you to creep into your dark room and develop me a roll of film."

"More of your Nazi trash?"

"Possibly."

I listened to Ezra expel a heavy sigh on the other end of the line. "What's wrong with your usual lab flunkeys? They don't print fascist films?"

"Not with your flair and speed, they don't." I could feel my hand tightening on the receiver, my discomfort growing. "I need them dry, in an envelope and waiting for me at our usual collection spot by three. Okay?"

"Do I have a choice in the matter?"

"No."

I listened to Lieberman mumble some Hebraic curse down the line before he replied. "Drop the damn cannister off to me now. I'll see what I can do."

"Thanks." I was about to drop the handset back into its cradle when Lieberman called out to me.

"Take my advice. Shit-can this black shirt madness before you start regretting it. Move to Albania. Buy a boat and fish. Live out your remaining years, happy and content, safe in the knowledge that you didn't defile your hands with such filth."

"My hands were sullied long ago."

"Not with this kind of muck they haven't been. The scum you're meddling with taints indelibly, Remis. You just remember that."

The line went dead.

I set the phone down and stood rooted to the spot, staring out of the booth into the street, the old Jew's sombre counsel echoing in my ears.

. . .

After dropping off the film at Lieberman's place I had some time to kill. I wasn't in the mood for booze, food or the agitation of police headquarters so I headed back across town to hole-up at my place for a couple of hours. As I turned into Pileos Avenue I was greeted by the sight of two men waiting in the street outside of my apartment. They were wearing fedora hats and double-breasted suits that were buttoned up the way you do when you've got more than just a fountain pen in your pocket. I told myself this pair looked more like intelligence officers than mobsters. Most crooks wear broken noses and cauliflower ears the way some men wear watch chains and carry canes. There was all that and the fact that they looked pleased to see me. When you've been in the zoo as long as I have you kind of get to know when an animal is going to attack.

It gets all nervous and agitated because, for most creatures, it's upsetting to kill. But these two were calm and self-assured and not eager to draw blood.

When I got out of the car the bigger of the two men took a step backwards towards the gutter whilst the other flashed a poised smile my way. I braced myself as he threw away his cigarette and walked towards me.

"Major Remis?"

"That all depends?"

"On what?"

"On what you say next?"

"Someone wants to talk to you."

"So why isn't someone here?"

"Because, at this very moment he's at the Rotary Club awaiting your arrival."

"Does this someone have a name?"

"I think you know this gentleman's name already."

"Well, maybe you could tell this gentleman I'm the shy type. Or maybe that I'm not suitably dressed for the Rotary." I glanced down at my wristwatch. "Besides it's a little early to be out at a club."

The stranger showed his teeth in a wide and happy grin. "Let's just say that the gentleman in questioned wished to speak to you in surroundings which were free of interruption. Somewhere private you can hear yourself think."

"I get all sorts of ideas when I hear myself thinking ... like there's some point to my existence." I watched the smiley goon slowly lift open the front of his jacket. I caught sight of the butt of an automatic pistol holstered on his trouser belt. I heard the bigger man close in behind me then felt the palm of his sizable hand cup the underneath of my elbow. I shrugged my shoulders and let the tension slip out of my coiled frame. "But since there isn't, we better get along to the Rotary." I winked at the big man who had taken my arm. "I'm glad you're coming along. I never normally meet strange men without a companion." My escort's face remained numb; his gaze fixed. He quickly ushered me along the pavement towards a dark-blue Mercedes-Benz convertible whilst the man who had been doing all the talking followed on after us. Our heavy footsteps sounded along the concrete-like hammers pounding inside a submarine. Smiley opened the back door of the swanky motor and gestured with a nod of his head for me to get in. I climbed inside without a word. Another gargoyle was already sat behind the wheel, his eyes focussing in on me through the rear-view mirror with cold hostility. My two newfound companions joined me on the back seat, the big man placing the flat of his hand against my chest, forcing me back against the plush leather upholstery. His stubby fingers curled around the lapel of my jacket. Smiley reached inside to relieve me of my service Walther. I watched him pocket the semi-automatic. The smug expression of his face informing me that he was content in the knowledge that I no longer carried a threat to anyone onboard. The two men quickly closed in, their bodies muscling up against my own. The big car's engine fired up, the driver pulling away from the curb with all the urgency of a funeral cortege.

As we drove away at a snail's pace the prickling dread I'd felt earlier suddenly returned. The gentleman wanting to see me was clearly the kind of individual who enjoyed getting his opponents on the backfoot. This was a man who derived great pleasure from toying with another person's mind. Just like the three-card monte dealers fleecing the easy marks in the old bazaar.

Whoever I was now at the beckoned call of wasn't that kind of grifter. No scam artist out to put the frighteners on me. This was an altogether different kind of predator. I knew I was in trouble. Anyone stupid enough to lift me off the streets was either clinically insane or connected to the kind of people who were used to digging your grave before you'd even sat down to pow-wow with them.

I kept my eyes looking directly ahead, ignoring the two men positioned either side of me. I'd been on this same kind of journey before. But this time the tables had been turned, the shoe now very much on the other foot.

I'd snatched up more than my fair share of unsuspecting individuals over the years. Once these poor bastards had been in my clutches, every one of them knew that they were beat. All knew they were to be taken off to be interrogated, perhaps tortured, most probably executed and that their bodies would end up either being dumped out at sea or slung into a deep, lime-coated pit. A hushed stillness always took over these people. The same series of grim emotions playing out over their petrified faces. First there was hatred, then an animal horror at what was about to happen to them. Slowly there was a sense of stunned amazement, a crippling fear holding them still and taciturn. I'd seen the last gasps at calculation creep into their shocked gaze then the stark realisation that all their cunning or well-connected protection would not be to coming to their assistance. I saw a strange wistfulness play out in their glare. A sadness as they realised what they could have accomplished with their lives. An amusement at the irony of their own downfall would set in, followed by an existential sickness, an atavistic loathing, and then a swift cosmic resignation at their forthcoming demise.

For every one of them, that all happened in silence.

I was no different.

CHAPTER
SIXTEEN

The Rotary Club of Thessaloniki is the second oldest members' club in Greece. The Rotarians' objectives were to promote and foster understanding and inter-community service. The fellowship believes that nobody can be a good member unless he adheres strongly to his religion and is a loyal citizen of his country. I more or less had the latter covered but was struggling with the devout and pious bit. The exclusive club was *the* place in the city where even I'd had a difficult time getting membership. Not only did I have to stick my thumb in a certain place, I had to press hard too. Some of the most important business in Salonica was undertaken at the Rotary. The atmosphere in the inky mahogany dining room, with its view over the sea, its hushed meals, rituals, subdued conversation and just the barest music of china and silverware, was privilege transcendent.

Octovriou Street rose like a slope in purgatory from the poor lower town to a hilltop section of fine homes. The grand clubhouse stood proud and immaculate at the very top of the gradient in the north-eastern part of the city. The huge

Ottoman-era building came complete with spacious lawns that were shadowed by huge olive trees and well-clipped shrubbery. The Mercedes entered this elite domain without having to stop at the gatehouse. We drove along a smooth, tarmac driveway and into a walled courtyard before pulling up beside a large fountain that was gushing crystal-clear water. The three-storey building came complete with a pair of chary, skeletally thin, uniformed footmen, arched windows the size of elephants and a white-washed paintjob that hurt your eyes to look at. Our muted driver got out, opened the door and watched Smiley and I clamber out. I was quickly shepherded across the buffed shingle and ushered inside. The club's interior was ornate and grand, decorated with Greek caryatids and ceiling-hanging polished-brass luminaires.

The young, dark-haired receptionist at the main desk turned from her switchboard and gave a curt nod when we walked across the carpeted lobby between the glass-cased tanker models and clipper ship prints. I winked at her and she spun on her swivel chair to show me her back as well as her disdain for my flippant greeting. Smiley raised an eyebrow, gently took my arm and glinted his well-polished incisors at me again. "If you'd like to follow me, Major."

We made our way up a wide staircase and along a cream corridor to a room at the extreme western wing of the building. The décor in the hallway was as ostentatious as the club's fancy anteroom. Smiley tapped gently on a large door and without waiting for a reply, motioned me through. It was dark inside the room with just enough light filtering through the window from the courtyard outside to see where I was standing. As my eyes grew accustomed to the murky conditions, I saw that the far side of the room was filled with a silvery sheen. I took a couple more steps into the pitch and heard the door behind me click shut.

"Ah, Mister Remis." Eric Hodt's Teutonic voiced boomed like an amplifier. There was a click from the other side of the room and a yellow tungsten light came on underneath the shade of a small table lamp. The German was sitting in the centre of an upholstered leather sofa almost obscured by a dense cloud of cigarette smoke. Around him, pieces of fine antique French furniture, carefully positioned to best show-boat each pieces hefty price-tag. Hodt's face emerged from the fog. He rose to his feet and inched forward giving me chance to admire his fancy grey-granite suit. We shook hands in wary silence, like two chess players about to do battle. His hand was strong but quickly rotated over mine so that his palm was facing down and mine up, as if he meant to show that he intended to have the upper hand during our meeting. That was fine by me; it was Hodt's interrogation after all.

"My apologies for having to drag you across town to see me. I do hope that I haven't caused you great inconvenience. As you no doubt deduced during our previous encounter my Greek is rather shaky and I'm unsure if you speak any German. May I suggest that we meet in the middle ground and converse in English?"

I shrugged, feigned a brief smile. "Fine by me."

"Good." Hodt sat back down and exhaled another great billow of grey smoke before unfurling the palm of his hand towards a chair opposite. "Please, do sit." I sank down into a matching leather, high-backed wing chair. An onyx and gilt metal coffee table acted as a polite barrier between the two of us. "And how is life treating an earnest public highway's official?"

"Me? Oh, I'm as busy as a German tobacco salesman."

Hodt nodded, amused. "Touché. Better a clever lie than a foolish truth, don't you think?"

"Maybe." I sat back in my seat. If I was going to be given the third degree, I thought I may as well endure it in comfort. "What can I do for you, Herr Hodt?"

"I wanted to speak to you privately." Hodt spoke with his cigarette clenched between his lips. "On a rather ... delicate matter."

"Delicate?" There was a sudden tap at the door. Hodt made a grunting sound. A young waiter entered and moved across the room like a wounded crow. He placed a silver tray on the table. In the centre of the tray was a Briki pot, filled to the brim with steaming coffee. Two small malachite-coloured fine-china cups sat on equally delicate saucers.

"Will you join me?"

"Why not."

I watched Hodt pour the drinks and heap four spoonfuls of coarse sugar into his coffee. He pushed one cup toward me then stirred the contents of his own brew as though he was putting an extra rod into an atomic pile.

"We appear to share something of a common concern."

"We do?"

"Yes." Hodt took a sip of his coffee, then looked up and met my eyes. "Konrad Tafel."

I let the sound of a car rumble away outside before replying. "Now that is a surprise."

My host ignored the venom. "This is all very embarrassing, Mister Remis."

"Oh, I can see how you're blushing."

Hodt lowered his voice a little. "I am an intermediary. The

people I act on behalf of wish me to discreetly confer with you on the rather sensitive issue of Tafel's demise."

"And who do you represent, Herr Hodt?"

"Shareholders and investors."

"I've never heard them called that before."

"Call them what you will. Superiors, masters, controllers. Whatever the title it all boils down to the same thing. One's betters instructing the likes of you and I to get our hands dirty, so they don't have to."

"And what muck are you bringing my way today?"

Hodt gave me a smug look. I watched him stub out his cigarette then hang another on his lower lip like a close peg. He lit the end with a match, got to his feet and walked across the room. He opened one of the big wooden shutters then stood looking out of the window for a moment before turning to face me. "I, nor those that I speak on behalf of, wish to muddy the waters any further than they already are."

"Well, that's very considerate of you all. At the moment it feels like you're peddling me the lies and truth spiel. Bankers and sneaky government agents generally trade in both."

"And I'm guessing that you don't think that I come across like the financier type?"

"Herr Hodt, from where I'm sitting you look more beagle than broker. And for what it's worth, I'd say that you make a shitty smokes salesman too."

I watched Hodt bite at the corner of his bottom lip before continuing. "Perhaps I could best be summed up as something of an enigma to you then?"

I took a swig of my coffee and shifted in my seat. "Enigma ... Gimme a break, will you. I can smell a spook like a camel sniffs out water. You know I don't run gangs of hairy-arsed road-workers any more than you shift tobacco for a living. So, let's cut telling lies to old liars. If I had to take a guess, I'd say that you were German Federal Intelligence Service, right?"

Hodt looked vague and waved his teaspoon at me. "What I am and who I work for isn't the issue here. What is, is how we can mutually be of assistance to each other. What I can tell you for now is that Konrad Tafel had been a person of interest to the people I represent for some time?"

"Tafel was an American citizen, not German. At least that's what his passport told me."

"Of sorts, he was both. He was resident and worked in the United States. Maryland, to be precise. He was educated and lived for many years in Munich. Granted dual citizenship by both nations. However, Konrad Tafel was born in Haifa, what is now Israel."

"Jewish and under the watchful eye of the B.N.D, that sounds messy?"

"The deceased and the organisation I work for had a complicated relationship."

"And you're not going to spill the beans to me in regards this thorny alliance, are you?"

"For the moment, no, I am not." Eric Hodt turned back towards the window and continued to look down into the courtyard. "Would you call yourself a trusting sort of man?"

"Ah, now, here's the thing about trust. In my opinion, there's not a great deal to it. Trusting anyone is simply about ignoring your gut instincts, your experience. Trusting another human being in my business is like suspending disbelief. If you're wanting me to swallow any of your patter you can begin by telling me about how, as you say, we can mutually be of assistance to each other."

Hodt spun on his heel and walked back towards me, nodding thoughtfully to himself. "At some point the disappearance of Tafel's body is going to require some kind of detailed explanation. This is not a Greek national that has disappeared without trace from one of your morgues. The people I work for can be of useful assistance in mediating with the American government, and, in time, with the Israelis, whilst you go about the arduous task of locating the corpse and tracking down those that snatched the body. We could make your life a great deal easier. Lighten the load, so to speak."

"How did you know that Tafel's body had gone walkabouts?"

"Informers are everywhere. You, of all people should know that. It's common knowledge, even to a foreigner like me, a man who works in a rather specialist field, that the Hellenic Gendarmerie is something of a snake pit. You have rampant factionalism and feudal warlord cops. Your city hall is hot wired to the station house and visa-versa. The detective bureau is full of listening devices and recording instruments that I'm pretty sure filter back to the Greek *N.I.S.* Officers at police headquarters. Fellow officers keep tabs on each other. Smart cops like you make your calls from pay phones."

"You seem to know a great deal about who I work for."

"That's my point, Major Remis. You don't mingle with the commoners. You are blessed with a certain freedom of movement. I know that the man you serve ensures that the work you undertake on his behalf rarely suffers or endures the eyes, ears and blabbering mouths that so many of your fellow officers within the Gendarmerie must tolerate. This is one of the important reasons that we find ourselves together today. You are in an enviable position, one that could aid me, and yourself, considerably."

Hearing Hodt refer to me by my rank threw me for a moment. It was a nice touch, deftly played by the German spy. I threaded my fingers together and rested my palms on my stomach. "And what are you expecting me to throw your way in this proposed sly little pact of yours?

"A little information. Insight ..."

"Infidelity?"

Hodt shook his head sombrely. "I wouldn't go that far. All I am seeking from you is that you keep me in the loop with regards your investigation into Tafel's disappearance. Nothing more."

"Nothing more? Sounds to me like you're asking me to perform a Judas kiss."

"That is a little dramatic, don't you think? Let me be clear. What I'm asking for is a simple and transparent collaboration. One that will exist for only a very brief period of time. A temporary alliance, which I trust will be advantageous to all concerned."

"You make duplicity sound very simple."

"Your reputation proceeds you, Major. I hear that you have an acute penchant for deceit. Double-dealing. Sharp practice. Not the usual qualities one expects from a serving police officer, wouldn't you say?"

I shifted forward in my seat. "No comment."

Hodt grinned, almost enjoying my insolence. "That's what I hoped you'd say. I realise that what I am asking of you is hardly by the book. Which is why I felt confident to approach you in this manner. With the limited amount of risk, our colluding could be extremely beneficial."

"Yeah? Maybe for you. The way I see it, Herr Hodt or whatever your damn name is, I'd be putting my head on the block, for what? To keep the German secret service primed about the offing and vanishing act of some dead Jew. That sounds like a pretty poor fucking deal to me."

Hodt wagged a finger at me. "Like I said, I can guarantee you a high-level of assistance. Iron out some of the misery with the very people who will want to make your life very difficult. You know the sorts. Bureaucrats. Embassy busybodies. Diplomatic envoys. I could take some of the heat off in the coming days. Allow you a little breathing space whilst you begin turning over stones.

"What makes you think I want to start poking around in some political hornets' nest?

Hodt placed his empty cup onto the table in front of me. "I'm not saying you should become Mata Hari. You're clearly involved in an investigation of some sort, especially in light of the recent death of your friend the coroner."

Hodt's remark touched a raw nerve. I could tell from the edgy look shifting across the German's face that he knew he'd pushed a button in me. Rather than bite, I continued with our pragmatic exchange. "I've just been doing what I'm paid to do. Nothing more, nothing less."

"And that's not far from what I am asking you to continue doing. Look, I was once a police officer. I served within the *Bundeskriminalamt*. My lengthy career mirroring your own tenebrous one, to some degree. And like yourself, the organisation I now work for entrusts me with somewhat dubious undertakings, rather like the one I find myself accorded with currently. I know what I am asking you to risk, and that's coming from a former dumb policeman."

"Now that I don't believe. That you were ever a dumb policeman."

"We'll, let's just say that we're both still working for our betters, so we must be doing something right."

"What kind of cop were you?"

Hodt rubbed at his chin thoughtfully. "The honest kind. Most of the time."

"What does that mean?"

"Like I said. I prided myself on my probity. That should tell you something about me as a man and what I'm appealing you to consider."

"Something else tells me that you know a little bit about murder, Herr Hodt."

"All Germans know about murder. As a Greek you should know that."

"Oh, believe me, we do".

Hodt produced a packet of his favoured Juno cigarettes from his jacket pocket, lit one and handed a cigarette to me. As I sparked up my lighter, I watched Hodt drag hard on his smoke then exhale slowly through his thin nostrils. "Major, correct me if I'm wrong, but my gut tells me that you enjoy being a policeman. That the detection art of the job, equals, even betters, the chase. I think you treat your work like a favourite jacket. One that you rarely take off unless it is either worn out or you have no further use for. From what I can see of you, you are a man of great tenacity with a solid propensity for obstinacy – those are forensic qualities which I admire greatly, and ones which, as I have said, could in the coming days be fortuitous for both of us. What do you say?"

"I'll think about it."

Eric Hodt smiled a decayed smile, which only served to

reinforce the likelihood of how rotten his soul most probably was. I judged him as a threat and chose to let him know it in my own way.

"The business card I gave you the other evening. Do you still have it?"

I nodded my head.

"Good. If you have any information for me, anything at all, contact me on that number. Likewise, if I can be of assistance to you during your investigation, please, do not hesitate to let me know. You can be assured of my gratitude."

I got to my feet. "Caught together, hanged together, right?"

"I wouldn't have it any other way, Major."

I bet you wouldn't, you slimy, kraut prick, was what I was thinking as I walked across the room to leave.

CHAPTER SEVENTEEN

IN ANY GIVEN SITUATION, MOST PEOPLE BELIEVE WHATEVER THEY NEED to: up is down, black is white, sun for day, moon for night and that dog shit tastes great with baked potatoes. Eric Hodt wanted me to believe that he was one of the good guys, a real kindred spirit. The oily bastard had all the attributes of an accomplished card shark; disciplined, focused, intelligent. A man imbued with the honed ability to control his emotions, all whilst keeping his winning hand close to his chest. He was prepared to grease a few wheels and made it clear he was the type of guy that I could rely on if the going got tough. An ally when I needed one most. I didn't believe a word of it.

Hodt's flunkeys had driven me back across town and dumped me in the same spot they'd snatched me from. They'd even thrown back my gun, just to show me that there were no hard feelings. My car was still where I'd left it, parked down the street from my apartment door. I checked the door handles and key-slot with my fingers for nicks in the metal. The match I always rigged inside the driver's door hinge fell away when I opened it. The Lancia hadn't been touched.

I got in, started up and headed toward the Karamanli district, north-west of the city. The Macedonian Tomb Park on Papanastasiou Street was a secure and little visited spot which Ezra Lieberman and I had long ago chosen for him as a drop off point for any under-the-counter wiretapping recordings or illicit information I had strong-armed him to obtain. I checked the few cars behind me, turned right then made a quick left, rechecking in my rear-view mirror. My motor hadn't been searched whilst I'd been over at the Rotary Club, but it had been watched.

I claim to always know when I am being followed on foot. Flushing a tail by car is more difficult, sometimes impossible, because the traffic conditions occupy too much of your attention. I knew I was being tailed within the first couple of minutes of being back on the road. The car doing the sneak work was a sun-bleached gunmetal-blue Citroen, with what looked to be only the driver onboard. Whoever was behind the wheel was carefully keeping one or two vehicles between us.

I was also dead set on making sure that whoever was trailing me wasn't able to stick around long enough to track me back to Lieberman's drop site. Rather than start any high-speed antics to try and throw whoever it was off the scent, I decided to take my peeper for a longer drive. I'd head someplace quiet, an area with a succession of sharp corners and tight back alleys which would help me establish how determined my new-found hanger-on was and to hopefully lose him along the way.

Half an hour passed. Forty-five minutes turned into an hour and after driving back and forth across the town's busy main arteries and around the narrow side roads that crisscrossed the port area, the Citroen was still holding on to my rear-end well. The driver was clearly skilled at keeping tabs on his chosen quarry and any hopes that I may have had of losing him in the provinces or down by the boondocks were quickly dwindling.

Realising that I wasn't going to rid myself of such a dogged shadow any time soon, I decide to change tack. Rather than scurrying about town, I'd draw my pursuer into a less familiar, more unwelcome domain in the hope of throwing them off my scent.

See how the hound liked being stalked by the hare.

The Dragoumi Street *Kata* slums on the western side of the city, also known as the *Kataraménos* were home to some of the worst criminal animals in Salonika. A so-called rent ghetto that occupied a little over two blocks of derelict wasteland, it was a series of hovel tenement tower blocks built just after the second-world war with more entrances and exits than a hunk of Swiss cheese. The rats ran along the balconies and stairwells of the labyrinthine six-storey doss houses and were hunted for sport or food by gang-owned fighting dogs and feral children with air rifles or catapults. Prostitution and drug-dealing were rife. Acts of brutality, rape and murder commonplace. Cellar dives housed illegal Tsipouro stills while, on the concrete back courts that were laughingly called 'gardens', packing case colonies of shanty huts housing some of the city's many home-less and unemployed squatted under lines of filthy washing.

I drove out of the city with the window wound down. The gulf was dark blue, the afternoon sun high in the sky, its warm rays a marked and pleasant change from the heavy cloud and heavy rain of previous days. I headed along the harbour road, keeping my speed to a steady forty. Rainbow-coloured sailboats stuffed the harbours, fishing trawlers, their nets draped from jibs like cobwebs. Fishermen mingled with down-and-outs in the shade of palms. The trees were shorn of leaves and looked like gnawed ribs plunged into the dirt. A bony dog limped alongside an old woman pushing a handcart loaded with oranges. The brown beaches were strewn with washed-up seaweed stretched out in a ragged line along the tide break. Signs of history followed. A Greek orthodox church on the headland, white stone and blue brick. A three-masted ship from the 1900's, full of false pride as it rotted out in the bay. After a couple of miles of cruising, the Citroen on my rear end became the only vehicle on the road with me. Another mile out and the highway veered away from the seaport quarter and the Aegean basin into a less built-up hinterland of warehouses and half-built, breeze-blocked domestic properties. I passed sulphur and petroleum tankers, a kingdom of piping and noxious odours.

I felt a wave of heat spreading across the back of my neck as I slowly picked up speed and motored over a crossroads. I took a quick look in my rear-view mirror, then stepped on the gas, whipping through the gears, increasing the gap between myself and the car behind by half a block before swinging sharp left and heading down a single-track, beaten-up asphalt road which led into the ghetto. A quarter mile more and I was speeding along narrower thruways which penetrated deeper into the projects. With my tail still locked in tight on me, I took a series of dives through the back streets, my speed increasing because I knew the skid row turf. I now had an advantage. I could go where I liked, whereas whoever was hunting me had to be thinking my moves before I made them, and I had no idea where I was going myself until the very last second. I kept my foot on the peddle, slinging the Lancia through a series of sharp left and right turns before veering on to a thin stretch of waste ground. My quick-fire stalker, unable to brake in time, shot past me, giving me just enough time to pinwheel round and get myself back on the road.

The driver of the Citroen quickly realised I'd duped him when I glided up on his tail. He immediately reduced his speed and continued to travel along the road for around another hundred metres or so before pulling over at the kerb. I took my foot off the accelerator, drawing up likewise on the other side of the street. I kept the engine running and waited. Whilst he was deciding on his next move, I took a quick look at the street through the mirror. It was empty apart from a lone cruising hooker who was staggering in and out of doorways, coked up to her eyeballs. I watched her drop into the gutter then lurch, arms flailing, back across the pavement into a red-brick entry. The avenue at my rear became still again, the same couldn't be said when I focussed back on the car in front.

The driver had climbed out of his vehicle and was moving at a pace, heading across the street towards the rundown housing projects. A trilby was pulled down on his head. His fast-moving frame hidden beneath a black trench coat tied at the waist. The way I saw it, a botched trailing assignment was now quickly turning into a bait and lure job; one that was being undertaken to either throw me off the scent or do me harm. I knew that if I chose to follow the stranger, I'd most probably be walking into trouble. Whoever he was, he was clearly hoping that I was an easy mark. That I could be fleeced rather than followed. I decided to let him hook me in, see how things played out.

I got out of the car just as the man was disappearing down a passageway that cut between two of the apartment buildings. I moved quickly, unholstering my Walther as I went because as soon as I crossed over the road into the Kata, I knew that I would be in the heart of gang territory. I might have lacked caution, but I wasn't stupid. I worked the slide on the nine-millimetre, put a round in the chamber, went through a narrow archway and down the footpath that led up to a tiled entrance with the door busted off at the hinges. On a dark, shit-splattered stairwell I found a bunch of junk addicts flopped out, sharing a needle and stumps of cigarette ends. I looked at the burnouts and they stared at the Walther I was holding in my hand.

"Did any of you see a man come in here just now. I'm not talking about a renter. This is a blow-in wearing a dark-coloured mac and a hat?"

Nobody said anything. But they were still listening. High or not; it pays to listen when it's a man with a gun doing the talking. To loosen up their vocal cords I pulled the gun's hammer and pointed the barrel into their faces. One of the men hastily jabbed a thumb over his shoulder. "Some guy just went out across the courtyard."

I ran down a set of steps and out into open ground. The austere grey surroundings of the back-court area looked like a granite frame for the brilliantly blue sky. I'd taken less than a dozen paces across the squalid cement enclosure when something zipped passed my left ear. I instinctively ducked my head low and heard the unmistakable 'phut' noise of a suppressed rifle bullet. Half a second later my brain registered the subliminal image of a flash from a third-floor balcony and impelled my body to take cover behind some bedsheets that were flapping on a clothesline. I didn't stay put. As soon as I had crawled several metres on my hands and knees, I heard another dull thumping sound, and something flicked through the sheet I'd been kneeling behind. I scrambled to the end of the line of washing and sprinted into the relative safety of another stairwell. Several ragged-looking drifters already wasted and cowering in the shadows stared at me fearfully, backing away as I darted toward them. I raised the Walther, my arms extended in front of me and hared up the stairs to the third floor.

The was no sign of the gunman, but I soon heard his heavy footfall as he began rapidly descending another set of stairs, three or four steps at a time. I went after the sound of the shoes. A few of the natives had come out on to the Kata's balconies to see what the hell was going on, but the sensible ones stayed hidden deep in their warrens.

Reaching the bottom of the stairwell I drew to a halt and pushed a couple of small metal oil drums that were leaning against the wall down onto the courtyard to draw the rifleman's fire. By now I had a good idea that it was a German rifle. I guessed it was a Schalldämpfer Karabiner. During my time in the army, I'd heard its partially silenced voice often enough to remember its name. The muffled weapon had a distinctive recoil and was accurate, but it was unsuited to rapid fire on account of its particular bolt arrangement. And, in the split-second it took the gunman to put another round in the spout I was out of the stairwell and firing. There's nothing slow about a nine-millimetre Walther.

The first shot missed him. The next too. By the time the Walther was ready for a fourth I could see the pattern on his necktie. This matched the design on his shirt and his coat. Red polka-dot isn't normally a favourite of mine, but on this guy they looked fine. Especially as their dappled source was from the hole I'd made just below his right cheek. He was dead before he hit the concrete.

I held the Walther at my side and moved along the walkway toward the sniper with my back facing the wall. I stood over the body for a moment. I didn't recognise the bloody mess looking up at me. I turned to check that I wasn't being crept up on by any of the locals or worse still, another deadeye, and holstered my pistol. The gunman was tall, thin with dark hair that was fashioned in a military-style crew cut. He had already lost his upper front teeth. At the moment of his death his tongue must have forced the dental plate from his mouth and now it sat like a pink, plastic false chin.

It was a cursed kill, and I was already kicking myself for having just blown a hole the size of a grapefruit out of the back of the dead man's head. I'd wanted to wound rather than terminate, then grill the shooter to find out who had put him up to the hit. Instead, I had to go through the miserable bastard's pockets and all under the curious eyes of a gathering crowd of vultures on the verandas above.

I found his wallet. The dead man's name was Ezo Dovas; I got that little nugget from his N.I.S identity card. What the hell was the National Security Service doing sending one of theirs to take me out at the neck? Perhaps the more crucial question; Was it its head, Brigadier Grivas, that wanted me dead?

I took the dead man's billfold – and his rifle – and left him sprawled out on the ground to start stinking.

The vultures were already taking his teeth and ripping his shoes and trousers off as I walked back down the stairs and out on to the street. False teeth and clothes were an expensive perk for the Kata hyenas.

Who was I to deprive them of such simple luxuries?

CHAPTER EIGHTEEN

I DIDN'T WASTE ANY TIME GETTING OUT OF THE GHETTO. A BLOOD-soaked stiff found in the Kata was a commonplace affair. Butchered or shot corpses were a dime-a-dozen, but that wasn't an excuse for me not covering my tracks. Stripping the man of his papers, personal possessions and firearm was just a start. I needed to make doubly sure that I didn't leave any trace that would link me to his death. Torching the dead agent's Ford Zephyr, which he'd followed me in was my next move. The car was thankfully unlocked. There was no two-way radio installed. An empty glovebox. No worldly-goods. No paper-work, photographs or files uncovered. In other words, it was a typical spook mobile. Swept clean daily and devoid of anything that could mark it out as being different from any other shitbox on the road. Satisfied it was clean, I walked back to my own motor, fished an old rag out of the trunk and returned to the Zephyr. I unscrewed the petrol cap, stuck the cloth into the tank, lit the end of it with a match and didn't hang about to watch it go up in flames.

The sun was still beating strong as I drove back toward

town. A sea breeze had turned into a steady, low wind and it felt like there was rain in the air. Free of anyone on my tail for the moment I could pick up the package Ezra Lieberman had promised to leave for me and that meant swinging by into the Toumpa, a Jewish neighbourhood on the outskirts of Salonika.

The Macedonian tomb park was a disused cemetery on the farthest edges of the two-mile-long Papanastasiou boulevard. The ancient bone yard had last entrusted cold meat into its crumbly red earth when the Turks still ruled the city and was now little more than wildland. It was a walled, dormant necropolis, now depleted of visiting mourners or clergy, but still a dusty site where the black-hooded crows would flock together.

Unlike the carrion birds, my only reasons to pay a visit to the old mausoleum were to snag up whatever Lieberman occasionally had secreted away between the brickwork of one of his favoured sarcophaguses. The small brown manilla envelope he'd concealed for me was camouflaged well; hidden underneath a small granite slab step that sat at the entrance to one of the old crypts. I pocketed the envelope and walked back to my car. Once inside I tore open the package to take a look at Vokos' handiwork.

Konrad Tafel's naked body, stretched out on the autopsy table had been meticulously photographed by the dead coroner from every possible angle. Every wound, ligature, cut, bruise and abrasion had been documented in graphic, forensic detail. Vokos had shot twenty-four separate ten-by-eight colour images, some zoomed-in offering close ups, most importantly of the six-pointed Star of David that was clearly visible, tattooed under the man's left armpit.

My body-snatched murder victim had become real again

and I had two dozen gory snapshots to prove of his past existence. I may have had the photos, but I still didn't have any concrete evidence of who Tafel really was. Was he a spy? Luckless banker to a bunch of Nazis? Mossad agent turned sour or just an unlucky Yid tourist? I had no real idea what Tafel had been doing in Greece or why he'd been killed so brutally.

All I had learnt in the past eight hours was that German intelligence wanted me to pitch in with them and that Greek N.I.S was having me followed and most probably sanctioned my liquidation. I thought about what my friend Lieberman had said to me earlier. His recommendation that I should forget the whole sorry affair. That I should pack a bag, get out of town and go buy a boat and fish in some far-off place.

If only life was that simple.

I needed a drink, I needed some female company, and after killing a member of the National Security Service, probably a new identity. As things turned out, I went to the best place for all three. The Capsis Hotel sat at a crossroads between Katouni and Oplopoiou Street in Ladadika district of the city.

The Capsis was both renowned for its elegant and palatial surroundings as well as being notorious as a hospitable rendezvous for corrupt politicians, sly businessmen, high-ranking police officers and the heads of Salonika's criminal fraternity. For the right kind of cash and with a respectful introduction, you could have a man killed or imprisoned, buy yourself protection or the love a good woman for the evening, procure a long-lasting favour and, should you wish, even obtain a new persona, passport and disappear off the face of the earth.

I parked my car in a side street and walked the short distance to the hotel. On the steps I peeled off a couple of notes and pressed them into the leathery hand of Pasha, the Capsis' watchful doorman who also moonlighted as one of my regular snitches. Inside the sumptuous lobby I looked around for Antonia Garbi, whom I hoped would have been working one of the bars. Instead, I found the manager, Akis Soulis. He was wearing black tie and tails and, in his lapel, a white rose that matched his woolly moustache. He wasn't a tall man but he was every inch a gentleman.

"Major Remis," he said. "How nice to see you. You must think me very rude for not taking the opportunity to thank you sooner for your kind assistance in dealing with that awful room theft last month. I was hoping to run into you to express my gratitude in person." He pointed to bar. "Do you have a minute?"

"For you Akis, I have several."

In the bar, Soulis waved for service but it was already on the way, the young barman moving towards us like an express train. "Metaxa for the Major," Soulis snapped. "The very best."

We sat down. The bar was quiet. The waiter brought over two cut-crystal shot glasses, filled to the brim. The elderly hotel manager raised his jigger and toasted me silently.

"I was hoping to find Antonia working this evening?"

"Ah, sadly not. She's not back on shift until after the weekend." Soulis quickly glanced over his shoulder, ensuring we were fully alone before speaking again. "However, I am aware that Miss Mercouri is with us this evening, should you wish a little company."

Soulis smiled and took another sip of his Metaxa. He rested himself back in his seat "There is an ancient Chinese curse that dictates, 'May you live in interesting times'. I'd say that Greece is going through interesting times, wouldn't you, Major?"

I grinned. "Yes, Akis, I certainly would."

"Given that is the case, and in light of some of the more unpalatable occupations your friend Miss Garbi has undertaken in the past, I just wanted to assure you that whatever happens, there will always be a job for her here at the Capsis. I know that you have Antonia's best interests at heart, and I wanted to assure you that any friend of Major Remis is a friend of the Capsis."

"Thank you, Akis. That's most kind."

Soulis' face flushed, he lowered his eyes, speaking into the carpet rather than at me. "Likewise, should you ever wish to take up the role as my head of security, you would be made most welcome."

"The way my day is going, I just might have to take you up on that."

Soulis, unsure of how to take my remark nervously rubbed a finger across the bridge his nose before continuing. "Most of the house detectives here are, as you know, retired policemen. We've had a number of unsavoury incidents over the last few months which have proved that one or two of the men are not equal to the task. Your experience and obvious connections would prove to be an advantageous combination. I could also offer an attractive salary ... with benefits."

"Akis, that is indeed a very generous offer." Soulis waved a hand at me in coy embarrassment. I leant forward, lit a cigarette; the only thing I could do in an attempt to hide my disinterest. "Let me chew it over, and we'll discuss the matter again, very soon, yes?"

Soulis was silent for a moment, unsure as to whether he'd

offended me with his proposition. "Of course, Major. That would be most agreeable."

We continued to indulge in the excellent aged brandy and chatted for a while longer. The old man, never one to outstay his welcome, bid me a good night and went to meet his wife and family for dinner whilst I went to search out Melina Mercouri. I found her on the second floor, on a corridor leading to the hotel's two exclusive bridal suites. She was wearing an elegant black evening gown and high patent-leather heels. But not for long. The smaller, less expensive rooms were on that floor. These had views of the harbour and, beyond it, the White Tower on the waterfront.

But I had the best view of all. And I wasn't even looking out of the window.

CHAPTER NINETEEN

I woke up feeling like the inside of someone's shoe. Little men with jackhammers and earth-moving machinery were rebuilding the inside of my head. The three empty bottles of Dom Pérignon, upturned in the silver-plate ice bucket on the bedside table, a cruel reminder as to why I was feeling as rough as I was. The room stank of sex, stale tobacco and the tail end scent of cut flowers. Melina Mercouri was crashed out next to me, the white sheet just about covering the top of her well-rounded backside. I stretched out my arm, grabbed up my cigarettes and lighter that were sat next to the dewy wine chiller, then rolled onto my back, shook the final coffin nail out of the packet and lit it. I wrestled my head up the pillow and took a deep pull on the last of Eric Hodt's gratis Junos and peered at the hands on my wristwatch; it was just after eight-twenty.

I stared up at the ornate coving and savoured the satisfying burn on the back of my throat before blowing a thick column of smoke into the air. The crystal chandelier above looked like a remote icy mountain top surrounded by an ermine collar of cloud. I'd never paid much attention to the ceiling before. My previous erotic encounters with Melina had often been furtive, hurried affairs, conducted with one eye on the clock and the other on the door handle, and I'd rarely ever had the chance to feel relaxed enough to fall asleep. The wooden window shutters were closed. The room remaining mercifully free from sunlight. As upmarket flophouses went, the place wasn't bad; I'd certainly slept in worst dives in my time. The furniture was tasteful but had seen better days. On the walls were some French prints depicting anodyne scenes of the Peloponnese islands, and at the foot of the bed, a decent-sized seating area for some pre-coitus entertaining. In the far left-hand corner of the room, an en suite bathroom for the punters to wash away the immorality, and a small sun terrace balcony for Melina to drape herself over once she'd kicked them out.

I felt Melina stirring underneath the covers, her body slowly coming to life, her arms and legs flexing out across the box spring. She finally turned on her side to face me. There was no smile, no warm look of affection or desire. "Sleep well?" she murmured curling her knees up towards her stomach. "No bad dreams?"

"No dreams at all." I ran my hand over her smooth olive flank, my hand cupping the back of her thigh, drawing her closer toward me. "That's good." Melina's warm breath fanned my neck. She leaned over me, kissing me on the mouth, before taking the cigarette from my fingers and smoking it with the exaggerated gestures of a drunk. I watched her nostrils flare as she drew a heavy hit of nicotine into her lungs.

The two of us lay together in silence, neither eager to engage in any further chit-chat, Melina no doubt impatient to end our previous night's congress. My companion for the evening had prudently demanded payment in full. The wad of folded Drachma notes I'd handed over had been quickly cached into the top drawer of the dressing table before we got down to any foreplay. I heard Melina sigh as she rolled back across the bed, reaching for the ashtray on the bedside table next to her, and stubbed out the cigarette. I twisted my body towards hers in a last-ditch attempt at intimacy, kissing the top of her behind, then the small of her back, then her shoulders. I was just about to sink my teeth into her neck when the telephone started to ring. Melina nudged me away with her shoulder and reached for the receiver, her head dropping down onto the duck-down bolster as she spoke into the handset.

"Yeah?"

I turned my head on the pillow and could just make out the low tone of a man's voice on the other end. I saw Melina chew the back of her lip, her checks and nose flushing bright red.

"Yes, he's here." Without making eye contact, Melina handed me the receiver. I pressed the phone to my ear.

"Had a fun night, Major?"

A German accent, the voice cold and calm. My reply to the stranger was terse. "Kind of early in the morning for games, isn't it?"

"Never too early for a little sport, Major." I heard the stranger snigger on the other end of the line. "Right now, you must be feeling pretty good shacked up next to that filthy tramp, huh?"

I struggled to sit up, my hangover thundering in my skull like nine-pins falling in a bowling alley. "What?"

The voice was silent. Only a dull crackling sound in the wires. Then after a short time the man said.

"You're looking for Konrad Tafel?"

I felt a cold sensation at the base of my spine, a tingling as though the nerves beneath my skin were opening up like tiny umbrellas.

"Who the hell is this?"

"Don't."

The line went dead.

CHAPTER
TWENTY

I'd left Melina Mercouri still in bed, Janus-faced and pleased to see the back of me. My wallet was five thousand drachma lighter. If a dead man could've shaken off his last repose, he'd have felt like I did. A steady swell of nausea rode down in the elevator with me. I was sweating like a long-distance runner on the last leg of a losing race, the stink of my own odour filling my nostrils – a ripe mixture of rut and whore's perfume, the musky perspiration oozing out of every pore.

I emerged out of the tiny vestibule-lift and padded across the lobby, the front of house clerk giving me the once-over like a government meat inspector grading a side of beef. On the steps of the Capsis I told myself I needed another drink. The hair of the dog. A double Metaxa – no ice, no chaser. Straight up and straight down. But instead I stepped out into the fire of a new day, deciding to hedge my bets on a little self-imposed temperance. An impulsive decision I'd no doubt be kicking myself over by midday.

The first few steps I took were a real pleasure. I was walking just as well as any other man; one footstep after another. That sense of elation didn't last for long. Every progressive stride I took made me feel a few years older and weaker than the last. By the time I'd hit the kerb at the end of the road it felt like I'd reached the century mark. The sun lanced into my eyes, making me squint. My skin itched, my face burned, my lungs working harder than a blacksmith's bellows against white fire. The sound of the traffic rang in my ears, the air around me so thick that breathing felt liquid, viscous. I had to get my act together. Get back to my place to shower, shave and put on some fresh clothes. No way could I head into the station house stinking like a polecat and looking like I'd been run through a meat grinder. I also needed to quickly staunch the beginnings of an all-day hangover.

On my way back to the car I stopped at a news kiosk and bought a packet of Tylenol and a bottle of water. I stood on the pavement, blood pounding in my head, loud and insistent, nursing my third hangover in as many days, amid the throngs of citizens and denizens, swallowing my medicine and feeling like shit.

Across the street, under a grove of olive trees, an old man was selling watermelons off the back of a truck. He'd lopped open one melon on the tailgate as an advertisement, the meat dark red in the shade. Seeing the hacked-in-two fruit did nothing to improve my splitting headache. I took another swig of water and looked back at the hotel, up to the second floor toward Melina's room and saw, for just a spilt-second, the figure of a man closing the shutters on the sunlight and the world outside.

. . .

The light was soft through the trees when I finally left my apartment and walked back across the street to my car. The air was still dense, a smell like salt and warm seawater on the breeze. Thirty minutes standing underneath the head of a cold shower had improved my banging head a little but not the nagging sense of unease that was biting at my insides.

The voice of the stranger on the phone warning me off earlier, Eric Hodt's fishy inside-man deal, knowing the N.I.S clearly had me in their sights and the fact I'd clipped one of their agents less than 24 hours earlier, wasn't doing anything for my peace of mind. Changing into a clean shirt and pressed suit couldn't mask the fact that I was in a tight spot. Whatever I had got myself mixed up in boiled down to more than the murder of one man. I knew that Konrad Tafel's death was never meant to be investigated but that hadn't stopped me from snooping around. The disappearance of his body was clearly meant as a wake-up call. An object lesson informing me to back off. The fact I'd kept pushing had clearly ruffled someone's feathers and now I was paying the price for sticking my beak where it wasn't wanted. The fact the security service had put a tail on me and were prepared to silence me meant that I'd clearly pissed off some faceless mandarin someplace.

Before leaving my flat I'd bagged up the evidence I'd gathered over the last few days. The petri dish containing the micro dot taken from Tafel's tooth, Ezra Lieberman's list of the Nazis he'd found inscribed on it and Vokos' mortuary slab photographs of the corpse. I knew it would only be a matter of time before my place was turned over. Somebody looking to incriminate me further or better still to destroy the material altogether. Thankfully, I'd taken possession of one of the few unofficial and concealed underfloor safes which I could deposit it all in, the combination known only to myself.

The traffic heading across town was pretty light and I made it over to police headquarters just a little after 11:30. The Gendarmerie building was built before the turn of the century; a four-storey, cream-coloured brick pile with a red pantile roof that was held together with soot and pigeon shit. I headed inside, ignoring the desk sergeant, and took the stairs to my office on the second floor. The station was alive with activity. Outside my office a dozen or more cops in plainclothes and uniform went about their business, taking statements, booking in new faces and regular customers alike. Station employees, thieves, muggers, city hall gawkers, attorneys at law, prostitutes and policemen all shifted around each other like a mass of army ants on a rampage, proving that the city's melting pot was not only a reality but sometimes a nightmare.

I spent the first hour of my day behind my desk trying to look busy, chugging back more painkillers whilst going through the internal mail that had piled up since I'd been out of the office. There were phone messages left on little yellow pieces of paper and a heap of new case files to delve into. But there was nothing important or which I felt had to be answered immediately. There was nothing concerning the Tafel investigation and for now, it looked like the body of the secret service agent I'd offed in the Kata was yet to be discovered. I knew that it was only a matter of time before the corpse would turn up someplace and his controllers started asking difficult questions which may well lead the N.I.S back to me. I sat back in my chair and swivelled around to look down on the *Via Egnatia.*

The early afternoon sunlight seemed to seep up around

everything. I had lived in the city almost my entire adult life, running wild for the Provost, committing almost every crime imaginable on his say-so, all whilst upholding the law in my own off-kilter manner.

For the last few years, I'd been hoping that I could find a way of climbing out of the dung pit I'd fallen into and wash myself clean, this latest madness had put paid to any hopes of future clean living. The duplicity and savagery of the past three days had once again made me realise how far down in the abyss I still was. Wrenching myself out of such a mire was never going to be easy no matter how much I wanted to try and redeem myself. Sat mulling over my current predicament, I suddenly understood the metaphor of baptism – how some truths hide away in a pocket or a forgotten drawer and show up when you think they hardly matter anymore.

Konrad Tafel's murder should have been the writing on the wall. A red flag warning me that if I wanted to fathom out what the hell was going on then I'd need to sink a lot lower into the dregs than I'd previously submerged myself in before. If I wanted to clean up my act, behave like a detective rather than a hired thug, I'd need to continue to tread on people's toes. I'd been foot stomping my whole career, why stop now.

Considering, and then giving up on, the notion of salvation had done little to improve my understanding of what I should do next or whose feet I should be squashing. I turned my restless thoughts again to the last twenty-four hours, replaying those brief words of warning I'd received on the phone earlier in my head, asking myself what connection there might be between Tafel's death and his disappearance and how the Greek intelligence services were involved?

I reached down for the bag containing the evidence I'd

brought in from the flat, opened the centre drawer underneath my desk and took out a black Ziploc envelope and began to transfer the petri dish and photographs into it. I picked out the scrap of torn notepaper Ezra Lieberman had written on, held it up in front of me, reading each of the names, one after the other.

Max Merten
Johann Robert Riss
Gerhard Sommer
Alfred Stark
Herbert Glebin
Helmut Beck-Broichsitter

I kept muttering those half-dozen names under my breath for the better part of two minutes before suddenly remembering what Ezra had said to me just before handing over his copperplate scrawl. The stuff about the "Expropriation of Jewish valuables and their property". I sank back in my seat, continuing to stare at the six names on the list, thinking about what may connect them to Konrad Tafel's death. I kept mulling over that conundrum until, for some reason, a seventh name suddenly sprang into my head. I picked up the phone and called down to the switchboard operator and asked for Lieutenant Colonel George Tsantes. After a long wait, he came on the line.

"George? Remis here. I want to drop a name by you."

"Yeah, who's that?"

"Dieter Lirtzman."

"That Jerry bastard."

I laughed, unsure how much I should tell him. Dissembling

had always kept me alive and more or less intact for a long time when nothing else could.

"What's he up to these days?"

"Great. I've got twelve unsolved murders, the makings of a student riot out at Valaoritou, I've got assorted pissed-off council officials on my tail like a hive of fucking bees and you call me up about some kraut prick."

"Then I guess I best leave you to get back to work," I said. "But you know, George that kind of talk's sort of unfashionable these days, if you know what I'm saying."

There was silence on the line for a moment, followed by a heavy sigh. "Okay, so he ain't a prick."

"I knew you'd see it my way."

I listened to Tsantes clear his throat before snapping back at me. "So, come on, spit it out. What do you want to know about the fucker?"

"Everything you got on the man."

"Everything? There's not that much to hawk up. Keeps himself to himself. A pillar of the community. Decorated war veteran, so I believe. Clean as far as this department is concerned. But just 'cause he's spotless on the outside doesn't mean he's not bent underneath that oily exterior of his."

"You're not painting a very pretty picture of the man."

"What do you want me to do, make him out to be Saint Gregory? Lirtzman's a banker. As far as I'm concerned that means he's dirty. He swims with some of Salonica's big criminal fishes but he's way too clever to get caught with his pants down associating in plain sight with any of them. He's got money, plenty of it and like I say, real pull. He's into everything that jingles or rustles, if you get my drift. He looks after the financial interests of this city's great and the good, as well as the heavy-movers up in Athens and back in Germany."

"So, you're telling me that Lirtzman is the one money launderer in this city we don't brace?"

"That's my point, Remis. There's not a single shred of dirt on him. Nothing to say that he's making his money on the sly. There's never been any improprieties reported, not a sniff of corruption or illegality directed toward him. If there was N.I.S surveillance on him, we'd sure as hell never hear about it, and as you're twisting my arm for the scoop on him, you've clearly never been ordered to sanction a wire-tap on his home or offices, right?"

"No, never."

"So, what's your interest?" Tsantes asked cagily.

"It's just a whisper I've picked up on the street."

"When did your snitches start rubbing shoulders with wealthy blackshirts?"

"Say what?"

"Herr Lirtzman was over here during the war. Officer of the Wehrmacht. Believe that shit, and you'll believe anything. There's not a Nazi over fifty left on the planet according to Germany. Every kraut you speak to pleads they were regular army."

I pressed my fingertips to my temple and began to massage the dulling ache inside my skull. "Sounds like an interesting man."

"He sounds like what he is Remis, a slimy, rich bastard. If I were you, I'd give him a good leaving alone. Prying around someone like Lirtzman can only lead to trouble. I'd forget the shit, besides there's plenty of crooked Greek brokers for you to stick your oar into."

The phone clicked in my ear, but I didn't lower the receiver immediately. I sat there, pondering on both Tsantes' advice and my own silent counsel. I'd heard Dieter Lirtzman's name occasionally mentioned in certain closed cabal circles, heard the rumours about his war time connections to Greece, but until now he'd stayed off the criminal radar and I'd had no dealings with him. I knew that a man like Lirtzman, so well connected politically, with his sticky fingers in all kinds of bureaucratic pies, could easily bring me a great deal of grief. Getting his back up, asking questions would be ill-advised.

That said, my job is, had always been, to investigate without let or hindrance, and that no-one in Greek society was above suspicion. It had been instilled into me to obey the orders of my superiors, either to soothe their fears or to fan the flames of their rage. And there were worse elements to my profession.

One of them was having to parlay with snakes like Eric Hodt and Dieter Lirtzman.

My call to George Tsantes, rather than warning me off, had only pushed me in deeper.

CHAPTER TWENTY-ONE

The offices of Dieter Lirtzman weren't pretty to look at. The modern six-floor rococo monstrosity had been built at the furthest edges of Koromila Street in the financial district of the city. The building stuck out like a sore thumb; the ornate, asymmetric design and pastel shades clashing with the unadorned plaster and breeze-block Greek premises that stood around it. Staring at it was doing nothing for my hangover, so instead I concentrated on how I was going to get inside the place without having to throw my weight around. There was a snappily dressed concierge outside the open, double copper doors and a uniformed deskman visible across the wide, green and white marble hall. The doorman was tall and tanned: a German, with broad shoulders, matching Max Schmeling muscles and nose and a nasty-looking predatory leer hanging off his top lip. He clocked me crossing the road, his huge shoulders rolling aggressively by way of a greeting as I made my way towards him.

"Yes?"

I broke out my warrant card, held it at arm's length just

long enough for him to gawk at my mugshot. "Major Michail Remis to see Dieter Lirtzman."

The ape nodded once. "Are you expected?"

"Yes," I lied.

"You sure?"

That question didn't seem to need an answer, so I didn't provide one. The doorman moved his lips around some more, waiting for, maybe even expecting, an answer to his nonquestion. When it finally became clear that our conversation was over the muscle said, "Wait here."

After some talking on the phone my new friend paced back across the wide floor. "Herr Lirtzman isn't expecting you. You need to call his secretary and make an appointment."

I shook my head. "What's your name?"

"Fuck you." The doorman was smiling like a chess grand master who was about to make a winning move. "No appointment. No way you're getting through this door. Simple as that, friend."

I took a step toward the German, fixing my eyes on his. "Here's what's simple, *friend*. I'm here on official police business. You need to get me in front of your boss in the next five minutes or I'm going to start ruining what's left of your day."

"You should have a little respect," the doorman advised.

"I give what I get. Now, go tell Herr Lirtzman he has a visitor."

The irate watchdog's jaw dropped like a cat-flap. I watched him clench the fingers of his left hand into a tight ball, his lips froze as he tried to hold his temper. He continued to eyeball me a second or two longer before going back to the deskman. They huddled a few moments, made another call, and then my temporary nemesis came marching back.

"Go down the hall and take the last set of elevators on your left," he snapped. "Sixth floor."

As I walked by him the doorman added, "I'd like to meet you on the street one day."

I stopped and turned toward him. This unexpected movement fostered uncertainty: the German minder suddenly unsure what to do with his big hands.

"I look forward to that with great anticipation."

The interior of the lift was understated, plain even. The walls were unadorned cherrywood and the lights above my head were bare bulbs nestled in mirror glass in the four upper corners. I pressed the sixth-floor button, clasped my hands at my back and enjoyed the short ride. I exited into a spacious room with a broad, blue-tinted window that looked down over the street with distant views of the harbour and seafront. There was only one door.

Rich people, in my experience don't share anything – not even a hallway in a glorified tenement block. I was looking for a doorbell when the oversized mahogany door swung inward. The woman standing there wore a utilitarian black dress adorned only by a thin white collar of modest lace. She was in her thirties, handsome, with similar skin-colour to that of the bolshie doorman downstairs.

"Inspector Remis?" she asked with only a hint of German encompassing the last syllable.

I nodded.

"Come in," she said with no smile. "This way."

The circular foyer was maybe twenty feet in diameter; it went up another thirty, with no stairs or ornamentation; just a domed skylight above. I followed the secretary into a smaller room, the centrepiece dominating this antechamber was a dark stone sculpture of two Greek wrestlers. There were no windows in this room and the walls were charcoal grey. The only illumination came from three stark-white spots, their thin beams cut across the walls like prison camp searchlights. Left to my own devices I would have hung around a while to admire the impressive statue, but my guide was eager to lead me forward.

We came to a sunken office area with a wall of glass that looked down on a large rear area and manicured garden. Surrounding the lawn was a ten-foot brick wall, edged in barbed wire with a single wrought-iron gate at its centre, which led out into a back street. The office was a big cubical room, with three identical brown leather sofas that faced one another across a solid-glass coffee table set upon shiny golden globed feet.

Embedded in the thick plate of crystal was a six by eight print of a World War Two German propaganda poster, which depicted an attractive blonde fraulein, dressed in a crisp white shirt and black necktie. Her hand was grasping a flagpole, the red, white and black pennant swirling at the top of the mast was only missing the swastika emblem. Centred in front of the huge window was an antique walnut desk with green-baize top; behind it, a matching leather-bound, swivel desk chair.

The secretary held out a hand toward one of the sofas. "Please, take a seat."

I dropped down on to the plush settee, sat forward, my elbows on my knees. I was oddly impressed by the tasteless Nazi print encased in the glass. A lot of good money had gone into creating such an extreme monument of wealth as well as all the other classy stuff that adorned the room. I was well on my way to hating Herr Lirtzman and I'd never even met him.

To the left of me a door opened and a man of around sixty came into the room. A pair of rimless glasses worn studiously at the end of a broad, Teutonic nose belied his robust frame. He snatched them off and stared awkwardly at me and then at his employee.

"Good afternoon, Major," the man said in a modulated Germanic tenor. He was tall and fit. His mottled, tanned skin seemed to come from sportsmanship rather than sun worshipping. His suit was khaki and the shirt, lime cotton. His feet were moccasined in Italian red-brown leather and his hair, onyx and silver as opposed to my own pedestrian salt and pepper mop. I rose to my feet.

"I'm Dieter Lirtzman," he said extending a hand.

The lines were drawn. I smiled at the possibly unconscious class strategy already at play. I shook hands with the Lirtzman and watched as he walked behind his desk and sat. I returned to my seat and reclined.

"Can I get you something to drink, Major?"

"Nothing for me, thank you." The was a moment of silence as Lirtzman's assistant departed through a door behind where he was sat.

"My secretary informs me that you are here on police business?"

I nodded my head. "That's correct."

"The kind of business that cannot be conducted over the telephone or prohibits a prior appointment to discuss?"

"I'm afraid so."

Lirtzman folded his hands thoughtfully, then unfolded them again before looking at me quizzically. "Very well, Major. You'll no doubt appreciate that I'm a busy man. Most important of all, you must understand that I am a very private one too."

"Yes. I got that impression from your concierge downstairs."

Lirtzman didn't like my tone. That was okay – I didn't like his doorman. He smiled grimly before giving me a little more of his well-oiled lecture. "My time is also very limited. I'm sure that you will appreciate that the governance of the wealth of others has certain obligations."

So, does an outside toilet, I thought. I leaned forward in my seat and smiled back at the broker. "I intend to take up as little of your precious time as possible."

There was a sulkiness about Lirtzman's mouth, and my limited acquaintance with the science of physiognomy told me that this was a man used to having his own way, mostly in cash. He stabbed a stout finger at my face from across his grand green baize. "That Major, would be greatly appreciated."

"I'm investigating the murder of a man called Konrad Tafel."

Lirtzman hesitated for a moment. "And?"

"I believe that, the dead man may have in some way been connected to your investment bank."

Lirtzman snorted with derision, affecting shock at my remark. "Really. And what evidence has led you to deduce such an unusual correlation?"

"The corpse unexpectedly gave up something."

"And what may I ask was that?" Lirtzman's voice sounded vaguely challenging, as if he was daring me to spill my guts but knew what I was going to say before I'd opened my mouth.

"A list of names. Six German names to be exact."

He raised his eyebrows. “And you think these half dozen epithets could be investors here at the bank, yes?”

I shrugged. “That’s what I’m here to find out.”

Lirtzman looked at me blankly. “All our patrons demand the highest levels of confidentiality. I’m in no position to divulge such restricted information to you.”

I held up a finger. “I haven’t told you their names, let alone asked you to breach any corporate discretion.” I watched the banker shift awkwardly in his seat. I got to my feet and took a couple of steps toward the desk. “Yet.” I fished out the slip of paper with the six names written on it from my jacket pocket and slid it across the desk toward the banker.

Lirtzman looked at the paper and pursed his lips, consulted the list and shook his head. “I have no knowledge of any of these men.”

“Not account holders with you then?”

“They are certainly not.”

I’ve heard lies told from the best and the worst of men. Lirtzman’s untruth was uttered with the kind of contempt and disdain that only a wealthy and powerful man could convey. His spirited deception was all the answer that I needed, but still the German tried to throw a little more sand in my eyes. “Why ever would you ask such a question?”

“I have it on good authority that your organisation handles some pretty large amounts of cash on a daily basis. Money that most other banks around here wouldn’t get a chance of loading into their vaults. I’m also reliably informed that the men on that list became very wealthy here in Greece during the occupation.”

“I haven’t the faintest idea what you are talking about.”

"No? Well, let me enlighten you." I moved around the side of Lirtzman's desk, so that I was standing directly over him. I leant forward, placing the palms of both hands on the polished surface, my mouth close to the German's ear. "I'm talking about hot money. The kind that belongs to some very unsavoury individuals. Men who were prepared to steal from others, and who like their dough, clean and hard for others to locate. If you know what I mean."

"I do not." Lirtzman's grey eyes became shifty and nervous, momentarily searching the floor as if he expected that at any moment, he would be lying flat out on it. I reached across for the list with the tips of my fingers and glided the torn notepaper back toward me, reciting the six names as I did.

"Merten, Riss, Sommer, Stark, Glebin, Broichsitter. Not customers of yours, then?"

"They are not."

I slipped the notepaper back into the inside pocket of my jacket and at the same time eased the Walther out of its cradle, then grasped a thick clump of hair at the back of Lirtzman's head, snatching his neck back and levelling the barrel at his right eye. "I really don't want to see your brains scattered all over this lovely office of yours, but unless you start telling me what I want to hear, your secretary is going to have one hell of a mopping up job on her hands." Lirtzman moved his shoulder ever so slightly. I cocked back the hammer on the automatic. It sounded like a bone breaking. "I wouldn't move if I were you, Herr Lirtzman. At the minute, if you were even to breathe too heavily, I'd blow your face off. Understand?"

The banker made a sound like he'd just swallowed his tongue before answering. "Yes."

I knotted up more hair, my fingernails grazing the German's scalp, and moved the muzzle of the gun close enough to touch Lirtzman's flickering eyelid. "Don't twitch now, I want you to see the bullet coming." Lirtzman's jaw trembled, his left eye half closed. "Now, think long and hard about those names and tell me what you know about them." I forced the barrel of the Walther against the side of the banker's clammy face and repeated the six surnames. "Merten ... Riss ... Sommer ... Stark ... Glebin ... Broichsitter"

"I've never heard of any of them!"

I didn't give the banker chance to see what came next, pistol-whipping him twice across the side of his head and face, both blows making a sickening crack. "MERTEN ... RISS ... SOMMER... STARK ... GLEBIN ... BROICHSITTER."

Lirtzman yelled out in pain. I quickly muffled his hollering by snapping his head back further and driving the barrel of the gun into his mouth, forcing the metal frame of the pistol against his tongue and lower row of front teeth. Dark blood gushed from a deep cut at the edge of his hairline. It poured in thick rivulets down the side of his face, pooling on the lapel and sleeve of his expensive made-to-measure suit. Once he'd quietened down again, I pressed the Walther's muzzle back against the side of his skull, all too aware that Lirtzman's belly-aching could well be attracting unwanted attention.

"What do you know about these men?"

"They were Rosenberg Sonderkommando!"

"They were what?"

"Rosenberg was a specialist taskforce set up by the Nazi party. A group dedicated to appropriating cultural property during the second world war."

"Go on."

Lirtzman blinked nervously a couple of times, his speech stuttering before he got back into a flow. “Back in ‘41, Merten and Riss plundered Jewish libraries for the Reichsleiter. They stole from homes, clubs and synagogues here in Salonica. They seized tens of thousands of books, archives, manuscripts ... rare objects and sent them back to Germany.”

“And Jewish money too?”

Blood covered the front of Lirtzman’s shirt, his body shaking. “Of course, they took fucking money!”

I tapped the muzzle of the gun against the banker’s skull. “Don’t crap around with me.” The man’s anger quickly disappeared, swiftly replaced by fear again. I let the pistol slowly slide down the side of Lirtzman’s cheek and let it rest underneath the soft part of his jaw. “And these Nazis laundered that stolen money through this company, yes?”

Lirtzman’s tried to shake his head. “Yes, but that was many years ago.”

“Bullshit.” I leant forward, applying more pressure, forcing the Walther deeper into the banker’s gullet.

“I’m telling you the truth,”

I reached down and took hold of the knot in his necktie, pinching it between my thumb and forefinger. Not much of a grip, but when I lifted him, he came up to meet me as easily as an empty husk. “Save yourself some trouble. Don’t make me squeeze or shoot the truth out of you.”

“I’ve told you all I can.”

He stupidly tried to pull away from me; I jerked the knot in his tie a touch tighter and pressed the gun’s muzzle deeper, letting the Walther bite at the centre of Lirtzman’s throat. That brought the man round to my way of thinking again.

“I don’t think you have.” I bullied him back into his seat

and kept the pistol stuck firmly in his windpipe. Lirtzman sank backward in his chair, his eyes closed, his trembling fingers pressed to his temples. I nudged his shoulder with a clenched fist and the banker reluctantly opened his eyes again to meet my gaze. When he began to speak it was slow, the words dragged out of the distance, filtered through layers of agitation and dread.

"These men you are asking about did at one time engage this company in matters of a financial nature, introduced to us through a third party. But that was more than a decade ago."

I shook a cigarette out of a pack and stuck it in my mouth but didn't light it. "A financial nature. You're talking about money laundering, yes?"

"No, not laundering. Investment."

I thumbed my Zippo, tilting the cigarette into the flame. "Investment?"

"Yes. We supplied services which allowed the client to invest capital across different portfolios. We were intermediaries, nothing more. We no longer handle those accounts."

I took a step back, withdrawing the gun barrel from Lirtzman's throat. His head and shoulders slumped forward, his arms sagging either side of him. I took a step backward and swiftly pounded him across the face, two heavy blows that almost knocked him out of his chair. The German lurched forward, blood and saliva spluttering from his mouth. I push him back in his seat and watched as he writhed in agony, gasping for breath like a fish out of water.

I leaned forward and blew a stream of smoke into Lirtzman's watery eyes. "Before you have another sudden amnesia attack on me. Tell me who the third party was that put you in touch with Merten and his cronies?"

"I'm unsure of the exact contact," Lirtzman shook his head, coughing. "Like I said, it's a long time ago. I remember it was the Union Bank of Switzerland who reached out to us. I'd need a little time to come up with a name."

I looked at my watch, then raised the Walther, pointing it directly into Lirtzman's face. His nose was streaming blood, the split on his forehead ridged up like an orange starfish. Fear was etched over every inch of the man's features, the kind of horror that went deep and couldn't be feigned. The sort of pain that travels up from the feet into the viscera.

"You have thirty seconds to recollect."

I watched the banker swallow hard, the beads of thick perspiration, heavy on his brow. "It was Roth ... Pierre Roth."

I smiled and took a couple of steps backwards, lowering the pistol to my side, never taking my eyes off the German once. "Thank you." I holstered the Walther. "Before I go, let's get something straight. If I find that you've lied to me, if none of what you have just said pans out, I'll be paying you a return visit. Understand?"

Lirtzman nodded his head like a berated child. I watched as he slowly sank forward in his seat, his quivering hands clutching the edge of his desk. I began to head back across the plush office turning again before making my way out into the foyer. "Remember, Herr Lirtzman. This is *my* town. Here you're a trespasser. Here, I can pick you up off the street and have you lost in a prison cell in the blink of an eye. I can visit you in the night and burn your house to the ground, fuck your wife, and kill your dog. And the only thing that'll protect you is if I can't *find* you. And I already found you."

Such words of warning would have normally had the desired effect on most hustlers and heavies. But my pep-talk had fallen on deaf ears. Dieter Lirtzman was no ordinary crook, and I should have known that.

Whilst I was mouthing off my threat to Herr Lirtzman, he was busy fumbling for the panic button underneath his desk.

CHAPTER
TWENTY-TWO

WHEN THE LIFT DOOR SWEPT BACK, I FELT A SUDDEN, STRANGE whoosh of heat hit my face, like someone had just opened a blast furnace door next to my head. Outside two men were tearing down the short corridor toward me: my friend the doorman and another heavy-set kraut carrying a Smith and Wesson .38. One behind the other, their sinewy frames dipped down low like predators on the hunt, and with less than ten feet of polished ground to cover before they were on top of me.

My Walther was already out of its holster and a shot fired as I was clearing the elevator door, the round hitting the first man as he was raising his own pistol. A tenth of a second later his rising gun hand hit mine, knocking the automatic from my grip. It was a posthumous act because he was already dead from the bullet entering his skull. The doorman dodging the still-falling corpse was holding a pearl-handled switchblade in his hand and pointing it at my guts. The flick knife's mechanism had sounded as harmless as a camera shutter. But the big German wasn't interested in getting a snapshot. He came slashing and jabbing at me, I shifted to my left as he darted forward, grabbing the wrist of the hand holding the knife and his throat with my right. He was at least five inches taller than me, but I still managed to heave him off the floor and barrel him against the wall on the other side of the narrow hallway.

I collapsed backwards towards the lift, my intention to latch back onto my gun and finish the job, but the doorman came snarling back at me like a rabid dog, the blade in his hand going for my jugular. I raised my forearm to prevent the switchblade slicing through my windpipe. The sleeve of my jacket managed to absorb most of the blade's sharp length as it came down, but it wasn't thick enough to stop the tip of the knife from stabbing my arm. I yelled in pain as the German took another jab at me, I twisted my arm and the knife to one side, and then lashed at him with my right. It was a good punch, a big uppercut that ought to have broken his jaw except that he ducked under it and came at me again.

There was fear and murder in his eyes and maybe just a hint of uncertainty about the outcome of the ruck he'd got himself into. He lunged at me again. The knife came within reach of my face, a few inches from my nose, and high enough for me to clap my two hands hard on opposite sides of his arms simultaneously – one on the back of his hand and the other on the inside of his forearm. I got lucky. Luckier than I deserved given how big and powerful my opponent was. My right hand stopped his wrist from moving and my left hammered down on the back of his mitt, forcing his fingers to open suddenly so that the blade flew out of his fist and clattered across the floor.

As he straightened up again, I swung with my right, and found my fist caught firmly in his huge paw. He snatched at my gullet and I headbutted him full in the face, which made him release my fist as he instinctively cupped his nose. I swung again and this time he ducked and seized me by my jacket labels. As he wrenched me toward him, I sank my head down toward his sternum, pummelling his ribs with a couple of short liver shots and at the same time burying my knee deep into his groin. The German creased forward as I stumbled backwards. The big bastard didn't stay doubled-up for long. As he fought to raise himself upright, one hand reached between his legs, the other lashing out at me, I lunged back at him, hammering him hard under the chin. I snatched at his necktie, my fingers knotting around the silk material and yanked his head toward the wall, cracking the side of his face against the polished plaster finish. As his skull bounced back, I tightened my grip on the man's tie, driving him back on his heels toward the front foyer, smashing at his nose with the heel of my hand a couple of times. The second blow carrying him down the remainder of the corridor and sent him crashing into a mirrored-glass lobby table. The security guard lay unconscious, sprawled out in an untidy heap of bloody face, nose and broken glass.

A terrible roaring filled my ears, as if a grenade had burst directly in front of my face. My heart felt the size of a watermelon inside my chest, hammering against my ribs, bursting with adrenaline. I spat a crimson wad of spittle onto the white marble floor and cursed myself, angry at not having had the chance to finish the son of a bitch off with a bullet.

I stood a moment longer, my breathing like a heaving sack of rabbits. I shook some life back into my stunned hand and then felt the blood slowly seeping into the fabric of my shirt sleeve from where I'd been stuck. Instinct told me that the wound wasn't as bad as it felt and a sudden gut feeling that it was time to clear out before more of Lirtzman's gorillas turned up. I quickly headed back toward the elevator and collected my gun and the knife off the floor. I pocketed the switchblade and holstered the Walther. I strode back down the hall, across the empty lobby and out into the street triumphant and trembling.

I would have been scared if it wasn't for the blood screaming through my veins.

CHAPTER
TWENTY-THREE

A BOXER TAKING A BEATING KNOWS HE HAS HIS CUTMAN WAITING IN the corner of the ring with a bruising iron and swabs at hand. Soldiers raging war depend on combat medics to treat their wounds. A ship's doctor diligently tends the sick and injured far out at sea when there's little hope of healing on dry land. When I've had the shit kicked out of me, I turn to Nia Garbi to apply the sticking plasters.

After leaving Lirtzman's place I drove out to her apartment in the Vardaris district, hoping that, at just after four in the afternoon she'd be home, no doubt still sleeping off her previous night's revelling. I parked up behind the dingy tenement building, climbed two short flights of concrete stairs at the pace of an asthmatic snail and rang the bell, then slouched against the sill and waited. I'd wrapped a rag I'd found in the back of my car around my arm, but it was soaked through now, and periodically thick gobbets of blood would squeeze their way out and fall along my wrist and over the back of my hand like fat slugs.

After a while I heard Nia coming to the door.

She opened up, grumbling obscenities and stared at me like I was stood on her doorstep to collect the rent. Her hair was tied up high in a bun, she was barefoot and wore a short, sky-blue kimono-like robe. She stared down at my blood-soaked sleeve, shaking her head, and made a disapproving sniffing noise before giving me one of her all too familiar damning looks.

"Don't tell me, Billy Krifakis asked you to cough up your bar tab?"

"Shut up."

"Who won this latest brawl?"

"I did."

"Yeah, then I don't think I want to see the state of the other guy. Aren't you getting a little old for playground squabbles?"

"Perhaps." I winced as a wave of pain shot up my arm. "There were two of them."

"Two he says, well, aren't you the tough guy. I'm really sorry I brought your age into it."

"Sorry enough to let me in to this rat hole?"

Gia gave me a blank stare before finally taking the hint. "What? Oh, sorry, man. Sure, be my guest." She turned and stepped away from the door. "You really do look like shit, by the way." I took a step forward. My head felt like it had been pumped with helium, my legs heavy, as if lead weights were tied to my ankles. I stopped for a moment, took a breath, then another step.

Nia took my elbow. "Are you okay?"

I shook her hand off my arm. "Just a little damaged in transit, as they say at the post office. You know, like when the cashier hands you this parcel that's taped back together three ways from Sunday and whatever was inside is crushed beyond recognition. That's how I'm feeling." I took another step further.

"Are you?"

"What? Crushed? At the minute, yeah. But you know me. I always spring back. Well, these days it's more like seeps back."

Nia laughed. "Stronger than before, right?"

"Not that I've noticed." I headed down the hallway and into the pokey living room. Nia's home these days was a damp, four-roomed dive on Mavilli Street where trams clanked by late at night and you could always smell the drains. It had a couple of overstuffed sofas , some knock-off Italian chairs, a king-size bed, a rundown kitchenette, even pictures on the walls. Mostly faded prints. I eased myself down onto one of the well-padded couches.

"You got anything to drink?

Nia looked around the spartan room. Pointed to a battered, red-lacquered wooden box sat in the corner. "Might be some brandy under that cabinet from when you were last here. Want me to look?"

"What do you think?"

There were a couple of inches left in the bottle she put on the coffee table before me. Ignoring the glass, I tilted the bottle up. It seemed easier that way: less movement, less pain.

"Shit. I feel like I just blinked and ten years went by. I tilted the bottle and sank what was left of the cognac. "Tell you what. I'm going into your bathroom, face up to some hot water and soap. Pay no attention to screams and if I'm not out in ten minutes, you can decide on your own whether to call for an ambulance or the funeral home." I struggled to my feet.

"Need any help?"

"Me? No, look what I've already accomplished, all by myself."

Nia smiled. Her eyes crinkled, threading with white lines at the corners. "I'll make coffee, then."

I nodded my appreciation and stepped carefully down the hall.

Five minutes later, my wash-down accomplished, my nerve ends singing like power lines in a hurricane, I came back and sat and watched as Nia poured yellow iodine into the cut, smeared an antibiotic salve and bound my arm tightly in gauze.

"That's going to need stitches. You're lucky you didn't cut a tendon or artery."

"It's not bleeding anymore. It'll be okay."

"Michail, don't you think you've worn your balls for a hat long enough for one day? Just get to the fucking hospital. Jesus!"

"Okay, okay. I'll get it seen to."

"Promise?"

I wagged my head obediently and she went back out to the kitchen, brought back a tin tray with two coffee mugs and the last dregs of milk that was swilling about in a grubby-looking bottle. She put the tray down, sniffed the contents, nodding to herself that the contents weren't going to give either of us the runs or worse, then poured for both of us. We sat there like some ancient married couple, sipping cheap coffee together without speaking. That silence told me that Nia had something on her mind, something other than getting in my face about a trip to the infirmary. I watched her light a cigarette, blowing the smoke up in the air, her eyes bright, her face suddenly tight with tension. She got up and wandered around the room, paced into the kitchen and bathroom and back again. After sitting again, finishing her coffee, pouring anew for both of us, she said quietly, "I hear you were looking for me at the Capsis last night?"

I said nothing and finally she laughed. "If you weren't looking to pump me for information you were obviously hanging around the joint looking to plug that favourite tom of yours, Melina, right?"

"Cut that shit out."

"Touched a raw nerve, have I? Looks like your friend Melina's got a loose tongue as well as slack thighs."

"Stop with all the fucking riddles." I saw hurt flicker across Nia's face, the skin denting at the corner of her mouth. She looked at my face, her gaze burning.

"I did as you asked me to the other night. I put out a few feelers, asked if any of the local leg-spreaders perhaps had a yid pay them a visit. One branded with a Jew star."

"And?"

"And, I got lucky."

"You did, how?"

Nia leaned in closer toward me, her previous tetchiness toward me swiftly dissipating, replaced by a sudden shimmer of mischief fixing in her eyes. I could smell the residue of last night's perfume and a hint of baby powder on her skin. Once she'd finished eye-balling me, she slumped back against the arm of the sofa shaking her head. "How, he says. You really do need to start hanging out with a better class of tramp, you know."

"What the hell are you talking about?"

She sat forward, picked up her cup and blew on her coffee. "I'm talking about your friend Melina Mercouri and that dead

American you asked me about. That girl clearly loves screwing yids as well as gendarmes."

"You're not any making sense."

Nia tried to keep her face empty of expression, but I saw her throat swallow slightly, as if the apprehension was caught in her windpipe. I watched her chest rise briefly against her dressing gown, her face turning to stone, the splashes of colour dying in her cheeks. She raised her cup again, balancing it between both hands, so that it partially concealed her mouth, Nia's eyes cut sideways at me "Major, there ain't no easy way of saying this."

"Spit it out!"

Her eyes shifted off mine. She looked straight ahead into the gloom, her voice low and hard. "If that slut is telling it straight, it looks like you've been dipping your dick in the same place as that missing stiff you're searching for."

The AHEPA hospital looked more like a tobacco warehouse than an institution that provided medical treatment and nursing care to the sick or injured. The white cinder-block building had all the exterior warmth and welcome of an abattoir, and rumour had it, what went on inside was little better than your average slaughterhouse. Many locals called the old sanatorium 'Quintessentially Thessalonian'; in other words, bleak-looking and gone to the dogs.

At the triage desk I gave my name and other information to the clerk, reluctantly answered that I was happy to wait to receive treatment, adding that I was more than happy to part with my own cash if that meant I'd get seen any quicker. That off-the-cuff remark earned me a lingering weighty glance, as though it was now moot whether I was a crook on the run or someone important who perhaps should be catered to. To move things along to my benefit, I offered up my warrant card. The snappy clerk, who was sporting the physique of an over-the-hill prize-fighter wasn't remotely interested in prestige or rank, he just wanted me out of his face.

"Please wait over there, Major." He pointed to row upon row of interlinked, crappy-looking plastic chairs. "A doctor will see you shortly."

Shortly turned out to be just under two hours.

The place was more like a bus station than an infirmary. The same sense of being cut off from real time, and much the same squalor and spread. Everything reeked of cigarette smoke, stale ash and bodies. Stains on the chairs, floor, most walls. Steady streams of people rolled in and out. Police and ambulance attendants pushed through the double-doors with drunks, car accident victims, vacuum-eyed young people, sexless street folk wound in layers of rags, resuscitations-in-progress, and slowly cooling bodies. Every quarter hour or so a poor swine's name would boom over the intercom and that person would vanish into the leviathan interior. None of them seemed to emerge. Nurses and other personnel strolled past me regularly on their way outdoors to smoke. The place reminded me of police headquarters.

Once the system finally got round to swallowing me up into one of its dank little ante-rooms I was ready to smash up the joint and the quack who was about to treat me. I finally escaped the place with a half dozen or so stitches, another splitting headache and an urgent desire to get blind drunk.

For better or worse, I decided not to stop off at the Tsinari bar. The prospect of getting both intoxicated and cranky alongside a roomful of other deadbeat barflies didn't fill me with a great deal of joy. Truth was, I'd be better off getting plastered alone rather than loaded and end up stretched out across Billy's beer-soaked counter. I finally got back to my apartment just a little after eight. I was walking toward the answering machine with its blinking red light when the phone rang.

"Remis," Nick Kampouris said. "You ever bother setting foot inside your office?"

"Not if I can help it, Captain. Why?"

"Why? Well, perhaps if you showed up at the station house once in a while you wouldn't be getting calls like this."

"What do you want?" There was silence on the line. A moment later the sound of a match striking and a long pull on a cigarette. A cough that died before having the chance to get going, rattling deep inside Kampouris' chest.

"Well, if it's okay with you, I'd like you to get your arse over to the Capsis hotel. *Sir*?"

"And why would I want to do that?"

"Melina Mercouri."

Hearing him use her name made my breath come hard in my throat. As the words came out of my mouth my heart twitched and my stomach turned. "Yeah, what about her?"

The line fell silent again for a moment. "Best come see for yourself."

I felt my skin tingle like I'd just walked out of an igloo. "See what?"

"How a tart's boudoir can be transformed into an abattoir overnight, that's what."

The line went dead. I cradled the phone listening to the burr of the disconnect tone and after a few moments hit the message button. After a brief pause, a momentary shush of tape noise then the unmistakable, icy tone of Manolis Callas identifying himself. "Call me as soon as you get this."

I dialled the mansion house, got a busy signal three times in a row, at last I got through and was put on hold. A few moments later I heard the line click in my ear.

"Where the fucking hell have you been?" barked Callas.

"Doing my job. Carrying out your orders."

"Really. Did I order you to pay a visit to Dieter Lirtzman's place of business today?"

"News travels fast."

"It does when you execute one of his men and beat another to a bloody pulp. What the hell are you playing at, man?"

"Last time I took a breath, I was searching for a missing American's body and trying to keep it under wraps, for you."

"And you think that raising hell at an investment bank and putting a gun to the chairman's head is keeping things under wraps?"

"Lirtzman is bent."

"Tell me something I don't already know, you idiot."

"And connected to Tafel's murder."

Callas' suddenly calm, metallic voice came back at me. "You have evidence to back up such a claim?"

"Some. And I'm acquiring more. A Swiss banker called Pierre Roth is involved somehow. I'm trying to find out to what extent."

"I didn't command you to go looking for Swiss bankers or proof. Nor did I want you to liquidate any Germans. I certainly didn't order you to undertake a damn murder investigation. My directive was explicit, Major. A delicate assignment. The American's body needed to be ousted from

Greek soil. Exiled. Banished. Deported. That was the mandate, yes?"

"Correct, Sir, that was the mandate. You also said that I'd be required to navigate through some rather unpleasant waters."

"Navigate, not muddy them."

"From what I've uncovered, this Mister Tafel or whatever his damn name is, has turned out to be anything but a man of no importance."

"So, it would seem." The Provost's stern tone unexpectedly became a little more pliant, almost reflective in its timbre. "You can appraise me fully in an hour. Don't come here. Join me at our prearranged rendezvous and be prompt." There was dead air for a couple seconds before the old man barked back at me. "That's once you've finished pouring over that whore's corpse at the Capsis."

The old bastard knew how to set the hook.

CHAPTER
TWENTY-FOUR

IF I WAS GOING TO HAVE TO STAND OVER ANOTHER DEAD BODY, I wanted to smell better than the stiff I'd be looking at. Before heading over to the Capsis Hotel I took a quick shower and changed into fresh clothes, slinging the bloodstained shirt into the bin on my way out to the car before heading back across town.

In the hotel's lobby I found two plainclothes N.I.S officers hanging around the front desk. Both were making a silent inventory of my face, my manner, the cut of my suit, the way I walked – their eyes were all over me like ants. I didn't recognise either of them but took a guess at them being a couple of Grivas's men. Like cops, most plainclothes spooks always appear a little to grubby in a grand hotel like the Capsis. Intelligence goons are the same the world over; they usually look as if they belong someplace else, like the Soviet Union or some backwater hellhole in the Baltic, where cheap suits, tight shoes and creased shirts with last year's colours are standard uniform. These two bastards looked like a couple of rotten apples floating in a silver punch bowl.

I took the lift and got off at the third floor. A wheeled stretcher sat in the hall. Two ambulance attendants slouched against the wall. The apartment door stood wide open. A flash-bulb popped inside. I walked in without a word. Tobacco smoke rolled about the room, thick as fog. Three uniformed cops paced around the lounge area with nothing to do. Melina Mercouri was where I'd left her, in bed. She was still naked, her body slumped against the headboard. Blood ran in thick rivulets down across her breasts and ribs and puddled between her thighs, soaking into the mattress. Most of what had been her head was splattered against the wall. Her hand had fallen into her lap, I smelled urine, faeces, the animal scent of blood and tissue. Bile rose in my throat. I felt my breathing quicken, my heart suddenly hammering like a metronome in overdrive, its percussive beating throbbing in my ears.

I cleared my throat, took a quick look around the place, saw that the balcony door had been pulled open again. The net curtains were billowing across the back of the sofa like a couple of comedy ghosts, blood was streaked across the middle of the fabric.

Another flashbulb went off. Captain Kampouris ignored my presence, he stood at the side of the bed staring at Melina's body, his hands dug deep in his overcoat pockets as the photographer knelt next to him for a closeup. I walked around the other side of the bed.

"Why'd you bring me over here to see this?"

Kampouris raised his eyebrows and regarded me with the same kind of silent scrutiny he'd been lavishing on both the corpse and the glut of empty champagne bottles sat next to it in the ice bucket. "Your name came up."

"Names have a way of doing that."

"Our mutual friend the concierge downstairs happened to mention to one of my men how he saw you in the foyer last night."

"Did he, now. That's very considerate of him."

"What, you think you're the only cop in this city that has snitches in this place?" The detective took a Marlboro from a packet and tapped it repeatedly against the side of a heavy Zippo lighter. He put the smoke in his mouth, thumbed the lighter's wheel and took a heavy pull on the filter then snapped the lid shut. "Word has it, you spent the evening with this lovely lady?"

"The word's wrong."

Kampouris turned his dead, cop's gaze on me. "Is that so? 'Cause, I've got two faces in this place telling me you were seen, and another on the front desk saying they put a call up to this room from some guy asking for you. You wanna explain that, Major?"

I shrugged my shoulders. "The front desk is mistaken."

"Mistaken, you say?" The Captain shifted a thumb over his shoulder toward Melina's body. "Well, if you weren't getting your kicks with her overnight, what were you doing here?"

"I like to add a touch of class to the place. Every now and then I'll stick my head inside, take a quick drink, admire the scenery."

The detective's nostrils flared, he rubbed the back of his neck and frowned. "All sounds very civilised. You know who this woman is, yes?"

I nodded my head "Yeah, I know her. You'd be hard pushed to find a cop in this city who didn't know Melina."

Kampouris pushed his sweat-stained hat back on his head and surveyed the carnage around him before returning his suspicious gaze on to me. "But you know her better than most of the grunts on the force, right?"

I rested my back against the wall, lit a cigarette and blew a plume of smoke at the ceiling. "We've had our moments."

"I suppose there's been enough of those ... *moments*, as you say, to leave some kind of trace of you being in this room, yes?"

I looked at Mercouri, at the hole in her eye, her brains spread across the counterpane. I fixed the scene in my mind like a photo then concentrated my focus back to Kampouris. "I'd say there was a good chance of you turning up something that could link me to being in here. Same as you could link any number of men to Melina's room. She liked company. Sadly, she didn't have mine last night."

"Is that so?"

"Would I lie to you, Captain? Look, it's no secret that I was downstairs last night. I came looking for one of my informants and ended up taking a drink with the hotel manager. After he went to dinner with his wife, I hung around in the bar a while longer before heading back home."

I watched Kampouris shift his weight aggressively and mutter through his tight ventriloquist's lips. "I already had a word with Akis Soulis. That slimy little bastard sounds like a spokesman for the Greek ministry of justice. He's backing-up the spiel you're giving me now."

"What can I say, Akis is an old friend. He's just telling you the truth."

"Truth, he says." Kampouris haughty glance was impatient and scornful. "In the time it's taken you to grace us with your presence, I've already had a call from one of the Provost's fancy mouthpieces at the Mansion House. It looks like you've got us over a barrel where this dead bitch is concerned. So, you can stay clammed up. Callas says the homicide division has to keep its hands off you." The detective glared at me as if I were something unpleasant he'd just stepped in. "The boss says I need to respect your rank, so that's what I'm gonna do. But if I find out you've had anything to do with this shit I'm gonna come down on you like a piledriver. You won't be able to hide under Callas' fucking apron forever."

I stubbed out the butt of my cigarette in the crystal ashtray on the bedside table. "You know me, Captain, I always obey the law."

"Bullshit! Men like you play jump rope with the system. Someday real soon you're gonna slip, and I'll be there waiting with open arms." The detective's lip curled over his crooked yellow teeth; his face flushed with anger. He spun on his heels, pushing past one of his officers, barking at the subordinate as he stomped past him. "Get this tramp bagged up."

"Always a pleasure to watch a true professional at work, Nick."

Kampouris turned, shot me a dagger's look and pulled his hat brim down. "I'll be waiting for you to step outta line, Remis." He stormed out of the room, slamming the door hard enough to dislodge a Louvtraki print from the hall wall.

CHAPTER
TWENTY-FIVE

Car headlights came up behind me not long after I'd left the Capsis – inside the vehicle were most probably the two shooflies who'd been weighing me up in the hotel's lobby. The front lamps winked into being far back in my rearview mirror, pinned in the distance at first before rushing in to close the gap, like something falling out of the sky. Less than a quarter of a mile across town and my new tail, a tan Volvo sedan, was trailing right behind me, filling the back windscreen and road.

I drove north, back out toward the Ano Poli district and Callas' secluded rallying point, the Pasha Gardens. Houses on the route I was taking were infrequent, nearly all set back off the road, simple wood and block structures built a foot off the ground, most of them long unpainted and patched with odd scraps of timber, corrugated tin and tar paper. Dusk was still another hour away, plenty of evening twilight for my latest companions to keep tabs on me. I was sick of trouble towing behind me, other mugs getting a boost on my every move. I had no intention of leading them to my meeting with Callas so decided to pull over. I'd go with the diplomatic approach first then move on to plain mean if things turned nasty.

My idea of tact and discretion came in the form of the leather cosh I kept stashed close to hand. I reached under my seat, took the sap out of the harness tied to the frame and stowed it up the sleeve of my jacket, my eyes already locked on the wing mirror as the Volvo drew up on the asphalt behind me. The driver and his partner riding shotgun didn't mess around, climbing out of their car double-quick, with purpose and both surprisingly empty-handed. I followed suit, hit the tarmac and stood by the boot of the car. The gorillas heading my way weren't Greek. Nor were they the plain-clothes cops I'd spotted from the Capsis. This pair were an altogether very different type of unpleasant.

The driver was one ugly looking big piece of work. A weightlifter type in a cheap suit and a perspiration calling card. Someone had been really creative with a razor down the left-hand side of his face and in one lone jagged pull of his neck. The nose had spent as much time taped up as not. His partner fared little better on the looks front and would have struck terror into most men's hearts if not for his stature; he was well under five feet tall. His body looked to be normal in size, but everything else seemed oddly foreshortened. Neck, arms, legs, fingers, temper.

The pint-sized guy opening his mouth told me all I needed to know about him and his bigger buddy. A familiar guttural Rhineland brogue spilled out from between his teeth, his tone hostile and exact.

"Herr Hodt is growing impatient."

"Excuse me," I looked straight over the head of the little

guy. "I'm hearing something but can't see who's doing the talking."

"That's not very polite, Major. Please if you would follow us." The midget held out a diminutive palm toward the Volvo, his open-handed gesture more order than request. His comrade had widened the gap between them, arching himself to my left, his mitts still thankfully free of any hardware.

"I've been chauffeured to meet with your boss once already. It's not happening a second time. If Hodt wants to speak to me, go tell him he can come by the station house and pay me a visit. He can jaw away at me to his heart's content."

"We've been asked to escort you without using force, unless you give us no alternative."

I took a step backwards. That's when any chance of diplomacy went out of the window.

The big guy came in fast, ready to sling the first punch. My cosh lashing across the bridge of his nose quickly put paid to his paws connecting with me. His dwarfish buddy was just as speedy, scrambling around my back like a chimp, hammering into my kidneys with considerable fervour. The taller one fell toward me, trying valiantly to get a knee to my groin whilst smothering one hand over his bloodied mug. I elbowed at the chimp's face and snatched at the big guy's nuts, crushing them together in my fist, dropping him to the floor like an epileptic. At the same time, still holding on to the kraut's balls, I lashed out my other hand and slammed the sap hard across the dwarf's mouth. I watched him crash to the ground and curl into himself. I put a heel down hard on the side of the ugly fella's face and put him out cold. Whilst both men were stretched out in the dirt, I shook the pair of them down, pocketing a couple of Luger P38 automatics for my trouble. Neither were carrying any form of I.D. No wallets. No cash. No passports.

I hooked my fingers around the dwarf's neck, yanked him onto his back and let the blackjack do another job on his now flailing arms and legs then smacked it hard against the side of his head. Whilst he wreathed in agony I stood astride the little man's torso, stomped the soul of my shoe against his shoulder then lodged the sap underneath his chin, lifting his head so we made eye contact.

"I've got some simple questions to ask. You're going to give me some bullshit-free answers or you're gonna find yourself buried beneath this soil rather than laid out on it. Understood?" I started backing off his windpipe to let him speak. A lip quivered, pain etched deep in his eyes, a defeated nod of the head settled my first enquiry. I rested my hand across the little man's throat, just easy, not squeezing yet.

"It was you who called me at the Capsis, right?"

The little man's grey eyes stared up at me as though they had no lids. His face frozen, his mouth hanging sideways like a fish caught on a hook. I could see the edges of his nostrils discolour. "Yes ... yes, that was me."

"You warned me off looking for Tafel, why?"

"Because Herr Hodt needed you to take him seriously. He was concerned that you may have been under pressure from your superiors to drop any investigation into Tafel's death and to stop searching for his body. We needed you to keep asking questions. Go to places we couldn't. Speak to people who would clam up if we started putting the squeeze on Greek officials and the likes. We'd have brought too much attention on ourselves."

"So, what's Hodt's real interest in Konrad Tafel?" I let my

hand tense then relax around his neck. His head came up off the ground, just a few inches, like a turtle, trying for air. Didn't get it. His head went back down and my grip momentarily tightened.

"Raubgold"

"Less of the kraut talk." I watched a bloody tongue moisten lips and eyes flickering toward a fallen comrade close by. I curled my fingers around the dwarf's neck, gave his head a shake, focussing him back on our little chat. "Forget your friend, he's away with the fairies."

"Raubgold ... it's ... it's, stolen gold."

"What's this Raubgold got to do with Tafel?"

A defeated reply was spat up in my face, along with a mouthful of red saliva. "I don't know. That's something you need to discuss with Hodt."

I pincered my fingers deep into the man's gullet, squeezing the neck flesh in my palm, restricting both air and movement. "Not good enough. Start talking to me about what you do you know?"

The little man hesitated, his arms raising at the elbows, panicked hands limply gesturing before the weakened wrists gave way to complete submission.. I pressed down on the neck, squeezing and releasing my hand around the larynx in quick succession. The man's eyes bulging in their sockets each time I applied a little more pressure. When he finally sputtered some kind of comeback, his words blurted out at me staccato and fearful.

"Tafel ... was ... Shin Bet."

"He was what?"

I got a little more blood and spittle sprayed up at me. "Israeli Security Agency. Tafel was part of some high-level repatriation team investigating Jewish property theft in the 1940's. He'd started sniffing around people the German government didn't want him getting close to." Blood bubbled up out of the little man's nose as he gasped for breath. "Hodt was sent to keep a close eye on him. That's ... that's all I know."

"Did Hodt have Tafel snuffed out?"

"No ... no, his execution didn't come at our hands."

"Then whose?"

The German squinted up at me, his monumental eyebrows sagging. "I give you my word ... I have no idea who took the Jew out. We were sent to Greece with Hodt to monitor Tafel's movements, not to eliminate him."

"Where exactly is your boss hiding out?"

I released my grip, let my hand fall away from the man's throat. He tried to speak but it came out a croak. His voice was buckling, the colour fading from his face. "Potamos. A villa on the coast road ...a place called Sephardim."

"And what about the girl back at the Capsis. Melina ... Did you kill her?"

"No ... that wasn't me. That, that was Scharff." The little fella snatched a fleeting glance at his unconscious companion. He swallowed hard before catching my glare with his own frightened, duplicitous gaze. I snatched him up by his lapel, twisting the fabric of his tweed jacket in my hand, drawing his face closer to my own. "Why'd you put a squeeze on Melina after I'd left?"

"Hodt had arranged to have you followed. He'd got a tip from some Greek insider that you and the Jew were screwing the same tart. I've got no idea who told him about the connection. Hodt wanted us to question the hooker, see if either you or Tafel had confided anything to her."

"And what did you find out?"

The man shook his head, the skin around his eyes stretched tight. "A big, fat zero. We braced her real hard and she gave us nothing."

"So why did she end up dead?"

"Scharff, he's got a real quick temper. After he'd slapped her around a little and got nowhere, she started to hiss and kick. That bitch really knows how to push the right buttons. She had one her filthy mouth on her. Scharff didn't like her attitude, tried to set her straight before we left. Things got out of hand. It was an accident." My head reeled like it had been slapped hard with a rolled newspaper. I could taste the bile rising uncontrollably from my stomach. I held on to the dwarf's lapel a while longer before throwing him back down into the soil.

Lies and cruelty come easy to some men. Slippery, double-dealing guys, like the one that was squirming at my feet. I put my hands around the German's neck again, and this time I didn't let go until the bastard had stopped breathing.

CHAPTER TWENTY-SIX

A WOLF'S HOWL OF WIND WHIPPED THROUGH THE OPEN WINDOW OF the car as I drove along the narrow winding road off the main highway towards the Pasha Gardens. The lamps of a half-dozen orange streetlights shimmered down onto the pavement and into the gutter, making the shadows between the trees and the half-ruined structures that ran up to the old park even deeper. Many a night when I was on the run from the orphanage and, for that matter, the police, I'd sleep in the hidden recesses of the Pasha. Nowadays, Manolis Callas had a secluded place inside the grounds where, on very rare occasions, he would command we meet. It was a secluded, ancient rendezvous, one for the Provost to dish out his scheming orders to me. Those unsanctioned decrees I knew he'd be wary of issuing whilst sat behind his stately desk up at the Mansion House.

I pulled into a rough tarmac parking lot at the rear of a dilapidated three-floor flophouse that overlooked the rear of the ancient walled garden, took a cigarette packet out of my jacket pocket, lit one, climbed out and headed across the pebbly bitumen toward the Pasha. A red-tiled lychgate that seemed innocuous enough from the outside offered access into the grounds. A screen of tall olive trees made it difficult to see what lay beyond. I knew there'd be the presence of a couple of Argus-eyed sentries on the other side, armed minders who would be waiting to escort me up to our mutual taskmaster.

Callas' concealed lair was the *Bensousan Han* a former travellers' lodge built during the Ottoman era. The derelict building's ironwork around the gate and balcony had long ago gone green, each storey, floor, room, door and window frame sat at its own particular angle; vegetation grew from cracks in the cement walls and from the rotten mortar between bricks. There was a bust of the Osman sultan, Mehmed V above the gate, and a sign which said, *Historical Monument.* ***CLOSED***. Cats wandered everywhere. Old Greek buildings and public parks attract alley cats like flies hovering around shit.

As expected, two gendarmes were loitering on the other side of the gate, both dressed in cheap, lightweight suits, one navy blue the other grey, the cut-rate material unable to disguise the holstered pistols hanging under their armpits. One of the men sized me up as I approached, the other stood staring back toward the door of the lodge, no doubt keeping an eye on our mutual master.

"Take no notice of the sign, sir. Just go straight on in." The officer in the grey suit held out the palm of his hand guiding me toward the ruinous den. He was tall, skeletally thin, his long, pale face lacking expression, like some plaster of Paris death-mask. I flicked my cigarette onto the ground, stubbed it out with the toe of my shoe and headed up the path, the two minders quickly flanking me. I walked inside the rundown lodge and immediately felt the floorboards creak under my feet. A few of the planks were still intact, many were missing. One vast corner column of plaster at the edge of the door frame had burst open, the tendrils of ivy plants snaking out from within. Callas' bodyguards moved in behind me, roused like hunting dogs expecting blood. The Provost was standing with his back to me, his heavy-set shoulders immediately recognisable. I came to a halt in the recess of a shuttered bay window and waited for the old man to turn and face me. When he spun on his heels and finally spoke, his voice came from deep within him, his chin dipping down to his broad chest like a cabaret tenor.

"I don't make common knowledge of it, but I have a small private residence on the Thermaic Gulf. Nothing specular, but it's a comfortable sanctuary when the time permits me to visit. Considering the sea air and the salt spray the place has a fine garden with, of all things, a croquet lawn. Are you familiar with the game, Major?"

I shook my head. "No, sir."

"It's an interesting pastime; I believe it's very popular in England. It also provides an interesting metaphor for the new Greece you and I find ourselves living in." Callas stepped carefully across the worn floorboards coming to a halt inches from where I was stood. He stared directly at me and forced himself to smile before continuing with his speech.

"Our current laws are merely hoops through which the people must be driven, with varying degrees of force, of course. But there can be no movement without the mallet – croquet really is a perfect game for a policeman." Callas nodded thoughtfully; his expression pleased with the comparison he'd just made. When his eyes met mine the satisfied look on his face had completely disappeared, replaced with his usual blank countenance. "And for a long time now you have wielded that hammer against both the people and our enemies very successfully." I watched as my boss's spine suddenly became ramrod straight. He continued to stare at me, saying nothing for a moment, a bitter look forming in his gaze. "However," he said eventually, "I get the feeling that you have been more than a little heavy-handed with your bludgeoning since we last met, yes?"

"I just lop and cleave as you order me to, sir." Callas' dead eyes turned even colder. I was thinking about saying something else that would get under his skin but decided against it.

"You can omit the impertinence and get on with illuminating me with the facts."

"The facts?"

"Yes man, the damn facts." Callas jabbed a forefinger against his lapel. "Tell me everything you know, right down to the last-minute fucking detail."

So, that's what the old man got. Everything.

I told him what I'd uncovered, procured or had yet to fathom out about the death of Konrad Tafel. Relayed the details about the microdot found in his tooth, the photographs of the dead man's corpse I had in my possession and the fact that I was in no doubt that Tafel was an undercover agent for Mossad. I spilled all I had on the inventory of Nazis' names listed on the scrap of paper and how I believed those men were linked to the theft of Jewish gold, precious gems and cash during World War II.

I gave the Provost the lowdown on Eric Hodt, telling him how he'd sought me out at the Tsinari bar and his seedy offer for me to inform for the German security services. I unveiled what I knew about Dieter Lirtzman's involvement brokering dirty money for fascists, how he'd squealed about the Union Bank of Switzerland's involvement and that he'd given me a name to go after, Pierre Roth. I also confessed to the fact that during the course of my investigation, I'd managed to kill two men, one of whom worked for Brigadier Kyril Grivas of the Salonica *N.I.S.*

"Good god, man." Callas shook his head bitterly. "You're not running some kind of private vendetta or investigation here. This is covert state business. I gave you a simple assignment. The repatriation of Tafel's corpse back on to home soil."

"Tafel's home, as you put it, is open to question."

"I didn't ask you to question," he said, his voice hardening. "I don't give a damn what stone Tafel crawled from under or why he was here, I just wanted his carcass shipped out of Greece and back to the USA on the next available flight. I commanded you to carry out my orders, objectively and professionally, not for you to drag the department into the mire and end up under the spotlight with the likes of German intelligence, let alone to have Grivas sniffing around. That slippery bastard was supposed to be involved, purely as an advisor, remember? I sent him along with you simply to appease the *N.I.S*, not for him to be running the fucking show and having my officers tailed."

I felt myself wince. "Grivas clearly has something to hide."

"Of course, he fucking well does! Most people in Greece have something to hide. Especially these days; Grivas more so. I let him tag along with you to Ptolemaida-Florina coal mine so that he could commandeer matters once he got there, which I'm reliably informed is exactly what the Brigadier did."

"I don't understand. I thought ..."

"You thought ...you imbecile." Callas shook his head, the

disgust all too evident in his voice. "I wanted that bastard Grivas to take Tafel's corpse off our hands, allow the Brigadier to clean up his own mess. I wanted him to dig himself deeper into his own grave. Instead, you take a trip up into the mountains with him, find yourself a conscience and start playing at fucking policemen."

"Look, I came into this latest shitshow blind. You always expect me to bring up the curtain and work the lights at the same time when you send me out to undertake your scut work. Something stank about how Tafel's body was found and the injuries that had been inflicted on him. I just wanted to make sure everything was on the level before fully carrying out your final orders."

Callas muttered an obscenity under his breath and folded his arms across his barrel-chest. "I expected you to use your head, not get yourself embroiled in matters that did not concern you." The Provost drummed the sole of his polished Italian leather shoe against the damp floorboard, the beats becoming quicker as the old man's temper escalated. "Damn it man, you're not green to this game. When Grivas stepped in as he did, instinct and experience should have told you to back off and let him reign supreme."

We were both silent for a moment. Callas' face adopted a less pained expression. "This can of worms that you've opened up means that Grivas and his dogs are looking to pull you down, make some kind of example and cover up what he doesn't want brought to light."

"Which is?"

"I rarely discuss personal beliefs or opinion in front of a subordinate, but we both know that Brigadier Grivas is one of the most unpleasant people it's ever been our mutual misfortunes to meet. Morally, socially, sexually. The man's a pig. His driving force is greed: for sex, food, drink, money and above all power. Power being the prerequisite of all the others. To achieve such power, he's been willing to do anything. I mean that quite literally. Most of it over the years has been the exploitation of criminals: business and politicians alike.

"During the war Grivas and I both worked for the Salonica police department. Young Kyril quickly found further employment with, how can one put it ... foreign masters. He quickly became intoxicated by the populist regime and chose to be swept up by its violence, its false promises, its hatred. He used a position of power to degrade the vulnerable, commit unspeakable crimes that he's never been punished for and for which it's been difficult to prove his involvement in. Nevertheless, ever since the 1940's, Grivas made it his lifelong work to hide the fact that he colluded with the Nazis." Callas smiled again. Twice in one night, a rarity in itself. "Cigarette?"

The Provost took out a pewter case, opened it and pulled a face as I bagged two of his precious *Georgopulo's*, slid one behind my ear for later, and let him light me. I took a lungful of smoke, which couldn't have tasted sweeter if I'd been facing a firing squad.

"As well as handing out hammer blows, you also have a way of always being around, looking up just as the pigeons fly over, don't you, Major."

I shrugged. "What can I say, it's a gift." I cupped the glowing ember in the palm of my hand, instinctively shielding the glare from the cigarette tip.

Callas gestured toward the *Georgopulo.* "Once a soldier, always a soldier, yes?"

I nodded my head. "Old habits die hard."

"If you want to come out of this madness on the winning side, as well as to stay alive you're going to need to become more soldier than gendarme in the coming days, Major."

"I am?"

"Yes, I'm afraid so. As much as you're not going to like it... you're going to have to get your hands far dirtier ... but not at my behest."

"Then who's?"

"You're out on your own."

"My own ... what are you talking about?"

"I've done a deal," he said in a calm voice. "Perhaps the nastiest deal of my career. I'm afraid you're leaving the *Matatzides.*"

"I'm what?"

"I can understand your surprise. I told you from the beginning that none of my men could ever put at risk the MAT division's importance to the powers that be. Those that work for me either obey and abide or they ..."

"Are resigned from service," I interrupted.

"No one ever resigns from my section. A rule without exception."

"But I'm to be an exception, yes?"

"In a way, yes. You're the best I've got, in fact, that's why Grivas wants you out of the way and no longer under my protection. The Brigadier has reached out to powerful men, insisted that you are relieved of your post, accusations of misconduct, criminal behaviour and treason have been cited."

"Is this some kind of April Fool's?"

"None of us are fools," said the Provost solemnly. "I mean what I'm saying Remis. I've had express orders from the Royal palace to relieve you of your post and for the *N.I.S* to arrest you this evening."

"For God's sake."

Callas raised a palm and shook at finger at me. "Please ... let me finish. It's in your own best interests. German intelligence has been sniffing around Grivas for some time. I've been aware of the fact for the better part of a decade and I've been keeping my own firm eye on the man. Grivas, being so well placed within the intelligence community, will likewise have been mindful that he was being kept tabs on.

"Konrad Tafel's covert assignment here in Salonica, his subsequent death and your snooping around post-mortem rather than doing as you were told has caused the Brigadier to panic and close ranks. Especially in light that you've been talking to a man like Eric Hodt."

"So, you're trading me in so that Grivas can stay out of the clutches of the German and American governments, and keep the motherland squeaky clean in the eyes of international law, yes?"

"I've made no such ruling, Major. Our betters have demanded this decision, not I. For them it was like weighing two diamonds. Each perfectly cut, each virtually flawless. Brigadier Grivas weighed in a few more carat's than you, I'm afraid."

"I bet he did."

"Grivas wants you dead. He wants it so badly that he's allowed German intelligence to sniff around, create the impression that you are the middleman in some sort of convoluted sting against him, one that could also bring shame on the state. Unwelcome questions that may well dredge up old skeletons inside the new Greek government. The one thing the old

Junta had going for it was the fact they knew how to keep a secret and where to hide the bodies of those that spoke out. The sooner the *N.I.S* has you in their grasp, the sooner he can silence you and fabricate another web of lies allowing the status quo to be maintained. The Brigadier has cleverly let you carry out his dirty work. You've snuffed out one his own men, as well as the Kraut operative this evening. The man now holds a great deal of hard evidence against you. The clock's ticking, Major."

"There were two plainclothes guys rubbernecking me in the lobby of the Capsis. I didn't recognise either of them. I was right to think that they're not on your private staff?"

"They are not. Those are more of Grivas' thugs. One can only assume that it won't take them long to locate and apprehend you."

"I'm pretty sure they didn't follow me out here. That being the case, I'm assuming you'll sanction that pair outside to take me over to *N.I.S* headquarters?"

"On the contrary. I said that I was letting you go, Remis. I'm not in the habit of killing off my rank and file, not even one as bolshie as you. I have other plans for you."

"Plans, by which you expect me to turn myself in?"

The Provost shook his head. "I have no such expectations ... just alternatives. A way in which you can dig yourself out of the very deep hole you've created for yourself." Callas reached into his lapel pocket, took out a small slip of paper and handed it to me. "This is where you can find the banker Pierre Roth. I think it may well be in your best interests to speak to him without delay." I glanced at the swanky Halkidiki address printed on the torn sheet before pocketing it. "And try not to create a diplomatic incident when you talk to the man. The last thing I need is the Swiss government breathing down my neck asking difficult questions. Understand?"

I remained silent and nodded my head. The old man cleared his throat before walking toward the hallway. He turned to face me when he reached the door, his face partially covered in shadow. "Get me the dirt on Roth and more importantly, Grivas. I want the man's secrets, uncover what he has to hide. Then you can bring me the Brigadier's head on a plate." I watched as Callas' hands clenched and unclenched as though he was attempting to keep some hidden anger in check. "We never met this evening. Never had this conversation. I gave you no orders to pursue or investigate the Brigadier or *N.I.S* business. Likewise, I don't expect the axe to fall across my neck if you foul things up. I'll expect you to keep your counsel if you're caught and the thumb screws are applied, understand? Should you be successful in your furtive, little search, we can talk about your future at some other time."

Callas stepped out into the hall and headed outside. I watched him come to a halt on the porch then heard him call back to me. "Oh, and by the way, it has not escaped my notice that you rarely extol the virtue of friendships with either your fellow man or woman. Grivas will have already discerned that you have no family and few, if any, friends. In light of that fact, one can assume that the Brigadier will be looking to house clean quite rapidly. He'll want to snuff out anything or anyone you may hold dear or could have confided in; that being the case, it would be perhaps prudent to take that nasty little bitch, Garbi along for the ride. You've been keeping her safe under your wing all these years. Be a shame to break the habit of a lifetime now, wouldn't it? Especially as we both know the woman has some rather dark skills that may well prove useful to you. Nia has always been so much more than just a whore and Judas. It would be advantageous to have her at your side. That's of course if Grivas's men haven't got to her already."

I listened to the sound of the Provost's footsteps has he began to traipse along the path toward the gate, his parting words sending the hairs on my arms and back of my neck up on end.

Adrenalin carried me out of the Pasha. I was heading across the street back to my car when a man wearing a filthy suit and speaking to himself stepped out from the rear of the old hotel and directly into my path. Bent with age, he turned his bleak, red eyes into my gaze and stared. As he closed in on me, I could see, pressed to his chest with both hands, that he was carrying a leather-bound bible which was as soiled and bereft as his suit. I could smell the hum of stale booze coming off his filthy skin and clothes long before he decided to regale me with his theological wisdom.

"Repent, and be baptized, every one of you, in the name of Jesus Christ for the forgiveness of sins, and you will receive the gift of the Holy Spirit."

When I failed to answer, he walked on, resuming his sotto voce conversation. As I climbed into my car and started up the engine a chill passed through me. Somehow, indefinably, I felt with the kind of implied understanding we sometimes have in dreams, that I had just glimpsed one future possible vision of how I may well end up. A drunk, on the streets, mumbling nonsense in the darkness.

To find out if that was the truth, all I had to do was stay alive long enough to allow fate to do its very worst.

CHAPTER TWENTY-SEVEN

I PULLED OVER AT A PAY PHONE ON THE AGIOU DIMITRIOU HIGHWAY just outside of the city and dialled Nia's home number. I counted the rings. On the tenth, I jammed my thumb on the cradle button, breaking the connection then dialled the reception of the Capsis hotel only to be told by the snotty desk clerk that she wasn't working the bar that night. When I gave The Deuce club a call there was no reply. I decided I'd check in on the dive before heading over to Nia's apartment.

Ten minutes later, as rain clouds churned thick and black overhead, like curds of smoke from an oil fire, I parked my car in the street opposite the strip club. I got out and headed across the road to find the place locked and in total darkness. I made my way down the garbage-littered alley at the side of the club and found the back door swung wide open. The rear windows either side of the entrance were boarded with slates from old packing cases. I couldn't see inside or hear any movement. I eased the Walther out of its holster, quietly chambered a round, held the pistol out in front of me, stared down the barrel and tiptoed inside. On the wall by the door was a light switch, I flicked it on, and a florescent strip stuttered to life and slowly lit up the hall with an opaque shimmer. The warped wooden floor creaked as I crept along the passageway, the tired panels covered with cigarette burns that resembled the stubbed-out remains of dead black insects.

The lounge and dancefloor were empty, but I could now see that a fight or a frantic attempt to flee the building had begun in the bar and looked like it had ended back down toward the small kitchen to my right. Bottles, ashtrays, and glassware were broken and strewn across the mezzanine and stage; the shards scattered along the corridor toward the annexe room behind me. Once I was happy the bar room was uninhabited, I made my way back to the kitchen. A weak light-bulb hung from the ceiling, its dull lustre more shadow inducing than useful illumination. A stack of porn magazines and cutlery from a wooden knife block had been toppled from a shelf and flung across the yellow-stained tile-effect linoleum.

The icebox was open, a carton of milk on its side leaking into the vegetable tray. The ancient air-conditioning unit was cranked up full blast, the noise deafening, the metal fins inside the cool box struggling to mask the unmistakable odour of death that was now filling my nostrils along with the competing whiff of spilt booze, cheap perfume and weed.

I stared woodenly at the mutilated body slumped in the chair on the other side of the room. My eyes suddenly felt seared, like there was sand in them, as though I had looked into the pure white fire of an arc welder's rod touching metal. My throat became dry, a pressure band forming on the right side of my head, my heart constricting as I took in a deep breath. I holstered the semi-automatic before moving closer toward the black and blue remains.

A corpse is a corpse; there can never be any mistake. The waxlike skin, the sternum still, the lips bone dry. Even in death, the Deuce's barman Sakis' face resembled an overcooked boiled egg, the eyes open, wide, disbelieving. His badly beaten body was sat in a chair, bare-chested, his limp arms fastened behind him with cord ligatures. An alcohol-soaked dishcloth had been shoved down his throat, the thick rag prizing up the chin. I doubted that was the cause of death. A leather loop, one with three knots tied into it, had been flipped over his neck. The burns digging a quarter inch into the ashen-white tissue.

Sakis had certainly gone out the hard way. In his time, he'd been a pimp, a predator, a thief, a degenerate, a sadist and a police informer. Whoever had taken him out had questions that needed quick answers. I knew only too well that the rat bartender would have given up the required information at full tilt. His interrogators extracting chapter and verse with ease. I was sure whoever had tortured and snuffed him out was looking for the same snitch that I was. I backed myself toward the door, sweating heavily, my unblinking stare remaining on the worked-over cadaver until I reached the hallway. I turned and stepped back out into the night; the image of butchery inflicted on the dead barman still haunting my vision. There are some inhuman sights, once seen, you can never get out of your head, this was one of them.

CHAPTER TWENTY-EIGHT

Cockroaches don't like sunlight. Despots and fanatics don't make appearances in environments they can't control. Elitists join clubs whose attraction is based not on their membership but on the types of people they are known to exclude, and hired killers keep on liquidating their targets until they are ordered to stop. It wasn't hard to work out that the butchers who had murdered the Deuce's barman had come looking for Nia Garbi. When they found she wasn't around, they'd tortured the miserable bastard to try and pin down her whereabouts. As Provost Callas had so coldly stated to me earlier that evening, "*Grivas wants you dead*". The Brigadier's triggermen had clearly been sanctioned to both wipe out any trace of those I had been in contact with in the past few days and to fit me up for each of the slayings they'd committed; all before putting a bullet in me.

After leaving Sakis stinking out the club's kitchen I'd returned to my car and retrieved a spring-loaded stiletto blade and a roll of duct tape that I always stashed in the glovebox. I pushed up the sleeve of my jacket and strapped the knife to my forearm. I hadn't used the thing in a while but when I twisted my wrist the nine-inch blade shot into my hand like a shard of cold lightning. I reached back into the glove compartment, took out a spare seven-round magazine and dropped it into my jacket pocket. Rather than trawl across town, checking out the various haunts Nia either hung out or hustled in, I decided it made sense to begin my search by checking out her home.

Heavy rain had begun to beat down on the roofs of the tenement buildings by the time I parked my car in a side street close to Nia's place, the downpour danced on the surface of the roads, the spray whipping at my car windshield. I climbed out and checked to see if anyone was lurking around, looking to see if anything seemed out of place. The alleyway was clear and the neighbourhood around quiet. The moon was down in the night sky, the olive trees shaking with a sudden white-green light when the wind blew out of the North and in the distance, I could just make out the dull rumble of thunder trembling in the gulf.

The narrow cobblestone lane at the back of Garbi's apartment ran with water. Rather than create more noise opening the clasp on the iron gate into the back yard, I placed my hands on the post and vaulted over the fence then headed across the small backyard. I drew my gun out of its leather cradle, let my arm hang loose at my side, the 9mm pistol resting against my lower thigh, then climbed the stairs to the backdoor. I didn't think about it at the time, but of all the houses on Nia's street, hers was the one that was unlit, draped in darkness. At that moment I had only one thing on my mind, getting to Garbi before anyone else did. I could hear water burbling from a stone pond behind me as I stood against the back door and listened. Inside I could just make out the sound of a man's voice mumbling something in a low tone. I stepped back, held the automatic out in front of me and counted three seconds. Then the heel of my shoe cracked the door and wood crashed inward. I charged into darkness blind. Something heavy thudded against my skull and red bloomed out of the darkness.

At that very moment, I lost time and the ability to stand on my own two feet.

I woke up when someone dropped me on the floor, a white-heat pain kicking in my head. My eyes took a moment to adjust to the low lighting. When the blurriness began to fade, I saw Nia sitting in a high-backed kitchen chair in the living room, her hands tied behind her back, her nose running with blood. I was in the hallway close to the front door, tinted mustard by a tiny lamp on the wall that gave off a scrap of light beneath orange glass. A man stood beside me, and another hanging over Nia. They wore olive-green army fatigues and rugged combat boots, and each man held a handgun fitted with a silencer.

Their eyes locked with mine. I heard the sound of the toilet flushing, followed by a door opening and closing then footsteps padding across the kitchen tiles. A third man walked around the corner, buckling the belt on his trousers. After he'd hitched his pants and pulled his gun from a side holster, he stabbed a gloved finger at me.

"Stand the major up." The accent was Greek. An unmistakeable earthy Athenian timbre.

The man beside me put his silencer to my temple. "On your feet!"

I rose slowly and his gun stayed on me. I eyeballed my Walther tucked into the front of his trouser waistband. I could feel they'd emptied my pockets, and as I got to my feet saw my warrant card, magazine clip, wallet and the slip of paper containing the banker Pierre Roth's address stashed on the edge of the coffee table in the living room. It was now close quarters and I was unarmed. The man beside me slapped the side of my head, then he shoved me forward and I acted like I stumbled and fell to one knee. When he tugged me to my feet, I flicked my wrist and whipped the stiletto into his neck. Blood geysered hot over my face and mouth.

I left the blade in and fell behind him as the other two raised their guns. One shot at me and smacked plaster on the wall behind as the round from the other gunman winged the frame of the living room door. Two further shots went *thwap* like pneumatic bolts and hit the man I'd stabbed. He spasmed at the bullets, the blade still lodged in his neck.

My gun was right in front of me, still stuck behind the man's belt. I snatched it out, raised it and fired through the blood fountain at the closest gunman. I didn't have time to actually aim, and I was half-blind with arterial spray, but I hit one of the men in the throat. The round hurled him backwards, his gun firing as he fell to the ground, the stray bullet hitting his comrade on the way down. The winged man gripped at his armpit and he slumped back hard against the wall. His gun sat a few feet from his boot. The wounded gunman looked at his foot, his gun, and then at me, just as I shot him in the head.

The whole thing took less than ten seconds.

The three men were laid out on the floor, thin tendrils of smoke rising from two bodies. The blade I'd skewered into the first guy stood out of his neck like a huge black thorn, the orange light made his flowing blood look like paint. Nia didn't move. She looked at me unblinking and at the floor. "It's a fucking good job you turned up when you did! I was just about to tear a hole through those three shitheads."

I wiped blood from my eyes. The sound of gunshots still ringing in my ears, my jaw rigid with adrenaline. Nia was wide-eyed and shivering. "You okay?" When she didn't answer I turned to the impaled corpse and yanked the blade from his neck. I wiped the edges of the knife on the dead man's sleeve then walked over to the chair and cut the cord from around Nia's wrists. "You're coming with me." When she didn't move, I held the gun to her face. She stared down the barrel and then at my eyes.

"Oh, yeah. That's what you think, ass'ole." Nia spat a wad of bloody spittle onto the carpet, pushed my arm and the gun away from her head then kneeled down off the chair and crouched around the bodies, going the through the pockets of the men I'd just killed. I reckoned she was searching for money or something they'd taken from her. She looked up at me, shaking her head. "No I. D's. No cash. No pretty photographs of the wife back home." She got to her feet, a fierce sober look on her face and slammed the toe of her shoe into the side of one of the bodies. "Who are these crazy fuckers?"

I ignored the question and picked my gear up off the coffee table and stepped over to the window. I eased back the fringe of the curtain and looked out. I was waiting for the sound of sirens but the night appeared as still and untroubled as when I'd arrived. I turned to face Nia. "I'll tell you everything once we've got the hell out of here and we're on the road." I quickly bobbed my head toward Nia's bedroom. "Go grab some clothes, enough for a couple of days."

"I'm not grabbing anything until you level with me, you prick."

I shook my head. Gave her a dagger's glare. "Once we're out of here." Nia's face lost its hard edge, and I could see in her eyes her sense of self-preservation and a knot of hard choices. I could have imagined it. Whatever I recognised only fluttered past me as instinct or stupid sentiment. Nia spat again then turned on her heels and began to head for the hall and her bedroom, I grabbed her wrist and pulled her toward me. "And pack that nasty little Russian Makarov automatic you keep stashed away behind your bathroom sink."

Garbi snatched her arm out of my own weakening grasp and marched out of the room. "Go fuck yourself!"

I followed Nia out into the passageway and called after her. "A little thanks for saving your life wouldn't hurt."

Nia raised her right arm, extending the middle finger of her hand high into the air.

I was about to snap back at her, but I didn't. My head was splitting. The stink of gunpowder and charred flesh clung to the insides of my nostrils and I could feel blood drying on my cheeks. I knew that savagery and anger had served us both poorly in the past, sometimes the hard and cruel situations we'd individually found ourselves in had not been of our own choosing, and we'd had little recourse or alternatives in our unspeakable actions. This was one of those situations. Credos aside, we both knew that when the mayhem and killing is over, you're always left with the same stark emotion.

You're glad you're alive and the others are dead instead of you.

CHAPTER TWENTY-NINE

I DROVE US TO MY APARTMENT. NIA HAD BEEN CLEANING UP HER bloodied nose and had already changed into a fresh black t-shirt on the ride over. We sat down the road across from my place for a while, in the dark with the car engine running. My flat looked just as I'd left it. The front gate closed. No vehicles outside that I didn't recognise. No light in the windows or torch beams strafing the interior. After five or so minutes we got out of the Lancia and walked on inside. Once in the hall with the front door locked, I pressed Nia ahead of me and kept the lights off. I heard Garbi mutter something under her breath before becoming more candid.

"You actually live in this shithole?"

"Shut up."

I wondered how long it would be before Grivas' hitmen were supposed to check in with their boss. Outside the world was almost too still; the rain had stopped, the earlier strong winds dying to a breeze. The trees outside didn't seem to rustle, their branches hung in the street in an unmoving air, the lights in the other tenements in the street didn't reveal any motion. No one passed in the windows, their lustreless glow lighting little more than the sills outside. I turned on the hall light and headed for the bathroom.

I left my gun on the lid of the toilet cistern and washed my hands in the sink, scrubbed my face, forearms and hands with soap and blistering water that drained in a pink whirl. I grabbed a clean shirt and a pair of trousers from my wardrobe and dug out a small lockbox like the kind used in banks for safe deposits. It contained a little over two thousand drachmas and a fake driver's licence and passport that Ezra Liebermann had made for me years ago. This cash and false identification were my retirement plan if I ever found myself in a really sticky situation.

I also took a box of .380 shells from one shelf, a clean licence plate, some more clothes and threw it all in my old army duffel bag. Before leaving my bedroom, I put my jacket back on and reached under the bed to retrieve my Mossberg shotgun and a bag of twelve-bore cartridges.

Nia sat in the living room's only armchair, the place where I'd end up sleeping most nights. A stack of *Fix* beer bottles covered the floor around the chair and at the foot of the beat-up cabinet that housed my *Duel* turntable, amp and vinyl collection. I had a couple of hundred jazz albums that had taken me a few years to put together.

I was sorry to leave them, especially as I knew my place would probably be turned over in the coming hours, my belongings and possessions tossed around and damaged, and that would include smashing up rare recordings by John Coltrane and Dizzy Gillespie.

"You've got a stack of records," she said. "But not a helluva lot of furniture." Her eyes scrutinised the bottles on the rug. "You know, you've really got a serious drink problem going on, Remis."

I wagged the gun at her. "Let's get back to the car. Move."

"We just got here. I'm still waiting to find out what the fuck is going on."

I took a stepped towards Garbi and kicked the foot of the chair. "Not here. I'll tell you everything I know when we're back on the road."

"Nah. I ain't buying that crap." Nia's tone was hard and without compromise. She settled back into the seat, pushed her legs out across the rug. "Go clip the tops off a couple of cold ones then come back in here and cough up what you gotta tell me, Major."

"Forget it. It's not safe here. Move, or we're gonna have a big fucking problem."

Before Nia had chance to open her mouth again, I reached down and snatched her by the arm up from the chair and pulled her out the front door, then across the street and into the shadows, where I still kept waiting to either hear sirens or the sound of gunfire.

At the car I pushed her into the passenger seat then used a screwdriver to switch my license plate. I dumped the shotgun in the boot and my duffel on the backseat next to Nia's faux crocodile-skin overnight bag, got behind the wheel, turned the key in the ignition and sped off down the road.

"So, come on, spit it out. Why'd those men want to kill both of us?"

"Some bullshit over a dead man." I smacked the steering

wheel. Callas' earlier warning to me to "*obey and not question my orders*" now finally hitting home.

"This the same dead guy you wanted me to ask around after, the Jew you found up at the mine?"

I nodded my head. "Yeah, that's the dude."

Nia had wanted me to cough up the full story, so that's what I did. Quickly recounting the facts, leaving nothing out. It was an almost exact repeat of the detailed account that I'd given to the Provost a few hours earlier. The only difference being that I ended my scoop to Garbi by telling her that the Deuce's bartender, Sakis, had been worked over and garrotted to give up her possible whereabouts.

Nia picked at her lip and stared out at the passing night with a face that quivered with anger. "Did Sakis suffer?" she said, ducking her eyes.

"He did."

I watched Garbi's face twist up in disgust before breaking into a smile, her muscled shoulders straightening defiantly. "Good. That slimy prick finally got what he had coming to him."

I kept at a steady forty, heading south out of the city, driving through the suburbs before making my way toward the quieter coast road in the direction of the Halkidiki peninsula. Whilst Nia was quiet for a moment, I found myself thinking about the idea of luck and how perfectly I'd shot those gunmen back at Garbi's place. How lucky I'd been that Grivas' men had not found the stiletto blade or that the trigger hadn't flipped when they knocked me out and dragged me down the hall. My buttoned-up thinking about good-fortune was suddenly shattered by a swift prod in the ribs from Nia's clenched fist.

"What the hell has all this cloak and dagger gotta do with me?"

"Because I made the big mistake poking my nose into the wrong people's business. Now I'm paying for snooping around, you've been dragged into this madness by association." Nia gave me a dumb look and shrugged her shoulders. "Look, nearly everyone I have spoken to about Konrad Tafel's murder is now dead. Those that aren't are probably the same people who want us both dead. You were part of a clean-up job. A way to implicate me in a string of murders and hopefully to rub me out too. Consider yourself lucky. If I hadn't have turned up, you wouldn't be breathing now."

I saw Nia grit her teeth and clutch her stomach like she'd been punched. "So, that's why I'm coming along for the ride is it. So you can play at being a fucking hero and keep me alive, yeah?"

I nodded my head. "Uh-huh." Our breathing was the only sound for a moment.

"And because I enjoy your scintillating company."

"Fuck off!" The heavy way Nia sank back into the seat was enough to tell me that she was reluctantly resigning herself to the situation I was forcing her into. A couple of random street-lights passed over her face, her eyes instantly glimmering in reaction to the fleeting bursts. I saw her chew her lip in a scheming way before she spoke again.

"Are you gonna tell me where the hell we're heading?"

"A place called Xina."

"Sounds like a dump. Why the fuck are we going there?"

"Because, I have an appointment with a Swiss banker."

"Jesus. Couldn't you try and be a little more cryptic?" I heard her give a heavy sigh. "Getting you to straight talk is like pulling hen's teeth." Nia made a loud huffing sound then suddenly shifted forward in her seat, pointing at me with her finger. "You've still got some blood on your face." I looked in the rear view and then her little finger touched under my jaw. "Right there," she said.

I wiped at it with a little spit then glanced across at Nia and saw that she was now holding a small compact mirror out in front of her face. She had a small make-up bag sat in her lap and was reapplying mascara to her eyelash. Her previously agitated demeanour now calm, tranquil almost.

We drove in silence for a little while. Depending on the places we passed, the night around us shaded from ink black to red and purple to a washed-out yellow that hung like gauze in front of the dark, like you could see the night sitting under the twilight, and then at a bend in the road would be back to pitch black. The further south we headed, out toward the Mediterranean, I noticed the air smell changes from pine pulp to sea salt to ammonia and burning oil. Olive trees and scrubland crowded us as we skirted along the edge of the coastline.

In the darkness I heard Nia suddenly chuckle to herself. "I am *so, so* glad you killed those fuckers, man."

The back of my neck grew hot and something caught in my throat, but I didn't let on. I felt myself smile. The spot on my jaw, where Nia had touched me earlier, unexpectedly began to pulse with a slight warmth.

"I am too."

CHAPTER THIRTY

KANISTRO WAS A SMALL PORT TOWN ON THE AEGEAN SEA THAT resembled every picture postcard of a Greek village I'd ever seen – all blueberry sea and Robin's-egg, sugar-lump houses and paper-white caïques. I parked the car and Nia and I stretched our legs for a while. It felt as if we were at the very edge of the known world. Walrus-faced fishermen tugged on cigarette pipes as big as clay pots while they mended their nets and watched us with ancient eyes that might have seen the Hellenic navy boarding their ships to fight mad King Xerxes. Flesh-coloured squid dried in the sun like wet swimming costumes on sagging lines and stray cats dozed on the quay-side or wandered between the tables of a lone café as if waiting upon the day's customers, who probably weren't going to come. The early morning air tasted of salt and smelled of Greek coffee and tobacco, and the otherwise perfect stillness was periodically jangled with the spilling-cutlery sound of a distant bouzouki band playing on a crackling transistor radio. It felt like a million miles from Salonica.

Earlier in the night I'd made the decision to pull over

midway during our journey. Travelling the eighty odd miles from Salonica along the Halkidiki peninsula wasn't an arduous drive but I could tell that Nia was beat after her earlier confrontation with Grivas' gunmen and I wasn't faring much better. Less than an hour out of the city I came off the main coast road and travelled into the heavily wooded Macedonian interior, out to a small village called Agio Mamas, and parked up in an expanse of olive groves away from the road and more importantly from prying eyes or possible local police patrols. A fresh number plate would only go so far in keeping us out of the reaches of local law enforcement. The last thing I needed was to have a patrol car pull us over in the small hours. There was also the risk that the *N.I.S* could well have issued some kind of all-points bulletin to be sent out across the wire demanding my arrest on any number of trumped-up charges, and for all I knew my mugshot was perhaps at this minute being telexed to every police station from Thessalonica to Ithaca.

It was a little after 6am. I was tired, my body tight with fatigue, my mouth as dry as an Arab's sandal, and rather than my usual hangover headache, the inside of my skull was throbbing as the result of being knocked unconscious ten or so hours previously. I need caffeine inside me to even attempt to stand up straight let alone break into the residence of a Swiss banker and then interrogate him. We left the car at the rear of a rusted-up corrugated, wood-frame boat house, walked a couple of minutes along the harbour front and sat and drank coffee in the lone harbourside café that had recently opened for the local fishermen. There I sank three mugsful of dark roast ellinikós kafé, read my road map and stroked the stray cats whilst Nia spoke to the old man who owned the place. He had a face that was a sun-baked mosaic of cracks and fissures and who proudly informed Garbi that she reminded him of his long-deceased wife.

When the old man returned to the kitchen at the rear of the café Nia emptied her coffee mug and filled it again from the pot, this time not bothering to stir sugar into the brew and knocking back the coffee as fast as she could swig it down.

"Do you still carry around that little roll pouch of brass lock-picks?"

Nia nodded her head. "Goes every place I do, along with a little leather coin sap."

"Good. I'm going to need you to flip a lock for me."

Nia shot me a dagger's stare. "Why can't you flip the fucking lock?"

I leaned in across the table, my voice down to a whisper. "Because I'm going to be keeping my eyes peeled making sure we're not about to get our damn heads blown off, that's why!"

"This locked door belongs to the Swiss banker you were talking about?"

"It does?"

"If I get you inside, can I toss the place?"

"Ah-ah ... you don't touch a fucking thing. I just need you to be my eyes and ears whilst I sweat Roth."

Nia bit at a hangnail at the edge of her thumb then spat it out on to the tile floor. "Sounds like a real shitty deal to me."

"You're doing as I say, that's the deal."

"No wiggle room to negotiate then, Major?"

I shook my head slowly. "No room. You either do as I say or

chances are, we're both gonna find ourselves laid out across a mortuary slab before the week's out."

Nia stuck a cigarette into the corner of her mouth, lit it, and slid the packet across to me. She inhaled deeply then blew a thick plume of grey smoke into my face. "You're a real fucking sweet talker, you know that, Remis?"

It took less than twenty minutes to drive and find ourselves in another back-water Greek port town. Xina was less picturesque than Kanistro. The harbour looked more sheltered than the one we'd just left behind and was perhaps shallower, too, as the sight of the fishing boat that was only half-sunk in the water confirmed. A single-track road led down to the waterfront that in turn opened out into the bay. A tiny Orthodox chapel stood on a sand and shingle promontory at the end of the causeway. Further along the road were a handful of beach front dwellings. I pulled the car into a shady area on the roadside and we walked down to the water's edge. The tide was on its way out, the strip of sandy beach slick and rilling with water and crustaceans in the sunrise, the bay glittering like a bronze shield. I took the slip of paper out of my inside jacket pocket, re-read Pierre Roth's address details and the brief instructions of where I'd find the place. Without speaking, I pointed up toward a lone building set back on a hillside that overlooked the bay. Nia gave a silent nod of her head and reached a hand behind her back to retrieve the Makarov pistol from underneath her t-shirt. She chambered a round, slipped it back into her waistband and pulled her shirt back over the butt.

. . .

We walked another five hundred yards along the remainder of the beach then headed inland. At the end of asphalt road that separated beach from road there was a wide sandy path that led up to the place I was looking for. Tyre tracks were clearly visible on the ground but I couldn't see any cars parked up any place. I unholstered my gun, the pistol heavy and warm in my hand. I pulled back the receiver, slid a round into the chamber and the two of us pushed on up the path.

The *Achilleion,* as Roth's shore-front residence was called, was not the grand mansion its title gave it the illusion to be, rather it was a tired-looking fisherman's cottage with two floors, and more or less typical of many of the houses right along the peninsula coastline. It was a little dilapidated and decidedly anonymous looking, a nondescript façade which I was sure the taciturn individual inside would have been more than happy to project. The curtains were still drawn and I noted that no one had come in or out, but there was wood smoke coming out of the kitchen chimney and a light still burning in one of the bedrooms.

Nia and I quickly reconnoitred the rest of the area, checked that no one was around and headed over to the cottage. There were no vehicles outside. The lower half of the residence was covered with bright blue tiles; above those the wall had been painted white, with large areas of the emulsion coating flaked away. An iron gate stood in front of a short gravel path. Either side of the gate were two stone pedestals on top of which stood a couple of ridiculous looking plaster fish painted grey; it looked like a cut-price version of the Gateway to India. Behind the gatepost was a box containing half a dozen empty scotch whisky bottles, which led me to suppose that Roth hadn't been entirely wasting his time during his stay in Greece.

We headed around to the rear of the cottage and Nia immediately began work on gaining entry. She popped open the lock on the back door in less than a minute and we headed on inside, my gun held out in front of me at arm's length. The place was pungent with the scent of expensive and distinctive Egyptian tobacco. There was a copy of the German magazine *Capital* on the kitchen table. A wood stove sat in one corner of the room and was still smouldering away from the night before; by the back door, a pristine-white new refrigerator.

A couple of china plates were washed and stacked on the draining board. The linoleum floor waxed to a shine. I opened up the refrigerator door and took a quick look inside. Next to the eggs and milk stood at least twenty 50cc phials of morphine. Enough to keep a dozen junkies stoned for a month.

I gestured for Nia to take a look, her face immediately breaking out into a huge smile when she clocked the stash of narcotics. I quietly closed the door and we moved through into the living room which we found to be as austere and clean as the kitchen. On the wall over the fireplace was a framed Imray chart of Greece and its islands. There was enough light coming through a crack in the curtains to easily conduct a simple search of the place. No weapons, no dogs, and importantly nobody guarding the joint downstairs. I whispered to Nia to stay put and keep an eye out for any unexpected visitors.

I headed for the carpeted stairs. Every step was furnished with a pile of books, as if the cottage belonged to a keen reader who didn't own any shelves; most of the books were cheap English-print paperbacks, crime novels and thrillers by English and American writers. I placed my foot on the first step and tested it for sound with my weight. The wooden step stayed silent so I tried another; and then another, until I was at the top of the stairs with my heart in my mouth. I turned and looked down and saw Nia looking back at me; she nodded her head sharply as if to say, *get a fucking shift on,* and I nodded back and prepared to open up one of the bedroom doors in the knowledge that Roth probably had a gun on the bedside table.

The master bedroom was empty and the bathroom door was open. I found a sterilizer steaming on the washstand. Inside, were a half dozen needles and three syringes. That only left the final room; that door was closed, but on the other side, I could hear a man snoring as loudly as an angry rhinoceros. I turned the loose doorknob and pushed firmly on through the sound of the creaking hinge and my own heavy breathing, until I could see Roth's body lying on its side in the bed. How he didn't wake up I didn't know. Possibly the racket caused by his own snoring was louder than any commotion I could have made. A Panzer tank would have made less noise.

At this point I could have gone for the easy option and cracked him over the head to stun him while I searched for a gun but I wanted to avoid this if I could, if only because questioning a man with a recently sustained head injury may prove to be difficult. On the bedside table was a copy of a Saint novel by Leslie Charteris, a pair of spectacles, a glass of something stronger than water, and, ominously, an open box of 9-millimetre ammunition.

Still looking for a gun I bent carefully over Roth's head; his loud snoring smelled strongly of cigarettes and whisky, while his rotund body was sour with the heady, unpleasant smell of sweat. From the way his hand was stuck underneath the thick, down pillow I concluded he was probably holding a pistol, which meant that unless he was very nervous indeed, or just foolhardy, the safety catch had to be on. If it was an older model of gun, like a Luger it would probably be stiff and might at a push give me another couple of vital seconds if the man woke and I had to wrestle him for it. I considered slinging him out of bed unceremoniously, but then rejected the idea, thinking he may still be holding the damn gun when he hit the floor on the other side of the bed and start firing wildly. I was considering my next option when Roth suddenly stirred, let out a loud grunt, and turned on his other side. As he did, I caught a glimpse of something black under the pillow. As the snoring resumed, I reached for the object quickly, and came up with a tatty, leather-bound copy of the New Testament, as if he'd been reading it before or after the Charteris novel. I wondered if perhaps he'd been viewing some useful text in there for the spiritual guidance for someone who was helping those who had engineered the deaths of millions of Jews after robbing them blind.

I stepped back from the bed and quickly glanced around the malodorous room and this time I spotted a Tokarev TT-33 automatic on an antique table by the window, next to it was a bottle of Johnny Walker and a familiar looking packet of Juno cigarettes, the brand which Herr Hodt pretended to smoke and liked to hand out to unguarded gendarme Majors. With some relief I snatched up the gun, checked the safety and dropped it into my jacket pocket.

Sweeping the table, I also found Roth's passport and a pair of Lufthansa airline tickets to Istanbul and from there, two first class ticket aboard the Orient Express to Innsbruck. From the dates on the tickets Roth would have been back in his homeland in just a few days. I pocketed these, too, thinking I might use them myself if things got desperate. Feeling a little more relaxed, I switched on the overhead light, helped myself to a drink and a cigarette, sat down in the room's armchair and, while I waited for the sleeping man to stir under the glare of the bare bulb, I glanced over his passport. Roth was only fifty years old but he looked ten years older. Not much of a testament for a man with a complete lack of conscience, I thought. After a minute Roth groaned, then suddenly sat up, yawned, belched, rubbed his bloodshot eyes, and frown at me blearily. He looked like a soused Swiss cheese salesman.

"Wha?" Roth said, scratching his pendulous white breasts and fat belly.

"What the fuck are you doing in here?"

Roth ... Swiss? I thought to myself. I sat back in the armchair and smiled as I raised the Walther up in front of me. The fat banker's broad Kraut accent couldn't have been more German if he'd had a black eagle with red legs perched on his shoulder and a snarling Alsatian on a length of piano wire.

CHAPTER THIRTY-ONE

Pierre Roth switched on an overhead lamp next to his bed and a rectangle of light pierced the dull room and illuminated my outstretched legs.

I pointed the Walther at the banker's chest and glanced down at my watch.

"About time for your breakfast hit, Herr Roth?"

"How the hell did you get in here?"

"Through the mail slot."

"Breaking and entering is a serious crime."

I stubbed my cigarette out in a crystal ashtray on the desk next to me, rose up out of the armchair and walked across to the foot of the bed. "I'll save you the trouble of calling the police." I took out my warrant card and held it at arm's length so Roth could properly see my credentials. "We both know you won't be calling the local law, think of the embarrassment if they found your opium den in your icebox."

Roth leaned forward, his eyes examining me, his chest ballooning as he took in deep breaths. "I have a debilitating condition. It's perfectly within my rights to store personal use pharmaceuticals for medical use."

"Come off of it, Roth, I saw the works cooking in the bathroom. How long have you been hooked?" I slid my warrant card back into my pocket and grabbed a chair that was sat next to the door, turned it around and straddled it, folding my left arm over the bentwood frame.

"I'm not ... an addict. I have chronic asthma and severe rheumatoid arthritis. Sometimes when the pain is overwhelming, I employ a mild narcotic analgesic. Roth inched himself up the bed and pointed a finger at me. Now, if you don't mind, I suggest you get the hell out of my house and go back to whatever stone you've just crawled from under."

"I think I'll stay put if that's alright with you?"

Roth scratched at his stubbly jaw, his face flushing crimson with anger. "Look here, you bastard. I'm good friends with the minister for public order. I warn you, all it will take is one call and I'll have you stood in front of your superiors so fast your boot heels will barely have chance to scrape the ground."

I jerked my head toward the telephone sitting on the bedside table. "Go ahead. I'll even dial Minister Karamalakis' number for you myself. I'm sure he'll get a real kick out of seeing your Nalline test as well as all the dirt I've got on you."

Roth sagged within the folds of his oversized silk pyjamas. "Dirt ... what dirt. What do you want with me?

I kicked the foot of the bed with the toe of my shoe. "Same thing I was after when I spoke to your friend, Dieter Lirtzman, a couple of days ago."

"Lirtzman ...the investment banker?"

"The very same."

Roth's haughty glance was impatient and scornful. "Lirtzman's no friend of mine. I barely know the man."

"Is that right? I suppose you don't have any idea who the likes of Herr Merten, Riss, Sommer, Stark, Glebin and Broichsitter are either?" I watched Roth's watery eyes as he slowly met my gaze. Not an eyelid flicker betrayed him as shuffled and reshuffled his cunning thoughts in his head.

"I've never heard of any of them."

"No? Well, I think you're a fucking liar." I got to my feet; my pistol still trained on Roth's wheezing torso. I turned the chair around and placed it so that the wood-frame backrest was facing the still draped window. I took another step backwards, my gun held out at arm's length. "Get your arse up out of that bed."

Roth shifted on the mattress, immediately raising a trembling hand, his huge palm outstretched in an attempt to placate me. "Please ... please be reasonable. Whatever it is you want. I'm sure that it doesn't require you to point that damn pistol at me."

"Move it!" I lowered my aim as Roth began to swing his fat legs out of the bed. "The first bullet goes through your kneecap. If I let you live, you'll be using a cane for the rest of your life."

Roth huffed to his feet, panting like an animal at bay. He dithered across the bedroom and dropped down in the chair holding his belly with both hands as if something might come loose if he let go. "Why are you doing this?" he moaned.

"Why? That's a good question. Let's just say that I've been

told you're the top man that certain people come to when they want their ill-gotten gains either cleaning up or hidden away."

Roth's face drained. "I haven't the faintest idea what you are talking about."

"No?" I shot forward, jamming the muzzle of the Walther under Roth's chin, forcing his head back. His eyes were as wide as a trapped dog. "I think you do, Herr Roth. So much so that I'm prepared to spray your brains all over these shitty bedroom curtains if you don't start telling me what I want to hear, do you understand me?"

"Have ... h-have you gone m-mad?" he stammered.

I stepped back, my gun trained on Roth's head and leant against the edge of the desk. "Mad? Too right I'm mad. I've been mad ever since I heard Dieter Lirtzman mention your name alongside a bunch of other Nazi's."

"You're making a mistake ... I'm ... I'm not a Nazi. I served with *Abteilung 5*, the Luftwaffe's Military Intelligence Branch. I never saw active service. Never took part in the Greek conflict." Roth looked up at me, a heavy frown on his face. I swung my arm out and backhanded him full strength across the mouth with my left, then struck the barrel of my gun across the back of his knee a couple of times. Roth screamed out in agony, his body crumpling forward, as he clutched at his leg.

"So, you were a spy, but not a Nazi. How come you're calling yourself Swiss these days?"

Roth rocked his huge trunk back and forth; his head tucked deep down in his lap. I reached for his shoulder, pinched the flesh through to the bone. He screamed some obscenity in German as I yanked him back into the chair, his face grimacing up at me, his body shaking. A long string of drool hung from the corner of his mouth, his brow and face dripping with sweat, he gasped in air a couple of times to catch his breath through the pain. When he finally answered me, he did so through clenched teeth. "My ... my mother ... was born in Lucerne ... I have dual citizenship."

"How convenient for you."

Roth shook his head, flinging a shower of sweat toward me. "It's ... it's not convenience, ... it's the truth, I tell you." I watched a bead of perspiration drip from the banker's chin and run down onto his bare chest.

"Oh, I believe you. I've already taken a look inside your passport; it says you're Swiss and most definitely not a Kraut." The banker stared into space, ignoring my remark. I let an edgy silence take over for a moment, a rank stink of perspiration beginning to filter across the room. Evil has a smell like copper coins on a hot stove, like offal burning, like a gangrenous-soaked bandage. It violates your glands and your senses. Its odour stays in your dreams, and you never fail to recognize it in your waking day. At that very moment I could have sworn that I smelt it coming off Roth's skin. I tapped the leg of the chair Roth was sitting in with the toe of my shoe settling the banker out of his two-yard stare. "I don't care what flag you're living under or how many showers a day you take, as far as I'm concerned you've still got shit on your nose."

Roth's body jerked at the coarseness of my language, His eyes suddenly looked like moons sunk deep in his skull, his voiced crackling with tension as he spoke. "My business hands may not be as clean as some. But I'm no dirtier than most men in my position."

"How noble of you to admit it."

"It has nothing to do with nobility. This is high-end

commerce I'm talking about. A world where you're expected to wash with the unclean."

I saw Roth flinch as I took a step toward him. "I've already spoken to the unwashed and it's led me to you. Now, I beat the information I wanted out of your friend, Lirtzman. It took me less than five minutes to get him to cough up your name. I'm not going to waste either my time or scuff anymore skin off my knuckles slapping the truth out of you." I aimed the Walther at Roth's knee cap again and pulled back the hammer. "I'm just going to start shooting parts off you until I get the answers I'm looking for."

"Wha ... what ... do you want to know?"

"Tell me about these investors of yours; the illusive Merten, Riss, Sommer, Stark, Glebin and Broichsitter."

Roth closed his eyes and pressed his trembling fingers to his temples. "It's been so long. Years and years. I've done my best to forget them."

"Bullshit! Don't you go pleading amnesia on me. My trigger finger's already starting to go numb, Herr Roth."

Roth gave me his best pleading orphan look. "At one time or another all those men required anonymous banking services."

"And you supplied those services, yes?"

"Yes. I arranged special accounts for them."

"Special, in what way?" I touched the tip of the Walther's barrel against Roth's ear-lobe, stroked the side of his cheek, left it there a moment before finally removing it when I heard the growl and rumble of the German's bowels beginning to turn over. Roth bit at his lip before speaking. His words at first, more stutter than speech.

"They ... w-were t-the v-very b-best ..."

. . .

I sank my fingers into Roth's shoulder, putting real weight into my grip, making the old man wince. "Go on."

"Swiss accounts use numbers and not names. Under our law, bankers do not have to disclose the existence of an account, who it belongs to, or any other information, without the account holder's explicit permission. This set up was the perfect solution for Merten and the vast sums he and the other men wanted to squirrel away."

"How much money are we talking about?"

"Over a three-year period of depositing, I'd have to say millions, and in different currencies and denominations. Dollars, Francs, Pounds Sterling. Then there were the gold and precious gem stones to put into safety deposit boxes. All innominate, all placed in various secure locations, in different branches right across Switzerland."

Roth was now on a roll, so I kept pushing. "How did all this business begin?"

"A long time ago now ... Max Merten came to see me back in the Winter of 1947. I'd recently relocated to Geneva and was then heading up a new investment department at Credit Suisse. Somehow, he knew I had been with *Abteilung 5,* knew I'd been an adjutant in the payroll department. He was privy to all kinds of undisclosed intelligence. He knew the men I'd worked for. The covert operations we'd undertaken. He was conversant in the kind of huge budgets that had been thrown at *Abteilung 5* during the war and how much of that money went missing before the ink on the Potsdam agreement was even dry." Roth suddenly froze, his reminiscing somehow interrupting his speech, his gaze immediately focused on nothing. I slapped the banker hard across the back of the head, bringing him back to the here and now.

"Keep going."

"To this day, I don't know how Marten knew so much about my past. How I'd had access to various accounts back then, that I had authorisation to counter-sign for large fund transfers, and although I never took as much as a Reichsmark, he said that he had evidence that could implicate me in misappropriation of vast amounts government funds."

"What kind of evidence?"

"He told me he knew that *Abteilung 5* had held various accounts which were actually at the time being used by the SS to deposit stolen cash and other currencies which were siphoned off into a slush fund. He said he could link me to those accounts."

"So, you're saying you were blackmailed into helping him?"

"Blackmail, extortion, coercion ... it all boils down to the same thing. I was encouraged to conspire with Merten so as to keep my own life, *uncomplicated*, as he put it. He told me that he'd leak my past association to *Abteilung 5* to my employers and to the world press. I told him to go to hell and do it."

"So, how did Merten get you to play ball?

"Money." Roth spat out the word as if it were a piece of rotten meat. "Isn't every man supposed to have a price? Well, back then, I had mine. "

"How much money did Merten buy you for?"

"Forty-five thousand dollars. Maybe that doesn't sound like a fortune now, but just after the war it was more money than I'd ever dreamed of."

"Yeah? Well, don't kid yourself. That kind of cash would still make for some sweet dreams these days."

Roth shook his head. "My dreams have long turned into nightmares; I can assure you."

"I couldn't give a shit about your nightmares. How does all this connect back to Dieter Lirtzman and his bank in Salonica?"

Roth coughed under his breath. A flicker in his eyes, as though someone were flicking a light switch on and off in his head. "It's a long and complicated paper trail to decipher."

I flashed Roth a grin. "Well, why don't you start unravelling it for me."

"Merten, as you may already know, was the German military administration counsellor for the city during the war. He was responsible for the deportation of more than 50,000 Jews. He and the other men you speak of stole millions from them before they were shipped out to the camps."

"You're right, I've already had this history lesson from Lirtzman. What I want to know is what does all of that have to do with his bank?"

"There were many Greeks who prospered from the illegal appropriation of goods, property and capital back then. Those same Greeks went on to filter stolen money through Lirtzman's bank."

"That's old news, Herr Roth. Tell me something I don't already know."

Roth's dull stare instantly became a lot more intense. "Lirtzman had a long-list of influential Salonican businessmen he looked after. Every one of them with chequered pasts and most of them the kind of people you probably rub shoulders with."

"Give me names?"

Roth looked up at the ceiling and shook his head violently. "No ... I will never see another sunrise if I divulge such information."

I gave him another crack across the skull with the back of my hand, flipping the face of my wrist watch toward Roth's eyes then dug the end of the Walther into the banker's ears. "You'll never see another hour of this day if you don't tell me what I want to know. Now, names!"

"There was the ... the former minister of the exterior Georgios Bakos, there was at least half dozen high-ranking army officers like Theodoros Pangalo, countless members of the former collaborationist security battalions who ran Salonica during the war, they all went to Lirtzman's. I can't remember their names. It really is so long ago."

"Don't give me that failing memory shit. You're holding back on me. Don't make me really hurt you, Roth."

"Tha ... t-that pig who runs your National security department ... h-he ...he ... has been hiding his fortune in Lirtzman's bank for years."

I felt a sick sensation bite at the pit of my stomach.

"The *N.I.S* ... Are you talking about Grivas?"

"Yes ... that's the bastard. The old Brigadier still runs the show, doesn't he?"

"He does."

"Then we're talking about the same monster."

"How the hell is Grivas part of all of this?"

Roth's bottom lip quivered; his teeth shiny with saliva as he sneered at me. "It's another history lesson, I'm afraid."

"Get on with it."

Roth looked straight ahead, rigid in his seat, his fists clenched like small hams on his knees, his face tight, his chest rising and falling as he prepared his speech for me.

"When Germany finally pulled out of Salonica in 1944, more than two weeks after the liberation of Athens, the country was in chaos, in turmoil. Grivas had been stashing money, gold, jewels in various secret hideaways for years. His plan was to drop out of sight after the war and resurface in another country then return at a later date, under a new name to reclaim his stolen spoils. Before he had chance to flee the country, as crazy as it sounds, Grivas somehow managed to get his feet under the table with the newly formed National Liberation Army.

He wheedled his way in, eventually heading up their department of restitution. From there he controlled the lists containing the city's collaborators and anyone who had been sympathetic to the Wehrmacht during the occupation. In all the confusion, Grivas was able to, in-effect, wipe both his name and his own dishonourable, treacherous past from history whilst charged with uncovering the kind of leeches that he was no different from. It has to be said the man's guile was quite brilliant."

I felt the anger grow in my chest; my lungs swell with air that was dense with the tang of Roth's sweat. "I can assure you; the Brigadier has lost none of that craftiness."

Roth grinned at me. "And Grivas wasn't the only one."

"What?"

"You opened up this can of words, I see no reason why all the names can't pour out now. There was Katsimitros, Seremetis, Callas, Bourantas."

I snatched the lapel of Roth's pyjama top and yanked him toward me. "Did you say Callas?"

Roth nodded his head repeatedly before brushing his wrist across his mouth, his eyes now staring disjointedly up at me. I let go of his silk nightshirt and staggered forward like a sleep-walker, not believing what I was hearing. I kept my pistol trained on Roth's head as I took hold of the edge of one of the curtains with my free hand, tearing it open, then doing the same with the other drape; the bedroom suddenly filled with bright sunlight. I reeled back against the desk, my pulse jumping in my neck. Roth began to bellyache at me like a man possessed. "The great Manolis Callas bent! The untouchable lawgiver of Salonica. He's as crooked as the rest of them. Dirty as Grivas, worse in fact."

I heard the disbelief crackle in my voice. "You expect me to swallow that?"

Roth sneered, clearly wallowing in the stupefied reaction he'd managed to draw out of me. He leant back in his seat, stretching one leg out in front of him. "Swallow it, spit it out; I don't give a damn. It's the truth. Callas was in a lot deeper than anyone around him would ever realise." The banker suddenly fell dumb. He arched his back, lifting his arms up to chest height, his palms open and turned up toward the ceiling, his stubby fingers stretching out into the air as if he was grasping for some unseen prize.

I turned away from him shaking my head, not fully trusting what I was hearing. The sudden silence, the lack of motion and the confines of the cramped bedroom seemed to contain an intensity on the brink of tearing itself apart. I stared out of the window and in that brief moment saw a man standing atop of the high dunes in front of the cottage, like a human lightening rod waiting to be struck. The figure was too far away to make out his features but I could just make out the rifle he held in his hands. A split-second later I caught in the corner of my eye the flare of the muzzle flash. A sound like a firecracker going off rang out and thought I saw the shapes of two other figures, but I couldn't be sure. I heard the rifle's report echo in the distance as I spun on my heels to push Roth out of his chair, but I was too late.

The first bullet cut a hole like a rose petal in the back the banker's neck and exited in a wide spray of blood and cartridge out of his throat. As I threw myself to the floor the second round had already penetrated through the window, struck the back of Roth's skull and blew his forehead apart like an exploding watermelon.

CHAPTER THIRTY-TWO

I WAS FLAT ON THE FLOOR IN A SPREADING POOL OF PIERRE ROTH'S blood, my back and hair covered with glass and splinters of wood. I was expecting a further burst of gunfire to pepper the room, yet nothing came. Outside I heard the faint sound of rain falling and a man's voice, but I couldn't make out any of the words. I began to crawl on my hands and knees across the carpet, I bawled out Nia's name, but got not reply. I kept my head down and edged my way toward the bedroom door. I shuffled up onto my haunches and squatted down at the base of the doorjamb and caught my breath, wiping the sweat out of my eyes with my knuckle before heaving myself to my feet. On the other side of the wall, I could hear movement, soft footsteps on the stairs. I held the Walther at an upward angle and quickly stuck my head round the door to snatch a look down the hall.

At the top of the stairs, I saw a shadow break across the landing. I swung my arm out, sighting the barrel down the passageway and let off a round before throwing myself out into the hall. As I was moving toward the stairs, I already knew that I'd fired too quickly, the shot high and wide, scouring a long trench in the wallpaper. There was no return fire. No big push of manpower toward me. I edged forward down the thin corridor, my back straight, my right arm outstretched, aiming the pistol in front of me, my eyes burning in my head, all my concentration focussing on the stairwell.

The passageway was hot and still. No further sound or activity coming from downstairs. I took another couple of tentative steps forward, breathing slowly and deeply through my mouth, all my attention focusing on what havoc may break out in front of me. Such an eagled-eye pose had made me forget an old admonition from my days in the army: *Don't let the bastards get behind you, Remis.*

The man came out of the first bedroom like a spring exploding from a broken clock, a long-bladed stiletto raised above his head, his face full of bone, his torso knotted with muscle under his black military fatigues. I tried to pivot, swing the Walther clear and aim at his chest but my knees popped and burned and seemed to have all the resilience of a cobweb. As I lost my balance and lurched backwards into the bathroom the knife came down toward my shoulder, raking through the cloth of my jacket sleeve, narrowly missing my arm and sending the Walther bouncing across the linoleum.

I rolled across the floor toward the sink, ending up on my back, panic rushing over me, my torso twisting toward the base of the shower, the man with the knife heading my way, his expression bone-plated and muddy-eyed. As I lashed out at him with one foot, I caught a glimpse of the butt of the Walther underneath the toilet bowl. I snatched at it with trembling fingers, frantically grasping at the grip and in one sweeping motion, raised it blindly and fired. I saw the man's shoulder jerk backward and his knees stumble. I fired again, the next round tearing into his upper chest sending him sprawling back out through the bathroom door and dropping him into the hall.

I was still stretched out on my back across the floor boards, my breath exploding in my lungs as two high-powered rifle slugs smashed through the tiled bathroom wall. I writhed on the ground, managing to wrench myself over onto my stomach as a third shot pounded through the plaster work, shattering the toilet bowl and tank in a cascade of water and fractured ceramic. A fourth round ricocheted off a metal towel rack and collapsed the shower door in a pile of frosted glass. The inside of my mouth was as dry as a bone. I ran my tongue across my lips and tried to speak; to yell out Nia's name again, but my words became a tangle of rusty nails in my throat. More gunfire. One blast after the other. A ragged salvo followed by an abrupt silence. My ears screeched with a sound like the sea, my breath rasping in my throat like a man whose lungs were perforated with holes.

I kept my head down, quickly scrabbling across the floor toward the wall at edge of the door. I heard a man's voice. Barely audible. Perhaps a three-syllable question. Maybe the words, *say again*? The kind of reply you got when someone issued a confusing order. I pulled myself back up on my feet, gripped the handle of the Walther with both hands, swallowed hard and stepped out again into the hall and immediately began firing at the figure crouched at the top of the stairs.

My first round punched through the man's throat. Still holding his gun, he clenched one hand over the wound, blood congealing immediately between his fingers. He made a choking sound, as if he'd swallowed a fish bone. The second shot made a hole less than the diameter of a pencil above his eyebrow and excited the back of his head in a spray of blood, bone and grey matter.

Behind the dead man, a second gunman crouched on one knee, two steps down from the landing. He squeezed off his automatic as I spun back inside the cover of the bathroom doorway and heard him break into a run toward me. Momentum and fear kept me rolling now. Rather than wait behind the wall, I took a chance and went hell for leather, darting back out into the corridor, dropping like a stone on one knee, firing at my fast-moving opponent. The roar of the nine-millimetre was deafening, the recoil powerful and palm numbing, the gun suddenly feeling weightless in my hand each time I pulled the trigger again and put two rounds into him, the second clipping off the top of the gunman's scalp. He went down hard on both knees, his jaw dropping, his arms dead at his sides before nose-driving in front of me.

I felt the breach of the Walther lock open on the empty clip. My hands were shaking as I ejected it and shoved a new one into the magazine and chambered the top round. I jumped over the gunman's corpse and ran down the hall. I felt a wave of nausea wash through my system as I reached the top step, pausing for a second, my eyes adjusting to the dim light. The way down was clear but I had no idea what would be waiting for me at the bottom. As I trod down the first couple of steps, I could hear the rain outside now coming down in a torrent. A sheet of lightening trembling in the distance.

Halfway down the stairs I heard a foot depress a board on the hardwood floor, then in the corner of my vision saw the silhouette of a man moving from the kitchen into the living room. As he turned toward the stairs, his rifle held at high port arms, I sunk down low, pressing myself against the wall, locking my sights on the top of the man's shoulder and pulled the trigger. The round hit him at an angle, blowing a hole in the side of his lower neck and collar bone. The impact spun him round, knocking him hard against the side of the wall at the foot of the stairs. His mouth hung open, his eyes fluttered and rolled in the back of his head as he slid to the ground, his blood smearing the plasterwork as he dropped.

That single shot of mine then unleased all hell. Out of nowhere heavy shotgun volleys erupted from outside, and at close range. As I threw myself down the remaining steps on the stairs and took cover against the kitchen doorjamb, I saw two more gunmen firing outside. The erupting flashes of cartridge flak leapt from behind the curtained living room windows, their pump-action shot guns clacking loudly back into place with each fresh shell, the explosions of flame visible as the buckshot blew window glass and curtain material into the living room.

As I heard the pumps clack back to feed another shell into the chambers and heaved myself into open ground, loosing off a couple of random shots before diving back into the spandrel underneath the staircase. As I was about to take another couple of aimless pot-shots, I saw Nia come up fast out of the red haze, positioning herself behind the two gunmen, partially hidden from them in the heavy rainfall. She began to fire into the back of one man, moving at speed, the ejected nine-millimetre casing flying into the air. Before I had time to break cover, push forward and return fire, Nia had dropped the first man and had already clipped the second gunman in the left shoulder. He'd spun around helplessly toward Nia, shocked, falling backward off balance, his body flailing frantically, his gun arm extending toward her just as she let off the next shot and caught him in the centre of the sternum.

Nia didn't stop there. She continued to fire with both hands gripped on the pistol. Each soft-nosed slug knocking him backwards with the force of a jackhammer, his black T-shirt exploding with scarlet flowers on his muscular chest, until the last round in the chamber hit him in the rib cage and virtually eviscerated him. The gunman dropped on crumpled legs as though the bones in his body had been surgically removed.

When Nia lowered her gun toward the ground, her cheeks look like they contained tiny red coals, her eyes frozen, as though she were staring into a howling storm, one that was filled with invisible forces and screams that only she could hear.

CHAPTER THIRTY-THREE

THE KILLING DIDN'T STOP THERE. HOW COULD IT? THE EXECUTIONERS sent to Xina to liquidate Pierre Roth and finish off Nia and I hadn't walked from Salonica or Athens to do their work, they'd travelled to do their 'wet job' in vehicles, with drivers and possibly more trigger men. My gut told me there was still more trouble to come. I could see in Nia's eyes a determination to continue to mete out summary justice regardless of the attrition. And I knew from all the times in the past that I'd gone into a firefight, under a black flag, that the only way to deal with these kinds of butchers, such as the ones who wanted us dead now, was to take the carnage to them, or end up a stiff.

I clicked my thumb and forefinger together a couple of times to grab Nia's attention, then pointed two fingers at my eyes before aiming them toward the thick line of pine trees that ran along the back of the cottage and extended down toward the edge of the dunes. I slowly mouthed the words. '*Head for the car.*'

Nia nodded her head as she released the empty magazine of the Makarov. She quickly slid in another clip, chambering a round, and headed out to her right, at a crouch, towards the side of the cottage and the tree line. Once she was out of sight, I holstered my Walther and snatched up one of the pump action shotguns from the ground, then rifled through the pockets of two of the dead men, collecting any spare cartridges they'd had stashed. I loaded a couple more rounds into the shotgun's port before heading down the path towards the harbour. Halfway along the track I found a thinner trail, which seemed like a better bet if I wanted to stay out of sight. Surprisingly I couldn't hear any voices. No cries or calls from disturbed locals after the heavy bursts of gunfire. In truth, anyone with any sense would have gone to ground after such a curtain of fire, but I knew there'd most likely be some damn fool stupid enough to be nosing around.

The sandy track I was on wound down toward the edge of the bay, taking me past the backs of the few sea-front buildings on the main street.

The footpath eventually brought me out into a back alley close to the marina. The sound of wind chimes tinkled, the solitary bell hanging outside the door of a tiny cabin at the foot of the alleyway. Beyond it I could see the jetty, the harbour still surprisingly deserted of either Xina's inhabitants or gunmen.

Rather than head into open ground, I decided to back track, running up the deserted little terrace and into the same tree line that Nia had already taken. Egrets clattered above my head as I worked my way silently through the sandy sloughs and troughs and piles of organic debris that squished under my feet and stank like fish roe. Even though we were on the cusp of winter, the air was dense with humidity, as though the environment itself was sweating. I pushed the moisture out of my eyes with the heel of my hand. I could hear the chop slapping against the hull of a boat at its moorings in the bay, but still no buzz of human life or chatter. On the edge of the pine canopy, I could see out along the harbour and the cars that were pulled up on the side of the road. I edged carefully along a white stone wall; my head dipped low, then moved down on to a strip of shingle waste ground, moving at speed until I reached a high mound of earth behind where I'd left my car.

I peered over the top of the soil and could just make out the silhouette of the head of a man sat at the driving seat of one dusty-looking vehicle. A second empty car, a flash, navy-blue S-class Mercedes Benz, was parked up ten yards behind the first. A man, within spitting distance, was leant against the wing of my Lancia, his back to me. Cigarette smoke billowed around his head, a Beretta nine millimetre was in his right hand, the barrel of the pistol resting lazily against the side of his thigh. I stooped back down into the gully, shifting along the sunken ridge quietly, my sly movements aided by a thin overhang of thorny foliage. I raised the shotgun at arm's length before reaching the end of the low trench. As I stepped up out of the channel onto higher ground, I thought I'd got the jump on him, the back of the man's skull already in my sights. Such brief hubris didn't take into account all the dry brushwood beneath my feet, and the giveaway loud snap that alerted my target I was about to strike.

I heard the startled man spit out the words "Son of a *bitch*," as he spun round to face me. That sudden, explicit vocal reaction was as far as he got in taking me on. As he attempted to raise the Beretta and I was about to pull the trigger, I saw Nia spring up out of the grass on the other side of the vehicle, the sound of her gun barking a single shot. The round entered the centre of the man's back and exited his chest in a violent plume of crimson, torn flesh, and cartilage. I watched the Beretta fall from his limp fingers, one hand suddenly extending as he stumbled forward. Bubbles of blood spotted his lips as he tried to gasp in air. A final, ruinous murmur slurred from his mouth as he collapsed toward the dirt, dead.

Nia's single shot ambush was enough to alert the remaining man that we were on to him. I began running, yelling at Nia to take out the rear tyres of the car, but the driver had already fired up his motor and was speeding off. We continued to give chase, spent cartridges flying from shotgun and pistol ejector ports alike, the rounds whanging off the retreating vehicle's bodywork. Any chance of our shooting the messenger was lost in a thick blanket of dust, flying stone and grit.

We both came to a breathless halt in the road, I could hear Nia's cursing between her wheezes and huffing. I kicked angrily at the ground with the toe of my shoe, eyes filled with water, my heaving lungs swelling with air that was dense with salt, the stark realisation that our failure to pull the plug on that last fleeing man had allowed him to get back to his superiors with his tail between his legs. He'd swiftly inform them that the operation had been bungled, that Nia and I were both still breathing. Roth's execution would still be up in the air, but it wouldn't take long before his corpse was discovered, and I'd be in the frame for his murder.

In the coming hours I knew that we'd have more predators on our tails, eager for the hunt and baying for our blood.

As I watched the car disappearing into the distance, I heard Nia say to me, "We need to get the fuck out of here."

I didn't argue.

CHAPTER THIRTY-FOUR

Nia was right in insisting that we blow town before fresh blood turned up. It wouldn't take the getaway driver long to find himself a pay phone, call in to the brass to report the botched operation and request back-up. A quick check in the boot of the Lancia confirmed that none of our belongings had been dug through or confiscated, and more surprisingly nor had the small cache of ammunition and the shotgun that I'd brought along for the ride either. The men sent to kill us had clearly been confident in their capabilities and that their hush-hush mission would be successful. I knew that the Provost hadn't just given me the scoop to where Pierre Roth was holing up, there'd be more he wanted me to uncover, I just wasn't sure I'd found it yet. Even with the clock ticking, the threat of reinforcements closing in on us, and Nia giving me the evil eye. My nose was telling me to head back to Roth's place and turn it over.

Before going with my hunch, I gave the ditched Mercedes a brisk forage; inside I found the keys sat in the ignition and more fuel in the tank than my old Lancia. I was in no doubt that the Merc would offer us a more comfortable ride and get us around a lot sharper, so I transferred all our gear into the plush saloon then drove us back down the harbour road, pulling up as close to Roth's residence as I could. I climbed out and stuck my head back into the car's interior.

"Take the wheel. I won't be long. You hear or see anything that doesn't feel right, honk the horn and fire the engine up, got it?"

Nia swung open the passenger door and scowled at me as I began to walk away. She called after me. "I get spooked, I'm flooring this fucker and you're on your own. That's what I'm doing."

"Just try it." I kept walking, my mind on other things, dark thoughts that boded well for no one, the scent of death and the tannic odour of late autumn on the wind.

Back inside the cottage, the unmistakable rank air of scorched flesh, dried blood and cordite immediately hit me. I didn't want to hang around and inhale the stink and I darted up the stairs, along the landing and into Roth's bedroom. The electric lamp was still burning on the bedside table, one of the few things that had not been shot to shit in the attack. Roth's corpse was still a few hours away from turning ripe, most of his brains were spread over the rug and part of the bed counterpane. Thankfully he was stretched out face down so at least my eyes didn't have to linger on whatever horrendous expression he'd been left with. Vague feelings of remorse began to trouble me. It had been a bad mistake to question the banker so close to the window. Unfortunate for Roth, and bad for me because I believed that he had so much more to tell.

I looked around what was left of the bedroom, fixing the place in my mind like a photo before starting my search. I began with the dresser, not finding anything other than the usual round of shirts, handkerchiefs and cotton underwear. Several expensive French suits hung behind a shoe rack in the closet. I felt the pockets without knowing why and didn't turn up a thing. Next to a bullet-ridden wooden antique bureau sat a brown attaché case which looked like it had managed to escape injury or ruin. I opened it and found it filled with bank statements and a heavy looking, hardback ledger. I took out the account book, quickly flicking through the pages. A few of the names listed on various pages, each one positioned against columns connecting them to various large sums of money told me I'd struck gold. I stuffed the ledger back inside the briefcase, took a look at my watch and headed for a small alcove at the furthest end of the bedroom. Inside the cramped spaced was a single metal filing cabinet crammed with files, most of them written in German, which meant nothing to me. I thumbed through all the documents hoping for some hidden scrap but drew a blank and headed back to Roth's desk.

Whilst I was searching among the remainder of the disordered papers, a small, printed card, edged in black, caught my attention. The familiar blue and white shield symbol of the Greek Intelligence Service was etched in the left-hand corner.

Below the shield talisman, written in Latin, was the service's ambiguous motto, "*Do Not Discuss Confidential Affairs*".

Engraved below that in bold italic print in the centre of the business card was the rank and name of an equally prominent figure who I was all too aware of, ***Brigadier Kyril Grivas.***

I picked up the card, immediately feeling my fingertips pressing hard against the edge of the stiff paper, my mouth suddenly feeling dry, my forehead beading with sweat. Roth's confession that Grivas was dirty was now being given a little more substance by the fact the dead banker had in some way had contact with the Brigadier. Grivas wasn't the kind of man to hand out his calling card carelessly, in that he only presented it to an individual personally. Provost Callas was equally as cautious in who he offered up his own credentials to, and, although Roth had implicated my boss in historical crimes and corruption, for now I had no real evidence that was the case. The Provost was slippery, devious, and controlling, perhaps he could even be described as 'bent', but I found it hard to believe he could have been a war criminal.

I kept looking, keeping an eye out for anything that could perhaps implicate Callas, but came up with nothing in the dossiers and deeds after quickly sifting through them. I decided to bundle all the paperwork that was on Roth's desk into the attaché case, then raked through the drawers and did likewise with any other document that took my fancy. As I turned from the desk to walk out of the bedroom, I caught a glimpse of the bottle of Johnny Walker whisky I'd taken a crafty nip out of earlier. It was lying on its side, tucked in close to the feet of the antique table, which had been kicked over in the earlier assault. I snatched up the bottle, pocketed it then made my way downstairs.

On my way out of the kitchen, I bumped my head on a set of keys hanging from a nail in one of the ceiling beams. I snatched them off the hook and stared around the tiny room. On the wall between the backdoor and the entrance into the living room hung a grubby-looking white linen curtain.

I dropped the briefcase on the oilcloth-covered table and yanked back the curtain. Behind it stood a low wooden door which was locked. I gave a couple of the skeleton keys a whirl and got nowhere, but my third attempt with a short, fancy bow affair gave me the lucky break I was after. I twisted the key clockwise, felt it rotate in the lock and opened it up. I found a light switch on the wall and flicked it on.

A low-watt bulb hanging from a scraggy rose above my head revealed a short flight of narrow stairs that were festooned with cobwebs, and which led down to a cellar. Thick dust powered every inch of the place, the musty stink of damp permeating what little air there was. I headed down, the wooden steps creaking below my feet. The basement was spartan in its lay out. Just a couple of old pieces of ponderous furniture arranged with little precision, and a small coal furnace crouched in the centre of the vault like a pagan idol. There was nothing remarkable, all except for the two pieces of pristine-looking luggage sat against the far wall. A pair of classy, leather suitcases, with gold catches that stuck out like a sore thumb amongst the rest of the cast-off crap.

I stood over both bags for a moment then grabbed the handle of one and was immediately shocked by the heavy weight of the contents. I lugged it over to the foot of the stairs, flipped it on its side and tried the gold catches either side of the handle; both were unsurprisingly, locked. I felt for the switchblade in my jacket pocket, released the stiletto blade and prized the tip into the hasp of the first lock, jemmied it open, and worked the other catch free. I lifted the lid and blew out a breath, my heart turning a sudden cartwheel, my eyes not quite believing what they were seeing.

I'd always assumed that high-rollers' baggage probably stowed pricey garments and possessions. The weighty contents of the travel bag I was now bug-eyeing was worth its weight in gold ... literally.

CHAPTER THIRTY-FIVE

Life moves at the speed of sound when there's gun smoke still hanging in the air over a dead body. In just a few seconds a gun changes time forever, and everything else that follows. Nia and I had not just left a single corpse laying on the ground back at Pierre Roth's seaside retreat, there was a heap of corpses, all of them either secret service men or hired muscle with military training. I'd not slain all of the assassins, but I wish I had. By drawing Nia into a fight not of her own making, I knew I'd brought down a whole world of trouble for her, the implications of which, could be grave. Manolis Callas had told me to seek out Nia, alluding that she may have already been a target for Grivas' men because of her association to me. What was it the old man had said, *"You've been keeping her safe under your wing all these years. Be a shame to break the habit of a lifetime now, wouldn't it?"*. Something didn't weigh up. Callas had never been so benevolent; so concerned for another human being's welfare, especially one of such little worth as Nia Garbi's life was. Instinct told me I was being played for a fool, but if not by Callas, then by who? Had the Provost directed me to keep Nia out of harm's way because he and not Grivas wanted us both silenced. If so, why? Could there possibly have been some kind of conspiratorial alliance between Callas and the Brigadier, some shady dealings, historical palm-greasing or worse that both men were eager should remain undiscovered and covert. Pierre Roth had insisted that the Provost was, *"As crooked as the rest of them. Dirty as Grivas, worse in fact"*.

Could I believe the word of a scared man, one who had himself much to hide and who I'd muscled to talk under extreme duress? Coercion played a valuable part in my work, it was part of my trusty toolkit, one I employed often. But at times I knew that such strong-arming could push a person the wrong way or too far; the titbits of information they coughed up, unreliable, their often-traitorous revelations misleading or fabricated to save their own scared necks. Had Roth given me a fish story to get me off his back and protect more important individuals, or was there some truth in the Janus-faced bastards' words?

Pierre Roth had been, after all, a banker. Not the most honourable of professions. And let's face it, who the hell in their right mind would trust a banker?

The men sent to liquidate Nia and I had also been ordered to silence Pierre Roth. There was no way the people who'd hired Roth to look after their crooked investments were going to let him talk and worse still, be taken into custody. After the sanctioned *wet job* had been carried out successfully, those same assassins would have been expected to 'clean' Roth's joint, removing any trace of our bodies and importantly, to retrieve the two-cases of bullion and the attaché of incriminating evidence that I now had in my possession.

I was dragged out of deep thought by the sound of Nia

suddenly slamming on the breaks. She switched off the engine, drumming the fingers of one hand against the edge of steering wheel, her upper body tight with agitation. We were in the middle of nowhere, on the outskirts of a village, surrounded by a landscape of stray farming equipment and rusting agricultural fuel tanks. In the distance I could just see the range of mountains that I knew we'd be heading up into soon. An old man carrying a large wooden rake over his shoulder wandered past the car. I watched him stop in his tracks, then turn and walk up to Nia's window, peering inside. She shook her head angrily at the man, mouthing an obscenity which quickly sent him scurrying away. She grabbed the steering wheel firmly and stared straight ahead. There was anger in her eyes, and when she finally spoke her voice sounded hoarse, like she was getting a cold.

Suddenly I was feeling pretty cold myself.

Nia snapped her head round and glared at me. "Where the hell are we going, Remis?"

"Vasilika."

"Vasilika! What, why in the name of Christ are we going up there?"

"Because, I said we are." For a moment the silence was deafening.

Nia spat into the footwell. "The place is full of inbreds and goat-fuckers."

"So, your kind of people then."

Before I had chance to say anything else Nia had got out of the car. She collected her bag off the back seat, slammed the door behind her, leaned back on the wing and lit a cigarette angrily. I followed her outside.

"We need to keep moving. It's not safe for us to be hanging around in the open like this. It's only a matter of time before we'll have more trouble on to us." I turned and pointed toward the mountains. "That's why we're going up there."

Nia stared down at the ground for almost a minute while I stumbled, badly through the rest of my explanation. I told her what Roth had said to me, and my fears that we were being targeted by a hit squad, and the possible reasons why. Nia said nothing. Didn't interrupt. I watched her take a long pull on her cigarette. When she looked back up at me, she blew a mouthful of grey smoke into my face. "So, what's in Vasilika that's so damn important?"

"There's someone up there, someone who can maybe help us." I walk backed toward the car, climbed behind the wheel, and fired up the engine. Nia followed, opened up the passenger door and stuck her head inside. I watched her check my expression nervously before she took a quick look behind her, towards the white-tipped alps in the distance. She turned back to face me.

"Whose up there?"

I ground the car into gear.

"A ghost from both our pasts."

The Monastery of Agia Anastasia sat both secluded and isolated in the southern foothills of Mount Ombrianos. The huge stone walls, constructed during the Byzantine Empire, reached up towards the heavens, its foundations built on a sheer drop. Three rows of ornate stained windows ran across the entrance, the huge oak door more in keeping with the protective gate of a medieval castle than that of a monastic place of God.

As I drove closer, the quadrangular form of the monastery offered, up at each of its corners, a heptagonal tower, each of the grand structures physically squared to the earth but clearly designed to spiritually raise toward the heavens.

I parked the Mercedes underneath a canopy of cypress trees. The air smelling of the branches, fresh sap and wet moss. The well-maintained lawn that lay either side, cut short, its borders crisply edged. We made our way down the stone path that led to the porch that hung over the monastery's entryway. I tugged a brass bellpull as big as a butcher's weight, and after a short while heard the sound of footsteps approaching.

When the door swung open, I was ready with my warrant card, held out at arm's length. A wizened, white-haired monk, dressed in a long, black, wide-sleeved cassock, sniffed the incensed air around him, before taking a couple of steps closer, peering at my identification indifferently before focussing his attention back to me, a bemused look on his face. "Good afternoon. My name is Remis. I'd very much like to speak to one of your brethren ... Rassophore Tolotos."

The monks ancient, watery eyes flickered nervously. "Tolotos, you say?"

I nodded my head. "That's correct."

The old man shook his head. "I'm sorry, I cannot help you. We have no one of that name within our sacred order."

I let my arm fall to my side. Smiled at the old man, but only for a moment. I took a step closer, a flickering kerosene lamp perched on a board shelf cast shifting shadows across the stone walls. "Oh, I think you have, padre. Michael's been bestowed the title of *Rassophore* since last we met. I know he's here, because it was me who sent him to you."

I watched the elderly brother ball one hand into a pudgy fist, the suspicious tone in his voice had a knot in it as tight as a wet rope. "That maybe so, but God nor this order now recognises the man you speak of by such a name any longer."

"I'm not surprised. The Michael I used to know, the one *man* we are speaking of, could never in anyone's wildest dreams have been identified as Christian."

The monk smiled back, placing the palm of his hand on the door, ready to slam it shut in our faces. "Sadly, I am afraid your police credentials offer no ingress to this private holy order, Major."

I inched forward, the toe of my shoe quickly resting itself against the bottom rail of the door. "It'd be better my badge affording me a right of entry rather than this, your holiness." I held open the lapel of my jacket for a moment, revealing the holstered Walther and watched the saintly expression on the old monk's face quickly run for cover. I slipped my wallet back into the inside pocket, buttoned up my coat and waited. I wanted to kill the little clown.

There was no one I hated more than a man of God. I fought off the urge to drive my fist into the venerable friar's face and edged forward, sending the old man lumbering backward.

"Bring Tolotos to me." My voice rasping with menace. "Now."

I watched the monk quickly turn on his heels and march away. I walked inside, Nia at my back, the two of us coming to a hole in a rectangular vestibule with a vaulted stone ceiling. The rough walls were studded with iron bolts. An ornate silk cloth edged in gold gilt covered an altar at one side of the portico, dozens of squat white candles ran along the ground and around its perimeter.

For a moment, I didn't move, my eyes adjusting to the darkness. A ceramic plaque on one wall identified the monastery's archaic order. I stared at the humble wooden benches lined up in an ante room to the left of me. The walls stank of mildew, the white alabaster paint job peeling in places. I felt a couple of Nia's fingers stab me sharply in the ribs, followed by her grim, matter of fact tone.

"What the fuck is Michael Tolotos doing in a convent?"

I pinch my eyes with my fingers, desperate not to react, but still ended up biting. "This is a monastery, you cretin. Convents are for nuns. Women, remember?"

"All I remember is that prick Michael Tolotos being a kiddy fiddler."

I could feel a weight the size of a brick in my chest. I rubbed my forehead and took a breath. "Yeah, well, we need the son of a bitch's help, so for now, just stow it!"

Nia grabbed my jacket sleeve, yanking me sideways, her implacable stare cutting into me. Her dark expression a mixture of hurt and rage. "You really must be desperate, coming all this way to ask for that cocksucker's help." Nia's monotone voice was full of hate for the man we were about to see. I knew we'd be lucky to leave without Garbi slitting Tolotos' throat. I snatched my arm from her grasp when I heard the sound of footsteps again. I turned to see a man walking slowly down the central stairway toward us. I watched as he pulled his cape anxiously up over his shoulders, his gait unsteady as he stepped off the bottom step and headed towards me, his exhaling breath clearly visible in the cold air. As the monk drew closer, I caught sight of the unmistakable profile of Michael Tolotos, his scarred, savage face materialising as he approached me. When he finally came to a halt, Tolotos made a deep bow, muttering the Latin words *"Nigrum Coal De Anima"* under his breath, before devoutly blessing himself with the sign of the cross with claw-like fingers.

"It's been a long time, Michael."

Tolotos' remained silent, still hunched over for a moment longer before raising his head to face both Nia and me. His scalp was hairless, not as the result of penance, but because of the alopecia he'd suffered since he was a young man... The eyes were set deep in his head, with tiny, mobile black pupils, his gaze both innocent and malign. Tolotos' nose could not really be called a nose, for it was only a bone that began between the eyes. As it rose from out of his face, it immediately sank again, transforming itself into two, black holes, broad nostrils thick with grey hair. His mouth, joined to the remainder of his nose by a scar, was wide and ill made, stretching more to the right than to the left, and in-between the upper lip, non-existent, and the lower, prominent and fleshy, there protruded, in irregular pattern, what was left of his yellowing, cracked teeth.

Unusually for a man with no nose, Tolotos' had a pair of horn-rimmed glasses hung around his neck on a gold chain. When he spoke, his voice sounded muffled and hollow. An involuntary shudder ran through me. Not fear, just deep revulsion.

"This is an unexpected visitation, Major."

I checked my watch. Five minutes past three. "We're not interrupting your afternoon prayers, I trust?"

Tolotos gave me a feral smirk, he shook his head passively, his attention quickly aiming towards Nia rather than myself, his eyes suddenly gleaming with predatory intelligence, a familiar cruel grin suddenly creeping out from between his mutilated lips. "I see that my appearance still offends you, Miss Garbi."

Rage darkened Nia's dusky complexion. Hot blood flowing swiftly into her cheeks. "Your fucking evil mug always did." Nia wiped her nose with her wrist, her eyes lighting up on Totolos's maimed countenance. "Like someone's been chopping wood on it!"

Tolotos ignored Nia's insult and lifted his chin towards her, proudly displaying his many lesions and disfigurements. "These wounds are my stigmata. Christ suffered injuries only to his hands and feet. A spear wound to his side. I bear dozens of such trophies."

I stepped in front of Tolotos and Nia, interrupting his line of sight. The rapist's wide, unfocused eyes leered at me. He bared his nasty incisors. A wolf in a trap. He stepped forward, his voice barely a whisper: "I was to be the man without a past, Major. That was your promise."

"Promises are meant to be broken, Michael." I stabbed two fingers into the centre of the child molesters stomach, snatching at the thick wool vestment that Tolotos was hiding behind, dragging him toward me. A Latin phrase I'd learned as a child at the orphanage, suddenly coming back to me out of the blue. "*Ut sementem feceris ita metes.*" I hammered a blow to Tolotos' guts before releasing him.

As you sow, so shall you reap.

The deviant stumbled back, clutching his mid-section spluttering and grunting, struggling for a minute to regain his breath and whatever little composure he could muster. He stood upright on unsteady feet, a line of sweat beaded across his brow, and lifted his specs to his face, his hand trembling, his cold, dead eyes magnified by the thick lenses.

"And what is it that you seek from me, Major?"

"Sanctuary, Michael." I felt my smile widen. "Nothing more than good, old fashioned Orthodox church sanctuary."

CHAPTER THIRTY-SIX

Sitting on the edge of a malodorous bed I lit a cigarette to help me keep my mind off the smell and stared around at the blank, monastic cell, my eyes slowly becoming accustomed to the gloom. The bed I was perched on looked like a medieval mantrap. Dirt clung to the walls. The curtains either side of a small, stained-glass window were little more than grey winding sheets. The shabby-looking room made me feel like I was already dead, or in limbo, or worse. I felt like a down-and-out and probably looked like one, too. The only thing preventing me from sinking into a true hobo's state of mind were the two trunks stuffed to the brim with gold bullion that were sat with the rest of our luggage on the other side of the squalid little chamber.

Nia was sat shivering at the foot of the bed, her back against the damp wall, holding on to Pierre Roth's bottle of Johnny Walker as if her life depended on it. She pointed at the cigarette in my hand and grunted. "Are you gonna give me one of those?" I tossed her the pack and my lighter and watched her light up, inhale deeply and take a disapproving look around the room.

"You know Remis, you should feel right at home in this shithole."

"Really?"

Nia was silent for a moment. "Yeah," She raised the whiskey to her lips, took a hefty swig, pulled a face then pushed the bottle in my direction. "This dump doesn't possess any fucking heating either."

I ignored Garbi's cheap shot and looked across at Roth's leather attaché case stood on top of one of the trunks. It was easier to keep my nose off the smell of the bed with the whiskey bottle under my nose, so I took another slug and put my cigarette back between my lips. Nia, emboldened by her first sniff of booze and eager to get a rise out of me was clearly not about to stop her taunting. She pointed at the whiskey bottle in my hand, a sly grin on her face. "Smoking and drinking, you know, it'll be the death of you, Remis."

I nodded my head blankly. "Funny, that's what my old friend, Vokos used to tell me." I took a double pull on the coffin nail before inhaling and blew out a thick plume of smoke. I listened to Nia snigger then watched as her head flopped back against the wall, her eyes looking up at the ceiling for a moment. She ran her fingers through her hair before focusing her attention back at me. "You ever take any notice of the good doctor's advice?"

I turned away and spoke at the wall. "All depends on the kind of advice he's dishing out."

"So, your gonna keep on smoking, drinking and screwing your brains loose until the end of your sorry days. Right?"

"Right." I felt myself grin. All that debauched living seems like a great way to go out, if you ask me."

Nia leant across and snatched the bottle out of my hands. "Jesus, I hope I don't end up like you."

"I hope you don't either." Out of the corner of my eye, I saw Nia broodily shaking her head.

"What the hell's the matter with you now?"

Garbi gave a shrug. "Nothing. I was just thinking, by the time I'm your age, I hope to be a little smarter."

"Well, it can't help to hope. You're off to a slow start, though, if getting smart is your goal."

Nia took another slug of whiskey and set the bottle down next to her. "What the fuck are we really doing here?"

I heaved myself up off the mattress and trudged across to the other side of the room. Perhaps the view of the monastic doss house would have a more favourable charm looking at it from a different angle. It didn't. "Biding our time."

"Yeah, well how long for?"

I rubbed at my face with the flat of my hand and turned to face Nia. "For a long as it takes me to figure out my next move."

Garbi took another drag on her cigarette and then looked at the glowing tip thoughtfully. "What was that crap Tolotos was whispering at you under his breath earlier?"

"Nigrum Coal De Anima."

Nia got to her feet; a shaft of weak sunlight shone on one side of her face; the other side buried in shadow. "Nigrum, what?"

"It's Latin for coal black soul." It's what Tolotos and the other lowlife's called me back when I was working the streets."

"Catchy, I might start calling you it."

I felt a sudden tremble in my right hand, sensed a flicker

behind my eyes, an annoying buzzing noise in my ear. "Don't bother."

Nia stepped closer to me, breathing hard. I could feel her breath on my face. Her eyes held mine, her jaw tightening, one hand propped on her hip. She peered over my shoulder toward the luggage on the floor. "So, are you going to tell me what's in those bags?"

"No." I turned and snatched up the briefcase, pushed Garbi out of my way and sat the case on the bed. I flipped the catches, took out the large ledger and opened it up. Nia didn't waste any time gluing herself to my back, clearly as eager to view the contents of the account book as I was. Staring at Pierre Roth's handwriting instantly made me hear his voice again and see his duplicitous grin, brimming with possible untruths and false leads. A few turns of the balance sheet's pages quickly revealed that the dead banker had revealed more of the truth to me than I'd perhaps given him credit for. As I began to scroll down the long list of names, some Greek, many German, the harsh reality of both what I'd gotten myself mixed up in, and why so many people either wanted me or others silenced hit home. My heart began to race when I came to the column where Brigadier Grivas' moniker had been inked in.

Next to his name, were various sums of money, nothing less than three thousand drachma, all being deposited into a bank account each month. Despite Roth's insistence that Manolis Callas was as dirty as Grivas, my boss's name wasn't, up to now, turning up in any of the columns.

I couldn't see Eric Hodt's name mentioned in the inventory either. The kraut spymaster's involvement in the madness of the last few days was becoming clearer the more I continued to leaf through the ledger's pages. Hodt's fellow countrymen, many, I suspected, well-respected, uniquely placed and no doubt influential back home, were being mentioned in the balance sheets. If the BND handler wasn't receiving any back-handers, then his earlier attempts to recruit me, and his operatives muscling in from the off were starting to make a lot more sense. Hodt was clearly looking to cover-up any evidence of German involvement in the historical Nazi looting of Salonica's Jews. I'd have taken a guess that some very serious operators could be linked to benefiting financially from payments listed in the log I was now pouring over. What I was seeing wasn't just about German national security interests or for that matter Hodt's earlier claim that he wanted to create some kind of temporary alliance with me. The contents of the journal were proof that the BND's interest in Konrad Tafel's murder was little more than a smokescreen. Hodt was in Salonica to bury the truth. Sent to gag those who may have wished to jeopardise the future good name of any number of his country's well-heeled and powerful citizens. Hodt needed an inside man to do his dirty work whilst he was on foreign soil and, as I'd already guessed, he'd chosen me to be his sucker.

As I turned another page, I felt Nia's finger give me a prod in the back. "Any of that scrawl making sense to you?"

Without turning to reply, I gave Nia a cagey nod, quickly focusing my attention back to the lined pages of the register again, continuing to run my finger back down more of the names and the corresponding huge sums of money paid out to them. As I reached the bottom, one unexpected name suddenly drew my attention.

Captain Nicholas Kampouris.

I ran my finger across where Kampouris' name had been penned in. Nick was raking in a tidy monthly pay-off. Not big money like some of the book's other recipients, but enough cash to confirm he was in the pocket of someone other than Callas or his own precinct chief. Why the hell was a greasy, low-ranking police detective from the Salonica homicide division in a banker's account book rubbing shoulders with the likes of Brigadier Grivas and a bunch of German heavy hitters?

My brooding was interrupted by the sound of footsteps thudding on the stone floor in the corridor outside. I heard Nia about to speak again, any utterance abruptly interrupted by a solid, single knock on the other side of the door. I closed up the ledger, dropped it back into the briefcase, snapped the case shut and walked across to the door. As I took hold of the brass latch, Garbi called back at me.

"Whatever's written inside that ledger is going to bring us more trouble, right?"

I didn't answer, turning the handle in my palm.

"You know, Remis, even silence sounds like a lie when it's caught inside your damn mouth."

CHAPTER THIRTY-SEVEN

I SWUNG OPEN THE DOOR TO REVEAL A SCRAWNY-LOOKING MONK wearing a black habit with a bald head and a long, dark beard. The young friar bowed politely and smiled. “Rassophore Tolotos has had a meal prepared for you.” He took a step forward and held out a slender hand. “If you’d both like to follow me.”

I pointed at the rusty warded lock set underneath the brass door handle. “Any chance you could roll a key through this whilst we’re gone?”

The brother shot me a bemused look before squinting into the chamber to eye the two trunks and briefcase. “You can rest assure; your belongings will be safe.”

“Well, that’s good to hear.” The young monk went to walk away. “But I’d still like the door locked.” The novice turned to face me again, his expression cold. He gave a curt nod of his head. “As you wish.“ He took a step back as Nia and I walked out into the hallway. “I will return shortly to secure the cell.”

Away from our makeshift bullpen, the rest of the inside of Agia Anastasia looked as downcast as the cloistered chamber we'd been sat in. The monastery was an uncomfortable, hollow place of long echoes, semi-darkness, hidden eyes, tangible silences and the sour smell of baking bread. We walked the length of a long, uncarpeted corridor, the abbey looking and feeling more like a prison than a place where pious men lived by choice. The hallway we trod along ran between clammy walls painted in institutional tones of green and beige, and past doors of unembellished wood that were without adornment of any sort. Above our heads, bare lightbulbs hung from plain ceilings.

As we headed deeper into the old building, I caught sight of another austere-looking monk sweeping the unvarnished floorboards with a rush broom, and somewhere behind me a small bell was striking the hour. A hatch in some faraway chamber banged shut as Nia and I marched behind the bearded novice, our heels clicking on the stone flooring, the loudest thing to be heard and sounding almost profane.

At the end of one long corridor, we passed by the open door of a barely furnished refectory where twenty or thirty men of various ages were silently eating bread and soup, and in a distant room a man began to loudly recite a monotonous prayer in Latin, which felt more superstitious than holy. I didn't get the impression that the cloistered building was a place of retreat or contemplation, more like some cold anteroom of purgatory that felt like it was a very long way from heaven. I wouldn't have liked to have to stay in the place for long. The monk showed us into a plain room with a few comfortable but threadbare armchairs, and a small dining table.

The walls of the monastic drawing room were made up of floor-to-ceiling wooden bookshelves, each ledge laden with volumes of dusty, leather-bound, ancient books and religious texts. The young monk bowed at me again and asked us to wait whilst he fetched Tolotos with our food. Nia dropped down in one of the armchairs and clicked her fingers at me. "Cigarette." I tossed her the pack and my lighter and walked across the room and stared out of one of the grimy windows, the view outside looking as bleak as it did indoors. Uninspired by the desolate view I joined Garbi, sitting down in the chair next to her and lit up as well. If in doubt or bored, smoke; that's the soldier's way, I thought to myself.

When Tolotos crept into the room his shifty blue eyes were already regarding us with justifiable suspicion. Strangers were rare visitors to any monastery. Women rarer still. Policemen who knew of a certain monk's nasty-little past, as rare as wooden horse shit. The little toad nervously carried a tray, two earthenware bowls of soup and a dish of olives were set at its centre, a thin plate containing a stack of dry-looking bread perched at one edge. He rested the tray on the table and raised his hand in benediction, crossed the air above our heads and said: "God bless all here."

I stood up. Nia stayed smoking in the armchair.

Tolotos smiled at Nia. "Could I trouble you for a cigarette?" Garbi gave him a dirty look then shot a finger at me.

"He's the one you should be asking."

I tapped a smoke out of the packet, handed it over to Tolotos and cranked the wheel on my lighter. I watched him nervously puff the cigarette into life.

He stared into the flame for a moment before sitting down in the chair I'd just got out of. He gestured his head toward me, a shifty smirk curling from his cracked lips.

"The pistol that you'll no doubt be carrying underneath your jacket. I assume it's loaded, even in a house of God?"

"There wouldn't be much point in carrying it if it wasn't loaded."

Tolotos was silent for a moment. He looked thoughtfully at the glowing ember at the end of his cigarette for a moment then returned his gaze back to me. "Cigarettes and bullets. Both of them so small and yet so efficient. If only we spent more time using one more than the other, life would be far less complicated, don't you think?" Tolotos cocked another nervous grin at me.

"Perhaps." I took a couple of paces towards the monk and let the tip of my shoe rest on top of the bare toes that were sticking out of the end of his sandal.

"In my experience bullets don't care about the targets they find." The joy went out of Tolotos' face as if someone had clicked off a light. I took a step back, lifting the sole of my shoe off his foot and watched his Adam's apple nervously sink and rise in his throat before he looked up into my face.

"You are welcome to stay the night in our humble quarters, Major. The Abbot reminded me when I told him of your request for sanctuary that it is a true monk's duty to offer refuge. For the Bible reminds us to entertain strangers." Tolotos' eyes lowered toward the floor, his lips muttering the words, "*for thereby some have entertained angels unawares*" then was silent for a moment. When he moved his head back up toward me, it was in an avian sort of way, staring like some scared carrion crow. I listened to him clear his throat before he uttered anymore of his spiel. "Hebrews chapter thirteen, verse two".

I took a breath before inching back toward Tolotos. As I

moved, I saw him veil his eyes again and flinch in his seat. I wagged a finger at the monk's face. "I don't need to remind you, I'm a very long way from being an angel."

Tolotos continued to fidget uneasily for a moment, his gaze still averting my own, now staring into space, his pupils suddenly becoming like black marbles, devoid of expression as though he had deliberately floated away into a serene environment that neither I nor Nia could see. A few seconds later I watched him blink back to life then rest one hand on the arm of the chair before smiling up at me. "Only God knows the truth of a man, my son."

That unruffled, cloistral beam was enough to send my hands flying down toward Tolotos' scrawny throat. Instead of grasping for his jugular I snagged hold of the front of his woollen cowl, yanking him up out of the seat, the cigarette flying out of his fingers and bouncing across the wood-panelled floor. I pulled his petrified face close toward mine and felt his fetid breath blow hot against my check.

"I know your truth better than any God, Tolotos, so you can cut the holy crap. Just remember who stowed you away in this consecrated shithouse in the first place. I could very easily drag you back to the same gutter I hauled you out of. See how long it takes for your old friends to come sniffing after you." I waited for him to speak but he didn't. I knotted Tolotos' rough monastic tunic in my fists, drawing him closer toward me. "By the time I'd dumped you in this place your name was already sullied by charges of rape, kidnap and child molestation. God may have forgiven you. But I certainly haven't." I tightened my grip on Tolotos' smock and felt the pulse in my right wrist beating. "Apart from the Abbott and the man who collected us from our room and brought us here, have you spoken to anyone else about us being here?" Tolotos scratched at the row of moles that seemed to leak from his eye and shook his head. I kept my eyes on his, watched the perspiration prickling across his face. He took a sideswipe glance across at Nia whose silent presence was clearly unnerving the monk as much as my strong-arming. I tightened my grip on the fabric of Tolotos' habit, his attention fixing back on me. "Made any telephone calls to anyone? Tolotos shook his head again, a vein pulsing in his temple, his watery eyes now staring at the floor. His voice crackled when he spoke, his speech solemn, a fog of body odour wafting off his skin. "Only the Abbott has access to the telephone."

I released my grip on Tolotos' tunic and pushed him away. He stumbled backwards on his heels, his calves knocking against the edge of the armchair.

"If you want to remain hidden here with your dirty little secrets, safe from the monsters out there in the real world, then you're going to have to keep working off that old debt you still owe me."

Tolotos' face turned the colour of a toadstool, his voice quavering as though he did not want to hear the answer to his own question. "What do you want, Remis?"

"Just a little Christian good turn, that's all."

The monk shuffled defensively and nodded his head, his eyes flat and somehow empty. The only thing they were telling me was what I already knew; that the bastard couldn't be trusted. I watched him flinch as I moved towards him. I rested the palm of my hand across the nape of his neck and felt the heat rise off his clammy skin. I pinched at his flesh with my thumb and forefinger and guided him toward the door.

"I need to get that car outside out of sight until the morning. Can you do that?"

Tolotos nodded his head. "We have a workshop. It can be safely concealed in there."

"Good." I eased the monk further towards the door, my mouth close to his ear as we walked. "No one is to disturb us this evening, understood?" I got another pliant bow. "You are not to speak about us to any of your fellow brethren, nor for that matter to anyone else. We were never even here. Got it?" Tolotos was about to bob his head again, tightening my pincer brace around his collar stopped him in his tracks. I pushed him out into the hall and watched as he began to flounder along the corridor.

"And."

The sneaky monk stopped dead in his tracks, his body swaying slightly.

"No God or prayer will save you if you try to cross me."

Tolotos didn't turn around but I could see the rigidity in his back and the blood rising in his neck like the red fluid in a thermometer.

CHAPTER
THIRTY-EIGHT

THAT NASTY LITTLE BASTARD TOLOTOS WAS PLAYING HEAVILY ON MY mind, as was the thought of what I was going to do with all that gold sitting on the other side of the room.

Priests and I hadn't had what you'd call a happy history. Nia hated the church and clerics, especially when monks were hiding the kind of dirty secrets that Michael Tolotos had stashed away. When you grow up in an orphanage or children's home, a man of the cloth is usually the first person you do your level best to stay out of the way of. I knew that the phony monk wasn't to be trusted. I scoured my memory, dredging up Tolotos' previous unsavoury criminal form in my head. In his time, he'd been both pimp and predator. Informer and Judas, incriminating or denouncing the rich or poor to meet his own grasping and aberrant ends. He was a sneak of the lowest order and in the past, I'd made good use of his duplicitous, snake-in-the-grass nature. Over the years, he's assisted me to fit up, frame, bribe and coerce anyone the state saw fit to manipulate or break. A filthy beast, willing to drag his victims into the gutter on my say-so, just as long as he earned his thirty pieces of silver on the way down.

When Tolotos found himself on a government hit list, I'd foolishly stepped forward to save his scrawny, worthless neck. I bundled him off the streets and found him asylum with the brothers of Agia Anastasia. Monastic vows were taken. A lifelong commitment to God had been sworn. The pederast was now a priest. But such oaths and covenants didn't fool me. A leopard doesn't change its spots, and Michael Tolotos was not to be trusted.

Knowing the kind of man he was, had it deterred me from seeking out Tolotos to give me a helping hand?

Had it fuck.

Was I deluding myself? Was I banking on age-old fear and intimidation to keep the shady monk on his toes? You betcha.

Deluding myself is what I do best.

I sat staring at that bullion-filled luggage until my eyes hurt. I knew walking away with the gold had compounded an already messy situation. But, in the heat of the moment, legging it with a dead man's fortune seemed like a good idea.

If I'd have had any sense, I'd have left the gold where it was, bundled Nia into the Mercedes and then headed for the Turkish border. I had a couple of fake passports and enough money to keep the wolf from the door for the next six months. In less than 24 hours we could have been on a train heading towards France or Spain. Out of the grasp of gunmen and my possibly duplicitous and vengeful employer.

But, like the fool I am I didn't run. I didn't look out for Number One, nor did I think for a moment how things could pan out for Nia. I'd determined to stick with the case. To do my job. But at what cost? It wasn't just my own life that was on the line, I'd been cajoled into dragging an innocent along for the ride too. Although I'd never told her as much, I saw Nia as a kindred spirit, who, like me, was a loner with no family. My relationship to her could, at best, be described as that of a corrupt father figure. She often jokingly referred to me as 'Uncle Michail', especially if we were in the company of those with a prying nature. We never spoke of friendship nor, over the years, had either of us looked for anything that could have suggested intimacy. Mutual trust had been found years back when she'd asked me to teach her to shoot a pistol, a skill she showed great aptitude for. As well as having a keen eye and a steady hand, Nia was adept with a throwing knife and could handle herself in a fistfight.

I'd gone on to employ those unique talents to great success, and on more than one occasion Nia had been a useful and very capable asset. The Provost had known that when he'd advised me to take Nia along for the ride. Callas was all too aware that Garbi may well have proven useful if I found myself in a tight spot.

In the past, I knew that Nia understood the risks posed in undertaking a job for me. She knew the level of threat and danger that was on the cards when I came knocking at her door. She was no fool and I knew she could look after herself. But in drawing her into this latest bloody mess I was starting to think I'd crossed a line. I'd now put her in more jeopardy than she deserved.

And if she knew the truth about what was really going on she'd certainly agree on one thing ...

That I was a cheap, lying, manipulative pig.

Shit ... friendships have flourished on less.

Had I known the kind of trouble I'd have been getting both of us into when sat in the Provost's office, gazing into the dark and deceitful heart of my master's soul, would I have turned away to protect Garbi from harm?

Probably not.

I never had before.

That pain-in-the-arse adage about those who ignore the past being doomed to repeat it – they wrote that bullshit for me. If I'd have considered all the torments that had gone before, reflected on the double-dealing the Provost was capable of, took time to reflect on the cruelties, the humiliations and shame he'd metered out to others and pondered upon the ruinous and brutal deeds I'd undertaken on his behalf, would I have acted differently to my superiors' orders that day? With knowledge aforethought, would I have said to Callas, "Nope, this assignment's not for me, thanks sir, give it to another chump. I'll preserve what little dignity and sanity I have left, thanks."

Alas, I was still walking that road of unhappy destiny and I was dragging an innocent along for company too.

Why?

Because I'm an idiot and worse, a stubborn one.

CHAPTER THIRTY-NINE

The past is no insubstantial, thready thing, sunlight slanting through shutters into cool rooms, pools, and standards of mist adrift at roadsides, memories that flutter from our hands the minute we open them. Rather, it is all too substantial, bluntly physical, like a boulder or cement block growing ever denser, ever larger, there behind us, displacing and pushing us forward.

And yes, in its mindless, rocklike, solid, unstoppable way, it pursues us.

Michael Tolotos had once again become an unwelcome presence in my life. A freakish reminder of darker days from both my own and Nia's past. Long dead and buried in my mind, the former predatory flesh-peddler was now at the forefront of my thoughts again. Once met, never forgotten. The man gave off an unnatural aura of depravity. He was fox-like; cunning and sly, remorseless and cruel. Neither his cassock nor the glass rosary beads I'd seen him grasping between his fingers earlier in the evening, nor the vows of chastity, poverty, and obedience that he'd taken, hide those starkly miserable truths. Being around Tolotos earlier had brought back all those old grim memories of the monster I'd happily placed into exile. No one who ever stood up close and looked into Tolotos' eyes ever quite forgot them. They flared with an icy light for no reason, looked back at you with a reptilian, lidless hunger that made you feel a sense of sexual ill ease, regardless of your gender. Canine orbs skilled in deception, the cold gaze they omitted, never to be trusted.

I was tired, unshaven, my mind going over everything that had happened, weary of allowing old foes and ghosts to dictate how things would play out, so I got off my ass and decided to do something about it. It was a little after four-thirty. I pulled on my coat, collected the two cases and crept quietly out of the damp cell into a cold corridor. Nia was dead to the world, asleep on the cot, a rough grey blanket pulled high over her head.

I wanted to be away from the abbey at first light, put some distance between Tolotos, and any plot or angle he may have been cooking up, and find someplace safe to stash the gold ingots before Brigadier Grivas, his lacky Kampouris or the men who had dispatched Pierre Roth were back on to me.

As I lugged the two heavy cases down the hallway, I was greeted by the sonorous sound of bells beginning to peal, commanding the brothers of the abbey to early morning Lauds prayer. Even for an outright atheist like me, I had to admit that the inside of the abbey was magnificent. I headed toward the main entrance of the building; only the occasional muffled cough disturbed the cloistered hush. The overpowering scent of burning candles and musty incense hung heavy all around me.

Before heading outside, I quickly turned to look back at the pulpit and altar area. A handful of the monks were already sat on hand-carved teak wooden pews, their heads bowed in silent prayer. I quietly nudged open the huge door with the toe of my shoe and, before heading out caught sight of the celestial scenes on the walls either side of the door. Paintings depicting Christ's passion in the garden of Gethsemane and his ordeal by scourge, mockery, spittle and finally crucifixion; images to make the devout swallow in reverence and trepidation.

Outside, dawn was about to break. The courtyard was surfaced with red flagstones, dead leaves somersaulted across the ground. Their dry rustle suggesting a light frost in the night. A few chickens were up and scratching around the abbey's gardens, the air, cool, full of moths and the sweet smell of oregano and rosemary.

I headed toward the rear of the abbey, and at the foot of a long path cut between thick laurel bushes, found the workshop Tolotos had spoken of earlier. It looked more beat-up garage than monastic sanctum and, despite the early hour, I could see a light was burning inside. I took a couple of paces backward and heaved both cases against the trunk of a mastic tree. My hand was in my jacket, on the butt of my gun. I worked the slide, thumbed the hammer back, aware that my clacking heels could be a liability. I began to walk quietly, inching closer toward the old building.

A sign in Latin above the door read, *Hic opus Illic Praemium hic certamen Illic coronae.*

Here is the work, there the reward; here the struggle, there the crowns.

The door was already open a crack, and, using my foot I eased it open farther and went on in, with my gun leading the way.

I found Michael Tolotos on his hands and knees with his head stuck inside the passenger seat of the car.

The Mercedes was parked over an inspection pit lit with an electric light illuminating its underside. The car looked as if a small grenade had exploded inside it. The bonnet and boot and all the doors were open. The spare tyre was on the hay-strewn floor. The leather panels had been removed from inside the doors, the rocker panels under the doors opened up.

"Find anything of interest, Michael?"

Tolotos, startled, shot backwards, out from the motor's interior. He turned slowly and fixed me with a sidelong glance, didn't say anything, just panicked. He looked like a scared animal, one which had the traces of a plan half-formed in its head, but which went against all its survival instincts. He was staring at the gun in my hand as he stumbled back on to his feet, his knees popping, and took a few tentative steps toward me, pointing at the debris around him.

"This was a bad idea, I know." Tolotos' eyes were red around the rims, the whites threaded with tiny veins. He raised a trembling hand to his face and began fingering at his cheek as though he had toothache, his scheming eyes quickly darting from clocking the partially opened door behind me to focussing back onto my face. I closed in on him, coming to a standstill when I was in reaching distance of the nervous monk.

"You've had better, I'm sure." I gave a nod toward the car. "Wanna tell me what you were looking for?"

"Insurance."

"Against what?"

"Any unpleasant demands, perhaps?"

"Demands? The only thing I asked for was sanctuary."

Tolotos nodded. "And that was granted." The monk choked back a grimace. "I feared you may have requested favours of which I could not satisfy." The Janus-faced monk flashed a nervous smile at me. His stained, chipped front teeth just breaking through parched, treacherous lips.

"If you are seeking leverage against me or reward, Michael, I'd suggest a sly root through my luggage would be to your advantage."

"It had crossed my mind to take a quick look whilst you were having breakfast."

"Oh, I bet it did." I inched a step closer. Near enough now to see the monk trembling. "I don't eat breakfast."

Tolotos looked at the ground for a moment, then locked those sneaky peepers back on me. I watched as he rolled his tongue over dried lips. When he finally spoke, his words came at me; edgy: "Can't you see, you backed me into this corner, Remis. I've not heard from you in years. Not a sniff." Tolotos held out his arms, palms open in a desperate attempt to somehow placate me from doing him any harm. "And ... and then you turn up out of the blue. Asking to hideout, bringing that whore with you. I knew it had to be bad news." Tolotos gestured with his hand at the mess he'd created. "The kind of trouble I know clings to you, generally involves two things."

"And what would they be?"

"Death and money."

"And you were looking for the latter, yes?"

Tolotos shook his head slowly. Swallowed hard. "I give you my word, I had no intention of stealing from you." The monk gulped again. "Just to try to gain the upper hand."

"And we both know how reliable your word is, don't we Michael?"

Tolotos tried to clear his throat. He shook his head and gave me his best attempt at a hard stare. "Look, whatever the real reason is for you coming here, we both know you'd have killed me before you left this place."

"And, what makes you think that?"

Tolotos laughed. "Come on, we both know a leopard doesn't change its spots."

"Well, I can't argue with that." I smiled at Tolotos and holstered the Walther. I saw the monk breathe a sudden sigh of relief, his perspiration-soaked face contorting for a moment, as though he'd just fled a burning building. He brushed at his nose with one knuckle, huffed air out a nostril, flicked his eyes off my face then looked at nothing, all with the same degree of thought or its absence. He trained his focus back toward me, raising his head ever so slightly, so that his jaw stuck out an inch or two higher than usual, the skin around his scrawny neck growing taut. He was about to speak again but stopped when he saw me take another pace toward him. Whatever Tolotos was about to say to me had been lost to him. Snatched away when in that briefest of moments, the tumblers inside his warped little head finally fell into place. That's when Michael Tolotos realised that he was about to die.

Before he had chance to fight or flee, I'd placed all my weight down on my right foot and in a split second my right hand had shot up in a three-fingered strike that stabbed exactly in the centre of Tolotos' larynx.

I watched the monk's head snap backwards, and then immediately drop forward, his face seeming to burn with a fear he was unable to express. He rocked on the tips of his heels for a moment, his neck twisting from side to side, his unsteady hands rising in a futile attempt to clutch at his snapped gullet.

I heard him make a grinding noise in his throat then saw a thin layer of blood begin to ooze from his mouth and line the edges of his lips. As he fell toward me, I unleashed a follow up blow, slamming the edge of my hand across the side of Totolos's exposed neck; all my strength meeting the man's now descending weight, holding it fractionally so that my final throat punch, another right-hander, pushed Tolotos backwards again.

He dropped to the ground fast and hard.

I stood and watched the life quickly drain out of his twitching carcass, confident in the knowledge that a bastard like Michael Tolotos would not present himself to me again, at least not outside the bright edges of my sleep.

CHAPTER FORTY

My body felt as if I'd just touched a live electrical wire. A familiar, hair-trigger reaction. The one which always kicked in after I'd snuffed out a life.

Now the clock was against me. No time for introspection or to mull over my brutal act. My next reflex was to haul Tolotos' limp corpse off the ground and throw it into the boot of the Mercedes.

And as I was doing that, I'd already decided on what I was going to do with the two cases of luggage filled with gold.

I headed back outside, heaved both bags into the workshop, then began snatching the bullion out of the rugged leather holdalls, placing them inside the stolen motor: eighty ingots jammed side by side inside the rocker panels or stacked one on top of the other underneath the back seat. I put the bars into every spare inch of the car's opened-up bodywork. Totolos's fruitless attempt to uncover either rich bounties or the dirt on me had offered up a simple solution to conceal the gold. Concealing a motor, even a big bucket like the Merc would be a damn sight easier than trying to go underground with a couple of cases filled with stolen bullion. I knew that whoever it belonged to, they'd be desperate to get it back and equally hungry to rid themselves of the problem of Nia and myself. I knew the gold had to be somehow linked to Konrad Tafel's murder, I just didn't know how.

Stashing the precious metal had been simple, putting the car back together, after Tolotos had ransacked the damn thing, took up time I could have done without losing. I kept one ingot back, wrapping it in a piece of cloth, dropped it on the passenger seat then screwed the rocker plates on top of the gold bars and put the inside panels back on the doors.

I glanced at my wristwatch; it was a little after six-thirty. First light had hit, and I knew the monastery would be starting to come alive. There'd be curious monks who'd soon notice one of their brethren was missing. I didn't want to be around when they started asking awkward questions. I quickly washed myself in a sink at the back of the workshop, straightened my tie, brushed off my suit then started back toward the abbey to collect Nia.

I'd expected Garbi to move like a cat when I tried to shake her from sleep. No such luck. The first couple of attempts to bring her to life, I listened to Nia swear and mutter under her breath. I gave her another firm nudge and before slumbering pussycat became savage tiger.

"Fuck off!"

I snatched the corner of the blanket and threw it across the cell.

"Get your arse up." I picked her jacket up off the floor. Threw it at her head. Nia's head shot off the bunk pillow, her gluey eyes trying to focus in on me. "We're leaving now." Garbi opened her mouth, a string of obscenities about to be unleashed. I kicked the foot of the bunk. “Save your bullshit for later.” I yanked open the door and heard Nia chunter to herself as she swung her legs off the mattress.

She put on her boots, grabbed her jacket and followed me out into the hall. She was cursing and mumbling profanities under her breath until we got back to the car.

I opened up the passenger door, stuck my head inside and unwrapped the gold bar I’d left on the seat. I turned to Nia and pointed at the ingot.

“Take a look.”

I watched Garbi’s brow furrow, she hesitated, but only for a second then strode toward the vehicle. I watched her clock the gold.

“What? Are you telling me that this fucking heap’s owned by Rumpelstiltskin?”

I shook my head. Said nothing. Nia sniffed the air as if smelling for trouble then reached into the passenger seat and withdrew the gold bar, hefting it in her hand.

“Must way at least ten kilos.”

I reached across, snatching the ingot out of her fingers. “More like twelve”

Nia whistled. “At sixty-five dollars an ounce that’s gotta be worth seventeen thousand dollars?”

“When did you become such an expert on international gold prices?”

Nia shrugged. “I don’t just get paid in cash, Major. Worth remembering next time you’re in my debt.” She pointed at the ingot. “That the only bar?”

I shook my head again, slower this time.”

“How many?”

“Twenty.”

"Fuck me." Nia broke out a smile and kicked at the edge of one of the front tyres with the toe of her shoe. "Where's the rest?"

I tapped the rear door panel with a couple of fingers. "In here and under the rear deck, and the rockers."

Garbi grinned and rested the crook of her arm on the roof of the car. "And before it ended up inside of here it was stowed away in those flashy two suitcases, yeah?"

"Yeah."

Garbi pointed at the gold bar in my hand. "Somebody'll be wanting to get that and the rest of their belongings back."

"Then we best not let the rightful owner find it, right?"

Nia grimaced for a moment, before a keen eye took another look at the gold in my hand. She gave me a curt nod. "Right."

I wrapped the ingot back up in the rag, opened up the back door and tossed it inside, then curled a finger toward Garbi.

"Follow me. I've got something else to show you."

I walked to the rear of the Mercedes, popped open the boot. Garbi followed, stood next to me and peered inside.

"Oh, Jesus." Nia spat at her feet before eyeballing me. "You gotta be fucking kidding me."

"I found him sniffing around the car. He didn't give me any other choice."

Nia began to shake her head. "There's no fucking way on God's clean earth that I'm gonna dig a hole to put that piece of shit in. You hear me?"

"I hear you." I slammed the lid of the boot down and patted the paintwork with the palm of my hand. "There'll be no cold, hard ground for our friend Michael."

I took a couple of cigarettes, lit both and handed one to Nia, and watched her inhale deeply before beginning to laugh through a thick plume of smoke. I walked around the other side of the car, opened up and gestured my head toward the workshop's huge wooden double doors. "Get those for me."

Garbi took another pull on her cigarette. I got behind the wheel and watched Nia pull open the doors. I turned the key in the ignition, fired up the engine and listened to the old beast cough and splutter as Garbi climbed in next to me. She closed her door too, looked at the leather covered panel for a moment then shifted her gaze over to me. "You do know you've got the better part of six and a half million rattling around in this shitbox."

I pushed down on the clutch and put the car into first gear. "Then the steering is going to feel real heavy." I raised the clutch to the point that the engine began to growl. Nia wound down the window and took another hit on her cigarette, letting the smoke escape from the corner of her mouth.

"Never mind the fucking steering. Think how much petrol we're gonna use carting both a stiff and all this gold around."

CHAPTER

FORTY-ONE

THE SUNRISE WAS SLOW IN COMING. THE SKY OVERHEAD WAS CLEAR, but there were clouds far away and they lit up pink and orange. Nia remained silent as I drove. She occupied her time either chain smoking or nodding off every ten miles or so. I kept off the main arteries that would lead back to Salonica, driving along back roads and isolated mountain passes, parts of remote Macedonia that, whilst familiar to me, were not areas I'd travelled through often. Thirty miles north of the abbey, just outside of the village of Vasiloudi, we crossed the Vardar river via an old arched stone bridge. I pulled over underneath an overhang of dense Carob trees close to the water's edge.

The Vardar was faster and bigger than I'd remembered, at least thirty metres across, about half as deep and as brown as my leather belt.

Nia threw her cigarette out of the car window and then wound it up again. She scowled at me like a chess grand master who was about to make a winning move, turned her head back to face the bridge, and pointed toward the river.

"This where you're intending to ditch Tolotos' worthless carcass, yes?"

"Uh-huh." I nodded. "Seems as good a place as any, don't you think?"

Nia shrugged. "What I think is that you can dump that miserable piece of shit on your own. That's what I think." Garbi wiped at her nose with the back of her hand. "You clipped him, you dump the stiff."

I knew better than to argue with her. As I got out of the car, I heard Nia light up another smoke and mutter another obscenity under her breath. The road in either direction was free of traffic as I walked around the bonnet of the Mercedes and looked down the slope at the side of the road toward the fast-moving water. The Vardar's a tidal river that swelled up on the banks each day and receded with the influences of the moon.

The surface was swollen and churning with mud, leaves and tree branches scattered by high winds that had swept through the area overnight. A rowboat was tied to the root of a rotting elm a few feet down the bank. On the far side of the river was a weathered boathouse with sagging wood decking that was slowly eroding into the water. Thankfully, there wasn't a soul around. Not even a solitary fisherman hoping to catch an early morning bite. I turned and took a moment to rifle along a short stretch of the verge and undergrowth next to the road, searching for a couple of sizable rocks, the type best used to weigh a bag of bones down with. A few minutes later I was resting the last of three chunks of hefty limestone on to the parapet of the bridge.

I walked back to the boot of the car and popped the trunk.

As the lid lifted, I was immediately hit by the familiar stink of death. Michael Tolotos' lay on his side, sunken eyes still open, glazed over with a thin milky film. I reached inside, knotting the coarse, black, woollen fabric of the monk's cowl in one hand, and lifting each leg out of the boot with the other. I took a deep breath and heaved the corpse up out of the trunk, balancing the already rigidifying remains against my chest for a moment before taking hold of the upper legs and unceremoniously slinging the body over my right shoulder.

With the road ahead and behind me still clear I didn't waste any time in heading back along the bridge and dropping the body onto the wide slab balustrade. I placed two of the limestone boulders in the deep scoop pockets of Tolotos cowl and the final one twisted inside the hood, then shoved the corpse over the side.

I watched Michael Tolotos' remains fall the sixty or so feet into the water and quickly sink without trace. No committal prayers. No minute's silence. Good riddance to bad rubbish, was the best I could muster. I turned and leant against the side of the bridge's rough stonework, stared up at the foreboding mountain range that was part of the vast *Kedrinos Lofos* national park, knowing that I had to journey up into its outlying, lonely heart.

I remembered the first time I'd seen the fabled promontories, back when I was first on manoeuvres during my army training. Back then, I'd tried to find words to describe it. But I couldn't. Nothing had prepared me. No books. No teachers. Not even the officers who'd taken us up into its mysterious interior to learn to survive in the wilderness for days on end. I heard a thousand stories, but none could describe the place.

The *Kedrinos Lofos* must be witnessed from deep within its heart to be understood. I'd been there, born witness to its savage and hostile landscape. And now gazing back up into its malevolent peaks I understood it less than when I first cast eyes on the place all those years before. Some called it the Greek alps. Others, the dark kingdom of death, but those phrases were invented by scholars at universities, surrounded by the illusion of order and the fantasy of right and wrong. To know the *Lofos*, you had to endure it, trek its thin paths and lose yourself in its bleak hinterland. If caught in its backwoods or snow-capped crags, there's nothing else you can do but climb, scrabble and bleed to get out. And if you're unlucky, you fall or drown, or are left for dead in its tors and rivers.

If you survive the *Kedrinos Lofos,* its true name becomes clear.

It is Hell. And there are demons everywhere.

And if what I was looking up at was Hell, and I was about to return to its unwelcoming domain, then I must be a demon, too.

And knowing that, I too must already be dead.

I trudged back to the car; our next destination already carved into my mind. I sank behind the wheel and turned the key in the ignition. I looked back up toward the alpine terrain.

"Where now?" Nia said, her voice little more than a crackle.

I pointed upward. "Into the mountains ... a place called Sephardim."

"And what's there?"

"A dangerous man."

Nia wound down her window and spat out a wad of white phlegm.

"Christ, not another?"

The remote, sparsely populated alpine village of Chortiatis stood over six hundred metres, tucked into the sloping, barren terrain of Mount Chortiatis, from which it took its name. In times of antiquity, both mountain and town were known as *Cissus* and the Greek author and poet Homer wrote that the infamous Thracian king, *Cisseus* had once been ruler of the rugged and inhospitable realm.

The dangerous man I needed to see was Jonas Zacharia.

Zacharia was a soldier of fortune. An arms trafficker and assassin. Another unwelcome ghost from my past whom I thought I'd long been well rid of. For as long as I could remember, from time to time, I did him favours, and Jonas paid me back in kind. I hadn't seen Zacharia since deciding to go from crooked to only slightly bent, so it would be a tricky business, me asking for a favour today when I might well have to turn him down tomorrow. But the way I saw it, I had to live through today in order to suffer the ramifications of later.

It took a little over an hour to traverse the serpentine pass and by the time we reached Chortiatis it was a little before midday. There were a few dwellings dotted about, mainly rundown hillside goat farmers' abodes, joined together by a series of stone-paved donkey tracks. *Sephardim,* Zacharia's nest, was set back amongst a thick pine grove. The concrete monstrosity looked totally out of place even tucked away amongst all the trees. The building resembled a military bunker more than residential mountain retreat. There were no guards or doormen at the gates or inside the grounds of the utilitarian bastion. The fort-like building didn't have a house number, nor did it display the property's title on the rampart-like retaining wall that ran along the length of the imposing building.

I drove inside and headed up the dusty cement drive, pulling up underneath a series of wall-mounted security cameras. *Sephardim* held its secrets below ground, with most of its living quarters dug out of the rock below our feet. The walls inside were concrete, at least thirty-inches thick, and some I'd been told were lined with copper. The rooms were sound and transmission-proof. There was food and fresh water to last for six months and an armoury that would have been the envy of most NATO countries. Few were ever foolish enough to enter without summons or assignation. I was going out on a limb, pushing my luck to try and get an audience with the devil inside. I saw Nia give the grey-walled building a dirty look as she opened up the passenger door and went to climb out.

"You might want to stay here."

Nia ignored me, got out of the car, stretching out her arms and rolling her head to shake the tension of the journey out of her limbs and muscles. She threaded her fingers together, cracked the joints and gestured her head toward the open double doors. "Lead the way."

"The man I want to see doesn't take kindly to smart mouths."

Nia winked at me. "Then I'll try and be on my best behaviour, Major."

"Try hard." I reached over onto the back seat to retrieve the gold ingot wrapped in the cloth. Once out of the car I unwrapped the gold bar, dropped it into my jacket pocket and made my way toward the bunker.

Nia spat on the ground and followed me.

We entered the stronghold by way of its front door, which was, surprisingly, always left open to the elements. Inside was a small plain, chalk-white lobby. No vase of flowers. No framed prints on the walls. Just an alabaster corridor on the lefthand side, which we headed for. At the end of the hallway, we turned right, following another slender passage past five doors to rooms that I knew would be locked. It was only the unremarkable sixth door that had any life behind it.

I knocked and waited. Thirty seconds went by but I didn't knock again. Another half minute passed, and I waited patiently. A few seconds later there came a loud click. The portal opened on its own and we walked in.

The antechamber to the dangerous man's inner sanctum was as bare as a room could get while still serving a function. The was a stainless-steel desk with a no-frills swivel chair behind it and another folding chair set up in one corner. Behind the desk was a black, leather-padded, seven feet by four, casted, bullet-proof door. Above the frame, hung a small Panasonic observation camera.

The were no paintings or photographs on the blanched walls, no carpeting on the unstained but sealed hardwood floor. There weren't any light fixtures, just two high-wattage stand-up lamps set in opposite corners.

Behind the desk, as erect as a high school teacher in a Norman Rockwell painting, an epicene, forty-something, oriental-featured man wearing gold rim glasses and no smile was seated. His black necktie was thin enough to qualify as string and his black dress suit was tight fitting with polished satin lapels.

This man was Tobias Jin.

"Major Remis," he said, neither in greeting nor as a question.

"Mr. Jin."

"You don't have an appointment."

"I didn't have the leisure to make one."

"That's unfortunate." Jin nodded unsympathetically.

I held the Korean doorman's keen gaze as he eyeballed Nia and me.

"I need to see Jonas."

The crisp gatekeeper bobbed his head at me again. I looked away, staring up into the lens of the camera above our heads for a moment then focussing back in on Jin.

"Now."

I liked Jin. He looked righteous sat inside his cramped little room. He had one very important job; to keep undesirables like me out, using whatever means necessary. Tobias Jin was in no way nonplussed by his anonymity. The Korean bodyguard was a hatchet-man whose sole employ and responsibility was to protect an even deadlier killer on the other side of the door I needed to go through.

Even though I liked him, Mr. Jin did not approve of me. I was course and gruff, hard drinking and corrupt. Unpalatable qualities that endeared me to his baneful employer.

There was a black box on Jin's metal desk. There was a small aperture in the top through which light of any primary and secondary hues of the colour wheel could shine. The hole shone a brilliant blue. Jin glanced at it, looked up at the camera above him and let his lip curl slightly.

"Mister Zacharia will see you now."

I heard the electronic click of the locking mechanism snap open on the other side of the door. I headed toward the partially opened portal, Nia tight on my heels.

The Korean held out a slender hand as I passed. Shook his head at Garbi then pointed to the folding chair.

"Just the Major."

I looked back at Nia and gestured toward the seat in the corner. She grimaced back at me and reluctantly surrendered to the offer of the metal chair. I felt my hands tremble with fatigue, my cortex aching as if I had been pounded with a meat-tenderizer.

CHAPTER FORTY-TWO

Where Jin's cubicle was barren and undersized, his boss's grand hall of an office was a study in opulence. Thick burgundy carpets run between royal-blue walls upon which hung Renaissance masterpieces lit from the ceiling by spotlights; artworks which I assumed had been gifted in part payment for services rendered.

Ten steps into the room I passed a fully stocked mahogany bar built into the wall on the right. Across the way, on the left, was an altar carved from a solid block of apple green and white jadeite. This sacred stand was as tall as a man and twice as wide. Images of oriental faces and animal forms, gracefully understated, flowed across the priceless sculpture.

There was no window, no portal to the outside world, but a green, orange, and blue kingfisher with metal-like glistening feathers gave a short, sharp whistle, repeated two or three times as I passed. It was a greeting or possibly a warning, but regardless, the tune subsided before I had taken the final twenty steps to Jonas Zacharia's desk.

He was standing behind a dining-table-sized piece of

furniture made from a single plank of unfamiliar dark wood. On the rare occasions I'd visited his home, Zacharia always stood when I entered the room. Maybe he did that to everyone – I didn't care. He was of medium height with flawless olive skin, black hair, and dark, hard eyes. Known in the underworld as 'Siopí', the Greek word for 'hush', he was a silent and ruthless killer, who commanded huge fees for the hits he undertook. Rumour had it that Jonas could hide naked in a snowstorm or talk a blushing bride out of her virginity on her wedding day to get to his target, at least that's how the stories have it. He never missed, never failed, that much was fact. If he had your name scribbled on the back of his bus ticket, you were as good as dead.

To the casual observer he might have seemed to be of a mild temper, but many of the worst monsters I've known were like that: pleasant even in the regrettable act of murder. His hair, which was neither long nor short, was perfectly coiffed, and his suit would have turned Christian Dior's head.

"Have a seat, Major Remis." If quicksilver could talk it would sound like him.

The chair I preferred, Jonas had once told me, was an ancient Greek Klismos, carved ornately from a single huge piece of olive trunk.

"It was used in sacrifices."

There was a tray that led down from the rear of the seat to carry the blood to a gold urn. Knowing Jonas's ignoble profession, I must have looked uncomfortable hearing about the chair's bloody history. I remember the killer grinning at me. "Don't worry Remis, it was used exclusively on virgins." He had said.

"Thanks for seeing me at short notice."

"What can I do for you, Major?" Zacharia was all about business. I may have been granted an audience into his inner sanctum based on an unspoken and fragile mutual respect, but Jonas didn't care about my health or the kind of day I was having. I took my cigarettes out of my jacket pocket, lit one and slid the packet across the desk.

"I need a special kind of rifle." I watched the assassin take a deep breath and then a cigarette. He sat back, lit it, and inhaled gratefully. I didn't like to tell him the coffin nail in his mouth came my way via a German spy master. "The kind of firearm only a few gifted marksmen could easily lay their hands on."

Zacharia's eyes sought mine through the smoke. "You flatter me."

I knew that the arse-kissing wasn't necessary. But at the same time, I was feeling a little uncomfortable around Zacharia; maybe more than a little. He knew a hundred ways to kill a man and dozens of techniques to make the body disappear. Buttering him up a little wouldn't do any harm, I hoped.

"I'm in a jam. The kind of firepower I'm carrying isn't going to help me out of it."

Zacharia nodded. "Your plight must be considerable, Major. A man of your notable resources rarely requires assistance. Over what range will the weapon be fired?"

"I'm not too sure yet, but probably more than six hundred feet."

"Silenced?"

"Most definitely."

I took the gold ingot out of my pocket and pushed it across the desk. Zacharia ignored the bullion bar. "There'd be another five of those, offered in gratitude." For a long, hard minute, the killer stared at me. It was like watching war. Finally, he cleared his throat. "If I help you, will such goodwill leave an unwelcome trail back to my door?"

I shook my head. "It will not."

Zacharia shrugged. He took out a handkerchief from the top pocket of his jacket, leant across and covered the ingot, quickly drawing it across the polished desktop. He placed the bar into a drawer at his side and got to his feet. "Let's resume this conversation down in the pedío volís." There was no friendliness to his icy tone. The statement a command, not an invitation.

Zacharia led me through a door at the rear of his office, down a spiral staircase then through a further two thickly panelled, soundproofed, double-winged doors into the *pedío volís*, a huge underground firing range. Large stainless steel cabinets lined one wall with the rest encased in thick insulation. The only furniture was a waist-high wooden bench that was littered with guns, the only decoration, the human silhouette paper targets attached to wire pulleys at the furthest end of the room.

I looked around the shooting gallery and whistled approvingly. "Now I can see why you decamped all the way up here. You could let a mortar off in here and no one would hear it."

"I came here for the anonymity, not necessarily for the peace and quiet."

"So, you don't miss the old hussle of the city? Perhaps occasionally clamour to get back to civilisation?"

Zacharia gave me a cold stare. "Civilisation? What, here in

Greece? You must be joking." The assassin shook his head at me despondently. "I'm up here in the wilds for good reason. I believe our cities have weakened us as a species. There are no consequences there. Step onto the streets of London, Paris, Athens, even your precious Salonica, without looking and the car merely stops or swerves, the only consequence, an angry driver. But up here? Out in the wilderness, in these peaks above us, there can be no mistakes. Because *here* doesn't care. The rivers don't care if you can swim. The snake doesn't care how much you love your wife or children. And the wolf has no interest in your dreams. If you fail to beat the current, you will drown. If you get too close, you will be bitten. If you are too weak, you will be eaten. It's a simple as that."

"Sounds just like the city to me."

Zacharia waved off my flippant remark. He made his way over to the bench and glided a hand across the various firearms laid out on top. "Fancy a work-out, Major?"

I approached the counter. "What do you suggest?"

My question brought a wry grin to the killer's face. He scanned the tabletop for a moment then picked up a plain-looking automatic pistol, emptying the magazine clip into his hand then quickly re-inserting it into the grip with mindless deftness.

"Nine point two seven Makarov. Straight, blowback action, all steel construction, frame-fixed barrel." Zacharia weighed the pistol in his hand and offered it to me. I took hold of the grip and let my arm fall to my side, allowing myself a moment to get a feel of the gun's heft.

"I know. It's heavy. What can I say? It's Russian. The damn thing's built to last, like one of their tractors. It may be clunky, but it fires like a dream." Zacharia took a couple of paces away from the bench. I turned and stood with my back to the target, swirled around, arm extended, the gun a pointing, accusing finger. I fired off six rounds so fast they sounded like one continuous noise. Zacharia wound in the target and looked at it. The bull was obliterated; the rest of the paper silhouette unmarked.

"Looks like you've still got it, Mikhail." For just a split-second, hearing the assassin refer to me by my Christian name set me on edge, but Zacharia wasn't the kind of man who'd allow me time to get the jitters. He was already bored of my target skills and was quickly moving toward the cabinets behind me. Without hesitation he swung open the shiny doors of one locker to reveal a series of rifles, each one perched on a metal and black felt cradle, one on top of the other, ceiling to floor. Zacharia paused for a moment, viewing each weapon in silence. Finally, he reached inside to retrieve an impressive looking specimen and brought it back to the bench.

"L42A1. Bolt-action sniper rifle. Serial numbers with acid. This model is used by the British Army, Royal Marines, and their Royal Air Force's Regiment." Zacharia stood back. I moved in to get a better look. "It's chambered for the seven point six two NATO cartridge and takes a thirty-two three-point five telescopic sight."

I brushed my hand across the rifle's gleaming walnut stock admiringly. "And the barrel can be suppressed?"

"This one has been modified for a silencer."

I picked up the rifle and was immediately impressed with how light it was. Solid and safe with a wide trigger and ramp front sight. Zacharia inched closer and continued with his enthusiasm for the weapon.

"I can offer you as much ammunition as is required. The

bolt operation is as smooth as silk and the ejection of the case is spot on. The brass is ejected down. Drops close to the ground to aid with policing the case before leaving a final firing position." The killer flashed me a rare grin. "But I don't need to tell you about cleaning up after yourself, do I Major?"

I shook my head, placed the rifle back on the bench and turned to the sleek killer. "Nope, you don't, and neither will the person who'll be firing it."

Zacharia gave me a surprised look. "Then you're not the triggerman?"

"No."

"And you trust whoever will fire it to hit the mark?"

"I have no doubt."

"Very well. Then that concludes our business here today."

"Not quite."

Zacharia's black eyes zoned in on me. He opened out his arms, the whites of his palms facing upward, a thick dark scar running from thumb to little finger across the left hand. "There is something else you require from me?"

"Yeah." I looked back at the cabinets Zacharia had taken the rifle from. "Any chance you have some smoke grenades, a couple of boxes of shotgun shells and a decent pair of binoculars hidden in there?"

Jonas Zacharia lifted his shoulders with indifference. "Perhaps."

I nodded my appreciation and glanced across at the Makarov on the bench and flashed a cheeky grin at the stone-cold killer stood at my side. "And I don't suppose you'd consider throwing that old pile of Russian junk in, would you?"

The two of us stood staring at each other in silence for a

few seconds. Zacharia had already decided on his answer to my question, he just needed a short time for his decision to settle.

Just time enough for me to leave his killing house, go back outside and fetch him five more bars of knocked off Nazi gold.

CHAPTER FORTY-THREE

This time I was sat in the front seat whilst Nia drove. For twenty miles we rode in silence but as we came through another twisting mountain pass she began to speak in a voice so deep it seemed to be coming out of the ground.

"Are you going to tell me where we're going, or do you just want me to drive this fucking heap all the way to Turkey?"

"Kavala."

"And what's there?"

"Resolution."

"What?"

"Just keep driving. I'll tell you what you need to know when we get to Kavala."

"More fucking riddles and orders." She pulled to the roadside sharply, shifted in her seat to face me. Her eyes watery with anger, boring into my own. "Enough of your bullshit! You either level with me now, or I swear to God I'm gonna take this wreck over the edge of the next fucking cliff we come too."

"We need to keep moving."

"We move when you've been straight with me."

I dummied up. Held Nia's aggressive gaze in my own. Nia slammed the palm of her hand on the top of the steering wheel.

"Bastard!" She cracked the wheel another hefty blow with the heel of her hand. "I ain't moving another fucking inch, Mikhail. Not till I know what the hell is going on."

I remained tight-lipped and held on to the angry stare.

"*Bástardos*," Nia muttered under her breath. I watched her collapse back into her seat and grip the wheel tightly with both hands. "Okay, Major, while you're sitting there playing dumb fuck, let me spell out to you what I do know."

She turned away from me, fixating on something through the windscreen, her eyes forming tight slits, a thin purple vein running along the side of her temple, raised.

"We're sitting here, in this shitbox with enough gold underneath us to bankroll a small revolution. You've dragged me along on this whistle-stop junket without telling me what the hell is going on. We've got every pig and their mother baying for our blood, a ledger full of names you don't wanna tell me about. I've had men tear up my apartment and try and kill me."

Nia snatched a breath between her rantings.

"We've been shot at, left a dead German banker riddled with bullets back in Xina and I've spent the night freezing my ass off in God's waiting room back there. You've butchered a monk, then dumped the stiff off the side of a bridge. You then drive us into the middle of nowhere, where the air was thin enough to choke a mountain goat and leave me sat with Fu Man Chu whilst you go catch up with some thug in a locked room. Then, like everything is good in the world, you come out smiling and fill the trunk with enough artillery to start World War Three."

I watched as she took another sharp intake of breath.

"I've not eaten a proper meal in days, my arse is hanging off from being sat in this fucking car for miles on end, I stink like a polecat and because of you, I've killed at least two men!"

"And I'm gonna need you to off a few more before we're done."

Nia was staring at me. Her eyes tightened as she began to shake her head.

"Oh, no ... no way. I ain't firing another fucking shot at nobody. Not until you tell me exactly what's going on."

"I've dropped you into a whole world of trouble, that's what's going on."

"Tell me something I don't already know."

I reached across and took hold of her small but surprisingly strong hand, opened it and, like a gypsy reading a palm, I took each finger, starting with her pinkie, and divulged everything about the Konrad Tafel case that I could. I told her that even Faust hadn't been offered a more damning deal than the one my boss Manolis Callas had handed out to me. I apologised for getting her involved in the whole sorry mess. Told her that Callas had given me little choice, insisting that she tag along with me. I told her about the German intelligence man, Eric Hodt, and his double dealing and how the murder of Konrad Tafel was probably linked in some way to both men. But the real clincher came as I took hold of her forefinger. I held onto that for quite a while as I explained about Brigadier Grivas, his connection to countless war crimes and the cache of gold that we were sat on.

"I've had to make deals with more than one devil, and I

could do with an angel to intervene when one of them comes to collect on my debt. That's where you come in."

"Killing devils?" she muttered under her breath.

"Yes." I nodded and let go of her hand. "We get to them before they hit us." I watched Nia's eyes flickering from side to side as she weighed up everything, I'd been telling her. "And they'll all need slaying in one fell swoop." I added.

"How'd you intend doing that?"

"By encouraging them it's in their best interests to come together."

"That's gonna be a tall order. Why would they do that?"

"Because I have what they want. I have the gold and I have the ledger. That's why. These particular devils have too many skeletons in their closet. Too many dirty secrets they'd much prefer remained secret. Transgressions that they know I'm now aware of. Grivas thought he could manipulate or strong-arm me. Neither of those tactics worked, so he has to take me out at the neck. Hodt and German intelligence wanted an inside man, me, to do his dirty work on foreign soil. Now that's not panned out as Hodt would have liked it to, my gut feeling is they'll take a back seat and leave me to hang."

"And Callas?" Nia interrupted.

"The Provost is the blank canvas. If he's dirty, then he's covered his tracks as I'd have expected him to. Bent or not, for now, he's just another devil that I need to reunite with all these other demons."

"Sounds complicated, and risky. We could just make a run for it. A car full of gold ingots. Head for Spain or maybe North Africa?"

I shook my head. "We try that, and we'll be looking over our shoulders for the rest of our short lives. It wouldn't take

Grivas, or whoever, long to find us and put a bullet in the back of our heads."

Nia gave my grave words some thought for a moment or two before replying.

"Okay, so, where's this gathering of demons gonna take place?"

"Kavala."

"Why there?"

"Because there's high ground amongst all the side streets and tiny back alleys. I need to put you someplace with that high-powered sniper's rifle that's sat back there in the boot. I want you to have a clear line of sight, give us both a fighting chance to get out of this fucking mess alive. We hole you up in Kavala whilst I go and stir up a hornets' nest."

"Where's the nest?

"Back in the city. I need to have words with a cop called, Kampouris."

Nia chuckled to herself. "Good luck with that one."

"Why, you know him?"

"Only from what the girls on the street say."

"And what's that?"

"That he's a nasty piece of work and as slick as shit on olive oil."

I nodded in agreement. "That's our man."

"So, Kavala it is, then." Nia turned the key in the ignition and turned to face me again. "I wanna stay in a hotel. No more shitty convents or whatever you call 'em. I want someplace nice. A room with a decent, soft bed, clean sheets, with food brought up to me. Something that doesn't look like a donkey's just puked on the plate ... and I want a bath big enough to drown in."

I slouched back in my seat. "Anything else?"

Nia opened the car door and swung her legs out.

"Yeah, you can get behind the wheel of this pile of crap." She climbed out and made her way around the dusty bonnet, stopping as she got to the wing of the car to holler at me through the windscreen.

"You might have me over a barrel doing your dirty work, but I draw a line at being your fucking chauffeur!"

CHAPTER FORTY-FOUR

THE DRIVE TO KAVALA GAVE ME TIME TO THINK ABOUT THE DEPTHS OF the investigation, such as it was. Usually, handling criminal cases, I spent the lion's share of my exertions in the shadows, unknown and unsuspected by the people I was up against. Most of the time my targets never knew I was on to them. And on the rare occasions when I had been revealed, I was still the most dangerous man in the room.

That wouldn't be the case taking on Grivas and his secret service gorillas or for that matter my own boss, Callas. Both men knew me well enough to be versed in my strengths and weaknesses and how I operated when my back was against the wall. Both men would have sent operatives to muscle in on my old contacts and allies, bear down on them for information; seeking word on my whereabouts or if I'd reached out to anyone. And they'd have people watching my apartment and the places I would go to ground if I was forced to.

Heading for Kavala would, I hoped, offer the chance to level up the playing field a little against Grivas or anyone else wanting to take me out at the neck. I knew I'd be fair game if I returned to home turf in Salonica. Neutral territory was what I needed; a grey area to stay one step ahead of the N.I.S, German intelligence, and possibly, my own people in the MAT division. I needed someplace off the beaten track where I could take a breath and quietly hole Nia up for a short while before having to call her into play to help me out at a later date.

Where better to hold out and parry against an enemy of unknown numbers than an ancient, fortified city; one that had once held out against both the Roman hordes and the Ottoman empire.

Kavala was built at the foot of the slopes of Mount Symvolo. The road into the city was littered with a straggle of newly-built holiday villas; pretty, chalk-white buildings, each set back from the road by high stone walls and huge, wrought iron gates, all probably owned by wealthy Greeks who used the properties as holiday homes.

With Nia still dead to the world next to me, I drove into the old town. The place had clearly changed from the quiet and remote fishing port I'd vaguely remembered, into a busy and sophisticated tourist resort. I imagined that Kavala was not unlike one of the French holiday destinations I'd read about, St Tropez or the like, and like those faraway sun traps, I sensed that the final rot of greed and avarice was about to set in or already had. Kavala still retained some of its original charm and character, but you could tell that the writing was on the wall in the upmarket direction the city was taking; new hotels, pizzerias, superior arts and crafts shops, boutiques, and a nightclub or two, and where once there had been simple tavernas, there were now smart, new restaurants and bars. Most of the establishments that lined the main street and coast road were closed and shuttered for the end of the season.

I headed down a newly laid stretch of asphalt road which cut through the almost deserted centre and pulled up at a junction which appeared to separate Kavala into two distinct districts. To my left, stood more, flashy, three-storey buildings; a small casino and, next to that, a row of swanky looking dress shops and jewellers. On the right, stood a tall metal road sign which read, *The Panagia Quarter*. I put the car into gear and drove out along the narrow coast road down toward what looked like the city's rundown port area.

I needed to keep Nia out of sight. As low key as possible, and despite my earlier assurance to her of a big-ticket hotel to stay in, I liked the sound of the word quarter, it had an anonymous ring about it. The Panagia spoke to me in the same way the doss houses and dives of Salonica's red-light district always did. I wanted an indistinct-looking joint. Out of sight. Out of mind. Somewhere no busybody cops would bother patrolling or be poking their noses about, day or night.

A fleabag lodging with no questions asked. Just someplace to put your head down for the night, undisturbed, unremarkable, and better still, cheap.

The Panagia Quarter was a series of tangled streets each lined by pretty pastel houses all of which had seemed to have escaped the worse effects of redevelopment and tourism. Tiny, white-painted stone fishermen's cottages rose in steps up to the top of a hill, which faced a wide, sheltered lagoon, at the northern end of which loomed the Acropolis of Kavala, a Byzantine-built, granite-walled castle. I found a space to park on a dusty, tree-dotted open space, one side of which was open to the sea and served as a quay and moorings for the local fleet of fishing caiques, three of which had been hauled up out of the water for repainting or repair.

I stretched at the wheel and tried to work a tension knot out of my neck by rotating my head before getting out of the car and looking around. There were very few people about. Three men sitting grouped around the foot of one of the trees close to the water's edge mending fishing nets and, beyond them, some children playing on a spit of sand. I glanced at my watch and saw that it was a little after two and remembered how, even during the autumn and winter months, locals on the coast and those in the mountain villages retired to their homes for a two-hour siesta.

To my left was an old attractive-looking taverna flanked and backed by a large garden and an expanse of orange, lemon, and olive trees. Outside the entrance was a small forecourt on which there were a half dozen tables shaded by an old canopy of bamboo. Hanging from the wall above the main door hung a wooden sign which simply read, *Megali.*

I moved slowly away from the car and heard Nia grumbling to herself and get out. "What the fuck is the Megali?"

"Hopefully, it's your new home for the next few days."

"Like hell is it!"

I headed across the road and entered the taverna. Inside was a spacious bar with rough-wooden tables and chairs ranged along two sides leading down to a counter at the far end of the room. In front of the counter stood a half dozen tall stools and to one side of the worktop there was an archway hung with a bead curtain.

Built into the right-hand wall, about two thirds of the way down the length of the bar, glass doors stood open revealing a tree shaded patio. The area was ringed with more tables and chairs and at the back of the courtyard there was a flight of steps that led up to an ornate metal balcony.

The taverna was bright and clean but sparsely furnished with few frills.

"What a shithole," piped up Nia behind me.

The place clearly catered mainly for locals and the few concessions which had been made for the tourist who stayed there were a display of Minoan pottery standing on a shelf, four original but amateurish paintings of local scenes and a rack of picture postcards on the counter.

The bar was empty. The only sound was of a man and woman arguing somewhere beyond the curtained archway. The argument was fierce and voluble. I moved down the bar to the counter, looked around for Nia to join me and we waited. The argument reached a peak of ferocity. The man swore and the woman yelled back at him with equal vehemence.

Moments later the beaded strands of the curtain were brusquely swept to one side and a middle-aged woman flounced into the bar, looking over her shoulder and yelling more obscenities defiantly at her opponent in the other room.

"I don't care! Whatever you say, you bastard!" she cried out in anger. When she turned to face me, I could see she was close to tears. She reacted with a start of surprise before suddenly becoming embarrassed. The woman was slim, fair-haired and, despite the red face and bitter demeanour, attractive.

"Oh, please, excuse me," she stammered. "I did not know anyone was here."

"You have rooms to rent?"

The woman nodded. "We do." She glanced across at Nia before quickly returning her gaze back to me. "A room for two?"

I gestured an open palm back toward Nia. "No, it would be for my friend here."

The woman smiled. "Of course."

"Elena!" a man called angrily from beyond the archway.

Elena frowned and her mouth hardened.

"How long will you need the room for?"

"Only a couple of nights."

The man called again. Louder this time. "Elena!" And then he thrust through the curtain and into the bar. He was in his mid-forties, tall, muscular, and deeply tanned. He had the appearance of a boxer, his face scarred, his bulbous nose knocked out of joint. He was carrying a kitchen knife in his right hand and his bad temper showed in his expression. He caught sight of me and pulled up sharply, his scowl momentarily deepening, then he made a visible effort to check his temper, for the time being at least. His pride would clearly not allow him to continue the argument in front of customers. And strangers too.

Elena looked at him icily and said: "This gentleman is seeking a room for the young lady."

"Excuse me," the man muttered.

"My husband," said Elena.

I smiled back at him. The man acknowledged my greeting with a curt nod, then turned and darted back through the curtained archway.

I watched Elena alter her stance after her husband was gone, resting all her weight on one leg, and focussing her attention on Nia. "We have a downstairs guestroom if you'd like to see it?"

I butted in before Nia had chance to open her mouth. "I'm

sure it'll be perfect." I smiled at Elena, then back at Nia. "Lead the way."

The large room Elena showed us into was light and airy. Basic was perhaps the politest way of describing what was little more than a cave with windows. The walls and stone benches which were built into them were painted white. On one wall there was a fireplace with a canopy and chimney of beaten copper, the grate was cleaned out and a tall pile of fresh kindling was stacked up in the hearth. The furniture in the compact living room and the bed were new but obviously made by local craftsmen to traditional Greek designs. The air conditioner-cum-electric heater above the door rattled busily but was unlikely to be able to either cool or warm up the room. A tiny bathroom housed a basin and cramped shower stall, the head of which was rusted and dripped red-stained water. The shade on the bedside lamp had small cigarette burns in a couple of places and the one picture in the room, an unsettling composition depicting an ancient sailing ship crewed entirely by toga wearing, grinning and possibly homicidal Macedonian sailors, hung crooked.

Thankfully Nia hadn't said a word since stepping inside.

"This will do fine. I'm happy to pay for the room in advance," I said.

Elena frowned and shook her head. "Oh, no, that won't be necessary." She took a couple of steps backwards toward the door before addressing Nia. "Do you have any luggage which you'd like me to bring in for you?"

Nia smiled at Elena through gritted teeth and glared across at me. Bile and venom laced her words when she spoke. "Thank you, but my friend here will happily bring my cases in for me."

Elena nodded politely and stepped out of the room without speaking again. Nia waited for her to close the door. As soon as the latch bolt had hit the strike, she spun on her heels to face me, her right arm outstretched, a tense forefinger stabbed toward my face.

"Don't you utter a fucking word!"

CHAPTER
FORTY-FIVE

NIA AND I SAT ALONE IN THE TAVERNA AT A TABLE BY THE WINDOW that faced out on to the thin stretch of beach and the tiny dock across the road. My friend had already polished off a starter of grilled sardines followed by a massive plate of chicken gyros and was now tucking into a mountain of lemon ice cream, while I made do downing another cold beer. She was scraping the glass bowl so clean with her spoon that it wouldn't need to be returned to the kitchen sink for washing.

The impressive banquet I'd shelled out for, up to now, had done little to improve Nia's mood or sate her fiery temper. I'd spent the last forty minutes explaining in great detail, why I'd chosen the taverna's rough and ready accommodation and how I needed her to keep her head down for the next twenty-four hours or so. She'd already hauled me over the coals earlier for going back on my word to set her up for the night in a five-star pad. The taverna's rooms were a step up from the dank monastery cell we'd bunked down in the night before, but not by much.

"So, how long before you head back to Salonica?"

I glanced at my watch. "Maybe an hour or so."

Nia shoved the empty ice cream dish across the table toward me. I watched her light a cigarette, slump in her seat and blow a thick plume of smoke out.

"You think you can get Kampouris to play ball?

I put my beer down and pitched my head forward, my forearms resting on the edge of the table.

"Who knows ... I've never known the slippery bastard do anything he didn't want to unless there's something in it for him. I need to spook him just enough to get him running to his master with his tail between his legs."

Nia took a deep pull on her cigarette, holding the smoke in for a long time before allowing it to escape from the corner of her mouth.

"And what if he doesn't spook?"

"Then the two of us are going to be constantly checking over our shoulders for the rest of our days."

Nia shot me a dirty look. "Ain't no way I'm gonna be doing that."

I felt the skin tighten around my temples. "We might not have any choice. If this doesn't pan out the way I need it to with Kampouris, we could end up with no place to go and find ourselves with a bullet in the back of our heads."

"What is all this *'we'* jive?" Nia slouched forward, her chin dipped low, her eyes focussing on mine. "Let's get something straight. If you can't put the frighteners on Kampouris and sort this madness out, there is no fucking *'we'*!"

I felt my face redden and shifted in my seat, my agitation rising.

"That's what you think?"

I saw fear suddenly start to creep into Nia's eyes. "I'll tell you what I think Major ... I think if it a tossup between going it alone or hanging around with you waiting for some executioner to show up, I'll take my chances out there on my own."

I stabbed my finger across the table. "And how long do you think you'd last solo?"

She sat in silence for a moment, weighing up the prospect. When she replied her words lacked conviction. "Long enough."

I reached my hand further across the table, my index finger jabbing angrily. "You really think that Grivas will let you walk away Scot-free?"

"I think if you keep sticking your finger in my face like that I'm gonna break it off, copper or not." Nia swallowed and peered into space, her face empty, as though the words she had just voiced had been said by someone else. She blinked and her mouth flexed uncertainly before she spoke again. "You got me into this fucking mess, Major. If you can't find a way out of it, I'm gone." Nia's eyes bore straight into mine. She started to get up, and I placed my hand on the top of her arm to get her to stay.

"Just hear me out, for Christ sakes."

Nia snatched her wrist from underneath my palm, the taut expression on her face like someone caught between anger and panic. I watched her slowly shake her head then reluctantly sat back in her chair.

"Look, I know the Provost is playing me, why, I don't exactly know, but I don't believe he wants either of us dead. Grivas on the other hand." I felt my face flush and I had to look away from Nia's eyes for a second.

I turned back to face her and watched her nervously draw on her cigarette again, holding the smoke down as though she was taking a hit on a reefer. "The Brigadier's wanted to rattle me from the off. He's wanted me off his scent from day one and when that didn't work, he put some muscle behind things. Now I'm getting closer to the truth, the man wants blood."

"Well, he ain't having mine."

"Which is exactly why Callas had you tag along with me. He knew without you, I'd have to go this alone. He also knows that you have a questionable history of being able to punch or shoot your way out of trouble when the shit hits the fan. Right?"

Nia let her cigarette hang from the corner of her mouth. She sat back, pulled her leg up onto the chair and brushed lint off her knee.

"Right."

"Callas rarely ever puts a foot wrong in my experience. I think he's figured the best hand he has to play against Grivas is to let me keep sniffing around the Brigadier's business and see what I can unearth."

"So you shed the blood, sweat and tears ..."Nia's voice was flat, distant. "And Callas hopefully gets the goods on Grivas, but still stays squeaky clean."

"Exactly." I looked at Nia's colourless, depleted face. "Just like he's always done."

Nia sighed, the merest flicker as her eyes strayed on mine, but I caught that glint.

It was the briefest twinkle, a spark that told me that Garbi hadn't totally given up on me.

Nia's eyes went from my eyes to my mouth and back, waiting for me to continue.

"The way I see it, for now Callas isn't the problem. If we..." I saw Nia's eyebrow raise when I mention the dirty *W* word. "If *I* want to still be breathing by the end of the week, I need to get the Provost what he wants and close the door on Grivas. Weld it shut and then burn his birth certificate."

Nia's voice suddenly intensified, like heat building in a furnace system. "And how'd you plan to do that?"

"If I can get you to shut up for the next five minutes, I'll tell you."

Nia stifled a half-hearted yawn then made a zipping movement across her lips with her thumb and forefinger.

"First off, you help me bring down Grivas and whoever else has it in for me and I'll make sure you never have to work another shift in any deadbeat Salonica joint ever again."

Nia laughed. "Promises, promises." I watched her face suddenly darken as she began to shake her head. "Bring down Grivas, he says. Can you hear yourself?" Her lips crimped on the end of her cigarette as she drew in another lungful.

"You're asking me to go toe to toe, up against the National Intelligence Service. You're fucking insane."

"Maybe." I ran my hand along the side of my head. I could feel a tightening in my veins, as though I had a hat on. I took a breath before I spoke. "Look, I never wanted you to get caught up in all of this. Asking for your help like I'm having to." I shrugged my shoulders and forced a smile. "And, for what it's worth, I'm sorry."

Nia glanced back at me in the warm shade, and her mouth parted slightly so I could see her white teeth. Her skin seemed coarse and grained, like that of a countrywoman or someone who had stepped into a cold wind.

"Sorry he says ... you bastard." Her face turned away to stare out into the street for a second before returning to glare some more at me.

"That's what you're good at, Remis. Forcing people to do

your bidding. Getting them to go along with whatever crazy stuff you want them to say or do for you, no matter what the cost. As long as I've known you, you've always been the guy that makes impossible demands for both yourself and any other fool around you. That's why you're in the mess you are today, and why I'm stupid enough to stick around and listen to all your bullshit."

I watched her stub out her cigarette into the glass ashtray in the centre of the table. She reached into her jacket pocket, took out another smoke, lit it and turned her face to look out into the street again. I could see the shiny film in her eyes but said nothing.

On rare occasions, I've learnt it's best to just shut up and leave a person alone for a moment or two.

This was one of those moments. I joined Nia and stared out of the window toward the beach and dock. On the ocean, close to where the water broke against the beach, a gannet lifted from a green trough and flew toward land, I could just make out a bloody fish dripping from its beak.

CHAPTER
FORTY-SIX

I NEEDED TO FIND SOMEPLACE SAFE TO STOW AWAY THE MERCEDES. Driving about in a stolen car was bad enough but being caught behind the wheel of a hot Mercedes owned by the N.I.S and loaded to the sills with knocked off Nazi gold was a different kind of stupid altogether.

It was Nia's host for the night, Elena, or rather her grumpy husband, Theo, who came to the rescue offering me the use of one of his *"discreet lock-ups"* located in a side street at the rear of the *Megali* taverna. I slipped him five thousand drachmas with the promise of another five if he kept tight-lipped about where the car was stashed, and if he could point me in the right direction to hire another vehicle for the rest of the day and overnight.

Half an hour later Theo returned to the taverna and parked a dingy, rusting, light-blue Datsun 120 outside. He blasted the horn a couple of times to announce his arrival. I went out front into the street to join him and found the taverna's owner leaning against the wing of the car. His taut body looked as if was made of whipcord, his thick, greasy hair combed in faint ducktails at the back. He wore oxblood tasselled loafers, beige slacks, a loose-fitting, navy-blue sports shirt with a white flower print on it. He spun a battered Panama hat on his finger, his huge thighs flexing against the fabric of his trousers, change and keys ringing in his pockets, the muscles on his shoulders as pronounced as oiled rope. As I approached him, he retrieved the car keys, placed them in the palm of his hand and grinned at me.

"This is my pride and joy. It's yours to take as a loan." Theo suddenly curled his stubby fingers tightly around the keys. "For the rock-bottom sum of four thousand drachmas."

I knew that there was little point in trying to haggle with the big man. I also knew I was being fleeced. But needs must when the Devil drives, even if it's in a shitty Japanese car. At least the motor was low-key. Whether the old wreck would get me to Salonica and back remained to be seen. I took out my wallet and reluctantly handed over the requested amount.

Theo studied the cash in his hand then me. At the corner of his eye was a coiled white scar. I watched as he fished out a piece of chewing gum from his shirt pocket. He took off the silver wrapping, threw it on the ground and put the gum in his mouth then threw the keys to me.

"Careful with the clutch." The edge of Theo's mouth twitched. "It's a little sensitive."

I nodded my head and turned to head back inside. Theo called after me.

"It's running low on juice. I recommend you fill her up before you leave."

I took a deep breath and swung round to face the crafty bar-keeper.

"Don't tell me. You own the local gas station as well as the Megali?"

Theo dropped his ratty Panama onto his head and grinned.

"The Greek millionaire, Yiannis Latsis said: 'To be successful, you must act big, think big, and talk big.'"

"I never knew Latsis got rich loaning out beat-up Datsun's and back-street lock-ups."

Theo shrugged his massive shoulders.

"A man's gotta start somewhere."

Who was I to argue with such erudite and scholarly thinking?

Before hitting the road, I spent another hour or so going over what I needed Nia to do for me whilst I was away, then handed over the L42A1 bolt-action sniper rifle, Roth's Tokarev TT-33 automatic and the holdall of ammunition for her to stash away safely in her room. I got Theo to write down the Megali's phone number in my notebook and told Nia I'd call her when I was heading back to Kavala.

Four hours later I was driving through the streets of Salonica again. As I headed across town, the darkening sky toward the bay was coral with skinny black clouds across it. Even if the heavens were brooding, it felt good to be back on home turf or at least it felt good for a moment or two before I started to mull over the downright foolish and dangerous reasons for returning.

I knew now wasn't the right time to be coming clean to the Provost and sharing my findings in the ledger I'd snatched from Pierre Roth's home with him, but I had little choice but to make contact with my boss whilst I was back in the city. I knew Callas would want my head on the block for not playing straight or appraising him as he'd ordered. The way I saw it, the Provost had hardly been on the level with me, so I didn't mind holding out on him a while longer. I knew I had enough dirt on Brigadier Grivas to bury him deep, but it wouldn't be easy to corner him without unleashing a whole world of trouble for me. I needed to throw both men a big enough bone to tempt them away from their dark lairs. I needed to spook them in such a way that left neither any other choice but to break cover. I desperately needed to get the upper hand.

And that wouldn't be easy.

How do you get the better of two extremely cunning men who have made it their life's mission to always be two steps ahead of the game?

I needed an Achilles' heel, a weakness in spite of both men's overall strength and guile. Something which could lead to their mutual downfall.

I was pinning all my hopes such a weakness would come in the shape of Captain Nicholas Kampouris.

The Bora Bora bar in the basement of the hotel Orestias was supposed to look like something on an exotic Polynesian island but it seemed a little gloomy to convince anyone that you were in the South Pacific instead of Salonica's Ladadika red light district. I don't know if the totem poles and tribal masks that lined the walls or the puffer fish hanging from the bamboo ceilings were the genuine article but the tropical rum punch, they served at the bar, always tasted real enough.

The Bora Bora was the last of five dives that I knew Kampouris regularly hung out in after work, or, for that matter, when he was on duty. I'd already trawled the other four joints and was hoping to strike lucky with this final cathouse.

A senior citizen was playing away on a battered upright piano. Long slab-like tables stood about the room surrounded by backless wooden stools. Aside from a couple of solitary drunks, most were unoccupied.

The smell of spilt booze, cheap aftershave and floor polish hit me as I walked through the door into the cellar cocktail lounge. Along the counter in front of the bar's mirror were row upon row of bottles – dark green and slender, stoppered with wet corks; obsidian black with arterial-red wax seals. Metaxa brandies took up one side of a shelf, followed by various vodka brands, all frosted-white in ice buckets filled to the brim and at least fifteen aged Scottish malt whiskies singing with heat and light.

The barman was a preoccupied, venal and skinny in his thirties called Matheos Viglis, who habitually had a cigarette hanging from his mouth, combed his jet-black hair straight back on his narrow head and kept the comb tucked inside the top pocket of his pressed white shirt. The glass tip jar on the shelf at the back of the bar was like a magnet to his eyes and he was well known for pocketing his customers' cash without ringing up a sale. I was hoping that the two, thousand drachma notes I was holding in my closed palm would distract him from the paltry gratuity pot and loosen his mercenary lips.

"Drink?" he asked me as I approached the bar.

I shook my head. "Information."

The barman's beady eyes focused on a spot inside his cigarette smoke as he considered my reply. I let the two, crisp bills slip up from my hand and fanned them out between my fingers. That got the man's attention.

"Has Nick Kampouris been through here tonight?"

Viglis raised his eyebrows and one eye glanced up toward the ceiling. "Been through and now relaxing upstairs." The barman sniffed the stale air. "If you get my drift."

"He usually stay the night?"

The corner of Viglis' mouth wrinkled slightly with the beginnings of a smile. He stirred the ashes in the ashtray with the tip of his cigarette.

Viglis peered at his wristwatch then turned his attention to the stairs I had just walked down. "Usually out of here by two." The barman took a quick peek at the cash I was holding, then shifted his hawklike, greedy gaze on me.

"You pour booze to customers with that hand?"

"Yes."

"Well, I don't want to have to come back here and break every bone in it if Kampouris finds out I've been asking about him. Got it?"

The barman's face turned white. He gave a brief nod of his head. I let go of the cash and felt the paper being snatched from my fingers.

CHAPTER FORTY-SEVEN

I PARKED ON THE CORNER OF NAVARINOU SQUARE IN THE CENTRE OF town and walked the rest of the way to Nick Kampouris' apartment. He lived in one of the many pre-war hovels that had been built along the entire length of Dimitriou Gounari Street close to the city's red-light district. The Captain's place was an unattractive four-storey pile arranged around open courts and malls. I found the entrance to his flat from a row of brass mailboxes set into the brick wall.

The front door was no problem. I got that open with my pocket knife blade in less than a minute. Kampouris lived on the third floor. I climbed the stairs and checked out his lock. That was as tight as a prison cell's, and there was no way I'd gain entry without making a hell of a lot of noise, so I sat on the steps leading up and waited.

I didn't have to wait long. I heard him puffing up the stairs and stubbed out the butt of my cigarette against the bottom of my shoe. He didn't see me and set the attaché case he was carrying down on the floor as he dug out his keys.

He was reaching for the leather brief case as I caught him from behind, grabbing his jacket collar with one hand and shoving him forward into the apartment with the other. He stumbled to his knees; the case flung rattling into the darkness like a sack full of snakes. I switched on the ceiling light and closed the door behind me.

"I'd like to have a little talk, Captain."

Kampouris slowly huffed to his feet, panting like an animal at bay, the stink of booze coming off his breath and filling the space between us. His right hand plunged into his jacket pocket and came out holding a straight razor. I shifted my weight. "Now, come on. I pointed at the blade in Kampouris' hand. "That's just plain stupid, Nick. Didn't you hear me? I just want to talk."

He muttered something I couldn't make out and lumbered forward, waving the razor. I caught his arm with my left hand and stepped in close, bringing my knee up hard, where it did the most good. Kampouris sagged and fell back with a loud grunt. I twisted his wrist, and he dropped the razor on the carpet. I kicked it against the wall.

"Like I said, Nick, stupid." I picked up the razor, folded it, and dropped it in my pocket then patted him down, half expecting to find a police issue nine-millimetre secured in its holster or a small throw-down revolver taped to his ankle. The Captain was thankfully carrying neither.

Kampouris sat holding his groin with both hands as if something might come loose if he let go. "What the fuck you want with me, Remis?" he moaned. "From what I hear, you're a dead man walking."

"Your buddy Kyril Grivas tell you that?"

"Go to hell!" Kampouris spat. He scrambled back on his heels across the carpet whilst still holding on to his crotch. "Why'd you have to dog shot me down there?"

"You're the one who came at me with a blade. What'd you expect a kiss?" I dragged a short red and black Moroccan leather ottoman over from behind him and snatched his bulk up off the floor by his lapels. "Take it easy. You'll be back screwing one of your whores in no time." Kampouris groaned, continuing to clutch at his balls as he sank down onto the seat. I offered him a smoke but he shook his head. I lit one myself and blew a little smoke in his face.

"You got something to say to me Remis, spit it out!"

"I need a favour."

"Yeah, well dream on, Major. I ain't in the favour business." Kampouris started to rise but sagged, grimacing, back onto the ottoman.

"I want you to relay a message to Grivas for me."

"I'm not your fucking errand boy. Go tell him yourself."

I set my cigarette down on the corner of the coffee table next to me then reached inside my jacket pocket. I withdrew a short length of brown leather strapping and began to wrap it around my right hand.

Kampouris looked up at me and laughed. "What's this, some kind of MAT division frightener?"

I remained silent, tightening the strap, and making a fist. The bulb hanging in the rose above my head drew the rooms shadows out long and spiny and fell across Kampouris' face in ghoulish markings. The aroma of cheap Retsina and musky sex rose from the Captain's oily, sweating skin as I took a step closer. The leather creaked around my knuckles. I didn't want to go so heavy on the man, but I knew he'd be hard to get into line. It was like beating a dog you love. It's important to teach it a lesson, it's just a shame this is how the stupid animal learns.

I snapped my arm back and drove two heavy, short blows into Kampouris' face.

The Captain's head and neck whipped backwards, the back of his skull cracking against the wall before he slumped forward, gasping for breath, then savage hacking, flecked with blood.

I grabbed Kampouris by the chin, hard, and tilted his face up. His blood-soaked nostrils flared and his gaze, paralysed, had a rabid fervour to it that looked to me a little like madness, barely constrained.

"I have your name listed in a very impressive-looking ledger next to some sizable financial donations that you've been receiving for some time now."

Kampouris wiped at his mouth with the back of his hand. His stared at his crimson-stained fingers and I watched his head sank forward. "I don't know what the hell you're talking about!"

"I didn't think you would." I snatched at Kampouris' scalp, clutching his slick hair in my hand and yanked his head back.

The double-barrelled impact of my leather-bound fist striking the bridge of his nose and top lip; the second blow knocked him off the ottoman and sent him sprawling across the floor.

The Captain tried to shout something at me, his words lost in pain and panic. He spat out a tooth, his tongue oozing blood. He kicked his heels out as I moved toward him. Kampouris shifted across the floor on his arse, finally pushing himself up against the wall. He brought both hands up to his bleeding nose and mouth and bellowed at me through his palms.

"You bastard!"

I kicked at the sole of the Captain's shoe.

"Tell me something I don't already know." I let Kampouris sit in a heap for a moment, heard him steady his breathing and I reached back down for his lapel again and set him straight against the wall. "This ledger I was just talking about. Apart from your nasty little name being scrawled across its pages, there's quite a few of Salonica's great and good in it too."

"Yeah ..." Kampouris wheezed. "Big deal."

"Oh, it's a real big deal alright, Nicky boy. Big numbers. Big names. And bad news running across every damn page." I watched a harsh reality suddenly shudder across Kampouris' face.

I picked up my cigarette, stuck it in my mouth and took a heavy pull on it. I watched my smoke break against the curling wallpaper before dropping the butt on the floor and stubbing it out with my heel.

"There's a lot of very bad people in that account book. The sort of names that would make most people's skin crawl and a few high court judges sit up and take notice."

"I told you, I haven't the faintest idea what you're talking about," Kampouris rasped.

"Nazis, Greek collaborators, bent politicians, local officials, state councillors, and your friend, Brigadier Grivas." I heard Kampouris snigger. I snaked forward and towered over him before abruptly sticking the toe of my shoe deep into the top of his thigh. He screamed out in pain and gripped at the top of his leg with both hands. I let him try massaging the hurt out of the muscle with his fingers before watching him shimmy a couple of inches down the wall in a futile attempt to put a bit of distance between his body and my all-to-eager foot.

The Captain peered up at me, pained. His brow furrowed; his mouth hung open, muted. He kept looking at my face for a moment, but there was nothing for him to read.

"Now, let's talk about that favour."

Kampouris' head sank again before reluctantly nodding in agreement.

"Whadda, ya want from me, Remis?"

"Nothing too taxing. Just to get up off your ass when I'm gone, and to call Grivas." Kampouris looked at me baffled but stiffened as I continued to speak. "Tell him what I've done to you tonight. Tell him that I know that you're both on the take for a lot of cash and that I can follow the meal ticket he's been holding his hand out to as far back as the end of the nineteen forties. Tell him that I'm not interested in creaming off his profits or muscling in with any kind of deal. Advise him that I've got enough evidence against the Brigadier to see him swing from a short length of rope from the wall of the Heptapyrgion." I reached back into my pocket, took out a folded piece of paper and dropped it into Kampouris lap. I pointed down at it. "Tell Grivas, if he wants what I have on both him and you to go away permanently, that he needs to come meet me tomorrow night. If he ignores me, if he thinks I'm not to be taken seriously, you tell him that I'll make it my life's work to ensure that his pox-dented face will be seen across the front of every newspaper in Greece by the weekend, and on the front pages of the world's press by the middle of next week." I saw a teardrop of blood drop onto the paper. "Nazi collaborators make for impressive headlines these days."

Kampouris struggled with trembling fingers to open up the sheet. When he finally did, I watched as he gawked at what I'd written.

"Kavala ... what the fuck is in Kavala?"

I winked at the Captain. "Me." I began to turn and head out.

"None of that shit would stick," Kampouris called. "Your trumped-up charges against Grivas. Not in a Greek court. Not for long anyway."

I turned and shrugged. "I don't see why not. There must be plenty of witnesses still alive. People here in Salonica who'd come forward, victims of genocide, men and women who came back from the camps who'll testify against him. Surely the Nazis didn't kill all of them."

. . .

Kampouris spat again. "You're so fucking naïve you know that? What you are doing has nothing to do with justice or genocide or crimes against humanity. There's too much more going on behind the scenes that you don't know about. People high up that want all this shit buried, and you with it if you keeping pushing."

"We'll see."

"Okay, let's say you do bring me and the Brigadier in without getting a bullet in the back of your head before you can slap the cuffs on. What next? The Greek authorities will go through the motions of giving Grivas a proper trial in open court. And the public will lap it up like cream. Koutsakos, the fat fuck of a state prosecutor, will sound like Aristotle at the trial when he narrates this country's misfortunes. The judge may even hand down a prison sentence to us. But Grivas has too many powerful friends in the government to serve any real jail time.

"Which government are you talking about?"

"Damn good question, Major. The Brigadier is well connected with a lot of heavy-hitters from here to Berlin, and he's not the only one at the N.I.S or in the police department who isn't well connected to other like-minded individuals right across Europe. Try asking yourself why we Greeks have never tried to extradite anyone from Germany for war crimes committed in this country."

. . .

"All right, I'll play along. Why?"

"Why, he says." Kampouris hawked up another mouthful of blood-stained saliva and spat it at my feet. "Look, it's fucking simple: the Greek government wanted the krauts to cough up reparations for its war crimes years ago. They proposed some kind of amnesty on all the atrocities and ethnic cleansing committed in Greece in return for around half a billion dollars. An important part of those reparations was all the stolen gold from the Jews of Salonica. But the government in Bonn refused. So did the squeaky-clean Swiss bankers. Both called it blackmail. Which is why that fucking Nazi Arthur Meissner was put on trial, as a small and unimportant example of what might follow if Germany continued to drag its dirty feet on the matter." Kampouris laughed, his front teeth and gums covered in bright red spittle. He rubbed at his eyes and held up his palms. "Remember, Greece is a NATO member state and it would be as embarrassing as hell if we started kicking up a stink and applying for the extradition of some small-time German national on the soil of other NATO members."

"Grivas is hardly small," I objected. "He's the real deal. And you know it. A genuine war criminal. Maybe he didn't summarily execute hundreds of Salonica Jews. But he extorted hundreds of millions of dollars in gold, diamonds, and cash from them and then abandoned them to their fate."

"Fate! Listen to yourself, for Christ sakes. Do you really think Grivas gives a shit about 30-year-old fate. It's nineteen seventy-six, Remis. You'd be doing yourself a real favour keeping the past where it belongs. In the fucking past."

My knuckles throbbed and I could feel a sharp pressure behind my eyes. I span round and made my way back across the room. As I opened the door, I reminded Kampouris of my demands without turning to face him.

"Call Grivas. Tell him exactly what I've said. He either meets me where I want him to or he can suffer the consequences in the coming hours. Tell him there are some Israelis who'll be coming to town who would be interested in what I have on him. Neither you nor Grivas would want to meet them, not because they're Jews, but because they're not as patient as me."

The room went silent as I walked out into the hallway. The only reason I'd gone to strongarm Kampouris was because he was the weakest link and I was afraid to show my face right now to the likes of Grivas or Callas. Believe me, sometimes bravery is just the very small space that exists between two kinds of fear. Outside, dawn smudged the night sky like rouge on a ballerina's cheek. Walking back to the car, I unfurled the bloodied leather strap from my hand, dropped that and Kampouris' pearl-handled razor into a trash can and headed for the nearest call box.

CHAPTER
FORTY-EIGHT

It had begun to rain softly, no downpour, just enough make the pavements shine beneath the streetlamps. I was fond of seeing Salonica in the dark, and at best, from a great height: the view from the Acropolis fortress high up on the edge of the city was unparalleled. But the world looks different when you're at street level at night, no higher than a dog's arse and no more significant than any of other schmucks around you. Walking toward the payphone on the corner of Nikis Avenue I felt like a vulnerable small child, one of the many street urchins I'd hung around with as a kid, who you'd see jumping naked into the sea or shouting to a friend to come hang out with them in some poor courtyard, where the sun rarely, if ever, shone.

I took shelter under the aluminium canopy of the call box, picked up the phone and dialled, and while I waited for my call to be answered, I took out a cigarette, lit up and listened to the ring tone buzz away in my ear. A woman finally answered. The familiar voice on the end of the line was testy and irritable and I hadn't uttered a word yet.

"This is Major Remis. Can you transfer me through to Salem mansion? It's urgent."

"About time. We've been trying to get hold of you for the past two days. Where the hell have you been?"

"Sunning myself on the Agia Triada." I waited a second or two for a short-fuse to blow, but all I got was dead air. "Go wake the Provost from his beauty sleep, will you?" The snotty telephonist was silent for moment or two longer. Finally she said: "Hold the line."

I was left with the sound of static and little else for the better part of two minutes. When Callas' voice finally broke the crackling atmospherics his timbre was pitched low and grim.

"Well, well, Remis, I thought you might've run out on me."

"No sir. Where would I go?"

"No further than I can reach, that's for sure."

"I've been kind of busy doing your bidding as ordered."

"Busy, but incommunicado." That cut the conversation for a beat. When the Provost spoke again it was suddenly in an almost forced calm and measured tone. "And what are your conclusions to my orders?"

"I haven't any. All I know is that Grivas and his men are running around bumping off everyone he knew who could finger him. I've had German intelligence lean on me. Their man Eric Hodt is over here posing as a tobacco salesman. He's been sniffing around for information. Looking for chapter and verse on the inside men in the Greek government and security services who might have been involved in illegal activities dating back to the second world war. Dirty stuff that they can use to strongarm the state somewhere down the line. I've uncovered all this dirt for you, and now it's me who's on the line for finding out. My gut is telling me that I'm being set up. I'm just not sure who by. I know that I've probably heard and seen too much for your liking."

Callas cleared his throat. "And what have you seen, Major?"

"People dead before their time for a start."

"That's the history of the world, Major. Some people die before their time so that others can live; it's the cornerstone of civilisation. War, religion, democracy... a hundred die so that a thousand may live. I asked for the dirt on Pierre Roth almost two days ago. Why has it taken you so long to report back and why are we speaking at this ungodly hour?"

I ignored Callas' questions and cut to the chase. "Roth's dead."

I heard Callas sigh deeply. "Really ... and did you kill him?"

"No ... but I strongly suspect Roth's demise was at the hands of the N.I.S."

"Perhaps." There was a moment's quiet. A couple of heartbeats whilst the Provost took in what I had said. "Were you able to talk to him before his unfortunate passing?"

"Yes."

"And?"

"And, he gave me a load of bull about him not being a Nazi. How he served with *Abteilung 5*, the Luftwaffe's Military Intelligence Branch. That he never saw active service; never took part in any kind of butchery here in Greece during the war. He said that the banker, Dieter Lirtzman, had been laundering and taking care of stolen money that had been originally stolen from the city's Jewish community. Lirtzman and Roth were looking after millions in illegally obtained cash, gold, and diamonds. And all for a long list of influential Salonican businessmen, politicians and high-ranking military and police officers."

"Is that so?"

"Brigadier Kyril Grivas was at the top of that list along with some other very interesting names."

"Who's names?"

"Some real heavy-hitters. Mostly men from the ministry, Katsimitros, Seremetis, Bourantas ..." I hesitated for a moment. "And yours, sir."

Callas breathed a curse that was both anger and surprise. "You're calling me in the small hours to tell me that you think I'm dirty like these other men you mention, yes?"

"I don't know what to think. This whole deal seems dirty. My job would be a whole lot easier, sir, if you'd stop holding out on me."

"I beg your pardon?"

"You haven't been much help at all. Everything I know about the dead man, Konrad Tafel I had to uncover off my own back. I think you knew Tafel was operating on Greek soil. I think you knew he was investigating Jewish property theft and a lot worse, and that he was close to lifting the lid on something you'd have rather stayed shut.

"I'm pretty certain that Tafel was Israeli intelligence. He was certainly snooping about into whatever the hell Grivas had been up to during the war. I know Tafel had uncovered that Grivas was connected to Nazi war criminals and it's sounding like the Brigadier was doing the German's bidding in

Salonica as soon as they marched into the city. Looks like he was making good money serving for both sides and he's continued to rake in the cash ever since."

"And now you think I've been raking it in too, do you?"

"I don't know what the hell to think." I felt myself swallow hard before continuing. "Maybe you have."

"I think you need to be more careful who you're pointing an accusatory finger at," Callas growled. He let silence castigate me a while longer before continuing. "All you need to know is that I'm a lot cleaner than you are, and I'm angelically whiter than white by comparison to Grivas."

I felt myself frown. "Did you know Roth?"

Callas snorted with derision. "Vaguely."

"Vaguely? I'm a little fed up with fucking vaguely. Vaguely is putting a noose around my neck and I'm starting to choke, so... did you know Roth or not?"

"Watch your language!" I heard Callas sniff indignantly. "I knew about Roth, who he worked for, his reputation in the banking world, his connections to business here in Greece". The Provost let those facts sink in with me for a second or two. "But I was never able to connect how deep his involvement was with either Dieter Lirtzman, Grivas or any of the other men you've just mentioned. Roth and Lirtzman were clever. They covered theirs and their clients' tracks very carefully over the years. Illegal off-shore accounts, money transfers to bogus names. The list goes on and on. I've had my suspicions over the years, but very little real evidence."

The Provost suddenly stopped talking. I imagined the glacial stare burning away. His cunning mind at play in the stillness as he kept me waiting. I heard the sound of an intercom buzz before Callas continued speaking. "I knew the answers were buried in the past. That the truth was sunk down deep. And I knew you'd be good for the spadework."

I began to shake my head. "You sent me to the Ptolemaida-Florina mine with Grivas to smoke him out, yes?"

"Let's just say that someone waved a red flag in my direction about how close Konrad Tafel was in uncovering the truth about the Brigadier. A sanction had been ordered to snuff out Tafel. I got word of that order."

"And did nothing to prevent the man's death?" I snapped.

"Tafel turning up dead was the break we needed to rattle Grivas' cage. He's not an easy man to spook. He wouldn't have anticipated that Tafel's body would have been found so easily or for his murder to be reported to the authorities so swiftly. I knew sending you was a risk. I was however hoping you would upset the apple cart and force the Brigadier out of the shadows for me. It really was as simple as that."

I rubbed at my neck wearily. "Simple ... nothing about this fiasco has been simple."

"Come on, Major. You know how it is when you swim with sharks. You've got to expect to get your balls bitten once in a while." Callas became quiet for so long that I began to wonder if he was still on the other end of the line. But then I heard him take a deep breath. "So now I've armed you with the facts. What do you intend to do next, Major?" Callas asked innocently.

"If I'm still being forced into the lion's den on your behalf, then I need to get to Grivas before he gets to me and perhaps uncovers your part in fashioning his possible downfall."

"Exactly." There was another short silence, then Callas' voice became cool. "And how do you intend to do that?"

"By offering him the chance to come and relieve me of a ledger with his name written on almost every page."

"Sounds very unenticing." Callas laughed. "I doubt the Brigadier will bite for a book."

"Maybe not." I hesitated before offering up the last ace up my sleeve. "Maybe he'll snap at the six and a half million dollars of Jewish gold bullion that I've got stashed away."

"What gold?" Callas asked frostily.

"The two cases I recovered from Pierre Roth's place before it was shot to pieces by the N.I.S."

"Um ... Grivas could find such a precious lure ..." I listened to another few seconds of hushed static before the Provost finished his sentence. "Seductive." I heard the sound of a match being struck. Heard Callas pull on one of his expensive *Aupa* menthol cigarettes. "If you are successful in coaxing our friend to take the bait and deal with our problem successfully, then that bullion will find its proper restitution if it's returned to me personally. Understood?"

I leant back against the side of the payphone and grasped at the corners of my temples with my fingers. "Understood," I muttered.

Callas fell tight-lipped again. Clearly savouring the silentious atmosphere he was creating. "Remis," the Provost abruptly barked, and not giving me a chance to drum up a rapid reply. "You remember how I warned you that I would not allow the axe to fall across my neck if you messed things up?""

I felt fear crawl across my skin. "Yes, sir. Yes, I remember."

"Good."

"There's one more thing," I blurted out before the Provost could hang up.

"What?" Callas snapped.

"I heard after all this is over, I might get a medal, if there are any left?"

"Screw this up, Major, and I'll be pinning the ribbon onto the lapel of your dress uniform just before the undertaker nails down the lid on your casket."

Callas slammed down his phone, leaving me staring at the handset with the curious sensation that the disembodied voice to which I had been speaking belonged nowhere outside my own imagination. I remained rooted to the spot; the receiver stuck to my hand with sweat.

CHAPTER FORTY-NINE

I knew overnight that I'd drawn myself into the murk and in doing so, stirred up a hornets' nest of trouble. Grivas, like any hornet, needed to be swatted at the first blow or better not to strike at all. Leaning on Nick Kampouris had been the safest way to get to the Brigadier and hopefully spook him, without actually getting myself stung. Forcing Kampouris to become my messenger boy, getting him to run back to Grivas with his tail between his legs, and my threats and ultimatums to recount, was, I hoped, the way to get the spymaster to play ball. My call to the Provost had done little to settle my nerves either. I wasn't sure if Callas was as dirty as the Brigadier. One thing I was sure of was that Callas wasn't rattled easily. I was pretty sure the Provost was the kind of man who covered his tracks thoroughly. Proving the Provost was bent would be a harder task than cornering Grivas and if I was stupid enough to point a finger at him, I was pretty sure I'd quickly end up on a mortuary slab alongside all the other poor stiffs.

My boss had certainly been interested in hearing about the six million-worth of bullion I was safekeeping, but that didn't necessarily mean he was corrupt. For now, I had to trust my instincts and tell myself Callas was clean.

Despite putting my plans into place, any sense of my own inner valour had quickly waned as I drove away out of the city. To stay as low-profile as possible, I made my way back toward Kavala taking the same mountain roads I'd travelled on earlier. It would add on the hours to get back, but the extra miles across fairly rough country would hopefully keep me under the radar; out of sight of the N.I.S or any police or army road blocks that Grivas may have ordered to be set up.

My progress back toward the coast was slowed even more as I traversed through dense woodland terrain, the alpine roads not much more than dirt tracks. I tried to remind myself that each kilometre I travelled away from the city, the nearer I was to arriving in an environment which I had a greater control over. Skid row Salonica may have been my stomping ground, but with few allies I could trust in the city, I knew that any chance I had of staying one step ahead of Grivas and his men and keeping myself alive had to be in a place where I could move freely and on the quiet.

I looked at my wrist watch, it was just after nine and the morning sun was already high in the sky. Around me everything was still. But not a stillness that made me feel at peace. It was a preternatural stillness, as if the forest either side of the road had hidden creatures eyeing me up hungrily. All I could hear was the sound of the car's engine and the occasional curse from me as the Datsun's front wheels hit another pothole.

On the edge of a backwater village called Zygos, I found a decaying call box on the side of the road. I pulled over, got out and stretched my legs.

I lit a cigarette and took my notebook out and flipped through the pages until I found the number for the Megali taverna and headed over to the payphone.

A half dozen rings later and I had the Megali's hot-under-the-collar owner, Theo grunting at me on the other end of the line.

"It's Remis," I said.

"How's my pride and joy?"

I turned and glanced back at the rusting Datsun. "If you're referring to that bucket you've rented out to me ..."

"Of course I am," interrupted Theo.

"I wouldn't fancy its chances in the Acropolis rally." I heard Theo curse something under his breath. Anticipating some kind of sullen comeback I snapped into the receiver. "Get Miss Garbi to come to the phone, quickly."

I heard Theo spout another string of obscenities then the phone clank against a hard surface. A couple minutes later the silence was broken and I had another happy soul swearing at me.

"I was just about to get into the fucking shower!" bellowed Nia.

I flicked my cigarette out into no-man's land. "Cut with the pissing and griping." I glanced at my watch. "Should be back just after midday."

"You want me call up a band and hang up some paper chains?"

"I want you to tell me that you've been putting that L42A1 through its paces whilst I've been gone."

"Uh-huh."

I felt a sharp reply rise in my throat. But instead kept my exasperation at bay. "And?"

Nia made a blowing sound down the line. "And, the fucking thing'll do the job."

"You care to expand?"

"Taking into consideration the targets you've selected for me to hit and the priority of who goes down first, whether they're moving or not and the fucking wind direction, I'd say the fuckers you want dead aren't gonna know what's hit 'em whilst I'm stood two and a half thousand feet away."

"And silenced?"

"At the same distance, I doubt anyone's gonna hear much more than a gnat's fart."

"Good." I took a look at my wrist watch again. "I want you to go back into Kavala later. Meet me at the Via Egnatia, the old arterial road close to the Acropolis at three. Pack your kit and clean down the room. Leave nothing behind. Understand?"

I heard another sharp release of air. "Yeah."

"Do you understand?"

"Yes. What you take me for, some kind of fucking imbecile?"

"Is Theo still around?"

"I can see him stood in the kitchen scratching his nuts. Why?"

"Just put him on. I'll see you at three." Nia didn't reply. She dropped the phone onto something solid. I could hear a whirring sound in the receiver as I waited, then footsteps; leather soles slapping against a stone floor.

"Whadda, you want?" barked Theo.

"How'd you fancy making another four thousand drachma?"

"Is it legal?"

"Almost."

"For *'almost'*, I'd expect five."

"Five it is ... You always peddle this hard, Theo?"

"Always." Theo began to cough. I listened to him hack, clear his throat, then spit phlegm from his mouth.

"Didn't you know since the end of the junta we're all part of the new get rich Greece." Theo chuckled. "For five thousand drachma, I can live better now and suffer the pain later. Every man finds his fortune where and when he can. One day, perhaps, if you're as poor as I am now, you'll remember that."

I placed the receiver into the cradle and headed back to the car, thinking to myself.

'I need to stay alive before I can ever dream of becoming poor.'

CHAPTER FIFTY

I PARKED THE DATSUN A FEW STREETS AWAY FROM THE VIA EGNATIA and walked along to the end of the road close to the foot of the Acropolis and the fortress that sat on top of it. The ancient Ottoman citadel was a sandstone, fifteenth century behemoth that almost resembled a comic-book fort wherein you might have discovered a company of dead legionnaires propped up along the crumbling castellated rooftop to hopefully ward off unwelcome invaders. It was a strange building to still find standing in an area now occupied by fishermen's shacks, ice warehouses and ramshackle boatbuilders' yards.

The streets surrounding the citadel and Via Egnatia were as quiet as the grave. Mid-afternoon brought the '*Hora Sexta*' or sixth hour. Since the hours of the day begin at dawn, the sixth hour is noon, which is when siestas often start. The siesta was still a sacred tradition for the Greeks, spanning back many centuries. In the less touristy parts of the country, towns and villages can be deserted between three to five during the summer months, longer in winter. There was even some decrepit law on the books ordering "hours of common silence" which imposes penalties on those breaking the rules. Siesta meant that Greeks could happily take a nap after lunch undeterred by distractions or obligations. It also meant that if, like me, you were about to raise hell, you had less chance of being seen or caught if everybody else around you is sleeping.

I headed for my meeting point with Nia at the corner of Jokaste Street and was greeted by a mangy-looking dog lying on the ground. Dogs sleeping on the streets of Salonica were a little bit neater and tidier about the way they dozed. You'd find them on the edges of pavements or tucked into the bottom of a wall or foot of a gutter, as if they were keen not to get in anyone's way. Some were so prim about how they bedded down you could almost take them for dead. But whether it was the city or here, on the coast, you stroked any of those flea-bitten mutts at your peril. Greece is the home of the very deserved expression, *'let sleeping dogs lie'*. It was good advice for everyone and anything.

If only I had taken it.

The sound of a car engine heading my way broke the serenity. I turned and saw a bright-red Toyota pickup truck kicking grit and powdery dirt up off the road. As it closed in, I could see Theo driving and Nia sat next to him in the passenger seat. Theo pulled up on the other side of the road, got out of the cab and moved around the other side of it to open up the door for Nia. She stepped out onto the road, looked around and then walked to the back of the truck with him where he unfastened the tailboard and let it fall noisily on its chains. Nia scowled at the big man.

"You wanna wake up the entire fucking neighbourhood?"

Theo gave her a sulky grunt and shrugged. Still scowling Nia reached in across the pick-up's floor panel and pulled out a beige canvas holdall and a matching leg of mutton rifle case. "Why don't you let off a couple of fucking fire crackers whilst you're at it," she snapped. Nia glanced in my direction whilst heaving the rifle case over her shoulder and headed over to me with Theo trailing after her like a scolded puppy. I reached into the inside pocket of my jacket, took out my fold of cash and removed three ten thousand drachma bills from the clip. I held the cash out in my hand as the two of them joined me. Theo, his face puzzled looked at the banknotes. "We agreed five thousand."

"I'm buying a little more of your precious time."

Theo raised an eyebrow, his dark wrinkled skin looking as if it had been supplied by the local leather tanning factory. "My time is clearly a valuable commodity to you?"

He took hold of the edges of the trio of bills. I kept a firm grip on them. "I'm also acquiring your silence and I'm going to need you to turn a blind eye."

The grumpy landlord studied me for a moment, his pull on the banknotes less firm, hesitation appearing in his eyes. Moments later he smiled and pulled the money from my fingers. "I've seen nor heard anything. You nor the woman were never here in Kavala as far as I'm concerned."

I nodded in agreement. "I going to keep hold of that death-trap you call a car a while longer. That okay?"

Theo shrugged again and grinned. "It was my late mother's. God rest her soul." I watched his stubby fingers begin to make the sign of the cross. "In truth, it was her pride and joy, not mine. Elena has always said that it is a heap of shit. Maybe she's right."

"When you've finished up here, I want you to take a fuel can to a gas station then go back to your lock-up and fill up the

Mercedes for me. I need the car ready for us to leave at short notice. Understand?"

Theo's smile faded. "I understand."

"Thank you."

Theo waved away my thanks and turned to head back to his car. He looked briefly at Nia and winked.

"Good hunting."

The afternoon air tasted of salt and smelled of thyme, Greek coffee, and tobacco. The otherwise perfect stillness of the day only periodically interrupted by the distant meow of a cat or the hypnotic rustle of cicadas in the olive trees that surrounded the citadel. We climbed up along the winding cobbled streets behind the old fort until we reached a thin dusty lane, which inclined and twisted at least another two hundred feet above the site of the fortress.

At the end of the pathway we clambered up a narrow, rock strewn former donkey trail that led up to the ruins of the Yperkalos tower. Set amongst the eroding foundations of an early Christian basilica, and the seminary, the tower offered an impressive two-hundred-and-sixty-degree panorama of both the citadel and the grounds inside, as well as giving a birds-eye view of the surrounding area, the Kavala dockland and, importantly, the artery road that led up to the fortress. Two black-winged kites slowly circled above our heads and wheeled across the upper ramparts of the old fortress, searching for new prey, sharp-eyed and merciless. I pointed up to them and looked at Nia.

"You're going to need to be as keen as that pair flying up there."

We walked across sixty yards of dusty, low scrub before climbing the stone steps up into the tower. Inside were two circular rooms, one above the other, connected by a narrow spiral staircase and constructed with local limestone. We headed up to the second floor. I pushed open a heavy wooden door, the bottom rail grinding against the floor. The harsh sunlight that burst through an arched window revealed a stark interior that was devoid of furniture. Dust and chalk was caught by the strong rays that cut through the circular room. The place echoed with its past like a chord of music that only the mind could hear. I rested the palms of my hands on the bare, stone sill and looked out past the fortress toward the cliffs and the ocean. The clear water, its hues of brilliant colour caught between sun and shadow, looked like a peacock's tail spread out along the coast. I turned to Nia.

"On a clear day the locals say that you can just about make out the island of Thassos, Mount Athos to the west and the shores of Keramoti to the east."

"I'm not up here to take in the view, Major," Nia said coldly as she set the sniper rifle and holdall down on the ground.

I brushed dust off my fingers and leant against the wall. "No, that's right, you're not."

"I need all your attention focussed down there." I pointed out of the window down onto the grass precinct that ran along the full length of the high-walled bastion.

Nia shifted in closer so that she could get a better look, her eyes blinking against the glare. "If all goes to plan Grivas and his men will be inside that compound just before seven. I'm also expecting a cop called Nick Kampouris to be joining him. Anybody other than me who steps foot inside that place needs to be in your sights and eliminated before they put a bullet in me. Got it?"

Nia gave a short, firm nod. She knelt down on the ground, unclipped the rifle case, drew out the L42A1 then opened up the holdall, took out a pair of binoculars and stood up. "And anyone who maybe waiting for you outside that field of fire?" She asked grimly.

I shrugged. "If you can't take 'em off the board, then it looks like I'm on my own and I take care of that problem myself."

Nia's face was expressionless. She rested the rifle against the wall, put the binoculars to her eyes studying the terrain outside for a moment then placed them on the window ledge. She snatched up the rifle, working the bolt to open and close the breach in quick time. Nia aimed out of the window, one eye staring into the telescopic sight. She turned to me and smiled. "And when it's all over?"

"Then we go our separate ways. You don't hang around and wait for me. You head back to the taverna, take the Mercedes and the gold and you get the hell out of here as fast as you can."

Nia's eyes narrowed warily. "Where will you go?"

"That's my business."

"And me?"

"You head for any place that's not Greece. Somewhere safe you can lie low."

"And what do I do once I reach this promise land?"

"You cover your tracks. You hunker down with your new found wealth and you stay hidden."

"And then?"

"And then you sit and watch a long, cold, and lonely winter pass by."

CHAPTER
FIFTY-ONE

As a police detective, I learned years ago a basic truth about all aberrant people: they're predictable. Their nemesis is not a lack of intelligence or creativity. Like the moth that wishes to live inside a flame, the obsession that drives them is never satiated, the revenge against a person, or the world for that matter never adequate.

My gut feeling that Brigadier Kyril Grivas would take the bait and rendezvous with me, albeit mob-handed, paid off. A little before seven, as the light started to fade, Grivas and three men came over a knoll and walked down into a depression that was flanked on each side by the walls of the citadel and a dense colonnade of olive and fir trees. Behind them on the road that led into the stronghold I could see the glow of a pair of headlights shining upwards through the trees. The men behind Grivas began to spread out, each one carrying a twelve-gauge, pump-action shotgun, all held at port arms.

I withdrew my Walther from its holster, held it at my side and watched the Brigadier and his gunmen make their slow, cautious approach. Out of the corner of my vision, I saw a movement beyond the trees and the high wall. Or at least I thought I did. Perhaps it was just more wishful thinking as I stood alone, I told myself. A moment later from across the open sea, I saw a faint flash of lightening, then the distant rumble of thunder. Seconds later, the wind blew in a violent gust and swept along the Panagia peninsula and over the Acropolis, shaking the trees, filling the air with pine needles and a smell like stagnant water and cold stone. I'd been in semi-nocturnal environments where snipers lurked inside foliage or in old buildings. The wind becomes their indispensable ally. When the trees, long grass and undergrowth begin to trash, the object that does not move or the shadow that remains like a tin cut-out becomes the entity that is out there in the darkness preparing to take your life.

Except in this case the presence on my perimeter, hidden out of sight, was my friend.

Nia may not have been military trained, but she was a natural and experienced shot who had killed before. She knew what to do when wind or pistol flare threatened to review her position. She'd settled herself quickly into her hide site, her arms freezing into sticks, her face down-turned so as not to reflect light. Nia was my safety net. A trump card I knew I'd have to play. Garbi hidden in that tower was the one thing that stood between me and an early demise. I just had to hope and pray that her reflexes were sharp, and her trigger finger was as quick as her mouth.

By anyone's reckoning, my plan to face Grivas in the open was a foolish idea, one that I was sure had its origins in my need to finally wipe the slate clean and be a law-keeper rather than bending it to suit my own dishonourable ways. Deep down I knew that if I didn't face the Brigadier in the way I'd chosen, confront him with the truth, I'd end up paying for my foot-dragging sooner rather than later. There are times when the probability of death in your life is so great that you step across a line and you no longer fear it. I'd just stepped over that line. I raised the Walther, the safety off, my arms outstretched, holding the grip firmly in both hands.

Grivas and his four musketeers came to a halt. He was focused on the gun pointing at his head whilst the men behind him made individual recces of the dusky terrain around them. He opened his palms, as though expecting grace from above, his head tilted, taking my measure as well as the surroundings around him.

"Well. What do we have here?" he said.

I could hear myself breathing and felt the oil and moisture on my finger inside the trigger guard.

"Keep working on it. You'll figure it out."

The Brigadier grinned and continued to scan the area around me. "This is a defining moment for you, Major. If everything works out nicely here this evening, we can all return to our separate worlds happy." Grivas looked at my feet and around me. "The articles you pledged to return in the note you had delivered to me. Where are they?"

"I have them safe. Everything you came for is close by. I'll take you to what you want when I have my assurances."

"Assurances. By which you mean I'll let you leave here this evening in one piece?"

"I mean, that once you have your blood money and the evidence of how you came by it, that I'll have your assurance I won't need to concern myself about either a bullet finding its way into the back of my head in the future or me being slung into one of your N.I.S cells for the rest of my days." Grivas remained silent. I stood my ground not taking my eyes off the Brigadier or his men. "Let's start by you making me feel a little less ill at ease. Use your left hand, reach into your jacket, and drop your weapon on the ground," I shouted.

Grivas slowly shook his head. "My men here are the only ones who are armed. I can assure you; I don't have a gun, Major."

I knew that was a lie.

"I suggest that it is you who drops your firearm."

I leant forward on the balls of my feet. Grivas' face firmly in my sights. I saw his top lip suddenly twitch, and his eyes briefly widened.

"I'm in no mood for games. The clock is ticking. The articles in your possession, Major. I want them. Either hand them over now or take us to where you've put them for safe keeping." Grivas slowly raised his left arm an inch or two, the sleeve of his coat rising ever so slightly to reveal the face of his wristwatch. He tapped the glass with his finger. "Tick-Tock."

"Then we're in for a long night. I'm not moving until you call off your pack dogs and I get those guarantees. Once I know you're on the level, you and I can take a short walk out of here and you can collect your two suitcases of gold bullion."

I saw Grivas wince when I mentioned the ingots. Hearing the word gold certainly got the Brigadier's and his lackeys attention. Eyes quickly widened and eyebrows raised.

A couple of travelling bags stuffed to the brim with gold was enough to change a man's life for the better. Perhaps a share in such wealth was enough to kill for. The Brigadier knew this only too well.

Like most cowards, I knew that Grivas had not truly anticipated the reality of me taking the fight so up close and personal. I knew that he could simply give the command for his men to open fire and wound me. Force me to talk and give up the whereabouts of the all-important ledger and gold. But he knew his men were watching him, expecting him to be more than the kind of posturing figure they'd followed during the Generals' junta uprising, to be more than just the man in charge wearing an expensive suit and using the martial rhetoric of just another cheap politician. He was now in the awkward position of having the true reason for our rendezvous disclosed and there was the possible risk of the very men he trusted to undertake his dirty work turning on him.

He also knew that I'd put a bullet in him before either him or his men got to me.

Grivas took an awkward step backwards, the breeze tousling his hair. The protrusion in his jacket now visible to me even if he thought it well hidden. The pistol he'd tucked away on his right-hand side. No doubt an imported, flash blue-black revolver with a pearl handle, which he'd have hung in a shoulder holster and hoped not to have to use.

I could feel my finger continue to tighten in the trigger guard. A line of sweat ran through my eyebrow. I told myself to stay calm; that when the time came, to squeeze off the trigger and not think about it. How many times had I fired a gun before at men just like Grivas. People I didn't even know.

I'd always just stepped over that line, letting conscience quickly disappear in the adrenaline rush of letting off one round after another. The only reality that mattered in the briefest of moments becomes the muzzle flashes, the clean smell of smokeless powder, the deadness in the ears that allows you to disconnect from the crumbling figure in the distance.

"So what's it to be Brigadier?"

"Don't tempt the devil, Remis."

"The devil wouldn't let a Nazi collaborator like you clean his piss pot."

Grivas glared at me. I saw his hand move toward the opening in his jacket. I took a step forward. Grivas came to a halt and the goons behind him started to become spooked. The Brigadier shook his head. He turned his face slightly revealing an ugly five-o-clock shadow, his whiskers like dirty smudges on his cheeks and chin. His eyes shifted sideways unsure if he should continue to allow me to speak or give the order to his men to shoot and prevent me revealing the truth about his shifty Third Reich connections. I held the Walther steady; my ears were filled with a sound like a train entering a tunnel, a taste like copper coins in my mouth; no matter how things played out, I was determined to spike Grivas' cannon before he or his men got to me.

"Grivas, I gotta know. How'd a piece of shit like you convince these guys you've dragged along to work for you? Do they know how you worked for the German occupation during the war? How you assisted the Nazis to plunder tens of thousands of cultural and artistic properties from Jewish academies, from their synagogues and their homes, and then sent the plunder back on trains to the Fatherland. Do they know about the forty-five-thousand Jews you helped deport from Salonica to concentration camps right across Europe? How you helped yourself to their stolen money; all the diamonds and gold you've pocketed since the forties? Do these guys behind you know about all the blood-stained cash that's been filtering its way into your bank accounts over the years?"

"I get it." The Brigadier smirked nervously. "This is your

finest hour, isn't it? This is the egalitarian police officer delivering his grand speech on justice to the multitudes just before his life is snuffed out. Unfortunately, Remis, with your dubious reputation, the role doesn't suit you well. And my men don't care for the nonsense you're spouting. Do you know, I've researched every aspect of your life, Major? I have trawled through your military records. Read all the sordid details of the pitiful history of your appalling childhood, your none too impressive police career, all those men and women you've blackmailed, coerced, or murdered for your employer, the Provost.

The common knowledge in the police department and the MATs division of your long-time belligerence and bolshiness with your superiors, the constant whining to them about the injustices visited upon you when you've been directed to carry out their orders. The fact that you take me to task about my past has established new standards in hypocrisy."

"The problem with you, Brigadier, is that after I'm dead and gone. You'll still be you," I said. "You'll wake every morning still knowing that you have the blood of thousands of Salonica Jews on your hands." I kept the pistol directed at Grivas' face.

"None of this rot matters. Behind me are your executioners. My men have been instructed to follow my orders without hesitation. Those orders are quite simple: either I get what I came here for or you die." Grivas glanced at his watch. "And your window of opportunity is quickly closing."

I swallowed and stared at the ground for a split second, then raised my head. I knew if I took a shot at Grivas and then began squeezing off rounds, I might get a couple of serious holes in two of the men behind the Brigadier. There were too many weapons in the game, and I was sure too many men on the ground for Nia to deal with. I suspected once I'd taken my first shot, I'd have about four or five seconds to live after Grivas went down.

Above me I saw an electrical flash in the clouds. It seemed to leap in the sky from the mountain range to the right of me and ripple through the heavens all the way to the horizon. In that brief moment I saw another flash to the right of me. The first of the four gunmen was hit in the neck, the bullet tearing a huge chunk of muscle and sinew beneath the man's head, almost decapitating him. As he was felled, the second of the two men began to spin round on his heels but barely made it a quarter of the way round before his skull cap was blown off and he dropped behind Grivas like a sack of rocks. Stunned and disorientated, I watched the third gunman stumble back a pace. Like most men who commit murder for hire, he'd probably concluded long ago that as the giver of death, he would never be its recipient. When he tried to aim at me, his mouth open in disbelief at the carnage erupting around him, he also made the childlike gesture I had seen others make in the last seconds on earth. He arrogantly extended his chin as though it could somehow save him from the bullet that he knew was about to explode from the muzzle of the gun pointing at him. As he went to fire, my first round clipped him just above his heart.

As he tumbled backwards my second hit him in the jaw. I dipped my head low, my lower half pivoting as I shifted to my right. I was about to put Grivas down just as he was raising his gun, that's when Nia fired for a final time.

The round was likely soft-nosed with a notched cross-hammer tapped into the lead for good measure. When it struck the back of Kyril Grivas skull it left a hole no bigger than the tip of my little finger but blew his forehead apart like an exploding watermelon. He fell forward onto the grass, a gurgling noise in his throat, his knees striking the ground simultaneously.

The lightning struck again and quickly died in the sky. I took a few steps forward and stood over the four slain bodies. I stared at Grivas' motionless body and sensed my shoulders slump and my breathing quicken. The pulse in my neck twitched in the vein and my heart pounded in my chest. I felt my stomach knot, the bile rise in my throat and then the urgent need to throw up. I was about to fall to my knees and puke when I caught sight of the thin beam from the car head-lights still blazing away on the road that ran up toward the entrance of the citadel.

And that's when I realised my terrible mistake.

I'd forgotten to question where the hell Nick Kampouris was in all this madness.

CHAPTER FIFTY-TWO

THE HEADLIGHTS FROM GRIVAS' CAR WERE NO LONGER GLOWING. THE two beams that had lit up the road outside the citadel had been suddenly extinguished leaving an eerie silence. The air was filled with smoke and cordite, the wind blowing coldly around my neck and ears. Dusk was encroaching, the twilight catching the top of the dark water of a spring-fed pool, its waning afterglow just picking out the frame of an ornate wooden jetty that extended from the pool's edge out across basin. I reached into my jacket pocket, ejected the empty magazine from the Walther, slammed a fresh one into the grip and starting walking towards the vehicle. I'd taken less than twenty paces when I knew something was wrong. I came to a halt, raising the Walther out in front of me, scanning the pond and fortress perimeter in front and either side of me. The give-away I was in trouble came from the sea breeze. It had quickly cleared the smell of gun smoke and left in its place an equally familiar and repellent stink.

The odour now coming from behind me was unmistakable. A heady mixture of sweat and testosterone. I slowly turned and looked into the face of Nick Kampouris. He was dressed in an olive-green army battledress combat jacket and matching trousers and carrying an M-1 carbine lightweight semi-automatic rifle, the muzzle of which was pressed firmly against the back of Nia's head.

"You missing something, Major?" Kampouris struck the back of Nia's knee with the sole of his boot and dropped her to her knees in front of me.

"I told myself earlier I needed to keep a firm eye out for you."

"You clearly weren't looking hard enough." Kampouris gestured toward me with the rifle barrel. "Why don't you lay that pop gun of yours on the ground."

"Don't do it, Mikhail." Nia said.

Kampouris turned and rapped the tip of the M-1 barrel across the side of Nia's head and winked at me. "Humour me."

"Whatever you say." I saw Nia glare at me as I slowly set the Walther down on the grass.

"Well done, Major." Kampouris glanced back at the four bodies that lay in the distance behind him. "It was a stroke of luck me unearthing this little minx. You and your friend here have had a busy night."

"Yeah. It's a real shame." I sniffed the air and got another whiff of the Captain's rank perspiration. "If you'd have turned up when Grivas did, you could have ended up sprawled out down there with the rest of the shit."

"Now that's not nice." Kampouris looked at Nia then at me and smiled. "Get on your knees."

"Sorry," I said.

"I can put you there if you wish." He glanced back at Nia. "Have you ever seen someone shot through both kneecaps?

Would you like to see your friend here brought down to size?"

"Go fuck yourself," snapped Nia. I sank down on the ground and saw Nia's shoulders slumped and her head fall forward so that her chin was almost resting against her chest. Kampouris took both our physical gestures as yielding to a stronger being. I saw my friend's arm go limp and her hand inch slyly toward the top of her boot.

Kampouris' rolled his shoulders, his smile never wavering. He took a single step closer to me, the odour that rose from his body almost made me gag. He quickly glanced back down at Nia and I saw him roll his tongue over his top lip. "Don't worry baby, when I've got what I want out of Remis, I have something very special lined up for you."

"Look at me, Kampouris." I barked.

The Captain slowly raised his head and fixed his eyes back on me. "Look at you. Why should I look at you when I have such a beauty at my feet? Do you think you can condescend to me and give me commands at a moment like this?

"You really are a fool, Remis. You've been chasing your tail for days and I've been one step ahead of your pathetic snooping just as soon as you dumped that Jew boy, Konrad Tafel's corpse at the morgue."

"You killed him?"

The Captain raised an eyebrow. "Maybe."

"And coroner, Vokos. You snuffed him out too?"

Kampouris shrugged. "I knew you and that old bastard were as thick as thieves. It was only a matter of time before he'd have smelt a rat and made waves. Grivas knew he was trouble and wanted him out of the picture."

"And you obliged your master by removing him, yes?"

Kampouris nodded. His eyes opened and closed as if, for a second, he were unsure where he was. "Orders are orders. You of all people know that."

"You're right about me being a fool," I said, holding my eyes on his. Kampouris kept beaming at me, as I watched Nia begin to slowly withdraw a thin silver blade from inside her boot. "You said just now, *'when you've got what you want'*. What do I have that you want so badly and what makes you think I'd give you a damn thing?"

I saw the Captain's chest rise and fall, his eyes narrowing and the blood drain from his mouth as his grin quickly disappeared. He raised a finger in the middle of my face "I want the fucking ledger and all –" he began.

That was as far as he got. I watched Nia swing her arm up from her side, the short xiphos blade appearing in her hand and plunge it deep into Kampouris' thigh. The Captain hollered in agony. As he slung the rifle toward Nia's face I sprang up off my knees and threw myself at Kampouris' waist knocking him off balance and sending him sprawling backwards. As he sank, I followed toppling over his body, the two of us tumbling across the grass.

I heard Kampouris scream again, the knife clearly embedding itself deeper into his flesh as he continue to roll. I dug my heels into the hard turf and managed to scrambled to my feet just as Nia was snatching up the M-1 from the ground.

I held out my arm and yelled. "Throw it to me!"

Nia, the rifle already held in her hands with the barrel facing the ground toward Kampouris' body, hesitated for a moment. She looked at me and shook her head. I saw Kampouris struggling to raise himself up onto his knees.

"You either drag yourself up on your feet and die or I can

put you down where you lay in the dirt. The choice is yours you bastard."

The Captain showed no reaction to Nia's threat. He clutched at the dagger embedded in his thigh, muttering obscenities under his breath. He spat on the ground and grimaced as he slowly began to rise to his feet. I moved in closer toward Nia, retrieving my Walther as I did. I raised the gun and aimed it at Kampouris' chest. I glanced across at Nia and smiled. "You've done enough." Nia shook her head, and bit at her bottom lip. "Enough is when I say it is."

I inched in closer, until our bodies were almost touching. "I'll finish this." I saw Nia's finger tighten around the trigger. The expression on her face as hard as granite. She took a step forward. Kampouris suddenly flinched and tried to limp a pace backward but quickly faltered as the knife in his leg worked deeper toward the bone. I suspected the pain was terrible. I also suspect that his suffering didn't begin to approach what he had inflicted on his victims in the past. I inched closer to my friend and held out my hand.

"Please Nia."

I didn't truly expect her to surrender the rifle; to relinquish something that in her eyes offered a finality to the bloodshed and mayhem that had just ensued. But as had often been the case, Nia had a habit of surprising me. Without uttering a word Nia gracefully conceded and offered me the M-1.

I grasped the rifle in one hand and dropped my Walther into my coat pocket then walked slowly toward Kampouris. "Let's me and you take a walk down by the water, Nick."

Kampouris remained poker-faced. He looked at Nia and grinned. "You not gonna join us, baby?"

Nia made a growling sound in her throat and shifted

forward toward Kampouris. I got in front of her and held up my hand. "Don't let him get under your skin," I whispered. "Stay here."

I moved toward Kampouris, nudging the rifle muzzle toward the pond. "Move."

Kampouris turned, blood pouring from the wound in his leg and began to hobble down the grass toward the edge of the jetty. I raised the M-1 and rested the butt in the crook of my shoulder.

I would be dishonest if I said my actions at that point were driven simply by the passion and heat of the moment. It would also be inaccurate if I said I had made a conscious decision about the immediate fate of Nick Kampouris. I created a blank space in my mind where I thought of absolutely nothing except the faces of the innocent people who the man had tortured and killed during the general's junta and his time on the force. Kampouris was on the jetty when I hit him in the back with the first round. I saw his shoulder jerk and his feet stumble.

Then I pulled the trigger over and over until the bolt locked open and the clip pinged into the night. Not one round went wide or high as he fell off the end of the dock.

As I approached the end of the walkway, I was greeted by an horrific sight. I thought Kampouris would go straight underneath and sink, the weight of his heavy combat fatigues and army boots dragging him down. Instead, I saw him roll on his back, his clothes ballooning with air. He looked at me and for the briefest of moments and I swear that I saw him grin before the black water closed over his head.

CHAPTER FIFTY-THREE

If there are angels who walk amongst us, then Nia Garbi hid her wings well. How do you find the words to truly thank somebody for saving your life? And if words of gratitude can never be enough, how do you fulfil such a burning sense of obligation?

Well, handing over six and a half million dollars' worth of stolen gold bullion is one way of showing your appreciation.

Nia and I walked out of the citadel leaving the bodies of Brigadier Kyril Grivas and his three cronies spread-eagled on the turf, and Nick Kampouris' bullet-ridden corpse laying at the bottom of an algae-covered pool. There were worse places the five men could have met their ends. The two of us were content in the knowledge we had taken their lives but neither of us felt inclined to bury or dispose of their bodies or for that matter, say any prayers. After collecting the sniper's rifle and her holdall from the Yperkalos tower, we headed back to the road outside of the fortress and the Chaika limousine which Grivas had travelled in. I found the keys still in the ignition and a packet of imported Marlboro American cigarettes unopened on the dashboard.

Who says that lady luck never smiles on the wicked?

I drove us back to the Megali taverna and, whilst Nia took her bag from the trunk of the car, I went inside and thanked Theo and Elena for all their help, then asked Theo to take Nia and I to where he'd concealed the Mercedes. I took the keys to Theo's Datsun out of my pocket and handed them to him. Before he had chance to close his fingers around them, I pressed a further twenty thousand drachma into his hand. The landlord looked at the money and then at me. Confused, he shrugged.

"What is this for?"

"Where I'm going, I doubt I'll need money."

I turned and began to walk away. Theo called after me.

"Where is there a place a man would not need money?"

I didn't have the inclination or the time to reply. I walked out into the street and waited for him to join me. Nia and I followed Theo through a maze of side streets and back alley's until we came to a single-floor, thatched barn that was tucked away at the end of a single-track lane. Theo unlocked the barn doors and swung them open. I walked inside and collected my bag containing the ledger from the trunk of the car then returned outside. Theo took a step back, and nodded at me, clearly realising that it was wise not to outstay his welcome. I thanked him again and we both bid him farewell. Nia and I watched him walk back down the lane until he was out of sight. I turned and held out my hand.

Nia stared at my open palm. "What's this?"

"It's farewell."

She frowned at me and continued to stare at my open hand a moment longer before finally offering her own. We held hands, rather than shake, standing in silence, looking at each other, neither of us knowing what to say. Then she lifted my hand, kissed it, and held it to her cheek. When she released my fingers, my arm fell to my side like a dead weight. Nia stepped away from me and smiled, then dipped her head toward the ground, the toe of her shoe kicking at the dirt.

"I still don't know where I'm supposed to go." she said without looking up.

I cleared a frog out of my throat. "Just get in that car and drive. Get as far away from here as possible. After that, you'll work it out. You always do." I began to turn to head back down the lane but Nia called out and I stopped in my tracks.

"Where will you go?"

I shrugged. "Same place I always end up going back to at the end of the day."

"And where's that?" Nia asked.

"That shithole of an apartment of mine." I stepped backwards and pointed at the Mercedes. "You'll find the keys in the glove compartment."

Nia looked at me in disbelief. "You left the fucking keys in the glove box with all that gold sitting underneath the chassis?"

I didn't reply. I turned, took a couple of steps, and heard the familiar sound of a match striking the surface of sand and powdered glass. I started to walk away and didn't look back until I reached the bottom of the lane.

The moon was beginning to rise high up behind the mountains. Silhouetted against it, Nia stood, a lit cigarette now hanging from the corner of her mouth. She leant against the hood of the car and gave me the thumbs-up sign with both hands.

I nodded a final goodbye, turned, and carried on walking, safe in the knowledge that I would never see my friend again.

CHAPTER
FIFTY-FOUR

My drive back to Salonica was a solemn one. Black storm clouds swollen with electricity had sealed the sky from Kavala all the way to the city. The last hour of my journey was made through torrential rain, hail, and loud rumbles of rolling thunder. By the time I'd eventually hit the suburbs the downpour had thankfully reduced itself to a heavy shower. Before skulking back to my apartment in the *Ano Poli* district, I decided to take a brief detour and deliver Pierre Roth's ledger to the Provost's gatekeeper at the *Salem Mansion*.

I pulled up outside the locked wrought-iron gates. The sentry was already out of his hut and heading toward the car, his approach cautious and sharp-eyed, the M3 sub-machine gun raised out in front of him. I wound down the window just enough for the guard to see my face and my MAT division identity card. The soldier scanned my credentials as I reached across and picked up the ledger from the passenger seat.

"An urgent delivery for the Provost. See he gets it immediately." I stuck the ledger through the gap in the window. The guard looked at the account book suspiciously for a moment.

The rain hitting the thick, crimson card cover. "If you hand that to him wet through, he'll have your balls made into earrings for one of his mistresses." The soldier snatched it out of my hand and gave a sharp nod.

I didn't hang around to say thank you or goodnight. I quickly swung the car out into the road and sped away along Vasilissis Street, thankful that I'd not been arrested on the spot.

Death comes in many forms. But it always comes. And for that reason, *'inevitability'* may be the lousiest word in the world.

Those were not thoughts that I should have been brooding upon on my drive back. But I was anticipating the very worst. If not, a gunman, I was half expecting to find a couple of unmarked police cars sitting outside my apartment when I pulled up.

But the street was quiet and practically empty of any vehicles. When I'd got in out of the rain, I'd dropped my damp jacket on to the back of the chair by the door, kicked off my shoes, threw off my clothes and took a lukewarm shower. Dry and in fresh underwear, the only things I could find in my refrigerator to eat were a half-bottle of chilled Metaxa brandy and some mouldy smoked cheese. I slung the cheese in the bin and downed the brandy in six long gulps, then I fell into bed.

As I'd expected. They came in the dark and knocked with closed fists.

The door shook as the clamour of beating knuckles filled my apartment. I switched on the bedside lamp, swung out of bed, wearing just my underwear and went to the door. Outside there were three uniformed army officers. Two of the soldiers were carrying Heckler & Koch G3A3 rifles and from their expressions they looked like they meant to do a lot more than draw my attention to the full moon outside.

"Major Remis?" said the captain in charge.

I glanced at my watch. "It's four-thirty in the morning don't you bastards ever sleep? Get the hell out of here."

"Come with us please, sir. You're under arrest."

My yawn turned to feigned surprise. "What for?"

"Just come with us, please sir."

"On whose orders am I being arrested? What's the charge?"

"Please do as you're told, sir. We haven't got all night."

I paused for a moment and considered my options, which didn't take that long after I noticed one of the privates had his finger on the trigger of his G3A3. Like a lot of police officers in Salonica, he looked like he was itching to shoot someone.

"Can I put some clothes on or is this a strictly come-as-you-are arrest?"

"My orders are that you're to come with us immediately, sir."

"All right. If that's the way, it's gotta be."

I picked my jacket up off the back of the chair and was about to put it on when the captain snatched it from me and started to search the pockets, which was when I remembered the Walther that was there, only he got to it first.

"That wasn't very sensible, was it, sir?"

I felt myself grin sheepishly. "I was just about to mention that, Captain."

"Oh, I bet you were." The officer gave the pistol to one of his subordinates. "You were going to remind me you had it when it was in your hand maybe and had the thing pointed at my gut. I don't like that you were attempting to bring a pistol along on my arrest detail." He took a step nearer – near enough for me to get a whiff of the sweat on his shirt and the supper on his breath. "You know, in my book that counts as resisting arrest."

"No, Captain, I was just putting on my coat. It's late and I forgot the gun was in my pocket."

"Like hell you did," said the officer in charge.

"We don't like people resisting arrest," said the policeman with the itchy trigger finger.

"Really, I'm not resisting arrest," I said. "The gun was an oversight."

"That's what they all say," said the captain.

"They? Whose they? You're army. Not police. You sound like you arrest people all the time, when it's plain as day that you haven't got the least fucking clue what you're doing. Now hand me my coat and let's go wherever it is you're taking me to so we can get this crap cleared up."

He handed me my jacket. I put it on, stuffed my feet into my wet shoes and stepped outside into the hall. They marched me out into the street and stood me at the tail of a canvas-covered dark green *Steyr* military vehicle.

"Where are we going?"

"Get in. You'll find out soon enough."

"I'm sure I will," I said, climbing up onto the back of the truck. The inside of the truck felt colder than outside in the street. "Any chance of turning the heating on?"

"Why don't you shut your mouth, sir?" The captain followed me, along with one of his minions.

"Sir. I like that. It's funny how respectful people sound when they're aching to crack you across the back of the head with a rifle butt."

The officer didn't contradict me, so I kept my mouth shut for a few minutes. We drove in silence for a good twenty minutes, long enough to know I was being taken out of the city, and certainly not to the Sedes military base, which was less than a couple of kilometres from the station house. The further away from Salonica we got the longer it was going to take me to reach out to my own people, who would hopefully intervene in my predicament, and not just that: I was easier to kill too. I knew what these army fellas were capable of, I just wasn't sure on whose orders they were operating.

"Look," I said. "When we get to wherever you are taking me, you need to let me make a call to Provost Callas."

None of them uttered a word – instead they just stared into space as if I didn't exist.

I looked at the soldier sat next to me. "You know I'd really appreciate it if you'd take that fucking rifle barrel out of my ear. If we hit a pothole, I might well end up with a serious hearing problem."

"I think you've already got a hearing problem," insisted the captain. "Didn't you hear me telling you to shut up?"

I folded my arms and shook my head. "You do know, I'm a police officer with the MAT division?"

I hated myself for saying that, but in truth I was starting to get the jitters. Life was starting to count for very little the further we drove away from the city. Life, I knew, could end all so abruptly in some ditch, shot in the back of the head by a short-tempered captain.

"I'm just obeying orders," snapped the officer, "and I don't give a fuck what you are or who you know. Someone like me – someone at the bottom of the heap after the Junta, I just do as

I'm told. And that's the end of it. So, fuck you and fuck your police credentials."

"You certainly have a way with words, Captain."

I checked my mouth and retreated into the remaining warmth of my jacket collar.

Ten minutes later I felt the wheels of the truck start to drive over gravel. Another couple of minutes listening to stones click and spit under the lorry's tyres and the vehicle came to a sudden halt. I heard the driver get out and walk to the tail gate. The captain climbed out and waited whilst I scrabbled out to join him with a rifle held a few inches from my back instead of in my ear.

A few minutes later we arrived at a red-bricked building. There was very little outdoor lighting except for a dull bulb which shone through a window in the distance. I had no idea where the hell I was. From the outside it looked a forbidding sort of place. Inside the forbidden had become downright condemned: damp and stinking to high-heaven, and that was just the entrance hall.

The cell where I was to spend what was the remainder of the night was through a heavy trapdoor in the floor and down a series of slippery stone steps. It was like descending into a very wet kind of hell. At the bottom of the steps, I realised that I was on my own and when I turned, I saw the soldiers' boots exiting through the trapdoor. It was the last thing I saw.

The next moment the heavy hatch dropped with a loud bang. It was like a hammer hitting tarmac and I was plunged into darkness that I could have cut with a knife.

When my eyes had adjusted to the dark, I slid down the rest of the stairs on my backside and then stood up. Now, straining to see, hands outstretched in front of me lest I came across some wall or door, I looked either way, but there was only darkness visible. I gulped down some of the cold damp air and called out. "Hey. Is there anyone down here?"

No answer came.

I was alone. Alone with the stark reality that I was deep in trouble, again.

Death itself could not have felt much worse.

I sat down and waited patiently for someone to bring me more bad news.

But it never arrived.

CHAPTER FIFTY-FIVE

I WAS RELEASED JUST BEFORE DAWN AND ESCORTED BY TWO SOLDIERS across a packed gravel parade ground over to a red-brick block of latrines. I was handed a comb, a bar of soap and a razor so that I might wash, shave, and then change into the police uniform that had been hung with a fresh shirt and pressed tie in the end stall. A folded cloth and tin of black boot polish had been left on top of the seat of the lavatory.

My guards waited outside by the entrance whilst I threw cold water over my face and ran the blade of a razor across my lathered cheeks and jowls. I changed into the uniform, polished my shoes, and combed my hair. I dropped the comb into the sink and walked back outside.

From the toilets, I was marched across the courtyard toward a two-story building built from the same red brick as the latrines. I was escorted inside and, avoiding the larger cracks in the lino, began the ascent. Both floors had their own distinguishing character, all of it miserable, all of it covered in aging paint varying from dark brown to dark green. The sickly-sweet smell of bleach and brass polish throughout the place was so strong it made the back of my throat sting. The lights above me dimmed tiredly as I was trooped down a long corridor and taken into a small windowless room that contained only a single wooden chair and a yellow-faced, Seiko electric clock hanging on the wall. I was told to sit, and I would be collected in due course.

I sat. A 200-watt bulb hung from the centre of the ceiling. Its light scaled my brain. I closed my eyes.

Due course turned out to be a five hour wait.

The same two soldiers returned and tramped me back down the corridor coming to a halt outside a room close to the stairwell I'd climbed earlier that day.

The sign on the door said *'Adjutant'* which seemed like a real joke as I knew that beyond that door the man waiting for me was anything but second-in-command. One of the soldiers knocked and a familiar voice bellowed "*come in*" from the other side.

Manolis Callas sat behind an antique brass, inlaid mahogany sofa table in an expensive, well-pressed suit as finically neat as ever; his long-nosed, thin-mouthed face raised in the air, his blue eyes fixing on me as soon as I stepped in front of him. On the table sat the ledger and a pair of the Provost's horn-rimmed reading glasses. He turned his attention to the soldier behind me. "That will be all for now."

"Sir!" snapped the guard.

I heard the soldier's boots stomp away and the door close quietly behind me. Callas remained seated. The expression on his face, blank. His stare hard. Finally, he spoke.

"I trust your overnight accommodation with us was satisfactory, Major?"

"I've been in worse ..."

Callas made a face at my lack of respect.

"Sir," I added in a beat.

There was a moment of silence whilst the old man continued to eye me up.

"It appears that you had quite a night in Kavala, Major."

"News travels fast."

"I had men tailing Grivas for days. Each one of them ordered to strictly observe his movements, nothing more. My informers and subordinates always ensure I'm never far from being appraised of the most up-to-date intelligence. You, of all people should know that." Callas paused and adjusted his tie. "I'm just off the phone with both the head of German intelligence and his Mossad counterpart in Tel Aviv. Both of them are asking me some very awkward questions."

"Such as?"

"Such as where in the name of hell the body of Konrad Tafel has disappeared to and what's become of the missing bullion that both countries are now claiming is rightfully theirs." Callas shifted in his seat. "Perhaps you can enlighten me?"

I pulled my shirt collar away from my neck – it was tight – and I took a long steady breath. "During my investigation I was able to ascertain that Captain Kampouris took Tafel's body from the mortuary on Kordelio Street and disposed of it. Where and how he got rid of the corpse, I have no idea." I felt my eye twitch and took a second before continuing. "Kampouris was also responsible for the murder of the coroner, Lakis Vokos."

Callas nodded to himself thoughtfully. "And the two cases of gold which, may I remind you, in our recent telephone conversation you informed me had an estimated value of six-and-a-half-million-dollars. What, may I ask, has become of that?"

"That appeared to go walkabout whilst I was in transit between Kavala and Salonica ... sir."

"Walkabout? Damn it! Do you honestly expect me to believe that you managed to lose over six million of gold bullion whilst you were galivanting from the coast to the city?" Callas gave me a calculated look designed to leave me with the feeling that that I was little more than a minor employee. He got to his feet and stood in front of the short, lacquered table. "Don't take me for a bloody idiot! Who has the gold?"

"I honestly don't know. I had it stashed away safely, hidden underneath the floorboards in a lock up down by the docks in Kavala," I lied. "It was safe under lock and key. By the time I went back to retrieve the ingots last night, they were gone. The place had been ransacked. Top to bottom. Whoever took the gold, clearly had me under surveillance, and when I was out of the way, they made their play for it."

"I don't believe a word of it! Has that little bitch Garbi got her thieving hands on it?"

I shook my head. "No sir," I lied again. "I let Nia go long before I found out the bullion had gone missing."

Callas pinched the bridge of his nose between finger and thumb. "What a fucking mess. None of what you're telling me rings true. How they hell do you expect me to explain away the fact over six million dollars of gold has gone going missing on Greek soil to either the Israeli or the German intelligence?"

"It wouldn't be the first time you've had to concoct a tale to placate a foreign nation who were turning the screws, sir. Besides, the Germans hardly have a legitimate claim to stolen Jewish loot."

"I don't give a damn about the Germans. I just want the truth from you."

My gaze drifted across the room to look out of the window for a moment before focussing back on the Provost. "And you've had the truth, sir."

Callas shook his head repeatedly. "*Have I really.*" He muttered to himself.

"So what now. A show trial?" I asked.

The Provost looked daggers at me. "Hardly. As far as I'm concerned, you've already been tried, Major and sentenced."

"Sentenced for what?"

Callas ticked them off on his fingers.

"The killing of Brigadier Grivas, the killing of three of his men, the unfortunate incidents involving the bankers Lirtzman and Roth, the two German intelligence officer you pummelled to bits. The questionable disappearance of Captain Kampouris. The missing bullion. Need I really go on?"

"But that all came about because of orders," I said. "Orders you initiated."

"And you carried out. All too unsuccessfully," blazed Callas.

"So, sir. Spell it out," I said.

"In short, I'm afraid you're leaving me, Remis," he said.

I felt a frown creep across my forehead. "You're saying I can resign?"

Callas made a rare physical reaction. He laughed. "I told you from the beginning that no-one has ever resigned from my section. A rule without exceptions."

"But I'm to be an exception?"

"In a way," he said. His face had become more and more static over the last few minutes, but now it had frozen stiff like a Notre-Dame gargoyle, his mouth clearly set to gush further bad news. He pointed to a polished oak table by the window. "Go pour yourself a drink."

I did I was told. Twelve-year-old Macallan malt and Waterford crystal glasses sat on a pressed white linen doily. I still had the bottle and glass in my hand when Callas spoke again. "The Israelis want you dead. The Germans don't care either way. The Israelis want it so badly they're prepared to forget about the missing gold. It would appear that Konrad Tafel was a much respected, prized agent of theirs. I have to admit, I do respect their position. I have little choice but to agree to Mossad's demands."

I looked at the bottle in my hand and poured more whisky into the glass. "So they want my corpse because Konrad Tafel's can't be found?"

"Exactly, Major."

I took a hefty swig. "So, you're snuffing me out for a quiet life, yes?"

"A quiet life for Greece. Not for me."

"Well, we can't go upsetting the motherland, can we?"

"In a nutshell, no we can't. Your execution will slake the Israelis' thirst to dig deeper into Tafel's demise. Your death in itself will likewise calm things with our German friends. The state can draw a line under Brigadier Grivas' and Captain Kampouris' unfortunate demises and I, in due course, can have my men continue to search for that missing gold," Callas said waspishly.

"You've got it all worked out, haven't you?"

"Of course I have. It was like weighing-in two diamonds," said Callas. "Each perfectly cut, each virtually flawless. It was the Israelis' dead, missing hero that weighed just one carat more. I'm very sorry, Mikhail."

"Sorry –" I sipped at the whisky.

"I'm incapable of expressing any kind of feeling other than in conventional terms," he said. "Like you with your assurances in regards the missing gold, I assure you that what I've just said is true. I am sorry."

"Won't ... won't this be bad for morale?" I stammered. If word gets around that you don't mind killing off the rank and file—"

"The word won't get around, I'll make certain of it."

"Is that why I've been brought here, to some God-forsaken army barracks in the middle of nowhere. So the army can put me against the wall and shoot me?"

"I know nothing of the *modus operandi*. However, I assume it will be quick and efficient. I could never agree to anyone in my section killing you," said Callas. "I told Mossad so."

I felt my whole body react to the Provost's last few words. "Did you tell them why?"

"I did not." Callas pulled an envelope out of his jacket pocket with two fingers and handed it to me. I felt the skin on my face tighten as I reached my hand out to take it. He looked at my glass. "Only read the contents of the letter in the moments just before ..." Callas fell silent for a moment, he smiled then gestured to the glass in my hand. "Won't you finish your drink, Major?"

"Why not," I said. "It'll be my last one."

I put the envelope in my back pocket. Callas drew close to me and looked at me as if he were seeing me for the first time.

He took a step nearer, putting his cheek close to mine then whispered in my ear.

"This is such a shame, Mikhail. I needed you by my side now, more than I ever did. God help me."

The Provost stepped away, turned, and called: "Guard."

The room fell into a deadly silence. I placed the empty glass on the table, took two paces backwards and before I could do or say another thing, I felt the hand of one of soldiers take my elbow and I was escorted toward the door.

The only sound I could hear, other the clack of mine and the guard's footsteps on the polished floor, was the sound of Manolis Callas' fingers drumming heavily on the wooden sill of the window frame.

I was handcuffed and taken down to a holding cell, told to sit on the metal-framed bunk in the corner of the room and I remained sat there until after dark. Before they left, I was given a jug of cold water and a pot mug to drink from by one the guards and then I didn't see or hear from another soul until the cell door swung open many hours later. The noise of thick-soled army boots stomping down the tiled corridor announced the arrival of more soldiers. I heard a key turn in the lock and the cell door swung open. Outside four guards, all armed to the teeth, stood in a line. A fifth man, an officer with the rank of major, walked down the hallway and came into the cell.

"Get up," he blared.

At first, I struggled to find either the necessary willingness, physical momentum nor strength to rise to my feet. I'd seen more than my fair share of military executions in my time and I was in no rush to take part in my own. The major rather than ball at me again to get up, gently placed his hand on my arm and offered his assistance. I got to my feet and felt my legs then body begin to tremble. The army major gestured with his hand to one of his men who calmly walked into the cell and from his back pocket produced a length of black cloth.

"Turn and face the wall," said the officer calmly.

I reluctantly did as he ordered and felt the cloth fall over my face and then tied across my eyes.

Everything went dark. *'Soon there'll only be darkness'*, I thought.

Aided by one of the guards I was paced out of the cell and back down the hallway. I heard the sound of bolts rattling followed by another locked door being prized open. Then I felt a cold breeze hit my face. I was aided up a series of steps and guided outside. I felt the gravel crunch under my feet. We seemed to be walking in a straight line for an age, in my mind's eye all I could see was the cold, stone wall that I was about to be stood against and shot. I felt my limbs become weaker, my legs and arms as heavy as lead, my mouth dried, and a piercing white noise filled my ears. I was drawn to a halt and told to raise my arms out in front of me and then felt the handcuffs being taken from round me wrists.

Then I heard the sound of an engine turning over. Not a car's, something bigger. A truck without a doubt. I smelt the exhaust fumes as I drew nearer to the unknown vehicle. I felt one of the guards take my arm and bring me to a halt. Then someone took my right leg and raised it. I felt the sole of my shoe touch something hard.

"Hold up your arm," barked another voice.

I did as I was told. Held out my arm and immediately felt cold fingers grasp at my hand and haul me upwards. Rising into the unknown was further aided by a firm push by more hands at my rear. Once inside the vehicle I was sat on a bench then felt the presence of another soul sit down next to me.

I listened to the truck drive over more gravel followed by metal gates swinging open and moments later we were driving at speed across smooth asphalt.

I had no idea how long the journey lasted. I had no idea what time it was. I only knew that when the truck finally came to a halt and the engine died, that I could smell the sea. I again heard the sound of hobnailed boots striking the boards on the floor of the lorry then sensed someone standing over me.

I felt fingers untying the blindfold and the cloth swiftly removed from my eyes. The army major nodded at me, took a step backwards and held his hand out toward the open tail gate of the trunk. "If you'd be so good as to step on down."

I got to my feet and climbed down onto wet concrete. As I turned, I heard the sound of water splashing against something solid, and the all too familiar smell of ozone. Even in the dead of night I knew without a doubt that I was standing on one of the many jetties at the port of Thessaloniki.

The soldiers who had accompanied me were stood along one side of the truck, not one of the men turned to looked at me. At the foot of the tailgate sat a suitcase, bulging at its seams, I quickly recognised it to be mine. The army major picked up the case and handed it to me, then once again held out his hand.

"If you'll follow me."

We walked without speaking to the entrance to an ANEK lines ferry terminal. The major guided me across the deserted building through an open door that led out to the passenger path that ran alongside a huge car ferry. The major escorted me outside, took a ticket and boarding pass from his tunic pocket and handed it to me. I stared at the travel documents in my hand and looked up at the major.

"I don't understand?"

"And I don't question my orders." The major looked at the ferry. "You need to be boarding right now. He stepped back a pace to allow me to pass and I walked out into the night. When I turned to thank the officer, he was already heading back toward the entrance we'd just come through.

I made my way down the slipway and climbed the gang-plank onto the ferry. Inside I was greeted by a young woman wearing a navy-blue ANEK uniform and a warm smile.

"Your ticket and boarding pass, please, sir."

I handed the documents over and watched her study them. "You have a cabin on the second deck, sir." The woman pointed toward the stairs.

"Cabin ... I don't understand. Where am I going?" I asked. As I said the words, I heard Nia's voice in my head asking me the very same question.

The stewardess, a bemused look on her face replied. "Your ticket says, Heraklion, Crete." She offered another smile and handed back my ticket and pass.

"Crete?"

The stewardess nodded. "We'll be arriving tomorrow after-noon, a little after three with any luck." She took a step back to allow me to move inside.

I climbed the metal stairs and followed the directions up to the ferry's viewing platform on the top deck. Once I was back outside, I dropped my case next to a bench and went and stood against the rail and peered out into the gloom.

The city lights glowed in the distance and the moon above my head lit a portion of the sky like a white flame. I stood staring into space until I heard the sound of the ferry's moorings being uncoupled and the vessel's massive engine power up.

Ten minutes later I was heading out across the calm waters of the Aegean. I remained stock-still listening to the water break against the side of the hull, my mind still unable to process what was happening to me.

And that's when I remembered the envelope the Provost had given me just before I left him. I reached my hand into my hip pocket to retrieve it. I tore open the flap, pulled out a folded piece of bonded, white paper, opened it and began to read.

Mikhail,
You're going back into the world.
Still a serving police officer, you'll be pleased to know.
Beyond my protection maybe, but not my all-seeing eye.
Remember that.
M.C

I grinned away my burgeoning tears. Not sure how to react to what the Provost had written. Even in the poor light, I stared at those words for the better part of an hour, my fingers numb with cold, the wind bruising my cheeks. Finally, I returned to the bench and picked up my case then headed back inside to go find my cabin and a bed for the night.

As I navigated my way along the thin passageway which led to my room, I thought once again of Nia. Of her bravery and where she may be heading.

I hoped that I would one day see her again.

I hoped that I would, in time, return to my home in Salonica.

I eventually found my cabin, opened the door, and walked into the tiny room. I dropped my case next to the door, kicked off my shoes and laid out on the bunk, my arm across my eyes.

Now, alone, I wept.

My tears would not cease until sleep finally took me by the hand and slowly drew me towards a never-ending blackness.

ACKNOWLEDGMENTS

Coal Black Soul is the first tale in a long-planned trilogy to feature the Greek Police detective, Major Mikhail Remis. As with all my previous work, there is more than a grain of historical truth generated from both the novel's geographic setting and in the characters themselves. The writer, Richard Cox considers *Coal* to be my best work to date. It's not for me to comment on such high praise other than to say that you, dear reader will ultimately be the judge.

As every writer knows, the success of a book involves many people whose names never find their way on to a book jacket. I am fortunate to have a wonderful group of people who whom I depend on daily. Some of them are old friends, some new. But without them, I would probably not have the career that I have been blessed with for more than a decade now, nor would I continue to have it.

I would like to thank my publishers and editor, Sumaira Wilson and Nikki East at Spellbound Books. The Wilson/East team have been integral in bringing *Coal Black Soul* and its sequel *Only Devils Left* to life. I am indebted to both for their enthusiasm and skill. Their individual passion for the book has been boundless.

It's now over ten years since I first met and was offered representation by my literary agent Philip Patterson at Marjacq

Scripts. Phil has been integral to the success of my writing. His guidance, wisdom and patience, invaluable. The same must of said of the rest of the Marjacq team: Guy Herbert, Leah Middleton & Sandra Sawicka who have been both supportive and encouraging over the years.

Printed in Great Britain
by Amazon

44643932R00229